What exposures will change their lives forever?

\\\\\\

BRETT LARSEN
Master photographer: Her art holds the magic that her life has yet to find.

JEFFREY UNDERWOOD
Corporate player: He wants it all—control of the Larsen fortune, destruction of the Larsen family.

BARBARA LARSEN
Society princess: Beautiful but betrayed by her father, proud yet envious of her daughter.

DAVID POWELL
Successful entrepreneur: He knows how to play the field, yet realizes that he has only one shot at real happiness—and it's in the arms of Brett Larsen.

\\\\\\

EXPOSURES

ATTENTION: SCHOOLS AND CORPORATIONS

POPULAR LIBRARY books are available at quantity discounts with bulk purchase for educational, business, or sales promotional use. For information, please write to SPECIAL SALES DEPARTMENT, POPULAR LIBRARY, 666 FIFTH AVENUE, NEW YORK, N Y 10103

**ARE THERE POPULAR LIBRARY BOOKS
YOU WANT BUT CANNOT FIND IN YOUR LOCAL STORES?**

You can get any POPULAR LIBRARY title in print. Simply send title and retail price, plus 50¢ per order and 50¢ per copy to cover mailing and handling costs for each book desired. New York State and California residents add applicable sales tax. Enclose check or money order only, no cash please, to POPULAR LIBRARY, P. O. BOX 690, NEW YORK, N Y 10019

EXPOSURES

MARIE JOYCE

POPULAR LIBRARY

An Imprint of Warner Books, Inc.

A Warner Communications Company

To our parents:
Gloria Frye
Juanita DeBerry, and the late John DeBerry
for the "right stuff."
To Hiram Bell
for his understanding and patience.
And to all the relatives and friends
who believed we could....

POPULAR LIBRARY EDITION

Copyright © 1990 by Virginia DeBerry & Donna Grant
All rights reserved.

Popular Library® and the fanciful P design are registered trademarks of Warner Books, Inc.

Cover design by Jackie Merri Meyer
Lettering by Dave Gatti
Cover photograph by Neal Barr

Popular Library books are published by
Warner Books, Inc.
666 Fifth Avenue
New York, N.Y. 10103

A Warner Communications Company

Printed in the United States of America

First Printing: March, 1990

10 9 8 7 6 5 4 3 2 1

— *Prologue* —

"You can't die! Please don't die!" Brett Larsen pleaded in an agonized, barely audible whisper. Lenox Hill Hospital seemed light-years away from her mother's Manhattan apartment, instead of only a few short blocks.

As the ambulance barreled through the steamy August rain, two medics worked feverishly to maintain vital signs. Brett knelt near the stretcher, holding her mother's feet, which were now cold and tinged a sickening blue.

It makes sense now, Brett thought. *Every twisted bit of it*. But it wasn't her mother's fault. Why hadn't she told someone? Everything could have been so different. But none of that mattered now. She had to pull through. "Mother, I love you."

The ambulance slammed to a halt and the doors flew open, as if by themselves. Before the stretcher could be lowered to the ground, the gloomy darkness came alive with a blaze of halogen lights and the whir of motor drives.

Brett jumped to the pavement and was assaulted by a barrage of questions from zealous reporters.

"Did your mother try to kill herself?"

"There are reports that your grandfather died tonight, too. Can you confirm this?"

"Were you aware of the reason for the rift between your mother and her father?"

"Will you leave fashion photography to head Larsen Enterprises?"

Brett, numb to the buzz of questions, let herself be swept through the double doors of the emergency room by the swarm of security guards that surrounded her. They whisked her to an empty lounge, and told her a doctor would be in as soon as there was news. Then she was alone.

Brett slumped into a cracked leather armchair, her clothes disheveled, her long dark hair damp and tangled. She drew her knees to her chest and rocked slowly back and forth, her green eyes staring into space. She hoped her fiancé and her dear Aunt Lillian would arrive soon. She could never have survived the hell of the last week without them, and she needed them now, she realized as she fought to control the panic that threatened to engulf her.

Glancing down at her watch for what must have been the hundredth time since she had left her mother's apartment, Brett was startled by the irony of the date. How could it be her birthday? So much had happened in twenty-six years. Somehow, her mother had always managed to upstage her on her birthday, she mused wearily as her thoughts drifted back to the party her mother had given when she was ten.

— *Chapter 1* —

"I got the ball over the net more times than you," giggled Brett as she scampered into the sun-drenched solarium, plunked herself on the blue-and-white-striped chaise, and twirled her thick brunette braid like a jump rope. Rush, the aptly named two-year-old Airedale, settled on the cool tile floor next to her.

"Yeah, but I beat you running up the hill from the beach," her best friend, Lizzie Powell, retorted as she scrambled onto a wicker settee and craned her neck to watch a crew of workers hoist a huge canvas tent on the south lawn of Cox Cove. The sprawling country estate in Sands Point, on Long Island's gold coast, had been a gift to Brett's great-aunt, Lillian, from her husband, the late Sir Nigel Cox.

"Who's the guy in the pink shirt?" Lizzie asked. She nearly fell over as she shifted her weight to follow his progress along the fieldstone terrace.

Brett bounded to the window for a better look. "That's Ian Wexford. Mother says he's a party architect."

"He's dreamy," Lizzie cooed.

"Dreamy!" Brett exclaimed. "He's a jerk! Why else would he wear a scarf around his neck in August?"

"It's called an ascot," Lizzie instructed, with a toss of her blond ringlets. "I saw it in a movie."

"Whatever you call it, I still think he's weird," Brett mumbled.

"Look at all of those trucks!" Lizzie said, now mesmerized by the caravan that lined the driveway from the access road to the service entrance. "This is going to be some party!" she gushed, dazzled by all the activity.

"Yeah, I guess so, but I always feel so lost at Mother's parties," Brett responded quietly.

"This isn't your mother's party. It's your birthday party," Lizzie protested.

Brett sighed. She didn't want to dampen her friend's enthusiasm for the day, but she knew her mother.

Suddenly, Rush leaped up and trotted through the door. In a moment he reappeared, wagging what tail he had, followed by his mistress, Lillian Larsen Cox. Lillian, an artist whose land- and seascapes had been acclaimed for decades, placed her easel, canvas, and a satchel containing her paints and brushes in a corner.

"Well, I think you rascals have earned some lunch. From the look of your clothes, I'd say you've had an active morning." She winked at them and smiled.

At fifty-six, Lillian was a handsome woman whose clear, azure-blue eyes reflected her warmth and spirit. Her thick blanket of blond hair was now subtly streaked with gray, and when people described her as statuesque, she jokingly took it to mean that at five feet eight inches her broad shoulders now supported a fuller figure than they used to. Lillian saw life as an extraordinary banquet, and to her, growing older meant she was finally getting to dessert.

"So, who won the tennis match?"

The girls erupted in a fit of giggles.

"I think we both lost," Brett finally managed.

"I hope you two will always weather defeat so well," Lillian chuckled and turned to supervise the cook, who had brought their afternoon meal.

"I love the way she talks," Lizzie whispered, admiring Lillian's charming mélange of Swedish, British, and American inflections, which never failed to impress her.

Brett nodded in agreement, her intense green eyes sparkling with affection. It was not so much how her aunt spoke as what she said that Brett loved. Lillian made more sense than any adult she knew.

Brett, Lizzie, and Lillian sat at a round table laid with starched white table linen and luncheon plates dappled with hand-painted strawberries. Lizzie swung her legs, causing her chair to squeak, until Brett shot her a look that made her stop midswing. Brett wasn't sure if she was bothered by the noise or the fact that Lizzie's feet did not reach the floor.

Lizzie was small and delicate, as fragile as a Dresden doll, which always made Brett acutely aware of her size. Brett stood more than a head taller than her best friend and, like a puppy, had hands and feet that indicated she would be very tall indeed. Lizzie, on the other hand, felt tiny and pale by comparison and secretly wished she had Brett's shiny dark hair and long, lean limbs.

As Lillian passed the herb dressing for the crabmeat and avocado salad, Lizzie said, "Everything looks so wonderful, Mrs. Cox. This is so exciting." She poked Brett, who was filling a glass with lemonade. "How can you be so calm? You'll be ten. That means you have two numbers!"

"But you have three numbers," Brett teased, referring to Lizzie's constant protestations that she was nine and a half.

Lizzie groaned. "You know what I mean. Do you feel almost like a teenager?" She turned to Lillian to illuminate her point. "Teenagers are so cool. My brother David is eighteen, and he goes to college all the way in California. He can even drive. He's driving here tonight."

"Are you sure he's really coming?" Brett tried not to sound too eager. Earlier that summer, David had tutored both Brett and Lizzie in math—his forte and their only problem subject at Dalton, the private school they attended. Lizzie was there on scholarship. Brett had grown very fond of David in those weeks and dreamed about having a brother like him.

"Yes, I'm sure," Lizzie answered for what she hoped was the last time. She couldn't figure out why Brett liked her older brother. David was okay, but not even close to dreamy.

The slam of the massive front door, followed by a torrent of commands issued in a throaty, insistent voice, interrupted the tranquility of the afternoon. The words, at first unintelligible, became clearer as the voice, making its way through the house, seemed to bring with it the frantic energy of an approaching hurricane. Brett stiffened in her chair, waiting for her mother to appear.

"I don't care, just do it!" Barbara snapped at one of the workers just before she reached the sun room.

Barbara Larsen North entered with all the melodrama of an MGM contract player. "Throwing a party always gives me the most dreadful headache," she said, putting her hand to her forehead to shade her blue eyes.

Barbara's face, dewy from her morning facial at Elizabeth Arden, was as mercurial and expressive as a child's. In fact, people found it hard to believe she was thirty-two. "It's a good thing I'm here. These people would never have had everything ready by the time the guests arrived. Hello, Aunt Lillian. Brett, you and Elizabeth are positively filthy! What possessed you to come to the table dressed like that!" She walked farther into the sun room, smoothing the folds of her orange-and-fuchsia halter dress, which revealed a figure that fashion dictated passé, men dreamed about, and women envied. "Where's my hello?"

Brett rose from her chair and dutifully planted a kiss on the cheek her mother offered, careful not to muss her hair. Her blond bouffant, a style that had faded from popularity a decade earlier, somehow suited her.

"Hello, Mother," Brett said cautiously, trying to gauge Barbara's mood.

To call Barbara beautiful was insufficient. To gaze at her, and everyone always did, brought a deep feeling of satisfaction, as though the gazer had somehow been fulfilled.

"The girls were playing all morning and I think they look perfectly fine for a casual lunch. It's not tea with the queen," Lillian intervened.

"You played all morning? You'll be exhausted before your party begins," Barbara said, exasperation evident in her voice.

Brett's face clouded. *Her party*. No one would even know she was there.

"We'll be fine for the party, Mrs. North," Lizzie said. "In fact, we'll go upstairs right now and rest. Come on, Brett."

Barbara settled herself in the chaise across the room from Lillian, crossed her legs at the ankles, and dropped her handbag beside her.

Lillian lit one of the brown-papered cigarettes she had smoked for years and began, "I'd like to talk to you about this party, Barbara. Your Ian Wexford has this household in an uproar, and I see little evidence of anything for children."

"Why, Aunt Lillian," Barbara began sweetly, "Ian Wexford does all of the most divine parties and balls. I was thrilled to death that he agreed to do this party for our Brett." She plucked a petal from a nearby daisy and rubbed it anxiously between her thumb and forefinger.

"I know all about Mr. Wexford's parties, Barbara, but I only agreed to the use of Cox Cove for Brett's tenth birthday celebration," Lillian said.

Leaning forward conspiratorially, Barbara confided, "Ten is such an important year, and you must admit that Ian's China theme is exciting. What with President Nixon's trip there this year, it's all the rage. Imagine, this party will have historical significance!" The daisy petal, now a tiny ball of mush, dropped from her fingers.

"Since when does the society page have historical significance?" Lillian snapped.

"There will be entertainment for the children," Barbara said defensively.

"Just how many children are you expecting?"

Barbara hesitated. "Oh . . . around a dozen."

"Twelve children out of two hundred guests!" Lillian stubbed out her cigarette for emphasis.

"So many of her little friends were out of town for the summer, and twelve children is like a hundred anyway," Barbara countered.

"Why didn't you wait a week or so? I'm sure Brett would have understood, and more of her friends would have been home by then," said Lillian.

"But, then it would be too late for the Feast of the August Moon," Barbara insisted.

"I don't care about the August Moon. I'm interested in Brett's birthday, which somehow seems to be the last thing on your mind!" She stood and moved toward the door. "It's too late to change anything, but I want you to know that you haven't fooled me, and I'm not so sure you've fooled Brett, either."

Relieved to finally be alone, Barbara crumpled the hem of her dress, trying to suppress the irritation she felt at Lillian's uncomfortably accurate observations. To calm herself she closed her eyes and replayed the months of shrewd maneuvering that would culminate in her triumph that evening.

The invitations—red scrolls hand lettered in gold—read, "The eighth month, the twenty-sixth day, nineteen hundred and seventy-two, six o'clock in the evening, your presence is most humbly requested at a banquet to celebrate the Feast of the August Moon and the tenth year of Miss Brett Larsen." Each was hand delivered to recipients as far away as Palm Beach and Newport. The guest list, calculated to shock and soothe, included Wall Street barons, movie stars, social register regulars, and a guru. Barbara had called strategically selected invitees and tantalized them with choice tidbits about the festivities and the guests who had already accepted. Soon the network buzzed with anticipation. How she enjoyed the discreet calls from those overlooked, trying to wangle an invitation. August had never been the high point of the social calendar, but Barbara had engineered an event, and she knew her name would be near the top of everybody's "in" list that fall.

Opening her eyes she reached for her purse and unearthed a rose-colored enamel pillbox, from which she shook two Valium, downing them with a swig from a glass of lemonade. *"This party will be unforgettable!"* she vowed and sauntered defiantly from the room.

— *Chapter 2* —

"Come in." Brett and Lizzie stared wide-eyed at all the paraphernalia Sergei carried into the bedroom. From the top of an enormous black leather tote they saw: a blow-dryer, curling irons, jars of gels and pomades, and cans of hair spray. He also carried what looked like a toolbox.

"It's your turn, birthday girl," Sergei said with an indistinguishable foreign accent. "I have just created a masterpiece for your mother, and now I shall work my magic on you."

"Wow! You must have brought the entire first floor of Bloomingdale's," Lizzie uttered in an awestruck whisper.

This might be fun, Brett thought, recalling how beautiful her mother always looked after having her hair done. She winked at Lizzie and asked, "Mr. Sergei, when you're through with me, could you do Lizzie too?"

"Of course, my angel. Anything for you on your birthday."

"He's cute," mouthed Lizzie to her friend, as Sergei worked vigorously to dry Brett's hair. Next, he applied the gel he hoped would tame its natural waves.

"What will it look like?" Brett asked.

"It is too complicated to explain. I must concentrate," Sergei said testily, as he looked over the array of ivory and jade combs and fresh flowers that were to be a part of his creation. "But you will look like a real China doll."

Too complicated, she thought. She didn't want people to stare at her hair all night.

"We studied China in school this year," Brett said. "Did you know that traditionally, young Chinese girls wear their hair down until they're ready to get married? I think it's supposed to be bad luck or something if you put it up."

"Bad luck?" Sergei asked nervously. Brett had no way of knowing, but he was extremely superstitious. "How did you say they wear their hair?"

Sergei placed a band of tiny pink-and-white flowers just behind the bangs that hid Brett's widow's peak. Her almost-black hair hung straight down her back and curled gently at the bottom. "You are going to be a beauty, a real beauty," he stated with certainty as he opened his kit and selected a pot of rosy pink lip gloss. "I hope a bit of lipstick is not bad luck, too."

Lizzie took Brett's seat and Sergei began to fluff her blond curls into a halo.

Brett peeked at herself in her dressing table mirror. She didn't see the girl who was too tall with gangly arms and legs, and hair that could only be controlled by braiding. Instead, she saw a pretty girl with skin that held the glow of summer sun, and whose thickly lashed emerald eyes revealed both wonder and knowing. She smiled warmly.

Sergei left quietly, muttering about bad luck.

Lizzie, pleased with her appearance, especially the lipstick, sat on the pink-and-white gingham spread that covered the hand-painted four-poster bed. She looked around the room and thought that she would never go anywhere if she had a room like this. She liked her room at home, but her parents' modest apartment on West Eighty-second Street in no way compared to Cox Cove or the luxurious Fifth Avenue apartment where Brett lived with her mother and Zachary Yarrow, her mother's current husband.

"What's wrong?" Lizzie asked, noticing Brett's serious expression.

"I just hope that everything goes all right tonight, and that my mother and Zachary don't have one of their fights," Brett replied.

"Don't worry so much, Brett. We're going to have a blast. Come on, let's get dressed."

Lizzie danced over to the closet and plucked her new yellow dotted swiss party dress from its hanger.

Brett stepped into her emerald green silk Chinese tunic and fastened the silver frogs along the neck and shoulders. Embroidered flowers of yellow, pink, and lilac, dotted with seed pearl centers, were gathered in clusters all over the dress. "Do I look silly?" she asked, feeling insecure about the extravagant costume Barbara had bought for her.

Lizzie clamped her hands over her mouth to hold in the squeal. "You look like a Chinese princess!"

Maybe even my mother will be pleased with the way I look tonight, Brett thought.

"Before we go downstairs, I want to give you your present." Lizzie went to her luggage and removed a gift-wrapped package.

Seconds later, Brett spritzed herself with Love's Fresh Lemon Scent cologne.

"I've never had perfume before. I love it! Oh, thank you, Lizzie."

Enveloped in a citrus cloud, they descended the stairs like ladies, meeting Lillian at the bottom. As the three approached the library, they could hear Barbara's voice.

"Why aren't you wearing the blazer?" she admonished.

"You may feel compelled to buy me clothes, but that doesn't mean I'm compelled to wear them," Zachary replied.

"I ordered that jacket for tonight," Barbara insisted.

"Dammit, Barbara, it's navy blue wool. Do you know what the temperature is?" Zachary asked.

"You look ridiculous, and I will have nothing to do with you the rest of the night!" Barbara said just as Brett, Lizzie, and Lillian came through the library doors.

Barbara posed in the center of the room, her arms akimbo, dressed in a mandarin-collared tunic—a wash of white satin trimmed in gold piping that oozed over her lazy curves. The skirt, slit up one side from hem to midthigh, revealed a silky leg and delicate foot balanced on perilously high, golden sandals. Her hair was indeed a masterpiece, created by the addition of a perfectly matched, pale blond switch that Sergei had coiled and lacquered into an elaborate figure eight and adorned with a cascade of crystals, pearls, and lily of the valley that danced and twinkled like the northern lights. Barbara was a study in contrasts. She seemed bathed in an almost serene, milky light, yet her eyes flashed and her cheeks burned with high color, the result of the several Dexedrine she had washed down with a glass of Cristal.

"Wow, Mrs. North!" Lizzie said.

"Thank you, Elizabeth. I take it you approve," Barbara said.

"May I present the guest of honor," Lillian said, intentionally shifting the group's attention to Brett.

"Brett! You look just like you've stepped from *Flower Drum Song*. Rogers and Hammerstein have done better, but the staging was inspired!" Zachary said enthusiastically, rising from his seat on the sienna leather sofa.

"Thanks, honorable Zach." Brett bowed ceremoniously, then grinning added, "You look nice, too."

Zachary wore white cotton gabardine trousers and a khaki safari jacket—his version of dressing for a summer party. He had never been handsome, and at fifty-three he was balding, with a fringe of gray hair and a slight paunch.

Zachary and Barbara had been married two years, and Brett liked him. He always managed to make her feel important by referring to plays and other adult things, just as if she were one of his cronies from the theater. He was witty, charming, and had been the wunderkind producer of the New York stage, but lately his projects had flopped. It seemed to Brett that her mother enjoyed his failures—she almost gloated with each defeat, despite the fact that it was her money he kept losing.

Brett felt Zachary was more like a grandfather than a father, but she had little knowledge of either. She had thought Brian North, the television star, was her father until she and Barbara had abruptly moved from California to New York four years ago. She was never allowed to see him again. When Brett asked Barbara why they left Brian or who her father really was, her inquiries were met with the same stony, "I don't wish to discuss it, ever!" as were her questions about her grandparents.

"That dress is almost too short. Will you ever stop growing?" Barbara asked, turning her attention to her daughter. "What on earth is that awful perfume you're wearing? I'd send you upstairs to wash it off, but there's no time. And I hoped Sergei would do more with your hair."

Inside, Brett stung from the harshness of her mother's critique, but her face revealed nothing. How could she have thought she looked pretty?

Appalled at Barbara's insensitivity, Lillian shot her a disdainful look, then remarked gently to Brett, "I have something I'd like to give you."

"Can't this wait?" Barbara snapped impatiently.

"No, it cannot," Lillian said. She reached into a drawer of her enormous mahogany desk and removed a small 35-mm camera. "Happy birthday, my dear!" She placed the strap around Brett's neck and kissed her forehead.

"Oh, Aunt Lillian! I love it! How did you know I wanted a camera?" Brett exclaimed, looking through the viewfinder to line up her first shot.

"Well, photography helped make me a better artist. I've spied you sketching down by the beach, and I thought it might be helpful to you."

"Can we go now?" Barbara asked bitingly.

"In a minute." Lillian handed Brett a tiny blue velvet jeweler's box. "This is from your grandfather."

"Why does he persist in this?" Barbara screeched. "He will never see her, no matter how many trinkets he sends!"

Brett placed the box back in the desk drawer. She would retrieve it later. She knew it contained a charm. It would be added to the other jeweled animals she had received annually from her grandfather since her sixth birthday. Barbara did not permit her to wear the bracelet, so she kept it hidden in her bureau.

"Barbara, his gifts do the child no harm," Lillian said.

"Harm? What do you know about harm?" Barbara fumed.

"I don't know what's been going on between you and your father for the last ten years, but I do know that it is his money that supports your extravagant life-style." After a tense moment, Lillian continued, "Shall we go and greet the guests?"

"Fine," Barbara said. "You go on. Brett and I will be right in."

Outside, a glorious amber sunset had bathed the evening in a golden light that made everything seem enchanted. Waves of luxurious stretch limousines and sleek sedans had deposited their shiny passengers at the stately Georgian mansion that was the heart of Cox Cove.

The pop of champagne corks and the ring of laughter was accompanied by the gentle rhythms of the Victor Parish Orchestra, whose dashing leader conducted the group from his perch at a gleaming white baby grand piano.

Anticipation had kissed the crowd as they hovered near the huge swimming pool, which twinkled with hundreds of floating candles shaped like lily pads. And they were fully aroused and ready as the torchbearers led them past the force-bloomed cherry trees that ringed the great lawn, where a muster of peacocks strutted, occasionally flaring their iridescent plumes. They proceeded down the jasmine-bordered red-velvet aisle and into the evening's banquet site, an enormous open-sided tent that resembled a pagoda. Gold silk streamers dangled from its sides, flickering in the gentle breeze, and a brilliant gilt finish made the roof gleam like a crown in the evening sun. An octet sporting traditional Chinese braids, and wearing red smocks gracefully trimmed in black, played lilting melodies while everyone awaited the guests of honor.

Finally, Lillian, Zachary, and Lizzie entered the tent and made their way through the maze of red-damask-covered tables. Each was centered with plump, double-finned goldfish, swimming languidly in wide glass orbs topped with pale pink lotus blossoms that delicately scented the air.

The tension of the past half hour had taken its toll on Lizzie, who was so relieved to see David that she broke into a run and threw her arms around her brother in a bear hug. "I'm so glad you're here," she said breathlessly.

"Whoa, Inchworm! What did I do to deserve a hug like that?" David asked, his brown eyes twinkling playfully.

"Oh, David, it was awful. You should have heard what Mrs. North said to Brett. And don't call me Inchworm," Lizzie said, quickly reverting to her customary sibling behavior.

"What was awful?" David asked.

Before she could respond, a gong sounded and the octet, which had been serenading the guests, launched into a fanfare fit for a coronation march.

Brett and Barbara, seated on the hand-embroidered cushion of a jinricksha, appeared. Oohs and aahs erupted into applause, which pleased Barbara and embarrassed Brett. Barbara waved as her bright blue eyes darted around to gauge the amount of attention she received. Her radar was infallible; she always knew when it was necessary to burn a little brighter.

Brett, mortified at being so conspicuous, took refuge behind her camera and began to snap pictures.

"Put that down!" Barbara hissed. "No one can see you!"

I know, Brett thought as she reluctantly placed the camera in her lap.

The sight of Barbara caused Zachary's earlier hostility to melt away. It was replaced by that feeling of apprehension and jealousy that was so often his companion when in her presence. Barbara was a drug, self-prescribed to ward off advancing middle age and failure. Zachary was hopelessly addicted. He ached for this breathtaking young woman, but he knew that to show it invited her scorn.

"Thou art most fair indeed." Zachary doffed an imaginary hat as he helped Barbara alight from the ricksha. "But isn't that dress a little tight?"

"Oh, Zachary, don't be such an old fuddy-duddy," Barbara responded, knowing that the reference to his age would keep Zachary at bay for the rest of the night.

David saw Brett, standing in the ricksha, awkward and forgotten, and rushed to her aid. At 6'2" he easily lifted her down and kissed her cheek. "Happy birthday, Brett! I'm sorry I don't have a present."

"That's okay." Brett blushed as she tried to refrain from stroking the cheek he had kissed. "Thanks for helping me down."

"It was nice of you to invite me." David had been touched when he had received his invitation, but had not planned to attend until he had heard how lavish an affair it would be. Through the years, David had heard about the cavernous apartment, the maids and limousines, that were a routine part of Brett's life, but he had never witnessed them firsthand. His curiosity about the rich had changed his mind.

"Everything is so beautiful! What's it like to ride in a ricksha?" Lizzie asked.

Brett took her place next to Lizzie. "Okay, I guess." She wanted to forget it had happened.

"It looked really neat. And look at my brother, Mr. Wizmo with the mustache. The last time I saw him in a suit, Mom and Dad made him wear it to graduation," Lizzie teased.

David had grown a mustache because it made him feel as old as his classmates, who were often two or three years his senior. Although only eighteen, he was about to start his junior year at Stanford, where he was the prodigy of the computer science department.

David was handsome in his tan summer suit, blue shirt, and Stanford tie, with its cardinal insignia. His hair grazed his shoulders and was curly like Lizzie's, but a rich, shiny brown.

"That's a pretty fancy camera," David said, ignoring his sister's remarks.

"I just got it for my birthday," Brett said proudly. "Can I take your picture?" She focused carefully, already comfortable behind the lens.

Across the room, Barbara assumed her coveted spot next to Avery Thornton, society editor of *NOW*, the bible of the social set. Avery, a pudgy little man of indeterminate years, was one of the most powerful men in New York. With a stroke of his pen, hostesses rose or fell from favor. He was either a valuable ally or a formidable opponent, and the ranks of those he had exiled to social Siberia were legion.

"Avery, darling, how are you?" Barbara asked sweetly, delivering the obligatory double-miss kiss. "And they said it couldn't be done," she added triumphantly.

A year ago, Avery had declared in *NOW* that there was no summer social season in New York, and insisted that no one could throw a major party during July or August. Barbara saw Avery's statement as a gauntlet laid down and accepted the challenge. She hired Ian Wexford to champion her cause and spent seven months planning *the* party of the summer season. Avery bet her a case of vintage Chateau Lafite Rothschild and prime coverage in *NOW* for a year that she could never pull it off.

Every moment of the banquet had been meticulously planned to include food, games, and entertainment. In authentic Chinese tradition, each of the nine courses presented a new and different taste sensation, ranging from mild and sweet to hot and spicy, the order carefully arranged to surprise the palate by Woo, the owner of the posh Manhattan restaurant that bore his name.

No detail had been overlooked and Barbara reveled in her soon-to-be-proclaimed victory. By the fourth course, eager to bask in kudos and compliments from her guests, she began circulating. Her white-sheathed figure drew either admiring glances or jealous snipes, but never went unnoticed.

As a troupe of acrobats in brightly colored costumes tumbled and cartwheeled down the aisle, Zachary anxiously watched his wife's every move.

Barbara reached a table engaged in a heated debate about the arrests at the Watergate. Sidling up to a young man ably defending his point, she interjected, "Frankly, I believe Martha Mitchell."

He pushed back his chair, gazing up at her with smoky blue eyes. "Mrs. North, you look very beautiful tonight."

"Thank you, kind sir," Barbara replied, and curtsied as much as her dress would allow. "How are, or should I say, where are your parents?"

"They're still skiing in the Andes. Mother will be distressed when she hears what she's missed. I hope you don't mind my coming tonight," he said.

One of the guests left the table and Barbara slipped into the temporarily vacant seat next to his. She crossed her legs, exhibiting a generous glimpse of thigh. "Of course I don't mind, but I'm sure a handsome young man like you has much more exciting things to do on a Saturday night," she said coyly as the Watergate discussion buzzed around them.

"I can't think of a thing I'd rather be doing. Well, maybe just one." His full-lipped smile invited mischief as he pushed back the lock of blond hair that dangled across his forehead.

"Only one?" asked Barbara seductively, realizing the game was on.

Barbara and Carson Gallagher had been having an affair since June.

Carson's lean, well-muscled body was the result of four years of crew and soccer at Harvard. He had graduated in May, and his position in his family's banking empire was waiting to be claimed, but Carson wasn't ready. This was going to be a year devoted to extracurricular activities, and Barbara was the first.

"Carson, you've barely touched a thing on your plate," Barbara teased.

"I'm afraid I can't get the hang of these chopsticks," he replied.

Barbara picked up a morsel of eight jewelled stuffed duck with her fingers and held it up to Carson's lips. "Sometimes the simplest way is best."

He looked directly into her eyes and accepted the offered tidbit, deliberately licking her fingertips as he took it into his mouth.

Having witnessed every moment of this performance, Zachary appeared and placed his hands possessively on Barbara's shoulders.

Without missing a beat, Barbara said, "Darling, have you met Carson Gallagher? Carson, this is my husband, Zachary Yarrow."

"Swell party, sir," said Carson, offering his hand.

Completely ignoring him, Zachary said stiffly, "Barbara, the Stuarts have been asking for you."

"Claudia does require so much attention," she said as she rose to follow Zachary. "You will be staying for the fireworks, won't you, Carson?" she asked with a gleam in her eye.

"I wouldn't miss them," Carson replied.

"Good." Barbara sashayed across the room.

Platters of moon cakes, sweet black beans, and salted duck egg yolks—the good luck foods for the Feast of the August Moon—were placed on each table. Then the lights dimmed, the band played "Happy Birthday," and four waiters carried in an enormous cake in the shape of a butterfly, ablaze with sparklers. Cymbals crashed and in danced a gigantic, multicolored dragon, the benevolent beast of Chinese folklore, who led the guests down to the waterfront for fireworks.

For thirty minutes the night sky was exalted with comets, pinwheels, and starbursts that could be seen for miles, then disappeared silently into the sea.

Lillian stepped up behind Brett, who was watching the spectacle with David and Lizzie. "Are you enjoying yourself, child?"

"This is the best part," Brett said enthusiastically.

"Why don't we go inside for some cake?" Lillian suggested.

"I think I'll stay out here a while longer," David said. Intrigued by all the people and activity, he headed over to the pool, where it seemed the party was just beginning.

In the living room, over cake and milk, the girls excitedly relived the evening's events.

Barbara had no trouble convincing Carson to slip away with her for a moonlit walk on the beach. He was six feet of young, handsome, virile, pleasure-seeking temptation, and Barbara could no more resist temptation than she could a challenge.

At the bottom of the stairs that led to the beach, Barbara sat down. "I have to take these sandals off."

Carson knelt in the sand and removed her delicate golden shoes. He let his strong, hot hand glide up her calf, and when he reached her milky thigh, he placed a long, slow kiss where the slit of her dress strained to open. Barbara made a low, throaty moan.

"I've wanted to do that all night," he said huskily.

Before Barbara could say a word, he lifted her to her feet, surrounding her in a powerful embrace. He pressed her round, gentle curves against his rippling muscles until there was no air between them. They kissed hungrily, his tongue exploring the deepest recesses of her mouth, his hands in constant motion, kneading her shoulders, her arms, her back. The insistence of his growing hardness ignited her, but before she succumbed completely to the burning between her legs, she pulled away. "Let's walk farther down the beach. I know a place."

When they passed the dunes, where a great outcropping of rock eclipsed the light of the moon and cast a shadow on the sand, she stopped. Carson came up behind her and nibbled her neck as he unfastened the clasps of her gown. Barbara closed her eyes, leaned against him, and let the pleasure envelop her. She pressed her palms against his thighs and moved them in leisurely circles, edging closer to his pulsing penis. Carson cupped her now bare breasts, massaging her stiff nipples with his thumbs. He slid a hand down her hip and through the slit that had tormented him so all night. Easing his fingers under the filmy silk fabric of her panties, he stroked the hard, swollen nub of her pleasure.

Lillian tapped Brett lightly, interrupting her conversation, and pointed to the corner of the blue velvet sofa, where Lizzie had fallen asleep.

Brett giggled, whispering, "She's always like that. One minute she's talking and then she's asleep."

"I think I'll take little Miss Powell up to bed. Why don't you come up, too, and I'll tuck you both in," Lillian said lovingly.

"Can I go out for a little while longer? I have a few pictures left and I'd like to take them."

"All right, but not too much longer," Lillian replied.

Brett grabbed her camera and trotted outside, where she ran into Zachary on the terrace.

"Can I take your . . ."

He brushed past as though he hadn't seen her and went inside.

Brett hiked up her dress the best she could and made her way across the lawn toward the beach. She knew the perfect place for her last few shots. Turtleback Rock was her favorite spot for watching the tide, sorting shells, and trying to make sense of the world. As she neared the outcropping of rock, she heard what sounded like a muffled gasp and stopped. For a moment there was only the lapping of water and traces of the music still being played by the orchestra. Then she heard rustling and a groan. She crept closer, and when the shadowed area underneath the rock was in full view, she saw her mother's back. At first, because Barbara was on her knees, Brett thought she may have been injured. But before she moved to help, she saw a man's legs, and she knew they weren't Zachary's.

Brett slowly backed away, but before she could leave, Zachary ran past her. "How dare you!" he raved.

Barbara sprang to her feet, clutching her dress to hide her nakedness.

"Zachary, let me explain . . ."

"Explain what? That you sleep with men behind my back! I know that already!" Zachary's voice came in gasps. "I love you! I need you, and you know it! You make me suffer for it!"

"You have to calm down," Carson intervened.

"Why? So you two can pat me on the head and laugh at the spineless old eunuch when I leave!"

"Zachary, listen," Barbara pleaded.

"No! No, you'll never laugh at me again!" Zachary drew the .32 automatic he had taken from the gun case in the house. Five crisp, hollow snaps slowly and deliberately punctuated the air, followed by a thick quiet that seemed to stop time.

"No!" Brett's wail echoed through the night air.

Barbara collapsed in a dead faint and Carson's lifeless body, legs splayed, lay on the cold sand.

Zachary let the empty gun fall from his hand. "I'm not going to hurt anyone else," he muttered.

Brett raced across the sand, stumbling, falling, tearing her gown. Sobbing, she mounted the stairs and ran into the throng gathered there. Hands grabbed at her, voices called her name, but Brett, seeing only Carson's body through her tears, plowed wildly into the crowd.

"Brett! What's the matter?" David grabbed her. She flailed, kicked, and screamed, until she realized it was David. Then her body went limp and she cried hysterically. "It's all right. It's all right," he repeated as he carried her into the house.

— *Chapter 3* —

The New York press had a field day, creating an epic tragedy with Brett, the innocent young eyewitness, at the center. Since the shooting, Lillian had harbored Brett at her Manhattan duplex in the San Remo, but Brett's days were plagued by zealous reporters and photographers hungry for a piece of her to take back to the newsroom, and her sleep was tormented by vivid dreams of the grisly event. So unrelenting was the media that in November, Lillian obtained a restraining order to shield Brett from the constant intrusion.

Undaunted, the press zeroed in on Barbara, who remained sequestered in her Fifth Avenue apartment. She saw no one, including her daughter. Barbara's radiant beauty was usurped by a haggard pallor. Valium and alcohol dulled her bright blue eyes and deep, dark circles lurked beneath them, like ominous shadows.

Articles chronicled the minutest developments in the case, never failing to mention that Barbara Larsen North was the only child of Sven Larsen, one of the country's wealthiest industrialists, as well as the ex-wife of reclusive sixties television star Brian North. Barbara took perverse pleasure in the discomfort the publicity would cause them.

In May, after weeks of testimony and lengthy deliberations, Zachary was convicted of manslaughter, but Barbara's trial by her peers dragged on. Some thought the whole mess unspeakable and banished her from their address books. Others felt empathy because they could imagine themselves in her place.

Barbara combed the pages of *NOW*, obsessively searching for some indication of the remaining value of her social currency, but her name had ceased to appear, as though she was bankrupt and forgotten. The days slid into weeks, then months, and she remained ensconced on the white suede sofa in her living room, her hair tangled and unwashed, a drink in hand, counting favors and IOU's and wondering if they would be enough tender to retain her seat on the New York Party Exchange.

"What are you doing here? I'm not seeing anyone!" Barbara said rudely, as her afternoon's machinations were interrupted by Lillian's unexpected arrival.

"I'm not anyone, I'm family. And in case you've forgotten, I have been taking care of Brett since this awful ordeal began." Lillian was appalled by her niece's appearance. "You have not seen her, called her, or returned her calls to you, and that is unforgivable. Yesterday was Brett's birthday, Barbara! You may be hell bent on destroying your life, but I will not allow you to ruin Brett's, as well. If you do not make an effort to pull yourself together, I am prepared to petition the court for permanent custody!"

Barbara shrugged her shoulders. "Go ahead."

Barbara seemed relieved at being stripped of her parental duties, and although she was granted unlimited visitation rights, she managed to see Brett no more than once a month, always at one of the posh East Side eateries she frequented. Brett, with the love and attention of her great-aunt, learned to insulate herself from her mother's cruel remarks. Even when Barbara requested during one of their outings that Brett call her by her first name, instead of mother, Brett agreed calmly. She was surprised at how free and happy she felt now that she no longer lived with Barbara. If leading a normal life meant that she no longer had someone to call mother, so be it.

Brett closed the semester's final edition of the *Middle School Media*, Dalton's newspaper, pleased with the four photographs she had taken. Seventh grade was exciting, but like most twelve-year-olds, she now counted the days until the end of the term, anxious for the freedom of summer.

She sprawled in one of her favorite spots for contemplation and daydreaming: beneath the fruitwood Steinway piano in the living room. Brett felt comfortable everywhere in the enormous duplex penthouse.

The room retained an intimate quality despite its massive dimensions. It was two stories high, with a balcony which overlooked the room and housed much of Lillian's art collection, as well as her studio. Towering windows, unencumbered by heavy drapes, dappled the room with genial sunlight for much of the day and revealed a panoramic view of Central Park.

The furniture was an eclectic combination of Scandinavian and antique, highlighted by an imposing Coromandel screen purchased when Lillian and Nigel had visited India. Easy groups of sofas, chairs and tables, casually arranged around Anatolian and Oushag rugs, marked conversation areas, but when guests gathered, no one ever gave a second thought to moving a chair or table to accommodate a new arrival.

"There you are." Lillian peered under the piano, then perched on the window seat and became silent for a moment.

"Is something wrong, Aunt Lillian?" Brett asked, aware of the concerned look on her aunt's face.

"Not at all, dear," Lillian said, a little too brightly. "As a matter of fact, on Saturday, we're going to meet someone you've often heard me mention." She slipped her hands into the pockets of her paint-spattered smock. Brett furrowed her brow, trying to guess who it might be. "It's someone I've known for a very long time," Lillian said.

Brett puzzled a bit longer, then said, "I give up."

"Come sit next to me." Lillian patted the needlepoint cushion. "We're going to meet your grandfather, dear."

"But, how?" Brett's voice trailed off. She didn't know what to say or think or feel.

"He's coming to New York on business, and he called and asked if he could see you," Lillian said.

"He wants to meet me?" Brett wondered about him often, but had never dreamed that he thought about her, too.

Lillian nodded and kissed her. "So, Saturday it is. Now, I've got to clean my brushes before supper."

What Lillian had told Brett about her grandfather provided little comfort. As a five-year-old in Wisconsin, Lillian had idolized her ten-year-old brother, wanting to follow him everywhere. He was aloof and distant then, and had remained that way as they grew up and pursued separate paths. She studied art abroad; he entered the Larsen family business, turning a prosperous railroad concern into a billion-dollar transportation conglomerate. But Brett knew his own daughter hated him so intensely that she could not abide the mention of his name. Did her grandfather hate Barbara, too? Would he hate her? What did he want with her?

She headed for her bedroom, closed the door, and dialed Lizzie's number. "Something really weird just happened."

"What do you mean, weird?" Lizzie asked.

"My grandfather wants to meet me. Lizzie, what am I going to do? What if he doesn't like me? What am I going to call him?" Brett asked.

"He's your grandfather—he has to like you," Lizzie said.

"But Barbara hates him," Brett objected.

"Brett, you know your mom's a little flaky. He's probably a nice man. My grandfathers are nice. One of them, Grandpa Powell, is really old. He smells like cough drops and can't hear much, but he's nice," Lizzie said.

"You've known him your whole life," Brett protested.

"So what?" Lizzie said. "He wouldn't have bothered if he didn't want to meet you. He always sends you stuff for your birthday and Christmas, and he's your aunt's brother, so how bad could he be?"

"Barbara would have a fit if she found out," Brett said.

"So, who's gonna tell her, you? How often do you see her, once a month? Come on, Brett, it'll be fine."

"You really think so?"

"Yeah. Hold on a second."

Brett could hear her friend's muffled voice, then she returned to the phone.

"Someone wants to say hello to you," Lizzie said.

"What's up, Brett? Inchworm showed me some of your pictures in the school paper. They're really good." It was Lizzie's brother.

"David, thanks. What are you doing home?" Brett sputtered,

glad David could not see that her cheeks had flushed bright pink at the sound of his voice.

"I flew in for a job interview." He had just received his master's degree in computer engineering from Stanford.

"Are you going to work in New York?" Brett asked. Already dreaming he would, her imagination raced ahead of the conversation. Of course, he would have his own apartment. She and Lizzie would visit often, maybe even help him fix it up. Brett was startled by the fluttering in her stomach. It felt as though she had just swooped down from the first big dive on a roller coaster, only nicer.

"Don't know yet. I've got offers out in California, too, so I'll have to decide. Anyway, see you around."

Brett still kept the picture she had taken at Cox Cove two summers ago on her dresser with those of her friends and small family. David didn't treat her like a know-nothing kid, and whenever she and Lizzie daydreamed about dating, proms, or their first kiss, it was always David that she imagined. That part she never shared with her best friend.

"Brett, don't worry about meeting your grandfather," Lizzie said again on the phone. "Everything will be fine. I'll see you tomorrow."

Eyes glued to the door, Brett waited in the sweet, peachy-pink comfort of Rumpelmayer's, the splendid ice cream parlor in the St. Moritz Hotel on Central Park South. She scanned the carnival of stuffed lions, rabbits, bears, and other beasts inhabiting the restaurant's front windows, fingering the jeweled menagerie on her wrist. She had never worn her grandfather's present until today.

"Suppose he doesn't come?" Brett asked, worried.

"Darling, he'll be here." Lillian tried to calm her niece with her steady blue gaze. "You mustn't worry so."

"But you're worried, too. You've been smoking cigarettes one after the other all morning."

Lillian lifted her hand from the cigarette case and patted Brett's arm reassuringly. "Everything will be fine."

They looked up each time a patron entered or exited Rumpelmayer's, but Sven slipped in from the entrance off the hotel lobby. Without warning, he just appeared.

"Hello, Lillian." His eyes were riveted on Brett. "My God, she is the image of Ingrid." He had not been prepared for the arresting similarities between his only grandchild and the wife whom he had loved so fiercely and had lost so long ago when she had given birth to their only child.

Brett, fighting apprehension and nervousness, rose from her seat and eyed him warily. Sven was the tallest, broadest man she had ever seen. He stood like a mountain, his bristly gray-blond hair its snowy summit. His presence, overwhelming and majestic, inspired awe and trepidation, as though to come too close tempted unnamed peril.

"Yes, Sven, she is," Lillian agreed. With some solemnity she faced her grand-niece. "Brett, this is your grandfather."

"Hello, sir." Brett looked directly into his eyes. They were the light, clear blue of a robin's egg, but startlingly transparent. His gaze was cool and penetrating. Brett felt as though he could see everything, and like the lens of her camera, capture all that could be observed in an instant. She wanted to touch him to make sure he was real, but could not bring herself to offer a hug or kiss. She extended her hand, and slowly he engulfed it with his own. The coldness of his grip surprised her.

Sven nodded in reply, seated himself, and continued talking to Lillian. "The photographs you have sent over the years only hinted at the resemblance." His voice, a deep, resonant baritone, was without a trace of the Swedish accent Brett had expected, and seemed to echo, as though it came from far away.

His somber brown, three-piece suit did not camouflage his girth, but made him seem more ponderous amid the peach and gold frivolity of the room. Aside from a gold pocket watch and chain, the brown homburg that he had placed on an empty chair had been his only adornment. A four-in-hand tie, the same color as his suit, was knotted snugly beneath the starched white collar of his shirt. Brett had no way of knowing that this was exactly how her grandfather had dressed every day for the past forty years. His only digression from sartorial sameness was that occasionally his suit and hat were black.

Brett decided to test the waters. "Do I really look like my grandmother?"

In a voice that seemed almost dreamy, Sven mused, "Yes, you are a very beautiful girl—as beautiful as my Ingrid. You have her face, her lovely hair . . ." He trailed off as he recalled how he had loved the feel of Ingrid's long, dark, wavy hair. "You even have her eyes. I never thought I'd see that face again." Sven's voice betrayed more emotion than he had intended. He remembered how intensely Ingrid's green eyes had flashed with golden sparks, as though she were trying to illuminate her subject from her own internal light. His granddaughter's eyes flashed that way now.

Brett and Sven exchanged timid smiles, and for the first time, she sensed a hint of warmth in his icy blue eyes. The word *beautiful* echoed in Brett's head. Barbara had always made her feel like a big, clumsy, hopelessly unattractive freak because Brett did not share her dainty blond beauty. But her grandfather had no reason to lie to her. He thought she was beautiful.

And now she knew she looked like her grandmother. Brett had always felt like a foundling in her family of blue-eyed blondes. She had assumed she looked like her father, whoever he was. She hated the thought of resembling someone who didn't have the guts to stay around, but now she was released from that painful idea.

"She had dark hair? Was she Swedish, too?" Brett asked.

"Yes. The story goes that dark-haired Swedes all descended from Bernadotte, one of Napoleon's marshals, who was named Crown Prince Karl John of Sweden back in 1810."

"Do you have a picture of her—my grandmother, I mean?" Brett asked cautiously.

"Yes. A wedding portrait. I'll send it when I get back to Racine." Sven cupped her cheek lovingly with his right hand. Noticing her wrist, he continued, "I see you're wearing your bracelet. Is there some kind of charm you'd like better than animals for your birthday?"

Brett puzzled for a moment. "You make trains, don't you . . . Grandfather?" The name sounded strange to them both.

"Yes, Brett, among other things. I make airplanes, too."

"I'd like a train. Maybe an engine with a smokestack and the funny metal fork at the front." Brett's face lit up with excitement and happiness.

Sven chuckled. "It's called a cowcatcher. We haven't made trains with those for a very long time, but if it's a cowcatcher you want, a cowcatcher you shall have!"

A red-jacketed waiter interrupted the merriment and asked if they were ready to order.

Lillian requested ice cream cake, a house specialty.

"I'll have whatever the young lady has," Sven said gallantly.

Brett had been about to order strawberries Romanoff, but changed her mind. "Vanilla ice cream, please," deciding it would be more to her grandfather's liking.

"Brett, I don't think I ever told you that your grandfather was quite the amateur boxer in his day. 'Swede' Larsen, they called him." Lillian smiled at her brother. She had not seen him so relaxed in years.

"A boxer, really?"

"And a tough one, I might add." Sven balled up his fists and sparred with the air. "I'd set them up with my right and finish them off with the left upper cut," he said, continuing to demonstrate his technique.

Brett laughed at her grandfather's antics. Lizzie was right—grandfathers were nice. When he unclenched his hands, and laid them on the table, Brett gasped audibly. She was horrified to see that the index and middle fingers of his left hand were no longer than his pinkie. The tips were gone. She was repulsed, and fascinated at the same time, and stared at his hand. With the candor of a twelve-year-old, she asked, "Did that happen boxing?"

Instantly, Sven's demeanor changed. He snatched his hands from the table and replied coldly, "No."

A frosty silence settled on the trio. The waiter reappeared balancing a tray with their selections. Brett looked at her grandfather, hoping to see some sign that he approved of her choice of dessert, but now his blue eyes seemed opaque and revealed nothing.

Directing his attention toward his sister, Sven spoke in a businesslike tone. "Lillian, since you're the child's legal guardian, my attorney will be in contact with you to go over some details of the trust I've established for her." He picked up his homburg and pushed back his chair. "I must leave now." He nodded at Lillian and Brett, looking past them both, then marched off in the direction from which he had come. Two dark-suited men, whom neither Brett nor Lillian had noticed earlier, closed ranks behind him.

Brett's face clouded. Her father, then Brian North and Zachary, were all gone. Now she'd driven her grandfather away. "I didn't mean to make him angry." Brett fought to hold back the tears.

"Nonsense, child, you did nothing of the sort. It's just his way," Lillian said, attempting to mask her own distress.

"No, I upset him. Everything was fine until I asked about his fingers," Brett insisted.

"I saw Sven with his hand still in bandages. I guess it was eleven or twelve years ago. When I asked what happened, I got the same reaction. Your grandfather is a hard man to understand. After all these years, I still don't," Lillian said sadly.

On the following Thursday, a package arrived for Brett. She opened it in her room and found two sealed boxes. The first contained an exquisitely framed, sepia-tone portrait of Ingrid, her grandmother, dated in the lower right-hand corner, April 12, 1939. Ingrid's hair was arranged in an upsweep with a pompadour in front. Her white lace dress bared her shoulders, and around her neck, on a white ribbon, she wore a cameo.

In the second box, cradled in cotton, Brett found the cameo, inscribed, "All my love, Sven."

Brett went to the mirror, fastened the cameo around her neck, unbuttoned the first three buttons of her blouse, and tugged it down around her shoulders. With one hand she lifted her long dark hair to the top of her head; in the other, she held the picture. Maybe she did look like her grandmother, she thought.

Tucked in one of the boxes, Brett found a note written on Larsen Enterprises stationery. It read, "As promised. Sven Larsen."

— *Chapter 4* —

"I know, I know, Diet 7-Up, extra Sweet & Low!" Brett yelled over the din of the Sex Pistols reverberating on the stereo. She passed the green and pink neon Christmas tree glowing in the front window and trotted down the hall, glancing occasionally at the rows of magazine covers, each in a silver art nouveau frame, which lined the glossy aubergine walls. Sometimes she still couldn't believe she worked for Malcolm Kent, the world-renowned fashion photographer.

Brett had filled her life to the brim and she thrived on it. Her senior year at Dalton held many academic challenges and she met them admirably, always maintaining her standing in the top ten percent of her class. Yet none of her subjects compelled her the way photography did.

In the last two years, fashion photography had become her passion. Every month she devoured American, French, British, and Italian *Vogue, Elle, Voilà!, Donna, Marie Claire*, and every other magazine she could get her hands on, keeping notebooks of the pages she admired.

In October of her junior year, while perusing the bulletin wall at Duggal, the photographers' film and processing lifeline in the heart of the photo district, she spied an ad that read, "Fashion photographer needs assistant for my assistant. Real grub work. Not much money, but never dull." She and Lizzie talked for hours about whether she should apply. Brett had learned many skills as a photographer. She knew the artistry and mechanics of composition and light, but she didn't know what happened between photographic concept and the newsstand. Whatever this job entailed, Brett was convinced that it would unlock the secrets of this "members-only" club.

So she called the number in the ad, and after being questioned briefly by a voice of indeterminate gender, she was told to bring her portfolio to the penthouse studio at 696 Sixth Avenue and ask for Gracie. Malcolm still teased her about the shock that flashed across her face when she discovered that the husky alto voice of Gracie belonged to Malcolm Kent, one of her idols. No one could move a photo the way he could, but this was not how she had expected him to look.

Seated at the burled mahogany desk in his office, he paged slowly and thoughtfully through her portfolio. Brett kept noticing his fingernails, which were polished a deep plum to match his silk kimono.

"Darling, these are very good," he said when he reached the end.

Brett couldn't believe it. Like most fledgling photographers, she had spent hours choosing which prints to include or remove from her portfolio, and had arranged it so that the pictures flowed pleasingly. But she had never dreamed that someone of Malcolm's stature would be looking through it.

"The textures, the light—really excellent. And you say you're in high school?" Malcolm was eccentric, but he knew good pictures, and he sensed a depth of understanding in Brett's brilliant green eyes. He could see from the way she dressed and spoke that she was a society girl, but she had exceptional talent for one so young. He needed someone three afternoons a week and some weekends to ferry color film back and forth to the lab, develop black and white film, clean and organize lenses and other equipment, tidy up the studio, and run general errands. If she was willing to work, the job was hers. If he was right, and he was rarely wrong, so was the future.

Brett begged and cajoled her aunt, promising that her studies would not suffer, that she really would be home at a reasonable hour, and with the drama of a teenager, insisted that this was the most important thing in her life and she would never have such a sterling opportunity again. Lillian, Brett's guardian, had her reservations about the job, but Lillian, the artist, understood the value of a mentor, and so Brett was allowed to work for Malcolm Kent.

Sweetened soda in hand, Brett strode back toward the makeup room. Her studio uniform of black cotton turtleneck, tucked into straight-leg blue jeans, made her look even taller than her five feet nine inches. Her hair, a joyous burst of brunette waves, was fastened at the nape of her neck by a silver Navajo clasp, a gift from Aunt Lillian. Despite her best efforts, tendrils had escaped and randomly graced her forehead, almost hiding her widow's peak. Thick, full brows lent a mischievous touch to her verdant green eyes and her skin shone with the healthy blush that cosmetics companies sought to package.

While working at the studio, hair and makeup people, clients, and other models often told Brett that she should lose ten or fifteen pounds and become a model, for while she wasn't overweight, hers was not the angular body of most models. Brett had inherited her mother's curves, but hers were not slow and lazy like Barbara's— they were racy and athletic. Brett always assumed her complimenters were being polite and dismissed the comments. Besides, she had no interest in modeling.

Brett spent little time thinking about her looks. In her own mind, she was not a beauty. She had accepted that, and instead of dwelling on her appearance, had started to build a full, exciting life for herself. Barbara's browbeatings when Brett was young still stung when she looked in the mirror. Whenever she pulled on a sweater or slacks she heard Barbara saying, "Your arms and legs poke out of everything. If I didn't know better, I'd swear you were growing up to be a boy." Each time she secured her waves into her customary braid she heard Barbara scolding, "Your hair was just brushed and now it's standing all over your head." Little Brett had been so awed by glamorous, dazzling Barbara that she never questioned her mother's assessments of her looks. But through no effort or contrivance, Brett had blossomed into a fresh and lovely young woman who had the effortless beauty of a wildflower blooming in a sun-kissed meadow. Her charm had always been apparent and her beauty would be there when she finally discovered it.

"I still don't know how you drink this." Brett handed Malcolm his soda.

Malcolm took the can without looking and continued his tirade. "It's still too pink!" he told the makeup artist, referring to the lip color of the blond model perched in the makeup chair. "Mauve—I want it more mauve. Here, give me that." Malcolm snatched the small black lacquered case that had compartments for thirty-two lip colors from the harried makeup artist. "Mix these two," he instructed, pointing out the shades with his own recently manicured red fingernails.

The hapless makeup artist did as she was told because she knew that Malcolm's eye for color was unerring.

"Much better, don't you agree, Brett?" he asked, indicating he was finally satisfied.

Brett did not respond because she was not expected to. She was just grateful not to be on Malcolm's hit list today. When she had arrived at the studio yesterday after school, Malcolm was on the warpath, ranting about film that should have been delivered by the lab. He had asked Brett to stop by Duggal on her way to work and pick up the film in question. Handing him the two oblong white boxes, Brett had reminded him of his instructions. He offered no apology. "Humph," he had uttered and strode away.

Then later, when he was shooting, Malcolm asked Brett for a 70-mm lens. She was certain that he meant a 110-mm, but having already evoked his ire, she gave him exactly what he asked for. Malcolm hit the ceiling. He insisted that he had requested the 110 and chided Brett for not listening to him. Brett was almost in tears, but during her first week at Kent Studios, she had seen him reduce a hairstylist to a sniveling mess, and she vowed that would never happen to her.

There were days when she wanted to quit and spend her after-school hours as she once had—taking pictures for the *Daltonian*. Sometimes she missed the relaxed camaraderie of working with her friends on the school paper. *But I'm learning so much*, she always told herself.

"Now she looks great, but I look horrible." Malcolm shifted his gaze from the model to himself. In the spirit of the season, he wore skin-tight red leather pants, a billowing white silk shirt tightly belted at the waist, white satin slippers with maribou trim, and a sprig of mistletoe suspended from a red satin ribbon around his neck.

"Why didn't someone tell me that my eyebrows looked so awful? I simply cannot take another picture looking like this." He held out his hand, and like a scrub nurse giving the surgeon a scalpel, the makeup artist slapped a pair of tweezers in his upturned palm.

He really is bizarre, Brett thought as Malcolm diligently tweezed his errant brows. Some days he was Gracie, some days he was Malcolm, and his wardrobe changed accordingly. She and Lizzie had endless discussions about Malcolm's sexual preferences, and Lizzie, who considered herself worldly in such matters, proclaimed, "He's bisexual with transvestite overtones, Brett." Brett didn't care. He was a genius with a camera, and in this business, Malcolm Kent was already legend.

Brett left the makeup room and moved around the studio, deftly performing her duties. First she inspected the white seamless paper used as a backdrop. Finding only three scuff marks, she removed her shoes, crawled across the paper, and covered them with chalk instead of rolling down fresh paper. She then cleared away the leftovers from the catered lunch, gathered half-empty soda cans and Styrofoam cups, and emptied ashtrays. When the makeup room was vacated, she swept up used Q-Tips, crumpled Kleenex, makeup-stained cotton balls, and the remnants of an emergency haircut. This was the last shot until the new year; she was glad for the brief hiatus.

Thinking of the holidays made Brett remember that she needed to confirm two models for the location trip to Cozumel in January. Closing herself in the relative quiet of the office, she called Ford and Elite with the necessary dates and rates, then called the travel agent to reserve flights for the models and crew. She sighed, wishing she could go along, but she would be back in school by then.

Over the year she had worked with Malcolm, he had come to rely on her greatly. She performed many of the functions of a studio manager for the hopelessly frantic and frequently difficult Malcolm, and in turn he critiqued her photographs, sometimes offering constructive suggestions and sometimes ripping them apart with pronouncements so scathing that she had to fight the urge to put down her camera for good. But when Malcolm was most difficult, she braced herself with the knowledge she was learning from the master; whatever price she paid was worth that.

"Brett, I need you!" She heard Vinnie Cambria, Malcolm's assistant, shout as soon as she hung up the phone and she hustled from the office.

"Stand in while I check the lights." Vinnie handed Brett the meter. The umbrella-shaded strobes flashed as Vinnie popped the power pack and Brett yelled out the readings over the driving, Eurosynthesized rhythms of Giorgio Moroder. Blaring music was part of the ambience at Kent Studios. Malcolm claimed the relentless sound blocked out everything but his "vision." Finally satisfied that everything was balanced, Vinnie beckoned to Brett.

"I'm doin' a test tonight. Wanna stay?" Vinnie whispered.

"Sure. I'll tell my aunt I'll be late." Brett never missed the opportunity to take part in a test.

She remembered the first time Vinnie had asked her to test. She had worried a good part of the afternoon, and finally asked him if she could have a day to study. Malcolm and Vinnie doubled over with laughter, then explained that they weren't going to test her. He told her that when a photographer has a new camera, different film, or unusual lighting that he wants to experiment with, he calls an agency and they send new models who need photos for their portfolios for him to choose from. Models get photographs, photographers get models, and everyone gets the pictures they need. Brett hadn't learned anything new from testing with Vinnie for a long time, but she felt the experience was valuable.

"But aren't you going to Malcolm's Christmas party?" she asked.

"Sure, but that won't start to cook until midnight. We'll be outta here way before that," Vinnie said.

Studio 54 would be closed to the general public for Malcolm's holiday soiree. The hottest, most outrageous, most beautiful people in New York would arrive in droves and party 'til the break of dawn. Brett's name appeared on the doorman's guest list, but she knew her aunt would never give in. *Next year*, she thought.

Just then the entourage, led by Malcolm, appeared. He paraded the two models, in their Bill Blass linen suits, before Phoebe Caswell, *Vogue's* fashion editor, who had been sitting imperiously in a director's chair, flanked by her two assistants, since the completion of the last shot. Waving her Mont Blanc pen like a scepter, she blessed the models with an emphatic, "They look fabulous!" The stylist made a last-minute adjustment to the double-stick tape he had placed under the lapel of the brunette model's suit and joined the hair and makeup people off the set.

The "Mighty Kent" surveyed the lights, the models, the makeup, the hair, the clothes, and silently nodded his head. Vinnie handed him his loaded Nikon, Brett turned up the stereo, Malcolm kicked off his satin mules and hollered, "Let's rock!"

The girls jumped, spun, danced, and cavorted across the seamless paper with the grace and abandon of wild things.

"Yes!" Malcolm wailed, the motor drive whirring, as he dropped to his knees.

Not all models could meet his challenge. Many a girl had been dismissed midshoot for not possessing the requisite vitality. Today, he worked with two of his favorites and they knew how to give Malcolm what he wanted.

"Film!" yelled Brett, who had been silently counting frames. Malcolm handed Vinnie the camera to reload, Brett rolled down fresh seamless, the stylist and hair and makeup artists descended on the breathless models to powder sweaty brows, comb stray hairs, and readjust disheveled garments, then disappeared.

"Jump higher!" Malcolm roared to the blond model who leaped across the seamless. And she did.

Now on his belly, Malcolm purred, "Unbutton the jackets." They didn't hesitate, and with each unfastened button, revealed more of their bare skin.

Sensing the change in mood, Brett switched the tape to Marvin Gaye's steamy "Let's Get It On."

"Work it," Malcolm moaned.

The blonde, her jacket held together by one button at her navel, stood with her hands on her hips, daring Malcolm with her body. The brunette hugged herself so that the roundness of her breasts peaked above her open jacket and she licked her lips tauntingly. They gyrated sensuously and Malcolm guided them skillfully, gently, never letting them stray into vulgarity.

Malcolm whipped through six rolls of film in no time, and with the drained but content look of a satisfied lover, he uttered, "I've got it."

Phoebe Caswell signed the models' vouchers with a scribble of her ever-present Mont Blanc and left in a flurry of double-miss kisses. She accepted Malcolm's eccentricities, as did fashion editors and art directors the world over, because the results were always vital photographs that never required compromise or costly reshoots.

Brett found Malcolm collapsed on the black leather chaise in his office. After the last shot he always disappeared immediately, never participating in the chitchat that inevitably accompanied clearing the studio of people and paraphernalia.

"You were great today. I don't know how you get exactly what you want from people," Brett said almost reverently.

"It's easy. You have to know what you want. Most people don't, but I think you do." Malcolm eyed her impishly. Brett was taken aback by her mentor's observation, but before she could question him further, he went on. "I need today's film late tomorrow afternoon. I don't imagine I'll be up much before then."

"I'll sort it by page and leave it for you by the light box," Brett replied.

Malcolm nodded, closed his eyes, and settled back into the cushions. Gently, Brett closed the door.

A short time later Malcolm burst from his office, a full length coyote coat thrown dramatically across his shoulders. He scurried out to prepare himself for the pre-Studio 54 dinner party he was throwing at his Greenwich Village brownstone.

"Why don't you jump around a little and I'll try to catch it," Vinnie offered lamely.

Randall, the golden-haired, sixteen-year-old six-footer, stood on the seamless and stared back at him incredulously. "I've been jumping around like a jackrabbit in heat, and if we've taken six pictures I'll be damned!" Randall fumed in her Alabama drawl.

Brett held the reflector in front of her face to hide her laughter. Vinnie was hopeless. He was a Malcolm clone and it just didn't work. The setting was the same, the music was as loud as it had been before, but Vinnie just didn't have the magic touch. Brett kept looking at Randall. She was special. She could easily become one of the girls who commanded $5,000 a day.

As the test dragged on, Brett became more impressed with Randall's natural, lazy ease with the camera—a quality Vinnie continued to miss completely. She bet Randall could tell a story with her face.

"I've got it," Vinnie exclaimed after his final click of the shutter.

In your dreams, Brett thought as Randall, the petulant, sexy, child-woman, stormed from the set.

Vinnie left the studio excitedly to take the film to the lab. He would be back to escort Randall to the party. Immediately, Brett turned the stereo off. The silence felt good to her.

"Thanks. That racket was driving me crazy," Randall declared as Brett walked into the dressing room where Randall stood naked in front of the fan, cooling down from Vinnie's forced aerobics.

"Sorry," Brett said as she turned quickly to leave the room.

"Aw, honey, it's all right," Randall said. "I never even think about it. With girls it doesn't matter, and most of these boys are a little light in their loafers, so I know I'm safe."

"I was just going to straighten up," Brett explained.

"Just what do you do?" Randall asked.

"I do a little bit of everything around here, but I'm a photographer, too," Brett said confidently.

"Well, I sure hope you don't shoot like Vinnie. He doesn't have the talent the good Lord gave a flea! This test was a waste of my time," Randall huffed as she snatched her black suede pants from a chair, and to Brett's surprise, stepped into them without putting on underwear.

"Oh, no, that's not my style," Brett asserted quickly.

"So, what is your style?" Randall asked as she dug in her model bag for her hairbrush.

"Well, it's more natural—relaxed, sort of," Brett explained. Before she could stop herself, she blurted, "I could show you."

"I've already wrestled one alligator tonight," Randall countered, vigorously brushing her waist-length hair.

"No, just keep doing what you're doing. Besides, if you've already wasted an evening, what's one more roll of film?" Brett coaxed playfully.

Randall laughed. "Are you sure this won't hurt?"

"Painless. Completely painless." Brett dashed from the dressing room. This had to be fast. Vinnie would be angry if he found her taking Randall's picture. She loaded her Nikon, grabbed two tungsten lights, a reflector, and a light meter, and went back to set up.

Randall remained sitting on the counter, one foot on a chair seat, one propped against its back. She was still bare from the waist up, her breasts covered only by a curtain of fine blond hair the color of corn silk.

"So, what do I do now?" Randall asked.

"Stay there. I need a minute," Brett answered. Her eyes darted about as she studied the room. She closed closet doors and grouped the makeup and brushes on the counter so they pleased her. She deposited Randall's open black leather model bag on the chair where her foot rested and arranged a few items so they spilled from the top, then stopped to check the scene through her camera. Satisfied with the composition, she placed the tungstens, creating planes of golden light and diffused shadows. Brett took a light reading and tried to ignore the tingling in her stomach. She wanted these to be good.

Gazing through the viewfinder, Brett said, "Powder your forehead and nose. You're a little shiny."

Randall reached for the brush, dipped it in the loose powder that sat open on the counter and swiveled to look in the mirror.

Click.

"But . . ." Randall sputtered.

"I told you this was easy," Brett said comfortingly.

Randall relaxed and powdered her face.

Click.

"So, where are you from?" Brett asked.

Randall turned and faced Brett head on, both hands at her sides on the counter. "Nowhere," she let slip in a whisper.

Click.

Regaining her spirited edge, Randall planted her elbow on her knee, propped her head in her hand, and continued, "Well, it might as well be nowhere. It's this teeny, tiny town called Headland, Alabama, that's next to a bigger tiny town called Dothan."

Click.

"Now, don't get me wrong—a lot of famous people came from Alabama. Helen Keller was born up in Tuscumbia, and Joe Louis was from Lafayette, but ain't nobody famous come from Headland 'til now. I'm gonna put it on the map!" Randall sat up defiantly.

Click.

Brett continued asking questions in a relaxed, calming voice, but she never heard the answers. It was as though she had no hearing or feeling, only sight, and she perceived everything in her viewfinder with intensity, clarity, and precision. She saw the light that flickered in the corners of Randall's eyes, the slight turn of her head, the arch of an eyebrow, that changed her expression ever so slightly. Brett seemed to anticipate these subtle shifts and click the shutter just as they occurred.

"Are you going home for the holidays?" Brett asked as she shifted her position to capture Randall's reflection in the mirror.

"I spent a lot of time getting away from home and I'm not going back now," Randall answered quietly, staring off into space.

Click.

Brett instructed Randall to continue dressing for the party. She put on her see-through black organza blouse, primping and arranging as though Brett wasn't there, and silently, unobtrusively, patiently, Brett waited for precisely the right moment to take each frame.

"Do you have an appointment book?" Brett asked.

"Sure," Randall replied, digging it out of her bag.

Click.

Brett gave Randall her phone number, still taking pictures as she wrote it down.

"You can call me tomorrow afternoon. I'll have film by then," Brett said brightly, finally lowering the camera from her face.

"We're done?" Randall blurted, surprised.

"See. I told you it wouldn't hurt." Brett breathed for the first time she remembered in ten minutes. She felt as though she'd just been in a trance. Before she had a chance to relax, she heard the elevator door open.

"That's Vinnie!" Brett sprang into action. She hid her camera on a closet shelf.

Knocking on the dressing room door, Vinnie asked, "Are you ready yet, Randall?"

"I'll be out in a minute, sugar," Randall cooed.

"Is Brett in there?" Vinnie continued.

"I'm cleaning up, Vinnie. I'll be done soon," Brett replied.

Brett tucked the lights in the closet; she would put them away tomorrow.

"Vinnie thinks I'm his date for Malcolm's party, but I'm losing him as soon as we walk through those big black doors," Randall confided. "This business is all about being seen, and I've got important people to meet," she finished, making one last adjustment to the gold link belt around her slender waist.

Minutes later the two young women emerged from the room, chattering merrily.

"You guys go ahead, I'll lock up," Brett offered, sending Randall and Vinnie off into the night. As soon as she was alone, she grabbed her coat and her camera, secured the studio, and nearly ran to Duggal to deposit her film.

"Malcolm! I didn't expect you so early." Brett anxiously looked up from the film she had shot of Randall. Quickly she removed the slides from the light table and returned them to their plastic box.

"Life is full of the unexpected, Brett," Malcolm said.

"The *Vogue* film is ready," she said, indicating the chromes neatly pocketed in clear vinyl slide pages and stacked beside her. "It looks great." She casually placed her film among the boxes of *Vogue* castoffs; she would retrieve it later.

Malcolm knew that Vinnie used the studio at off hours for testing—all assistants did. That was one of the perks the job offered. But as an assistant assistant, Brett had not yet been accorded that privilege, and she did not want to think about the possible consequences of using the studio without Malcolm's permission. "How was the party?"

"A great success, as usual, but exhausting. It's really very tiring keeping up with your image," Malcolm said with a touch of bitterness.

"But, you created that image," Brett said.

"I know, I know. I always become disenchanted after spending twenty thousand bucks to entertain people, half of whom I don't know, the other half I don't like," Malcolm snapped.

Brett stared at Malcolm, not knowing if this was again one of his conversations with himself or if he expected her participation. Today he was clearly Malcolm. Standing there in a quilted down vest over a fisherman-knit sweater, corduroy pants, argyle socks, and rubber slush-proof duck shoes, he looked like a suburban husband who had lost his wife in the mall. His brown hair, parted simply on the side, showed no evidence of mousse, spray, or gel. Even his fingernails were free of polish.

"So, why do you do it?" Brett asked after a moment.

"Because I can't do anything else. Never mind about me, it's just the Scrooge coming out. Let's see the *Vogue* film." Malcolm exchanged places with Brett and took a seat at the light table. He spent twenty minutes examining the slides in silence, then announced triumphantly, "These should blow Phoebe's dress up!"

"They really are amazing, Malcolm—especially the last roll," Brett volunteered.

"Pretty hot stuff, huh? You know, I'd like to see the castoffs of that roll."

Brett's heart pounded as Malcolm began to look through the slide boxes at the back of the table. He lifted each lid and removed one slide to examine as he searched for the right box. When his hand reached the one containing her chromes, Brett held her breath.

"What is this? Why is Vinnie's film mixed in with mine?" Malcolm asked loudly. "Did that twerp have his film processed on my account at Duggal?"

"It's not Vinnie's film," Brett answered quietly.

"Well, whose is it and why is it here?" Malcolm asked.

"It's mine." Brett braced herself for one of Malcolm's harangues.

"Yours! I thought Vinnie was testing last night."

"He was—I mean, he did," Brett fumbled. This was it—she was going to be fired, she knew it. "But I shot a roll of film when he took his to the lab."

Malcolm emptied her box of slides onto the light table and examined them with the loupe as he spoke. "So you thought you could do a better job than Vinnie, Miss Wonder Lens?"

"Yes . . . no. But this girl was so incredible, and Vinnie kept missing it."

"And Sally Shutterbug, girl photographer, thought she'd whip out her trusty Nikon and save this poor model from Vinnie's ineptitude," Malcolm said sarcastically.

Brett decided that since she was going to be fired anyway, she might as well say what she felt. In a firm, strong voice she replied, "I shot what I saw. Vinnie copies everything you do, from the loud music to the jumping around, except his pictures are flat and boring. This girl had such a quiet beauty that when I saw her sitting in the dressing room I had to take some pictures. If that was wrong, I'm sorry. It'll only take me a minute to clear my stuff out of the studio." Brett turned to leave, then said, "I'd like my film."

"So, you're a better photographer than Vinnie?" Malcolm asked, a hint of mischief creeping into his voice.

"Yes!" Brett answered defiantly, prepared for the onslaught.

"Well, you're right." Malcolm finally put down the loupe and spun around to face her.

"What?" Brett couldn't believe her ears. She eyed Malcolm in stunned silence, still not ready to let her guard down.

"Vinnie's an excellent assistant, which means he anticipates my needs and fulfills them without bothering me. Technically, he has the skills of a good photographer, but he has no soul. He doesn't know what he wants, so he'll never get it. But you're different, Brett."

"I knew what I wanted Randall to do. I just wasn't sure how to get her to do it, so I just asked her some questions, got her talking. I don't even remember what we said."

"But you knew what you were after, right? And when you saw

it, you knew it was right? That's what I mean. I can see it in these shots. They're breathtaking," Malcolm said exuberantly.

"You really think so?" Malcolm's praise made Brett's hands tingle.

"Is Malcolm Kent ever wrong about a photograph? Besides, you know as well as I do that you have talent. You just told me so in no uncertain terms."

"RISD should help a lot." Brett finally relaxed.

"What?" Malcolm asked incredulously.

"The Rhode Island School of Design. I've been accepted as a photography major. I start in September."

"I know what RISD is. Let me tell you something. The last thing you need is to study photography. You should go to Europe, learn about fashion, experience the world, and take pictures!"

"But RISD is a good school," Brett protested.

"Maybe I was wrong about you. When you first came here, I knew you were from money, but your pictures were good and you were willing to work hard, so I gave you a chance. It came to me shortly after I'd hired you why your name was familiar. I'd been reading about your mother in *NOW* for years."

Brett blanched at the mention of her mother. She had not tried to hide her background, but it had never been questioned or even discussed in all the time she had worked for Malcolm.

"But it wasn't until I read about your grandfather buying an airline or something that I put the whole picture together. You could buy this entire building with your allowance, and I had you working for minimum wage."

"But it's not like that. I'm not like that . . . them," Brett stammered.

"Oh, no? Then why go off to Rhode Island to study photography? To be up there with all those eligible Brown, Harvard, and MIT men with proper pedigrees?"

"I don't care about men with pedigrees. I care about photography," Brett insisted earnestly. "I just thought school would broaden my horizons." As soon as she said it, she realized how naive it sounded.

"I'll tell you about broadening your horizons, Brett. Remember, a little while ago, you said I created my image—the one I have to live up to? Well, I did create it—all of it. I'm not from England, as everyone supposes. I'm from a coal mining town in West Virginia—the name isn't important. When I left at fifteen, I'd already been working in the mines for two years, and I had nine brothers and sisters still home. One Friday, I didn't take my pay home. I bought a Trailways bus ticket to New York, and although I send money home regularly, I've never been back."

Brett tried to hide her shock at Malcolm's revelations. She had had no idea, but that's the way Malcolm had planned it. No one had any idea. As he continued, his eyes darted furtively, as if telling this story would resurrect ghosts he had long ago dismissed.

"When I stepped off the bus in New York, I looked up and saw a huge billboard in Times Square. It was an ad for Kent cigarettes. Down at the bottom of the board was a small sign that said, 'Malcolm & Mitchell Outdoor Advertising.' Over the next few years, I used all three names in different combinations while working at any menial job I could get. While I washed dishes and swept floors, I practiced speaking the way people in the movies spoke. I had never been to a movie before I came to New York.

"By the time I was nineteen, I had worked my way up to waiting tables at a tiny little restaurant in the theater district. One of my regular customers was a photographer. When he offered me a job as his assistant, I was sure it was my ticket to success. I accepted the job and soon found out what kind of photographer he was. He took pictures of working girls. You know what that is, Brett?"

She nodded silently, completely engrossed in the story.

"He worked for several British girlie magazines. The magazines paid him $100 a photograph; he paid the girls $15. After all, he said, they didn't have to do anything but show up and take their clothes off. He paid me $5 per photo. I worked for him for two years because it was the most money I'd ever made. I saved up, bought my own camera, and started offering girls $40 to pose for me. I got prettier girls because I paid more money. Then I approached the same British publisher with my pictures. I did that for ten years, Brett. My name was Kent Mitchell then.

"And I liked taking pictures. I could make magical things happen with a camera, but I wanted something more. The publisher offered me a job in England. They sent a plane ticket and an advance. I traded in the ticket to London, took the advance, and went to Paris. I changed my name to Malcolm Kent and started taking pictures of girls with their clothes on. Eight years later I returned to New York as the toast of the fashion world, the outrageous Malcolm Kent."

"Malcolm, that's amazing," Brett said.

"I didn't tell you that story to impress you. If I'd had all of your advantages, I would have used them in a minute. It would have saved me lots of time and a great deal of inconvenience. You can stay home and play tiddledywinks, knowing full well that you'll still have a handsome roof over your head and live happily ever after. But if you want to take pictures, you don't need me or some esteemed faculty to tell you how. You need the guts to go do it. The choice is yours," Malcolm finished and stood to walk away.

"Malcolm?" Brett called, her voice tinged with playfulness.

"Yes?" He turned to face her again.

"What's your real name?" Brett asked coyly.

Trying to appear stern, he crossed his arms and stared at her. She giggled and looked him directly in the eye.

"Well?"

Malcolm dropped his stance, put his hands on his hips, and suddenly became Gracie. "If you breathe a word of this to anyone—*anyone*—I shall find you and scratch your eyes out. Then you'll never take another picture." He paused a moment. "Earl . . . Earl Cooley. Now, isn't that a tacky name?"

— *Chapter 5* —

"Are you sure?" Lillian asked. She tried to appear composed, but her face showed all the concern she felt about Brett's surprise announcement.

"More sure than I've been of anything, Aunt Lillian. I just know it's the right thing for me," Brett answered, her green eyes alive with a newfound confidence.

Five months had passed since Brett's conversation with Malcolm, and although he never mentioned it again, she had thought of little else. She went through the Christmas holidays, including a ski trip to Sun Valley with Aunt Lillian and Lizzie, virtually in a fog. As winter thawed into spring and Brett's friends were aflutter, planning gowns and dates for the senior dance, she camped out at the library, devouring information about Paris, when she wasn't at the studio. She had even begun *reading* her French fashion magazines in an effort to improve her language skills.

Still she told no one of her discussion with Malcolm—not even Lizzie. In fact, the first person she told was a stranger, almost. He was a proper young man—a Groton alumnus, Princeton freshman, and neighbor at the San Remo, whom she asked, at the last minute, to be her escort for the senior dance. In her daydreams her date had always been David, but he was miles away in California, and besides, Brett was certain he still thought of her as a kid.

She was dancing in the arms of her proper young man under a papier-mâché moon, and imagining herself beneath the stars on a bateau-mouche cruising the Seine, when he asked her what college she was planning to attend.

"I'm not going to college. I'm going to live in Paris." She said the words without thinking.

"Wow, that's great!" he responded. "I envy you. My parents decided the day I was born that I would attend Princeton. It's a family tradition."

His reaction surprised her and she knew she had made her decision. *Now*, she thought, *I must tell Aunt Lillian. Maybe her reaction will surprise me, as well.*

"I certainly didn't expect this," Lillian said evenly.

"Life is full of the unexpected, Aunt Lillian," Brett said, unconsciously quoting Malcolm.

"I do have my reservations, but I understand, child. When I decided to go to London to study art, my parents were shocked, but they supported my decision and I shall do the same for you." Lillian paused for a moment, then added hesitantly, "I was older than seventeen, of course, but I guess these are different times."

Brett threw her arms around Lillian's neck. "I hoped you would understand!" Rush, the Airedale, had been napping under a coffee table during the discussion. At Brett's exclamations he came over and sat squarely on her feet, as though waiting to be apprised of the news.

"Heaven only knows what your grandfather will say," Lillian announced.

Since their first meeting six years ago, Sven had kept in touch with his only grandchild and saw her at least the two or three times a year that business required his presence in New York.

When she turned fifteen, Sven had begun to acquaint her with the magnitude of the Larsen holdings. She spent several days with him at the plush-hushed enclave of Larsen's New York headquarters on Park Avenue, just north of Grand Central Station. Brett remembered feeling uncomfortable, as grown men and women in crisply tailored suits, who referred to her as Miss Larsen, were called upon to give her reports on the various Larsen interests. Railroads, airlines, and shipping formed the backbone of the Larsen empire, and research into space transport was being pursued as the wave of the future.

50   Marie Joyce

She would hate to be staring across a conference table trying to make a deal with him, Brett thought while watching Sven during one of her briefings. It would be hard to come out on top. Many experienced negotiators thought the same thing.

Brett always listened attentively, but had no interest in following in her grandfather's footsteps.

"I'll tackle Grandfather in a few days," Brett explained. "First, I have to tell Lizzie."

"You mean, you haven't even discussed this with Lizzie?" Lillian asked.

"I had to make up my own mind this time. I just hope she understands," Brett replied.

"Well, when would you like to leave?" Lillian asked.

"As soon after graduation as possible. I'll miss Cox Cove, but there's no point in spending the summer in New York when I can spend it in Paris," Brett said.

"That's just a few weeks, child." Lillian thought for a moment. "How would you like me to go over with you and help you get settled? I haven't been to Paris since the summer we spent in France—what was it, four years ago?"

"Oh, Aunt Lillian, I'd love it! We'll have a wonderful time!"

"I'm not going to RISD in September," Brett said.

"You're not what?" Lizzie shouted into the telephone. Neither one of her parents had a degree and they had provided for their children admirably, but David had changed all that and Lizzie was determined to be the second Powell with a college education. She planned to put two of her natural talents—talking and asking questions—to good use as a broadcast journalism major at Syracuse University.

"I'm not going to RISD. I'm going to live in Paris, learn about fashion, and take pictures," Brett explained.

"But, what will . . . how can . . . ?" Lizzie fumbled for the right questions. "I thought . . ."

"I know it sounds crazy, but I've been thinking about this for almost six months, and I've made up my mind. Anyway, Malcolm says it's the only way I'll realize my potential," Brett said.

"Six months! And you never even told me?" Lizzie wasn't sure whether she was more distressed because Brett was going thousands of miles to live in a foreign country, or because she hadn't shared her plans. "When are you going?" Lizzie asked quietly.

"Next month. Aunt Lillian is coming to help me get settled," Brett said jubilantly. "I can't wait until you can come for a visit!"

"A visit to Paris? Brett, I'm a scholarship student, remember?" Lizzie said emphatically.

"Oh, we'll work something out. Think about it, Lizzie. What fun we'll have in Paris, surrounded by romantic Frenchmen." Brett hoped the possibility of an affaire du coeur would make Paris more inviting to Lizzie. She was right.

After fully discussing the Parisian campaign, Lizzie blurted, "Guess what?"

"You have a date with John Travolta?" Brett teased.

"Better!" Lizzie giggled.

"You've just been crowned the new Miss America?" Brett was enjoying her jest.

"No—David's engaged. He surprised us and flew home with Kate—that's her name, Kate. Really it's Kathryn, but David calls her Kate." Lizzie babbled on, but Brett did not hear her.

"They're gonna get married in August—in California, of course. Kate's family is there. She asked me to be a bridesmaid. Oh, Brett, she's really cool. She's a pianist—classical stuff. And she's really beautiful." Lizzie took Brett's silence for rapt attention and continued. "We're all going down to the Village tonight to wander around and maybe get something to eat. Do you wanna come? She's really great, you'll like her."

Fat chance, thought Brett. "I can't, Lizzie. I'm sorry, but I have plans with Aunt Lillian," Brett said quickly. "Maybe some other time."

"They're going back first thing in the morning. David's starting his own computer company, you know, and Kate has a recital coming up. You won't even be here for the wedding. I know David wanted you to come." Lizzie had never taken Brett's feelings for David seriously and had long since forgotten them, so she was puzzled by her friend's reticence.

"No, I won't. Tell David—and Kate—I said congratulations," Brett answered slowly. "I have to go now. Aunt Lillian is waiting." She knew the excuse sounded feeble, but she just couldn't spend the evening with David and his fiancée, trying to be perky and excited for them.

Brett gently placed the receiver down and lay across her bed. She knew her reaction was silly. How could she have been so stupid? While every other girl she knew daydreamed about movie stars, rock singers, and football players, she'd been thinking about David. She'd thought they were being crazy, but she had been no more realistic. David was kind and funny and honest, but he was almost ten years older than she. He was starting a business and getting married. She was just getting out of high school. Maybe she would have her own affaire du coeur in Paris, she thought wistfully.

The following week, during their monthly lunch at Lutece, Brett told Barbara of her plans.

"You don't have to go to college or work, you know, but you'll have a marvelous time in Paris," Barbara replied between nibbles of escargot swimming in butter. That was it—no questions, no words of encouragement. Then she ordered another Manhattan—a double. Barbara was only forty, but the years had not been kind to her, as she had not been kind to herself. In an effort to control her natural tendency to unfashionable roundness, she continued to take amphetamines and appetite suppressants, and because she couldn't sleep, she required more sedatives, which she washed down with Roederer Cristal or Manhattans. Her inner glow gone, she artfully applied her makeup in a vain attempt to restore what had once been natural beauty.

Though firmly headquartered in New York, Barbara followed the seasons in Bar Harbor and Palm Beach, with an occasional Washington gala thrown in for good measure, but as time passed, Barbara's indiscriminate sexual behavior and her pill-induced mood swings considerably lightened her social calendar.

Brett was saddened by her mother's apparently empty life, but more determined than ever to make a real life for herself. That meant doing *something*, and for Brett, that something was photography.

* * *

Brett settled into the luxurious back seat of the vintage Bentley and reached for Lillian's hand. Albert, the chauffeur, drove them to Kennedy Airport, where they would take a LARSair 747 to Paris, a newly acquired route for her grandfather's airline. He had surprised Brett by accepting her decision to pursue photography. His only comment was, "There's plenty of time for you to be creative. When you come back you'll be ready to settle down. I can wait." Brett had puzzled over the statement, but put it out of her mind. *At least he doesn't hate me*, she thought, as she reached up with her free hand and fingered her grandmother's cameo.

Brett and Lillian relaxed in the crimson-and-gold VIP lounge of the LARSair terminal, waiting to board their flight. Suddenly, there was a commotion at the door.

"I don't need a ticket! My father owns this damned airline!" they heard Barbara shout.

Brett and Lillian looked at each other; this was the last person they had expected to see.

Barbara pushed through the airline personnel like she owned the place and strode across the lounge, her gait unsteady. Her dress was too short and too tight, her makeup looked as if it had been applied with a trowel, and she was very obviously intoxicated.

"Barbara, what are you doing here?" Lillian asked.

"Can't I even wish my own daughter bon voyage?" she asked rudely.

Brett was appalled by Barbara's behavior. Her joy and anticipation of her new adventure dissipated, replaced by the old anxiety that usually accompanied her mother's presence. *This isn't fair*, Brett thought. *She can't spoil this for me.*

"Why don't you sit down?" Brett suggested, trying to keep the growing agitation out of her voice.

"I'm not staying. I have my car waiting," Barbara slurred. "I was out with friends when I remembered you were leaving tonight. I only came to say au revoir!" She waved farewell with such enthusiasm that she lost her balance and fell into an empty chair.

Brett rose from her seat and bent over Barbara. She could smell the stale, sour odor of alcohol on her mother's breath. "Are you all right?" Brett asked impatiently.

"Of course I'm all right. I just lost my balance, that's all," Barbara protested. She looked at Brett and realized, for the first time, that her daughter was indeed pretty. She had long ago grown out of her awkward stage, but Barbara hadn't noticed. Brett's long, dark hair settled in waves about her shoulders, and she wore a simple azure blue silk knit dress that made her emerald eyes look almost turquoise. Barbara was just about to offer her daughter a rare compliment when she saw the cameo.

"Where did you get that?" Barbara shrieked, pointing at the offending cameo. "You've seen him! That was my mother's. He's the only one who could have given it to you!"

"Barbara, calm down," Lillian interjected.

"You stay out of this, like you should have. You arranged for her to meet that bastard—I know you did!" Barbara screamed, sobering quickly. She stood and glared accusingly at her daughter and her aunt.

Brett, holding her grandmother's cameo tightly, stood toe to toe with Barbara. "Yes, I have met my grandfather," she said defiantly.

Barbara turned her fury to Lillian and said, "I forbade it! How dare you?"

"Barbara, stop making a scene," Lillian whispered angrily.

A ticketing agent left her post behind the counter and came over to them. "If this woman is bothering you, I can call Security," she said in a low, discreet voice. Her main goal was to keep the disturbance quiet so it did not annoy the other first-class passengers. But by now, every eye and ear in the lounge was fixed on the trio.

"I don't give a damn about a scene!" Barbara momentarily turned to face the young woman. "Or Security, for that matter. I hate him! I hate him and you know it!" she screamed at Brett and Lillian.

"So what if you do?" Brett said. "I've lived almost eighteen years with your blind hatred for a man who seems perfectly nice. I was forbidden to ask questions or even speak his name, and you never explained why—never! You told me nothing about your mother, or even my own father, for that matter. You took me away from Brian, and if it weren't for you, Zachary wouldn't be in jail!

I felt like an orphan, but that didn't matter to you." Years of silent anger and resentment erupted in Brett.

The elderly woman sitting across from them clutched tightly to her Louis Vuitton cosmetic case with one white-gloved hand and used the other one to try and catch the "Oh my," that slipped from her lips.

"Could you please keep it down? You're disturbing the other passengers." The ticket agent tugged her red blazer down and squared her shoulders in an effort to look more authoritative.

Barbara flinched at Brett's attack. "You don't know what you're talking about! My mother is *dead*, and so is your father. He died before you were born!" By now Barbara was trembling with anger. "Zachary was a fool! And Brian—I'll tell you about Brian! We were a convenient package for him, and everyone in Hollywood knew that—everyone but me. Brian North, macho sex symbol TV star, was a *faggot*! His producers told him to clean up his act or he would lose his show, so he found himself a wife and child and created a veneer of respectability. But I caught him! He thought we had gone to the Malibu house for the weekend, but I decided to come back early. When we got home, I found him in our pool with three young boys. They were all naked! I trusted Brian and he used me!"

The agent from the airline nodded to a co-worker behind the counter, who immediately picked up the white Security phone.

Brett held on to a chair back to steady her shaking hands. "You're lying! If Brian was so terrible, why did you keep his name? You just want to make everyone seem more evil than you!"

"Because he was a star. And don't you speak to your mother that way!"

"You made me stop calling you mother years ago, *Barbara*, and you stopped acting like my mother a long time before that." She pronounced her mother's name like an epithet. "You've hidden my father from me all my life, and now you tell me he's dead! Who is he—or do you even know?"

Barbara crumpled into a seat. Pathetically, she countered, "You can't talk to me that way."

Over the loudspeaker a soothing voice intoned, "This is the final boarding call for LARSair flight 406 to Paris." Brett and Lillian looked up and realized the lounge had emptied.

"Barbara, you have managed to destroy everything that mattered to me. I won't let you do it this time. I'm going to Paris, and I'm going to make something of my life, because I have no intention of ending up like you!"

"Then, you better stop seeing your grandfather!" Barbara said.

"Good-bye, Barbara," Brett said with finality as she and Lillian hurried out of the waiting room. Although she was shaken by the encounter, Brett refused to let her mother see it.

Barbara, stunned, watched their backs as they disappeared down the jetway. When she turned around, she stood face-to-face with a uniformed guard. "If you touch me, I'll sue!" she hissed. Then, hands trembling, she dug frantically in her handbag until she found her small enamel box.

— *Chapter 6* —

"Kristie, the energy is really good, but try to redirect it, make it less theatrical," Brett coached, drawing on her dwindling reserve of patience. "Forget the choreography. Just stroll around the square, maybe stop and read a menu board at a cafe. Try pretending that I'm not here and invent a story about where you might be going dressed like this." Brett squeezed the young model's shoulders for encouragement as they stood in the place du Tertre in Montmartre, amid a comfortable crowd that examined stacks of oil paintings, serigraphs, and pen-and-ink illustrations exhibited by young artists.

Brett had taken Malcolm's advice to heart. From the moment she had arrived in Paris more than two years ago, she had immersed herself in her new world and taken pictures with a vengeance. She spirited her cherry-red Peugeot, a surprise eighteenth birthday gift from Aunt Lillian, across the continent, meeting people and recording her insights on film. Not only did she test with beautiful models in the latest fashions, but lean-faced Basque fishermen at Saint-Jean-de-Luz, weighing anchor for their six-month quest for tuna, oil rig mechanics toughened by the fierce North Sea in Aberdeen, and sweating Danish brewery journeymen in Arhus, all opened up for her camera as though soothed and reassured by the honesty of her deep gaze.

Thanks to Lillian's international friendships, courtesy of her years spent abroad, Brett found open doors everywhere she went. Brett explored the vineyards of Burgundy's Côte d'Or region and acquired a healthy knowledge of wine. She skied the Alps in Austria with vicomtes and duchesses, thrilled by the rush of frosty air in her lungs as she traversed the slopes at breakneck speed. She felt as at home on the dazzling beaches of Monte Carlo as she did in the countryside of Nottinghamshire.

In two years of traveling, she discovered more about photography and about life than four years and a diploma could ever have afforded her. Now, at twenty, she ached with the impatience of youth and talent to see her work on the glossy pages of magazines. Diligently, she made the rounds, taking her book to every magazine in Paris, London, and Milan, but her only work so far was shooting a maternity catalog in Munich. Art directors and editors almost universally raved about her photos. "Darling, your work is fabulous!" they would marvel. "Come back and see me as soon as you have some tears!" Tearsheets, the actual pages from a magazine showing your pictures, were the key that let everyone know that someone else found your work unique, exciting, and worth paying for. Even in the world of fashion, where being first and most scandalous is often enough to guarantee fame, it took a person with extraordinary intuition and a willingness to stand apart from the pack to give you your first big break.

Brett knew she could have bought her way into a career. At eighteen, she started to receive a substantial income from the trust fund her grandfather had established, and although she could not touch the principal until she was twenty-five, she was, by all accounts, an exceptionally wealthy young woman. But she craved recognition for her talent, not for wealth she hadn't earned. More than anything, she wanted to avoid becoming like her mother: rich, spoiled, and useless. And since no father had wanted to give her his name, she vowed to make one for herself.

"Relax, Kristie. You're not going to the guillotine." Brett could see the storm clouds gathering. *She can't cry now*, Brett thought. Kristie looked sensational, and there was too much riding on these pictures.

Martine Gallet, one of the Left Bank designers who challenged the scions of the major couture houses on the Rue du Faubourg Saint-Honoré, had loaned Brett the navy taffeta reefer coat with satin lapels, pleated trousers, and white silk shirt that Kristie wore. This was Martine's version of "*le smoking*"—*the* fashion craze of the fall 1982 season. Martine liked Brett's work and if she liked the results of this test, she would book Brett to shoot publicity stills of her next collection. Brett knew the money would be negligible—young designers usually have low budgets—but the prestige was exactly what she needed, and the shots would be picked up by magazines and newspapers around the world.

Martine had selected the dark-haired, doe-eyed Kristie from the composite cards that Brett presented her. Kristie had the sleek, coltish look that made the clothes sizzle, but she was a "farm team" model. Barely three weeks ago, the seventeen-year-old had been whisked from Oregon by a scout for A-One, a New York agency. In New York, she had been scrubbed of frosted lipstick and pastel eye shadow, and her shaggy cheerleader hair had been clipped to a gamine bob. After some preliminary testing, they shipped her off to their Paris affiliate for six months to refine her look and build her book, in hopes that she would return to New York, where the real money was made, with enough clout, cachet, and tears to command high rates, repay A-One's initial investment, and add healthy dividends to their coffers.

But Kristie was nervous and her inexperience showed. She knew the day was not going well—she had no idea how to give Brett the pictures she wanted.

Brett shoved wisps of brunette hair from her forehead and slowly panned the crowd. She sighted several artists stationed at wooden easels, making a great show of concentration and effort as they labored over charcoal portraits of tourists.

"Wait here," Brett instructed Kristie. She strode across the square—as usual, oblivious to the admiring glances she received. Since her arrival in Paris, Brett's style of dressing had evolved from her uniform of jeans and a black turtleneck, which suggested she was an American college student backpacking her way through Europe. Now, she tucked the turtleneck into slim black wool leggings. Her garnet and gray Missoni cardigan, one of several sweaters she had purchased in Milan, was topped by her multipocketed photographer's vest, which contained the filters, film, meters, and other gadgets she needed to keep handy when she worked.

Brett approached one of the artists, a handsome young man with a mop of blond hair, who relaxed in the canvas director's chair normally reserved for the subject, his feet propped up on his folding stool. "*Pardon, Monsieur. Combien . . .*"

"My English is a lot better than my French, if that works for you," he interjected.

"Okay. How much for a portrait?" Brett asked as she sized him up.

"A charcoal is a hundred francs, but to do justice to those green eyes, I'd recommend a pastel. There's hardly a difference in price." He shifted over to his stool and waved. "Have a seat."

"It's not of me. I want you to draw that girl over there while I take her picture," Brett explained.

The artist lifted a puzzled eyebrow and repeated, "You want to take her picture while I draw her picture?"

"I know it sounds odd, but I'm a photographer, she's a model, and I've tried all afternoon to get her to act naturally, but either she doesn't know how or I've scared it out of her," Brett said, exasperated. She hoped she didn't sound too desperate, but the late-afternoon light was fading quickly.

"So I'm the decoy," he said.

"Exactly."

"Sounds good. And if she doesn't loosen up, I'll make her look laid back in the drawing so today won't be a total washout for you." He smiled. "By the way, photographer, my name is Joe Tate."

"I'll be right back. And I'm Brett Larsen."

Kristie sat ramrod stiff, staring blankly ahead as Brett took light readings. Joe turned to Kristie. "We could do the regular sketch, but for you, I think the super deluxe globe-trotter special is the ticket. You have your choice of the Eiffel Tower, the Arc de Triomphe, or my favorite, the statue of Winged Victory, in the background." From the back of his pad he pulled a stack of pages, predrawn with the landmarks. "I do a batch of these every night. They sell like crazy."

Kristie giggled before she could stop herself.

Joe continued to make conversation as he chose colors from a cigar box filled with pastels. Soon Kristie was chattering, gesturing, and laughing freely. Brett circled them, snapping pictures from every angle, pleased and relieved that her plan had worked. *He's really quite good-looking*, she thought, observing his dancing hazel eyes. His massive shoulders and arms seemed barely contained by the sleeves of his olive-green sack jacket.

After the shot was completed and Kristie was back in civilian clothes and on her way to the nearby Métro station, Brett settled up with Joe. He remarked, "If you happened to get me in any of those shots, I sure would like one to send home to my folks in Fort Wayne. They'd love a picture of their baby boy, the artist, at work."

"You came all the way from Fort Wayne to draw pictures of tourists?" Brett asked as she packed her equipment.

"There's more call for it in Paris than in Fort Wayne. Besides, I'm a sculptor, but the money's pretty lousy until you're Michelangelo or Henry Moore, and this pays better than waiting tables," Joe said as he folded his easel.

Brett liked Joe's unpretentious, easy manner immediately. "Well, if you give me a phone number, I'll get you a picture," she offered.

Joe ripped a corner from a sheet of sketch paper and jotted the number down. "You'll have to leave a message with my landlady.

She'll give you the third degree, but feel free to make up answers —the more outrageous, the better."

Joe helped Brett carry her gear to the car, easily shouldering the extra bags in addition to his own. Their conversation revealed they had a lot in common. Joe had left the University of Indiana after a year, feeling bored and stifled by college courses and campus life. He traveled through Europe, doing sketches to pay his modest living expenses and studying the artwork that he found all around him. Brett really felt he understood how anxious she was to get her career going.

"You have to go out every day, produce the best work you can, and hope that somebody has the sense to know it's good. Just keep taking pictures, keep showing them every chance you get, and be ready when opportunity knocks," he said in a voice filled with confidence.

Joe closed the car door soundly, then leaned through the open window and kissed Brett's cheek. "My agent will call you in the morning," he grinned and strolled off into the twilight.

Brett squeezed her Peugeot into the first parking space she saw on the rue de Seine and grabbed her camera bags from the backseat. She was still several blocks from home, but since many of the streets in her neighborhood were too narrow for cars, she felt lucky to have found a spot so quickly.

Walking through the open-air Buci market, Brett savored the confusion that characterized the colorful Saint-Germain-des-Prés institution. She stopped at several stalls, and after the expected haggling, purchased raspberries, pears, and a wedge of chabichou she hoped would add another dimension to last night's ragout.

Finally, she reached the three story, ivy-draped *maison de ville* on the narrow, cobblestoned rue de Bourbon le Château where she rented the top-floor apartment. Brett unlocked the front door and gazed contentedly at the geraniums hanging in their festive blue-and-white Limoges pot. A puddle of deep red petals had settled on the marble floor beneath them.

As she grabbed her mail from the bowfront commode in the hall and started up the stairs, she realized she loved this old house as much now as she had when she had first seen it. Her aunt had tried to steer her to more luxurious quarters near the rue de Rivoli or place de l'Opéra, but it was the Left Bank that Brett found irresistible. The moment she set foot in Saint-Germain-des-Prés, named for the oldest church in Paris, which sits at its heart, Brett knew this was where she must live. The neighborhood pulsed with the vitality and idealism of students from the nearby University of Paris, the Sorbonne, while maintaining the time-honored traditions of Parisians whose families had made Saint-Germain-des-Prés their home for centuries.

Brett and Lillian had ambled along the quaint winding streets and turned into the rue de Bourbon le Château when Brett spied a *"logement a louer"* sign. Brett insisted that this apartment, with its three terraces, beveled glass French doors, and two bedrooms, offered her beautiful light and enough space for a small studio, but more than that, it felt right.

During the rest of Lillian's stay, she and Brett combed antique stores, secondhand shops, and the famous Parisian flea market at Puces de St. Ouen, for pieces to finish the semifurnished rooms. They stopped at Boussac to order fabric to recover the deep, overstuffed sofa, tub chair, and ottoman that came with the apartment and hired an upholsterer in the neighborhood to do the job. Since then, Brett had picked up many items in her travels—the lace curtains in Normandy, a Sheraton side table in Cornwall, and a gold-veined, green marble plinth from Florence that currently held a temple jar filled with dried flowers, were among her finds.

Dropping the bags in the red-and-white kitchen, she poured herself a glass of Beaujolais. In spite of the troubled start, the shoot had gone well, thanks to Joe Tate, Brett thought as she turned on the brass candle lamp on the side table and curled up on the glazed chintz sofa in her living room to survey the mail: a lab bill, which she would pay tomorrow when she picked up the film from today's test, and two letters—one from Lillian, the other from Lizzie.

Lillian loved the Rigaud candles Brett sent for her birthday. Their delicate floral scent reminded Lillian of the gardens at Cox Cove in full bloom.

Lillian also mentioned that Barbara had remarried. Brett couldn't believe her mother had found another man that stupid, but she knew

Barbara would keep finding men. She had to. They were her career, her reason for getting up in the morning, her only measure of worth, and to Brett that was pathetic. She had not heard from Barbara since their fight at the airport. *I don't really care what she does, as long as she stays away from me*, Brett thought as she put the letter in the silver toast rack that she used to hold mail.

Lizzie's letter began with the revelation, "Now I really know what love means." Brett laughed aloud and tried to recall the number of times Lizzie had found the meaning of love since she had been at Syracuse. Brett sipped her wine and wondered how you know what love means when it's so hard finding out what love is, or more often isn't?

Brett had met many young men in Europe. Some were interesting, funny, and talented, and while others were less than riveting, they all seemed destined to become friends, not lovers—except for Paolo. She stretched out on the hollyhock-patterned sofa, crossing her legs at the ankles, and stuffed a pillow under her head.

Brett had gone to Milan, hoping to capture some of the frenzy of the collections on film, but because she was an unknown photographer and had no press credentials, she found herself barred from every showing. On her third frustrating day she stood outside the Valentino tent, ready to give up and return to Paris, when a young man wearing an obviously custom-tailored gray Armani suit over a white polo shirt approached her. "You want to go inside, no?" he said in perfect English. "I want to go inside, yes!" Brett had responded. He introduced himself as Paolo Bernini of Bernini Textiles, in Turin. He took her to every remaining show and to dinner every night. Paolo was witty, charming, and devilishly handsome. He was also a dedicated romantic.

After the collections they sailed the Mediterranean and the Aegean for two months on his family's yacht, the *Bella Fortuna*. They explored craggy volcanic islands by day and lay on the deck of the *Bella Fortuna* under starlit skies by night, lost in warm embraces and each other's eyes. From Paolo she learned the intimate joy of knowing a man. She had thought nothing could be more wonderful or perfect, until he started planning her life. She would come to Turin, where his family manufactured the finest woolens in all of

Italy, he announced as they sipped Bellinis and watched the sun set over the chalky-white villas of Santorini. Her work was in Paris or Milan, not Turin, Brett protested. Then Paolo insisted she would never have to work—photography would be her hobby. Her only job would be to stay beautiful and make him happy, and Brett knew it was over.

She had written to Lizzie about her affair with Paolo and declared that she could never, ever trade her own goals and ambitions for a wedding ring. And Brett knew that the right man would never ask her to.

— *Chapter 7* —

The techno-chic chrome-and-glass lobby of *Voilà!*, one of the oldest and most prestigious fashion magazines in Paris, was intimidating, but Brett was prepared for the ritual. She would add her portfolio to a mountain of others near the enormous semicircular brushed steel reception desk and retrieve it the following morning. But Brett sensed that no one at *Voilà!* ever looked at it, so like many photographers, she had rigged her book by slipping her business card between the fourth and fifth pages. If it was moved or missing when she picked it up, she would know her book had been seen by *someone*.

"*Entrez, entrez.*" The receptionist waved Brett impatiently past the accustomed stack of portfolios and toward the door that was open behind her. Brett stepped eagerly into the adjoining waiting room. She had never gotten this far before!

To her surprise, the room teemed with models. Every seat was taken; some were shared. Girls lounged on the gray-carpeted floor in clusters, repairing their makeup and chatting merrily. She took a chair vacated by an anemic-looking redhead wearing blue lipstick and skintight yellow spandex pants, who sauntered through the door at the opposite end of the room.

Brett pulled her appointment book from her black leather shoulder bag and checked to make sure she had come on the right day. Then she turned to the girl sitting next to her—a haughty-looking brunette whose hair was pulled back severely and gelled into the perfect French twist. The girl paged distractedly through American *Vogue*. "Excuse me. Do you know what this call is for?"

"My agency said they're looking for new faces, and I think it's about time. They always use the same girls in every issue." She removed a compact from her tan Hermès satchel and smoothed her dramatically arched eyebrows. *They always use the same photographers, too*, Brett thought as the model reapplied brick-red blush to her already well-defined cheeks. In a confidential whisper, the model continued, "Yesterday, around four-thirty, my booker said someone new called from *Voilà!*, canceled all of the regular girls who were on hold for the next issue, and asked to see every model in the agency. I know three girls who are booked all day today and they're planning to sneak out to come here."

When the blue-lipped model reemerged, Brett's seatmate rose. "Good luck!" she said and sailed across the floor.

Brett's heart raced. The receptionist's mistake had gotten her inside, but what would happen when she actually met the art director? She rearranged the folds of her red cashmere shawl, suddenly self-conscious amid the exquisitely beautiful, reed-thin young women surrounding her. Maybe she should go back to the front desk and put her book where she knew it belonged, but she felt too close to go back. If she could just talk to the art director, Brett knew she could convince her at least to examine her portfolio. It was a start!

Who am I kidding? she thought soberly. Stories routinely circulated on the photographers' hotline about *Voilà!*'s art director, an exceedingly opinionated Breton with an acid tongue and a short temper. She had been the magazine's guiding artistic force since the sixties, and had shaped it in her own, very exacting image. Impeccably tailored clothes were draped on perfectly coiffed and heavily made up models who posed stiffly in overdecorated rooms. *Voilà!* retained a core group of devoted readers and a respected place in the history of fashion magazines, but its reputation was now a little dusty. Since the early 1970s, time had stood still on the fashion pages of *Voilà!*

Besides, she'll hate my work, Brett thought as she turned the pages of her portfolio. Free, windblown hair, minimal makeup, and quirky but realistic settings were the hallmarks of her style. Each photograph was different, yet they shared a vision that was clearly her own. Her latest additions—the photos from the place du Tertre—were better than she had hoped. *If she's looking for new faces, maybe she's ready for new photographers, too. All she can do is call me names in French and throw me out*, Brett concluded as she snapped her book closed and waited her turn.

For an hour Brett waited, contemplating her strategy for the impending meeting. When a stately black model carrying a bichon frise in her carpetbag left the office, she knew she was next.

Brett marched confidently into the office, trying to ignore her sweating palms. In one glance she took in the two window walls that provided a magnificent view of the city below. Unexpectedly, the other walls were covered by a seemingly random assortment of plaques, citations, photographs, *Voilà!* covers, and baseball pennants. Stacks of correspondence, newspapers, and magazines littered every available surface, including the tops of the dozen or so putty-colored file cabinets that lined the room. Once inside she stopped in her tracks. Seated at a battered oak desk, his back to the door, engrossed in a vigorous phone conversation, was not the magazine's notorious art director, but Lawrence Chapin, *Voilà!*'s editor in chief.

The dashing expatriate American bachelor was often photographed attending gallery openings and charity benefits, and dining at chic bistros. Brett had even seen him once at a jazz club in Saint-Germain-des-Prés. Immediately she recognized his striking hair—thick waves as black and shiny as onyx, shot through with strands of silver.

"I am fully aware that our deadline is in two weeks!" he persisted, agitation in his voice. "Handle the advertisers however you like, but tell them *Voilà!* will be more exciting than it's been in fifteen years!"

Still embroiled in conversation, Lawrence spun his chair around, and without looking at her, stretched out his arm and motioned for Brett's portfolio.

His words gave substance to what Brett had sensed. The editor in chief never dealt with routine matters such as selecting models unless something radical was happening. Everything could be up for grabs, Brett thought excitedly as she waited to be noticed.

This may be the craziest thing I've ever done, she thought as he opened the book to the first page. Every nerve in Brett's body tingled. As soon as he turned the next page, he would know something was wrong.

"That's your *job*!" he exploded, emphatically turning two portfolio pages to punctuate his words. He still had not looked at the pictures.

Lawrence was already primed for a fight. Brett knew that she would have to have a quick response to his first volley; otherwise, the match was over.

"I don't have time for this!" Lawrence finished and hung up the phone. For the first time he looked at her, up and down, taking in every feature with a practiced eye.

Although Brett knew that he was critically analyzing the photographic potential of her face and body, as she herself had done hundreds of times with models, Brett felt suddenly exposed under his penetrating scrutiny.

She's quite beautiful, Lawrence thought. *The right height, excellent hair and skin, and truly amazing green eyes*. And after the parade of costumes he had seen this morning, Lawrence was impressed by the simplicity of her clothes. The red shawl provided striking contrast to the black cashmere sweater and midcalf skirt she wore with shiny, black flat-heeled boots. *She needs to lose a few pounds, but that's easily taken care of*. He flipped again through her book, looking at each page, then at Brett. "What's this all about?" he asked hostilely. "This isn't your book! These aren't even the same girl!" A scowl eclipsed his deep-set ebony eyes.

"No, they aren't, but it is my book. My name is Brett Larsen, and I'm a photographer."

"Photographers drop off books, Miss Larsen. I don't have the time or patience for pranks," Lawrence Chapin said irritably, but he continued to look at her portfolio.

"Neither do I, Mr. Chapin. This isn't a prank. Perhaps I should have left my book with the others out front, but when your receptionist assumed I was a model, I saw it as an opportunity to have my work actually seen by the art director. My book is usually returned unopened. I did not expect to see you," Brett admitted.

He paused in his perusal of her portfolio. "You've submitted work here before? That's exactly the problem," he muttered under his breath.

"Excuse me?" Brett could not clearly hear his comment.

"Nothing. I was talking to myself. These aren't bad. In fact, some are very good—especially this," he said, indicating the shots from the place du Tertre.

"Thank you," Brett said cautiously. She knew it was wrong to have gotten here under false pretenses, but she *was* here and *Voilà!*'s editor was complimenting her work!

"Tell me why I should consider booking you?" Lawrence asked. In spite of a less-than-auspicious introduction, he admired Brett's spunk and he liked her style.

"Because I'm good," Brett answered boldly and without hesitation. "I'm new, and nothing remotely like my work has ever appeared on *Voilà!*'s pages. I couldn't help overhearing your conversation. You are obviously making some big changes. You want to give *Voilà!* a new look, a different feel, and I can help do that." Brett exuded the enthusiasm and confidence she felt about her work. "When I worked with Malcolm Kent . . ."

"You worked with Malcolm?" The edge of impatience in Lawrence's voice had been replaced by a hint of interest.

"For two years in New York, and there isn't a better teacher of how to see what you want and get it on film."

Lawrence returned to her book and, in silence, reexamined every photo. Finally, he said, "You've seen the fashion forecast in the front of the magazine?"

"It's called '*Prévision du Mode*,' " Brett replied knowledgeably.

"Not anymore. And the rows of pictures in little boxes with adorable captions are out, too. It's now a three-page, full-color spread called '*Trop Chaud*.' I want the next one shot in an apartment that looks like someone below the age of ninety might actually live there, and I want film by next Wednesday. Can you do it?"

"I wouldn't be standing here if I couldn't."

"Good. I'll need you tomorrow at eleven o'clock for an editorial meeting. We'll discuss merchandise, location, and models. And who is the model in these pictures?" Lawrence pointed to Joe Tate.

"He's not a model. He's an artist."

"I like his look. Every male model I've seen looks like a product of some exclusive prep school. I want to use him in this spread. Can you get him to do it?" Lawrence asked.

"I'll try," Brett replied.

"Do better and let me know at the meeting tomorrow. And, Miss Larsen, I have no time for reshoots. If the pictures are good, we'll print them and talk about the next issue. If they're not, I'll print them anyway, but I'll never book you again."

Brett beamed, and almost ran along the boulevard Sébastopol. She wanted to shout her good news to everyone she passed, as if saying it aloud would make her believe it wasn't a dream. *I'm going to take the best photos Lawrence Chapin has ever seen*, she thought triumphantly.

"This is a pretty good-looking guy!" Joe, his café au lait steaming in the early morning chill, jokingly admired the print Brett gave him from the place du Tertre.

He had been pleasantly surprised the night before when he had returned to his room to find a message from Brett. He hadn't expected to hear from her again, but hoped in his heart that he would. From the start, he had felt at ease talking with her, almost as if she were an old friend, and he wanted to get to know her better. When he phoned around midnight, she was anxious to meet him wherever he would be the next morning. He was puzzled by the urgency in her voice, but grateful just to see her. He had planned to do some sketching for himself in the early light near the Pont

Neuf, and if Brett wanted to meet him at seven o'clock that was fine with him.

"Someone else thinks you're a pretty good-looking guy, too!" Brett peered at Joe, her green eyes bright and clear, even though she had only slept fitfully. The exhilaration she felt each time she recalled Lawrence Chapin's decision to hire her gave way to nervousness and apprehension when she realized that she needed Joe Tate to agree to work with her. Brett wanted to impress Lawrence as a person who could get the job done, and she knew this was her first challenge. But she barely knew Joe. He had seemed nice enough and he photographed well—even Martine had commented on his rugged attractiveness—but Brett had no idea what Joe's response would be, and when she had been unable to see him until the morning of the meeting, Brett had been nearly frantic. If he said no, she would only have a short time to devise a way to placate Lawrence. But Brett could already see her photographer's credit, the tiny black letters along the sides of her pictures in *Voilà!*. They would announce to the world that Brett Larsen had arrived. She was certain she could get Joe to help her realize her dream.

"Really? And which someone is that?" Joe propped an elbow on his easel and shot her his most charming look.

"Lawrence Chapin, the editor of *Voilà!* magazine," Brett replied.

"What?" Joe nearly toppled the easel.

Brett explained in great detail the circumstances of her booking with *Voilà!* and the importance of Lawrence's request.

"But, I'm not a model. I'm a farm boy from Indiana. Do you have any idea what it's like to announce to your parents that you've decided to become a sculptor and move to Paris? They still want me to be a high school art teacher. Now I'm supposed to tell them I'm a model? I'm not a pretty boy!" He turned and looked out across the Seine.

"It's only for one day, Joe," Brett coaxed. "I'll be there to talk you through it, and you just told me how handsome you are." Brett looked at Joe the same way Lawrence had scrutinized her yesterday. She noted how his thick, honey-blond hair accentuated his hazel eyes and framed the strong jaw he had not shaved this morning. In profile, his aquiline nose appeared to have been shaped by one of the master sculptors he so admired. Joe had the right combination —his looks appealed to women but did not threaten men.

"How did I get myself into this? Four days ago I was minding my own business, making my way as a struggling artist, and now you want me to embarrass myself on the pages of a magazine."

"Joe, I wouldn't let you look ridiculous. Think of it as a business proposition that happens to be a lot of fun. You do those tourist sketches to make money so you can afford to sculpt, right? Well, this is the same thing, but I know you'll make more money than you would in a day of drawing Henrys and Ethels in front of the Eiffel Tower."

Joe contemplated the offer for several moments. "I must be a damn fool to agree to this," he relented, chuckling self-effacingly.

"Oh, Joe, you won't regret it!" Brett exclaimed, throwing her arms around his neck enthusiastically.

"Let's get this meeting started," Lawrence announced, slamming the door as he strode into the conference room. He was fifteen minutes late, but no one dared to comment.

Around the smoked-glass table were assembled the people necessary to plan and execute the three pages Brett had been assigned. Those on the permanent staff of *Voilà!*—the fashion editor, chic and understated to the point of looking prim; the accessories editor, excessively scarved, belted and jeweled; the photo editor, in jeans and a sweatshirt with a loupe suspended from his neck; and the copy-editor, wearing a dark skirt, white blouse, no jewelry and a permanent squint—sat on one side. They fidgeted nervously with pens and notepads, like students faced with a pop quiz. Most of them had been with the magazine for years, and they realized from the tumultuous events of the past few days that their futures at *Voilà!* were at stake.

More relaxed, filled with anticipation instead of anxiety, all dressed in black and looking like refugees from the same heavy metal band, were the freelancers. The make-up artist, a young woman with a platinum crew cut and a nose ring; the hairdresser, who wore his own blond hair Rastafarian-style in dreadlocks; and the fashion stylist, overwhelmed by a shapeless neo-Japanese bag dress with one long and one short sleeve, and wearing men's oxfords; were all veterans of the business. Their interpretation of style appeared regularly in the leading European fashion magazines, including *Voilà!*, but under the former art director, their creative expression and innovative ideas had been stifled. They were anxious to hear what Lawrence Chapin had to say about *Voilà!*'s new direction.

Then there was Brett—the photographer, the fulcrum. Upon her arrival she had greeted everyone, but their reception had been cautious. They were wary of this newcomer. They knew nothing about her work and were painfully aware that no matter how well-conceived these pages were, the most beautiful models, the most exciting designers, the snappiest captions, would not make up for a bad photograph. But Brett was too excited to be nervous and too full of enthusiasm to contemplate failure. She had done her worrying the night before, and her final doubt had been erased when Joe had agreed to do the layout. This was her chance and Brett was ready.

"Good morning, Mr. Chapin," she said, shattering the tense silence around her.

Never taking his seat at the head of the table, Lawrence nodded in her direction, leaned forward, placing the palms of his hands on the table, and began.

"*Voilà!* is in trouble, and has been for several years. Circulation is down, both newsstand and subscription, and advertising revenue is way off. We spent a great deal of time and money redesigning our offices so they looked sleek and contemporary, but we failed to apply the same principles to our editorial pages.

"Part of the problem left with the dismissal of the art director, and I will be acting in that capacity for the next three issues. Three issues—that's what the publisher has given me to turn this magazine around, or there will be no more *Voilà!*."

Lawrence paused and eyeballed each person at the table for emphasis. Brett leaned forward, hanging on his every word.

Now Lawrence stood tall, hands clasped behind his back, and walked slowly around the table as he spoke. "So, the old look is gone!" He snatched a current issue of the magazine from the startled fashion editor, ripped it in two, and flung the pieces to the floor.

Brett felt ignited, compelled to participate rather than just listen. "There's a whole group of magazine buyers who don't pick up *Voilà!* even to browse through. If I weren't a photographer, I'd never buy it," Brett added, not intending to voice this last thought aloud. But she couldn't help it. This is what she'd felt about *Voilà!* for a long time.

There was a collective holding of breath. Everyone waited for Lawrence's response.

"Exactly! We've catered only to women who lunch at the Crillon and dine with the Mitterands. To women who have things *done*, not women who *do*.

"We've got to make every page of *Voilà!* jump out and grab the reader! Tickle her, shake her up, make her want more! Until now, our damned 'Fashion Forecast' wasn't even considered important enough to warrant an editorial meeting!"

Brett responded excitedly. "But by changing the forecast from '*Prévision du Mode*' to '*Trop Chaud*,' and really making it 'Too Hot,' you can show the reader a change instantly, and the rest of the book can build from there!"

"Yes!" Lawrence agreed. The meeting turned to the specifics of the pages to be shot. After the fashion and accessories editors showed Polaroids and samples of the items to be featured, Lawrence asked Brett for her suggestions. She outlined her ideas in detail, fielding questions from around the table with poise and confidence. Lawrence was impressed by the way Brett jumped right in, voicing her opinion without fear of reprisal. She gave shape and substance to his most rudimentary suggestions, as though she could somehow read his mind. *She's exactly what I need*, Lawrence thought.

The others were galvanized by the electricity that charged the air. There were few comments and even fewer questions as the meeting concluded. Although Lawrence and Brett had dominated the discussion, everyone understood what would be expected of them at next Tuesday's shoot.

Brett wondered how the magazine had ever gone into a tailspin with such a dynamic man at the helm, but the past was unimportant. Only the future mattered to her now.

— Chapter 8 —

"How soon can you get over here?"

It took Brett a moment to recognize Lawrence Chapin's voice. Exhausted from the day's shoot, she had showered and climbed into bed for a quick nap before dinner. "What time is it?" Brett asked sleepily as she sat up in her white ironwork bed.

"Ten o'clock," he replied tersely.

Brett couldn't believe she had been asleep for three hours, but more important, why did he want to see her now? What was wrong? A knot formed in the pit of her stomach. "I can be there in half an hour."

Her mind raced as she hastily pulled on jeans and a sweater, grabbed her bag and keys, and ran down the stairs, combing her hair with her fingers as she went. She drove through the still-busy Paris streets, recounting the events of the day. The location had been perfect, the models were pros who had given her exactly what she wanted, and in spite of his self-doubts, Joe was a natural.

The knot in her stomach grew as Brett waited anxiously for the security guard to call for clearance before she could proceed to the elevator banks, and when she stepped into the ghostly quiet of the empty *Voilà!* offices, Brett could hear her own heartbeat thundering in her ears.

She headed for the sliver of fluorescent light escaping beneath a door at the end of the corridor and found Lawrence hunched over a light table, mounds of discarded yellow chrome boxes at his feet.

"This is the worst shit I've ever seen!" he roared. "I can't find anything here worth printing!" With one swipe he knocked a batch of the chromes from the table to the floor.

This can't be happening, Brett thought. A blow to the gut could not have hit her harder. She was so close to tears that one more blink would send them spilling down her burning cheeks. "But they can't be that bad. I checked the clip test," she said bravely.

"Your film was great, but *this* . . . this looks like it was shot by a teenage boy with blue balls. Here, see for yourself." Lawrence picked up two slides from the floor and held them out to her.

Brett's tears receded. She placed her hands on her hips and her eyes blazed with outrage. "Wait a minute! You mean you dragged me down here in the middle of the night to complain about someone *else's* work?! You scared me to death over something that has nothing to do with me!"

"It has everything to do with you. You're going to reshoot it tomorrow night. These pictures are pornographic! I have two days before the film for this issue needs to go for color separation and a six-page hole where a lingerie story should be."

"Do you get some kind of perverse pleasure from keeping people off balance?" Brett examined Lawrence with an unflinching gaze. His clothes—a striped broadcloth shirt and comfortably tailored trousers—concealed a body with the sturdiness and explosive power of a quarter horse. His hands seemed strong; the chromes he held were dwarfed by their size. Brett estimated that he was in his late thirties and decided he had a face made more appealing by the crinkles and creases that mark the passage of time. In his youth, he would have been too blankly pretty. When she got to his dark, deep-set eyes, she was startled to find a hint of sadness, perhaps a faint reminder of some otherwise hidden pain.

Lawrence moved from the light table and stood in front of Brett. "I don't think it's perverse," he said, a glimmer of amusement now lighting his eyes. He waved the two slides at her tauntingly. "Wanna take a look at these now?"

Brett glowered at him a moment longer, then smirked and plucked the chromes from his hand.

"Welcome to the trenches," he said.

For the next hour they bandied about concepts for the story. Lawrence listened raptly as Brett brought the disparate ideas into focus.

This is crazy, but it couldn't be more exciting, Brett thought as she leaned her still-tingling body against the back wall of the elevator. Working with Lawrence Chapin was like standing in the path of a tornado, calm following chaos without missing a beat, but no one, not even Malcolm, had challenged her more.

"Don't spray!" Brett cautioned the hairstylist. "Women don't use hairspray before they go to bed. And somebody take those champagne glasses off the bedside table. She's not expecting Prince Charming. Women who sleep alone wear beautiful lingerie, too."

It was almost midnight. They had been at it for six hours and this was the next-to-the-last shot. Brett had meandered through the town house on the avenue Foch most of the afternoon. Friends of Lawrence's had given him permission to use it for a shoot while they were in the States, and Brett had been determined to take advantage of all the possibilities the magnificent house offered.

People expected a lingerie layout to be photographed in a bedroom, and there were eight to choose from, but Brett decided that she would not be restricted by convention. She had already used the kitchen, library, a bathroom, and even the wine cellar.

Lawrence spoke with Brett occasionally, but mostly he watched. It was obvious to him that she was in control here. He saw the concepts they had discussed the night before suddenly materialize. Brett kept up with every detail. In the bathroom, she wanted the water actually running in the sink as the model reached for a toothbrush. *She's so young to be so sure of herself*, he thought. *She's driven by something much more compelling than the fashion business*. He wondered what it might be.

"That looks great, but put the glasses *on*," Brett instructed. The model, wearing a column of jade green silk suspended from spaghetti straps, reclined against the headboard of the canopied bed with a book open on her lap. "Now, read," Brett said, and clicked the shutter.

Brett had planned the last shot carefully and saved it for the end because it was easy and dramatic. She was aware that Lawrence had been watching her performance all night and this would be the finale. She hadn't spent two years with Malcolm Kent for nothing.

The raven-haired model ran up the wide, curving staircase, her red chiffon peignoir billowing out behind her. Brett called out her name and the model automatically looked over her shoulder, directly into Brett's lens, her face alive with expectation.

"*C'est tout!*" Brett shouted, and Lawrence led the spontaneous burst of applause.

Brett was bone-tired, but savored the waves of exhilaration that engulfed her. She mingled with the crew, dispensing hugs and thank-yous for good work and cooperation. Her assistant, a spindly young man who studied at the École des Beaux-Arts, packed her equipment and listened intently to her instructions for the lab. Not long ago, that had been her job, she mused, but now she had shot nine pages for *Voilà!*

She sat cross-legged on the floor in the library, waiting for the house to be returned to its original pristine condition before she left. A fire, lit for an earlier shot, still burned in the marble fireplace.

"You look like you could use a cup of coffee or a drink," Lawrence said as he came up behind her.

"I'd love a glass of wine—white, if possible."

"Possible? You saw the wine cellar here. Anything is possible!" Lawrence disappeared, and returned a few minutes later with a chilled bottle of Le Batard-Montrachet and two glasses, then joined her on the floor. "That last shot is going to be sensational." He poured the wine, then lifted his glass in salute. "You did a good job, kid, but I have to tell you, there were missiles in your eyes last night when you blasted me." Lawrence stretched out on the carpet, propped up on one elbow.

"Thank you, Mr. Chapin."

"I don't sit on the floor and drink wine with people who call me that."

"Thank you, Lawrence." Brett touched his glass lightly with her own, then took a sip. The glow from the fire made the rich golden liquid appear almost amber. She sighed, unfolded her long legs, stretching them out in front of her, and leaned back on her hands. "This room is really beautiful. It reminds me of Cox Cove," Brett said wistfully. The high ceiling; richly paneled walls lined with shelves full of handsomely bound books; the stout, well-worn mahogany and leather furniture; combined with the aroma of crackling cherry wood and lemon oil; triggered her memory of the place where she had spent so many happy days.

"Cox Cove? Where's that?" Lawrence asked, realizing that he knew nothing about Brett Larsen, except that she was an American like him, and she was a damned good photographer—the best he'd seen in a long time—but still a little green for too much heady praise.

"New York—Long Island, actually," Brett responded.

"I lived in New York a while, but I never heard of a town called Cox Cove," Lawrence said.

"No, Cox Cove is my aunt's house. It's in Sands Point."

"That's pretty pricey real estate," Lawrence remarked.

Brett wasn't sure that she was ready to discuss the details of her background with a man she hardly knew. Except for those people she met through Aunt Lillian, she had, for the most part, been able to avoid the subject since she had been in Europe. She was obviously not a candidate for a bread line, but Europeans thought it was bad form to ask *where* your money came from. "So, you're a New Yorker?" Brett asked, turning to Lawrence.

Her pointed shift in focus did not escape him, but for some reason, he didn't mind—usually, he did. "I lived there for a few years, but I was born and raised in Buffalo."

"Is it really as cold as they say?"

Okay, Lawrence thought, *now we're talking about the weather*. "When you grow up there you become accustomed to it, but once you move away, you try not to visit during the winter."

"Do you go home often?" Brett felt the conversation disintegrating into a series of polite questions and answers, and wondered how long it could go on.

"No, the last time I was there was ten years ago, for my father's funeral. Wouldn't you know it, the old coot died in January." He saw the look of dismay on Brett's face at his apparently irreverent remark. She didn't know him well enough to see when he was joking. "I was kidding. My dad would have thought it was divine justice that I had to come home in January. He was crazy about that town, weather and all. He accepted my decision to live elsewhere, but he wouldn't have left on a bet. It was home." Lawrence couldn't remember the last time he had talked about his father—or himself, for that matter. So-and-so's latest collection, the hottest new cover girl, or who was fired from where and replaced by whom, were deemed more appropriate topics of conversation in his world.

"He sounds like a wonderful man. What did he do?" Brett liked the pride in Lawrence's voice when he spoke about his father, and she was disquieted by the thought that she would never have a father of whom she could be proud.

"He was a newspaper man. He published the *Daily Express*, so I grew up around printer's ink and deadlines. My sister runs the paper now." Why was he telling her this? What was it about this girl that made him want to open up? Brett had an intangible energy, a directness, that piqued his curiosity. She was straightforward, and in a business rife with affectations, he found her refreshing. He hadn't figured it all out, but he liked her.

Brett had rolled over on her side and rested her head in her hand, watching Lawrence as he talked. She was completely intrigued by this Lawrence Chapin. He seemed totally different from the brusque, mercurial man she knew. Brett was so fascinated that she failed to notice that the crew, having set the house to rights, had gone. "Why didn't you go into the newspaper business?" she asked quietly.

Her question was so measured, he turned to look at her. She had inclined her head toward the hearth and stared into the fire. So earnest was her expression that she seemed to be contemplating choices she had made in her own young life. For the second time since he had met her, Brett's uncomplicated, natural beauty struck him. The firelight added flecks of gold to her green eyes and he was possessed by a sudden desire to free her thick brunette wave from the confines of her long braid. Clearing his throat in an attempt to regain his composure, he answered her question.

"I did, for a while. But Vietnam changed my perspective on truth in the news. I guess I became disillusioned. That's pretty easy for a war correspondent who's covering a war that's not a war."

"You must have been awfully young," Brett commented.

"I suppose so, but youth was a privilege that didn't last very long over there."

Once again, Brett noticed the sadness in his eyes as she examined his face more closely. "Is that where you got this?" she asked, gently smoothing her fingertips over a scar nearly hidden by his left eyebrow. She drew her hand away, startled by her action. *What am I doing?* she thought. This was a client—her first client. How could she have been so forward? Was it the hour and all of the excitement that made her forget herself, or was it Lawrence?

"I'm sorry," she murmured softly.

"Don't be," he replied, fixing her in his gaze. Her touch sparked a yearning he had fought mightily to suppress. She was so young. This was business. He knew he was asking for trouble. He leaned closer to her, and after a long moment, continued. "It's not so noble as a war wound—I was hit in the head with a hockey puck." A smile frolicked at the corners of his mouth.

He was so close that Brett could count the tiny lines around his eyes, feel the warmth of his breath. "That must have hurt." She had barely finished speaking when Lawrence's lips met her own. He held her face, and the heat from his strong hands suffused through her body. His tongue probed the inside of her mouth, asking a question she was not ready to answer. Just as her body and her mind began to grapple over the double-edged sword that had been thrust upon her, Lawrence pulled away.

"It didn't hurt much. I had to sit out a period, but I went on to score the winning goal." He got up and pulled Brett to her feet. He held her hands a moment longer than necessary, then let them go, clumsily jamming his own into his trouser pockets.

"It's late, I should go." How had she let this happen? It was bad enough that she had gotten her first break because she was mistaken for a model. She could not afford to have Lawrence think she wanted to be his pet in exchange for future bookings.

They had not spoken as they gathered their belongings and left the house, their silence an acknowledgment of their ticklish circumstances. They stood awkwardly at the top of the hedge-lined circular driveway, their cars parked on opposite sides of the cobblestone arc. Hundreds of stars twinkled in the midnight-blue sky, and only the hum of traffic from the nearby, always congested place de Gaulle penetrated the quiet.

"Good night," Lawrence said, absently tapping his foot. "You really did do a good job tonight."

"'Night," Brett replied, and turned to walk down the sloping drive to her car.

The engine of Lawrence's black Citroën roared to life and he shifted into gear, recalling the softness of her cheek, imagining the feel of her body. He wondered if he had lost his mind.

Brett put her foot to the accelerator of her Peugeot, remembering the warmth of his touch and the urgency of his kiss. She had never been more confused.

At the top of the circle they passed each other, waved hesitantly, and drove off in opposite directions.

— *Chapter 9* —

Brett's photos for "Trop Chaud" were so impressive that she had been assigned that department for the next six issues—if *Voilà!* lasted that long. She had also shot an après-ski story on location in Lausanne for the January issue with a more willing Joe Tate booked for his second appearance in the magazine. He had decided to enjoy the fun for as long as it lasted. But aside from the editorial meetings prior to each shoot, she had barely seen Lawrence Chapin.

He had returned to his original gruff demeanor and dispatched the fashion editor to supervise Brett's bookings with the cryptic directive: "You know what I want." And Brett knew instinctively what he wanted . . . in a photograph. She knew enough not to expect the editor in chief of a magazine to attend every shoot, but his seeming avoidance confused her. Did he fault her for what had happened? Did he feel guilty? She tried to dismiss their brief digression, choosing to blame it on the risky combination of wine and exhaustion. Yet each time she saw him, she recalled every word of their conversation, how the sadness in his eyes had turned to longing, and most clearly, his kiss. Even though she missed their fiery discussions, she welcomed her reprieve. Brett needed to prove to herself that Lawrence was not rebooking her as an apology for his behavior.

Brett knew her work was good, but she found it hard to believe that the fashion grapevine in Paris was even shorter than the one in New York. The word was already out that there were big changes taking place at *Voilà!*, and that the magazine had found a talented new photographer. So as Brett continued to make her rounds, she found open doors and scheduled appointments at magazines where she previously had been anonymous. No longer was she just another photographer trying to make it in Paris. Her work had yet to hit the newsstands, but Brett Larsen was now welcomed as part of what was rumored to be "a revolution in the magazine industry, the likes of which had not been seen since Diana Vreeland took over *Vogue*."

Not only did she shoot the press kit for Martine Gallet's new collection, but with a casual mention of Martine to an editor at *Marie Claire*, Brett got the innovative young designer in a layout she did for them. If Brett thought Martine was going to be hot, then *Marie Claire* wanted to "discover" her.

Stylists and makeup artists Brett had never met began phoning for appointments to show her their portfolios so they might be considered for any work she had upcoming, and they even volunteered their services for tests she wanted to shoot.

And where in the past she had to beg bookers for copies of headsheets and model books, she now received a steady stream of comp cards and even some lunch invitations from agency directors, who were always eager to befriend a photographer who had work to dispense to their models.

At one of these lunches Gabriel Jarré, the shrewd but affable head of L'Étoile, asked Brett about the "hunk" she had discovered who would debut in December *Voilà!*. He wanted to know if Joe had an agent in Paris, and when Brett told him no, he ordered another vermouth and gave her a spiel about why Joe should come to L'Étoile.

Brett, too, had begun to think that Joe needed an agent. He was a natural charmer whose jocular, pleasant demeanor put people at ease immediately. He seemed responsible and level-headed, and with his blond good looks—a combination of wholesomeness with a healthy dose of adventure—Brett sensed that Joe would create quite a stir. Gabriel impressed her as a hard-working, aboveboard agent who would represent Joe well, pay him promptly, and not try to fill his off hours with lonely matrons willing to pay the price for a little entertainment, as some agents did.

Brett carefully crept down the rickety steps to Joe's cellar atelier. Rough sketches and more precise blueprints covered the grimy stone walls and at the center of the dirt floor Joe, mallet and chisel in hand, pondered a partially sculpted chunk of granite, his work in progress.

"So this is how Michelangelo got started!" Brett teased as she looked around Joe's work space. It was her first time there.

"It'll do for now. Sometimes I don't know whether it's day or night, but the rent is cheap. There's not as much call for dungeons as there used to be," he said, laughing. The space was not heated, but Joe worked in a T-shirt that revealed his well-muscled torso, and beads of sweat dotted his brow.

"No wonder you're in such great shape." Brett stretched both her hands around his right bicep, but her fingertips didn't meet. "I had no idea that a sculptor worked so hard. I guess I never thought about it." She examined a finished piece that resembled a series of undulating sand dunes. "This is really wonderful, Joe," she said, and swung her arm around his waist.

"You think so? But I could really do something wonderful if I could afford finer materials and better tools." Joe draped his arm around her shoulder and contemplated the sculpture he was working on.

Joe enjoyed the time he spent with Brett. Over the two months since they had met, their friendship had grown. At least once a week they met to share an evening meal and freewheeling conversation. They spoke honestly about how their work was going, voicing the excitement, fears, and frustrations they hid from less trusted companions.

In the beginning, Joe had pursued more than a platonic relationship. Brett gently explained that she did not feel the same way, but that she valued his friendship. Reluctantly, Joe accepted her decision. What she did not explain was that in many ways, Joe reminded her of David, and although she had come to terms with the impossibility of that relationship, she had convinced herself it would be unfair to become involved with Joe because he reminded her of someone else.

"It's funny you should mention that, because I have a proposition for you," Brett said.

"Oh, no! Close the barn door, Nellie, there's a storm brewing." Joe backed away in feigned horror.

To Brett's surprise, Joe was enthusiastic about Gabriel Jarré's offer.

"I felt strange about modeling, at first. But then I realized that it's not illegal or immoral, and I could make good money in a really short time. I love what I do in this damp, dirty basement, and if I can finance my work by mugging for pictures, so much the better. I just hope I can do it without you behind the camera." Joe said.

"I wouldn't worry," Brett said confidently.

Brett tested with Joe to give him the beginnings of a book. In another few weeks he would have his first tears. Gabriel welcomed him warmly and sent Brett flowers and tickets to the ballet for steering Joe his way.

Joe was amazed at the hard work of pursuing his new career. The agency would make ten appointments a day for him with photographers, magazine editors, designers, and ad agency casting directors, and at each meeting he had to be as witty and enthusiastic as he had been for the last, but Joe was philosophical. He figured he had been sculpting for six years and no one had paid him any attention yet, and he had some time to spend since alfresco drawing in winter was out of the question. He was willing to do the groundwork in the hopes it would pay off handsomely.

Joe and Brett celebrated when his first big assignment came in early December, just after his work in *Voilà!* appeared. *Homme du Monde* booked him for its April issue. He would spend the first two weeks of January in the Seychelles, a lush tropical paradise in the Indian Ocean.

When *Voilà!* hit the street, Brett's career went into orbit. More clients began calling in her book and she was wooed by photographer's reps—those combination P.R. agents and business managers whose job it is to garner plum assignments for their clients at a fee—but for the time being, Brett decided to handle her own affairs.

The magnitude of Brett's progress was driven home by her Christmas card from Malcolm. She knew he mailed five thousand of them, and that the whole procedure was orchestrated by computer. When she opened the pink flamingo with a red stocking cap she found a handwritten note: "Saw your *Voilà!* spread. Next you'll be back in New York coming after my clients! Nice work, babycakes! Gracie." In all of the frenzy, it hadn't occurred to Brett that her work would be seen in New York by the fashion posse who scoured everything between two covers that said "fashion" on it, first scrutinizing the masthead and credits for new players, then perusing pictures and articles.

Brett had planned a trip stateside for the holidays, but canceled at the last minute. As much as she wanted to see Lillian, she knew that in New York she would run herself ragged visiting friends and attending parties. Her social calendar would be busy in Paris, too, but she would have a better chance to unwind from the last few pressure-packed months and prepare for the January onslaught.

Brett and Joe decided to spend Christmas together. They invited a few friends, also holiday orphans, to dinner at Brett's apartment. Joe, having discovered that Brett was nearly helpless in the kitchen, did the cooking. The rich, woodsy bouquet of pine from the stately tree and the wreaths and garlands which graced doors and mantels, mingled with the piquant fragrance of numerous bayberry candles, the smoky-sweet scent of cherry wood logs burning in the fireplace and the spicy smell of mulled wine which emanated from the Georgian silver wassail bowl, to welcome the guests with the aromas of Christmas as soon as they entered Brett's apartment. The group reveled in the good food and the good cheer and ended the evening singing rousing, if off-key, renditions of their favorite carols.

After everyone left, Brett emptied the ashtrays into the silent butler, gathered the remaining glasses, and carried them into the kitchen. The maid, who came in twice a week, would be in Monday to clean, but Brett wanted to remove some of the clutter. The last strains of Nat King Cole's version of "The Christmas Song" played on the stereo, and the only illumination came from the flashing lights on the Christmas tree. All things considered, it had been a good Christmas, she thought as she returned to the living room and poured two fingers of calvados into a brandy snifter.

Drink in hand, she settled into the rose-colored *bergère* in front of the fireplace, only to realize that the fire was dying. Brett sat for a few moments thinking how fortunate she was to have good friends in Paris. When she decided not to go to New York for the holidays, she had been slightly depressed, knowing how much she would miss Lizzie, Aunt Lillian, and Christmas at Cox Cove, but the day had been fun in spite of her doubts.

She got up to stoke the embers and put on another log, and the Art Deco fire screen scraped against the bluestone hearth as she moved it aside. *It's not exactly a roaring blaze, but it'll do*, Brett thought as she resumed her seat.

Holiday greetings had arrived in bundles. She had heard from everyone at home, including her grandfather. Everyone except Barbara. *How long can she be angry because I've met my grandfather*, Brett wondered. But it had been two and a half years since the scene in the airport and her mother showed no signs of forgiveness. Brett tried to dismiss the disappointment and longing she felt at her mother's slights, but she wasn't always successful. She crossed her legs under her and stared into the hypnotic flames, fingering her grandmother's cameo. It wasn't just her mother's refusal to talk about her own father that disturbed Brett. Barbara was the only person who could answer questions about Brett's father, and she refused to talk about him, as well. Brett took a sip of the fruity cognac and remembered how warm and animated Lawrence Chapin's stories about his father had been that night on the avenue Foch. She respected Lawrence and she liked him. His kiss hadn't offended her, but based on his recent behavior, it had obviously bothered him.

The wind rattled the French doors that led onto the balcony, and she went over to secure them. She pulled the lace curtain aside and was delighted to see the swirling flakes of the first snowfall of winter. It didn't snow very often in Paris. Brett watched for several minutes. In spite of everything else, her career was going extraordinarily well—in fact, better than she had hoped. She knew many photographers who had knocked around Europe for years before anyone took real notice of their work, and some never made it at all. She let the curtain fall and unplugged the lights on the tree.

Later, in bed, as she snuggled under her down comforter, Brett found herself remembering Lawrence's kiss once again, but she decided that working for Lawrence Chapin had to be less problematic than having him as a lover.

January proved to be as hectic as Brett had expected. She spent a comparatively luxurious three days shooting seven pages for March *Voilà!*. Although the publisher had yet to decide if that issue would be released, the rejuvenated magazine had received good reviews and had generated reader and advertiser interest. Lawrence traveled extensively, cheerleading and whipping up interest for the book throughout Europe.

She shot her first retail ad for the Galleries Lafayette and snagged a prestigious location booking for *Elle* by default. Umberto di Santis, the original photographer, was arrested on New Year's Day for cocaine possession and could not leave the country. *Elle*'s roster of star photographers had prior commitments and could not accept the last-minute booking, so, based on her work and the most grueling interview she had survived to date, Brett, two assistants, three models, and a crew of six set off to capture exotic evening wear in the ancient city of Marrakech. The heat was oppressive, and she could only shoot in the early morning and evening hours when the temperature was a cool 98 degrees, but the scenery and landscape were incomparable. She took full advantage of the locale, using the majestic Atlas Mountains, the minaret of the Koutoubya Mosque, and the lush gardens of the fourteenth century sultan's palace as backdrops. On the trip she also heard rumors that *Elle* was planning to storm the gates of Condé Nast and start publishing in the U.S.

When she returned home at the beginning of February, Brett was anxious to touch base with Joe. She hadn't seen him for a month, and they both had travel stories to tell. They had made a dinner date, but at the last minute, Joe had called to cancel—his booking was running overtime. Brett was happy for Joe, because that meant time-and-a-half, but disappointed because their plans had been scotched. Before she could decide what to do with her evening, the phone rang. Mathilde, Lawrence Chapin's secretary, called to invite her to an impromptu celebration at the *Voilà!* offices. Based on revenue and circulation figures for December and January, the publisher had okayed another six-month run.

She drove across town through snarled Parisian traffic, made worse by a persistent rain. Brett arrived to find the party in full swing. The din of conversation was well-oiled by alcohol and relief. Champagne bottles and paper cups littered every horizontal surface, and a dense Gauloise fog hung in the air. A cheer arose when Brett entered. Although she was not the architect, she had been one of the engineers responsible for shoring up the dam. The staff had been granted a stay of execution, and they were jubilant. The usually controlled and proper fashion editor, who always spoke in terse, well-modulated French, had given up on language completely and greeted an astonished Brett with a kiss squarely on the mouth.

Brett mingled easily with her associates. Until then, she hadn't realized how much *Voilà!*'s success meant to her. Suddenly, across the room, she spotted Lawrence, leaning against the door frame of his office, head thrown back in hearty laughter, looking like he owned the world. She remembered the last time she had seen him look so happy—but she had been much closer then. *Stop it!* she thought. She was grateful to Lawrence Chapin for starting her career and happy for the success he was enjoying now, yet she still could not extinguish the ember of desire that seemed to ignite spontaneously within her whenever she was in his presence.

"Congratulations, Mr. Chapin." Brett offered her hand, bracing herself for his touch.

"The battle's not over yet." Lawrence gripped her hand, pumped it twice, then let go. He had known she would be there, but had chosen not to think about their meeting.

"Everybody in the business is talking about the changes you've made. Some people are getting nervous." The easiness of his manner seemed to evaporate, replaced by an apparent restlessness.

"Well, I'm not going to break my arm patting myself on the back yet." Lawrence did not intend to sound so short, but he needed to keep Brett at a distance. She was so creative and talented, so beautiful, and the sincerity, the lack of guile in her eyes, threatened to penetrate his shield of sophisticated detachment. It made him feel the potential for a wide-eyed love he had deemed impractical when he was a much younger man, but illogically, he was drawn to her. His transgression by the fire had been enough. He could not let that happen again. "If you'll excuse me, I have some phone calls I need to return." He escaped into his office, closing the door behind him.

Fine, Brett thought. She had fulfilled her obligation to be civil. *Voilà!* was a valued account that she intended to keep and she would address Lawrence Chapin as it was necessary, no more. How could she have been charmed by someone so arrogant?

After circulating for a while longer, Brett left, making her way to the underground garage where she had parked. The coughing and straining of a car engine struggling to turn over shattered the hollow silence. Brett started her car and headed for the exit when she heard the slam of a car door. "Shit!" Lawrence bellowed as he yanked open the hood of his Citroën. Brett's first impulse was to keep driving. She'd had enough of Lawrence Chapin for one evening, but he turned just as she was passing by and saw her.

"I paid a fortune for this damned car and I'm still under the hood like a kid with his first jalopy." He peered hopelessly at the huge engine.

"Can I give you a lift somewhere?" Brett offered reluctantly.

Lawrence listened to the insistent rainfall tapping the sidewalk outside. "My garage is closed and I'll never get a taxi. I guess you could give me a ride."

He sounds like he's doing me a favor, Brett thought as he secured his car and got in with her.

For a time they drove in silence. "Where are you going?" Brett asked, realizing they hadn't discussed a destination.

"I was planning a quiet dinner at Le Flore. Do you know where that is?" he asked.

"Certainly. It's only a few blocks from my apartment." *At least this will be convenient*, she thought.

"Then why don't you join me?" Lawrence wasn't sure what made him ask.

"Well, I have a very long day tomorrow," Brett said.

"So do I, but you have to eat, don't you? The least *Voilà!* can do is buy you dinner."

"That's very nice of you, Mr. Chapin." It would be a dinner with a client, sometimes a necessary evil, she reasoned.

Lawrence was aware that "Mr. Chapin" was a moat between them again. He had created the distance on purpose. It was what he had thought he wanted.

Again they lapsed into silence. Brett struggled to find words to begin a conversation, but her mind seemed stuck in neutral. She had to relax if she was going to make it through a meal with him.

Brett parked the car and reached for her umbrella. Lawrence pulled up his collar.

"Wait. You can't go outside like that," she said. They huddled under her umbrella, making their way against the rain, which came in sheets, propelled by an icy wind. Unexpectedly, the wind changed direction and the umbrella was blown out of Lawrence's grip and into the street, where it was flattened by a passing car.

"Run for it!" Lawrence exclaimed, and they dashed through the street, at first trying to avoid puddles, then realizing they were hopelessly wet anyway. When they entered Le Flore, they looked at each other and burst into laughter.

"Ah, Monsieur Chapin. Either you have no umbrella or you have been swimming in the Seine!" greeted the maître d'. "Let me get you and the lady a towel before you sit down. I will have them prepare your regular table."

When Brett slid onto the worn red leather banquette, a random profusion of shiny wet curls framed her face. "My feet are drenched. I can feel my toes sloshing around in my boots!"

"Take them off."

"My toes?"

They both snickered. The silliness seemed so natural.

"Here, give me your foot," Lawrence reached under the table

and yanked off her soggy boots. "I took the liberty of ordering Pineau de Charentes. I thought it might take the chill off."

Brett sipped the topaz-colored liquid, enjoying the lush bouquet of the heady wine-and-cognac blend and the warm feeling that budded on her lips and blossomed fully in her mouth. Brett had wanted to have an awful evening, but already that was not possible. "Excellent choice." She pondered a moment. "So, why did you give me a chance back in September?" It was really the question she needed answered. If she caught Lawrence off guard, so much the better.

"Your pictures were direct and compelling and you took a risk. I like risk-takers."

"If I'd left my book in the pile with the others, would you still have been drawn to it?"

"I can't answer that, because you didn't. Brett, your work is quite exceptional, and when I gave you that assignment, I wondered if I had lost the ability to make rational judgments, but part of life is learning when the irrational judgments are the right ones. And I am very satisfied with the call I made." His answer cleared the air.

They ordered the special, cassoulet Toulouse, a hearty stew of beans, sausage, mutton, and duck, which they savored hungrily while engrossed in conversation.

"Now it's my turn to ask a question," Lawrence announced. "What makes you so sure of yourself?"

Brett looked past him into her own reflection in the mirror. "Once someone tried to convince me that nothing I did was good enough. When I discovered that person was wrong, I decided that whatever I did was better than doing nothing at all."

When they left the restaurant, only a damp mist hung in the air. "I'll walk you home," Lawrence offered, so they strolled through the empty streets. Brett marveled at the antique dolls and marionettes in the window of Au Beau Noir, her nose nearly pressed to the glass. Lawrence stood behind her, his head at war with his feelings once again. Finally, going with his feelings, he placed his palms on the glass on either side of her. "Would you be offended if I kissed you again?" he whispered.

Brett turned to face him, "No," she said quietly. "I wasn't offended the first time."

He gently stroked her cheek, then cupped her chin and tilted her head until their eyes met. In that moment, all that had been misunderstood, everything that had put distance between them for months, dissolved, and what their eyes conveyed their lips confirmed—slowly, sweetly, tenderly. Silently, hand in hand, they reached Brett's apartment.

"Would you like to come up for coffee?" Brett asked.

Lawrence was struck by the coziness of Brett's apartment. From the simple, clean lines of her clothing and her modern, straightforward approach to her work, he had expected her living quarters to reflect the same attitude. The chintz-covered sofa and chairs, lace curtains, and antique tables and lamps were not at all cloying, but rather warm and inviting, as if a deliberate effort had been made to create a haven or preserve a tradition, and he wondered which it was.

Brett knew what she wanted now that Lawrence was there, but felt the curious thrill of not knowing what to expect. She removed her boots, hung up their coats, and went into the kitchen. Lawrence, who had settled into a corner of the overstuffed sofa, got up and followed her. "I don't really want coffee, Brett."

"Neither do I," she said.

Lawrence pulled her to him, and for the first time, their bodies met in an embrace. Their lips no longer asked, they demanded, passionately urging them on. Lawrence traced the planes of her back, moving his hands slowly down until he could slip them under her sweater. His touch quickened her and left her breathless with desire. She pressed her body into his, then drew away wordlessly and led him to her bedroom.

Brett began to disrobe hastily, but Lawrence stopped her. He laid her down on the hand-embroidered duvet and knelt at her side, undressing her reverently, revealing her body slowly and deliberately, nuzzling and nibbling as he exposed more and more of her silken skin.

From Brett's moans and whimpers he knew what pleased her most, and he continued until she could barely breathe before moving on to another sweet spot. She was a willing pupil to his learned touch. Brett had never felt such exquisite torture. She wanted him to hurry, yet couldn't bear relinquishing her newfound pleasures. Just when she thought she would lose her mind, Lawrence stopped and quickly undressed himself.

For what seemed to Brett an eternity, he sat beside her and made love to her with his eyes. The light, diffused by a peach silk shade, cast a warm glow over her supple form. Not an inch of her was spared his pilgrimage.

"Is something wrong?" Brett asked, suddenly aware of the insecurity she still felt about her body.

"No, I just can't look at you enough," Lawrence answered, aroused by her luxurious curves. Then he stretched out, pulled her close, and let his hands explore the terrain he had committed to memory, this time letting himself travel with her. Brett rubbed her hips insistently, rhythmically, against his fully engorged penis and it pulsed and throbbed as if it would explode. When she touched him there he closed his eyes and groaned from a place deep within. Finally, he slid himself inside her and she shuddered with waves of ecstasy.

"I can't go any farther," she said.

"Stay with me," Lawrence coaxed. And she did. Again and again he thrust, taking her almost to the summit, then pulling her back. Finally, and together, they reached a peak neither had known before.

They fell asleep entwined, sated, and spent.

— *Chapter 10* —

"Brett, we're in a high-profile business. For reasons I have yet to fathom, the French press zeroed in on me the moment I set foot in Paris, and they have yet to let me out of their sights. You'll get used to it," Lawrence explained.

They had reached the outskirts of the city and turned onto the auto route that would take them to Orly to meet Lizzie's plane. Brett had looked forward to her best friend's visit to Paris, and thought nothing could put a damper on her good spirits, until they picked up the latest edition of *Espion*, the gossipy French tabloid, on their way to the airport. The lead story covered Nureyev's opening night performance in *Giselle* at the Paris Opera Ballet, but there was only one photograph of the world-renowned dancer. The rest of the story was a pictorial who's who of those in attendance at the glitzy event and included "the fashion world's most elusive bachelor, Lawrence Chapin, and his latest, the beautiful young American photographer, Brett Larsen."

"But they implied that I seduced you to get my pictures published," Brett said angrily, a rumpled copy of the paper in her hands. Not only did it announce her liaison with Lawrence, but it detailed her ties to the Larsen fortune. For years Barbara had sought the very publicity that Brett now abhorred. "They're vultures, except they don't wait until you're dead!"

For the first few weeks of their relationship, Brett had turned down Lawrence's invitations to attend social events, deliberately avoiding the limelight. Instead, they spent quiet evenings, usually dining at a neighborhood brasserie, then returned to Brett's apartment, where they talked and made love until neither had words or energy left.

After Brett told him about her childhood and family history, Lawrence understood why she was so publicity-shy. "But I'm afraid you've chosen the wrong line of work if you want privacy. Perhaps you'd like to consider sheep-herding?" he had teased. He knew she needed a thicker skin to survive, but he was convinced that time would take care of that.

"Besides, we both know it's not true, so what does it matter?" He reached over and massaged her thigh. "Are you happy?"

"Yes, but . . ."

"Then ignore what people say. It means you're interesting enough to talk about."

Brett knew he was right. It was true—she was happier than she dared imagine. It was now May, and since the winter, her career had snowballed and her publication in *Elle* added considerable sheen to her reputation.

And in Lawrence she had found the one man who seemed to meet all of her needs. Unlike Paolo, he respected her work and offered her insights into the business of magazine publishing that broadened her professional horizons. He understood that her hectic schedule required frequent travel; it was much like his own. Lawrence exuded a worldly confidence she had not found in the younger men she had dated. He was not threatened by her ambitions. Instead, he guided her along paths that he had already walked, intuitively knowing when to take her hand and walk with her, and when to step aside and simply urge her on, his quick wit and strong arms his only prods. She trusted him. And Lawrence was the consummate lover —sensitive, patient, and skillful.

"Besides, they had to include at least one picture of someone pretty. The others look as though they've been sucking lemons." Lawrence pulled the paper from her hands and chucked it into the backseat.

Brett was like the fantasy Lawrence had not dared to entertain. When he had been young and bold, he had blazed new trails in his career with boundless energy, astounding those around him. Later, he had traded the excitement of exploring for the comfort and safety of routine. Now, with Brett, he thought he could share the adventure without taking the risk. In her he found sophistication, without the boredom of those who had seen it all. He could guide her, playing professor to his prize student, and she was eager and willing to learn from his experience. When he made love to her, he could recapture the thrill he had felt when bodies were all new and his to conquer. And when he let her go, he would be revitalized and ready to relax into his cozy routine again.

"You should go in while I park the car. I know it's hard to believe, but the plane may be on time," Lawrence said as they pulled up in front of the LARSair terminal.

"Okay, I'll be right outside customs."

Lizzie was the first one through the gate, and Brett couldn't imagine how she had managed that feat, considering the tower of suitcases she pushed on an airport-issue luggage cart. Brett could count four, plus the carry-on bag slung over her shoulder. Lizzie was planning to stay for six weeks, but she had obviously brought her entire closet.

"I can't believe I'm in Paris! I'm so glad to see you!" Lizzie said as they hugged, laughed, and almost cried. Then Lizzie was off. "Brett, the flight was amazing! It was like going to a private club! The seats in first class are already like sofas. Then you can go upstairs to the lounge like you're in some grand *maison*, instead of thirty-five thousand feet in the air. When the stewardess brought me the menu and the wine list, I just about passed out!" Taking a breath, she continued, "Brett, you look so . . . well, what I mean is, you look like you're in love. Are you? Where is he?" she whispered, her head swiveling like a compass needle gone wild.

At that moment, Lawrence emerged from the crowd. "You must be Lizzie. Did you have a good flight?"

"Uh . . . yes. It was great," Lizzie said.

"Here, let me take that. I'll meet you two out front with the car," Lawrence said as he steered the cart through the throng.

"Brett, he's a *man*! Is he really forty?"

"Actually, he's forty-one, but I never think about it."

"He's so handsome!" Lizzie said.

"I know," Brett responded, pleased that Lizzie was so impressed.

In the car, Lizzie discovered the discarded copy of *Espion*. "Wow! This is great—you're a celebrity. Brett, you look beautiful. I love this dress. Lawrence, what kind of car is this?" Lizzie chattered nonstop all the way back to Paris.

Lawrence pulled Brett aside while Lizzie unpacked in the guest room. "Does that young woman ever *not* talk?" he asked in exasperation.

"Well, maybe not in her sleep," Brett said.

It's going to be an interminable six weeks, Lawrence thought.

That night they dined at La Tour d'Argent and Lizzie saved the number from their duck as a memento of her first night in Paris. While Brett and Lizzie reminisced and occasionally giggled like schoolgirls during dinner, Lawrence felt acutely aware of his age. Had he made another choice, he could have children almost Brett's age.

Brett could see from the distant look on his face that he was not enjoying the evening. And she knew something was wrong when he double-parked his car on the rue de Seine, walked them to her door, and said good night with only a perfunctory kiss on the cheek.

"I'll talk to you tomorrow," he said briskly and walked away.

Over the next four days, Brett and Lizzie did the official tour, seeing the Paris of travel brochures and postcards. Lizzie had saved for two years to make this trip, and since her ticket had been a gift from Brett, she allocated a large portion of her funds to adding continental flair to her collegiate wardrobe.

On the fifth day, a footsore Brett paused just beyond the perfume department of Au Printemps, trying to convince Lizzie that they had six whole weeks to visit every store on her well-researched shopping itinerary.

Lizzie spotted a woman pushing a sleeping infant in a stroller and said, "I forgot to tell you—I'm going to be an aunt! David and Kate are expecting a baby in December." David's company, Hands On, had its first personal computer—Fingertips-I—on the market and sales were good. "He's been crazy busy—they didn't even get home this winter for the holidays—but hopefully, the baby will be here by this Christmas and I'll go to California with my folks."

For the first time she could remember, Brett was happy for David and his wife without the undercurrent of longing and misplaced hope she had always felt when she thought about them. *I guess I've finally grown up*, she mused. David deserved the happiness he had found, and she knew he would be a wonderful father.

"I think that's great, but I'll have to get used to Aunt Lizzie," she said as they marched off to the Caron counter.

"I've planned a picnic for Sunday," Brett said as they rode the Métro back to Saint-Germain-des-Prés. She usually spent Sundays with Lawrence, and she hadn't seen him all week. Although she had purposely lightened her work schedule for Lizzie's visit, Lawrence had been busy at *Voilà!*. Besides, she knew he had no interest in tagging along on their jaunts. She had, however, persuaded him that a day in the country with a picnic lunch would at least give them a chance to see each other.

On Saturday, Joe, just back from a working trip to London,

phoned Brett. "You won't believe what I've got to tell you because I don't believe it, so I thought if I said it out loud it might sound real."

"I take it you've got good news," Brett said.

"I'm about to bust a gusset."

"Tape your gusset and hold it until tomorrow," she said, laughing, and invited him along on the outing. She wanted Joe, one of her dearest friends in Paris, to meet Lizzie, her oldest and closest friend.

On Sunday morning Lawrence met Brett, Joe, and Lizzie, and they drove through the countryside to the forest of Compiègne, a former hunting ground of French kings, that sits on the river Oise, stopping first at La Bonne Idée, a cozy restaurant in the hamlet of Vieux-Moulin, to claim a picnic hamper full of cheeses, cold meats, fruit, baguettes, and a pâté with cornichons and several bottles of wine. They found a grassy spot in a clearing shaded by a towering oak, spread out a bright red blanket, weighting down the corners with rocks, and settled in for the afternoon.

It was one of those singular, arbitrary days in May when nature's benevolent promise supersedes her whimsy and caprice. The young sun warmed newly minted leaves and blades of grass, encouraging growth, and lighting their transition from the virgin green of springtime to the lush, dark verdancy of summer. Dense, puffy clouds floated lazily through a perfect sky, providing fuel for fanciful imaginations and daydreams. From a clump of tall marsh grass on the other side of the river a honking flight of geese rose in formation, and soared across the horizon.

Brett lounged against the tree trunk with Lawrence's head in her lap. "Okay, Joe, what's the good news you don't believe?" she asked.

Joe lay on his stomach, propped on his elbows, and explained, "Last week Gabriel sent me to see this company called Clik Claque. They make these silly plastic watches in all colors with squiggles, stars, dots, and everything else on them. I didn't think much about it until Gabriel tracked me down just before I left London to tell me they want me to be their spokesman. Kind of like Mr. Claque,

I guess. Anyway, they want me to do print ads, commercials, and public appearances all over Europe and in the States. Brett, I can't believe the money they're talking about, and Gabriel is holding out for more."

"Joe, that's fantastic!" Brett said.

"Sounds like a pretty good deal. I guess *Voilà!* should book you again quickly, before your rates go up and we can't afford you anymore," Lawrence said.

"I'm a little worried about all of this activity," Joe confided, reaching for an apple.

Brett said, "Joe, it will be fine. You could make a tree limb feel at ease, so personal appearances should be a snap. And I know it sounds like a heavy schedule, but think of all the time you can afford to take for your real work."

During this conversation, Lizzie's blond curls bounced as her head turned from speaker to speaker. She twisted her legs into a tighter and tighter pretzel beneath her eyelet peasant skirt. Here she was with the editor of an international fashion magazine, a photographer at the beginning of what promised to be an illustrious career, and a model with his first international contract, and she was just a college senior. Lizzie felt insecure, as though she had to find some way to merit inclusion in this group.

"Well, the most important thing to remember with television is to relax. TV cameras read things still cameras don't, like nervousness, and you have to be really careful with gestures or you'll look like you're trying to land a plane," Lizzie said with authority.

"Oh, yeah, I remember. Brett told me you're a broadcasting major," Joe said.

"Yes. I'm the weekend features reporter for WSTM in Syracuse. I graduate in December—six months early—and they've already offered me a job, but I have a pretty good reel and I want to consider all my options—maybe check out L.A. and New York—before I lock myself in."

Brett, realizing that Lizzie had felt left out of the conversation, added, "Lizzie's brother lives in L.A."

"Well, actually, he's in Santa Clara, up in the Silicon Valley.

He started his own computer company and he's quite successful." Lizzie offered up a healthy serving of her brother's accomplishments, estimating how wealthy he would be eventually.

Joe was amused. Rarely had he seen anyone talk so fast and with such animation.

Lawrence was bored and agitated. All this talk of youthful goals and aspirations made him aware that more of his life had gone by than he cared to think about.

"I'm going for a walk." Lawrence rose and headed for a path that led through a grove of beech trees.

"I think I'll go, too." Brett followed him out of sight.

As much as Lizzie talked about men and love, both made her nervous. When she was attracted to a particular man, that nervousness was multiplied tenfold, which usually made her talk twice as fast as she normally did, often before her brain could process what she had just said.

"You and Brett are certainly different," Joe said, taking a bite of his apple.

"Why? Because I'm not rich and famous? I will be someday. Jane Pauley is my role model. She started on the 'Today Show' when she was in her twenties. She's from Indiana, too, you know."

"Wait, wait. That's not what I meant. Brett's work is getting her known in some circles, but it doesn't seem to have changed her much and I don't think it will. And I don't think wealth will change her, either," Joe said.

"Change her! Brett's been rich all her life. I flew here on her grandfather's airline!"

He paused a moment to digest what Lizzie had revealed.

"That Larsen?" Joe had never connected Brett with Larsen Enterprises, a name he knew from news reports. He had had no reason to. Brett worked as hard as any young artist he knew, and he had certainly never seen her throw her money around. He respected her for that. "Lizzie, all I really meant was that you're physically so different. Brett's so tall, and you're . . ."

"Short! There's nothing wrong with being short. Sally Field and Susan Lucci aren't more than 5'2" and I don't think Jane Pauley is really very tall."

"Okay, Lizzie. How about you're blonde and she's brunette? Is that offensive? And don't give me a list of famous blondes. I was just trying to make conversation." Joe sat up and looked off into the distance.

"Oh." Lizzie felt silly and tried to redeem herself. "I can't wait to get out of school next year. I think a college education is important if a person wants to get ahead in the world."

"Well, I left after my first year. I'm not sure college is the only way to learn what you need to know. Your friend Brett didn't seem to need it."

Lizzie was now sure that she had killed any chance she might have had with Joe.

"Would you like to go for a walk?" Joe asked. He thought that Lizzie was probably a nice girl, if she would just calm down.

"Sure!" Lizzie wasn't really dressed for walking in the woods. Brett had suggested that she wear casual slacks and sneakers, but Lizzie was going on a picnic in the French forest with a male model, and she somehow felt she had to dress the part, so with her eyelet skirt and embroidered top, she had worn white leather ballerina flats.

Much of Joe's work as a sculptor evolved from forms in nature, so as they strolled, he stopped to look at moss-covered rocks and carefully examined a fallen bird's nest. "This looks like it might be a thrush's nest. They're fairly common in this part of Europe."

Okay, he likes nature, Lizzie noted.

They came to a winding rivulet and followed its sloping banks. At a narrow point in the stream, an alder tree had fallen and become wedged in mud and rocks.

"Let's cross to the other side. Maybe there are more nests and things to look at," Lizzie suggested.

"That's probably not a good idea. Your shoes won't give you enough traction," Joe warned.

"Oh, I can do it." Lizzie hopped on the tree trunk. "I have very good balance. It comes from taking gymnastics for six years when I was younger." She took two more steps, attempted a pirouette, and slipped off into the muck.

Joe tried to hold in his laughter, but the sight of Lizzie, forlorn and covered in slime, was more than he could bear, and he laughed heartily as he scrambled to help her.

"No . . . I'm fine. I can get up!" She hoisted herself out of the water and stomped onto the shore, mortified.

"I didn't mean to laugh. Really." Joe tried to adopt a more sober demeanor, but as she stormed along, looking for all the world like the Swamp Thing, he began to chuckle again.

Lizzie didn't blame him. *I deserve this*, she thought.

Joe ran ahead and stopped in her path. "Lizzie, you're wet and muddy and that's got to be uncomfortable. Why don't you take my shirt. You can change over behind those trees." Joe removed his navy cotton shirt and handed it to her.

"I feel so ridiculous."

"You look pretty silly, too," he teased. "Just relax."

Lizzie looked into Joe's hazel eyes, smiled sheepishly, and headed off toward the trees, shirt in hand. In a few minutes she returned, in what appeared to be a fashionable, if oversized, dress.

Joe, eyes twinkling, offered his hand. "How about a truce?"

"You've got a deal," Lizzie agreed, and they shook on it.

"What's the matter?" Brett asked when she caught up to Lawrence.

Lawrence continued to walk, as if she weren't there.

Brett grabbed his arm. "You've been impossible for a week. What is it?"

Brett was prepared for an argument. She knew his behavior had something to do with Lizzie, and she had decided that he was jealous of the time she was spending with her friend.

He stopped and leaned against the smooth silvery-gray bark of a nearby beech and looked past her as he spoke. "I see you with Lizzie and I can't help thinking you could both be my daughters."

"But you know that doesn't matter—not to me. We've talked about that before."

"You're right, we did. I didn't think it was important before."

"Then, why have you suddenly changed your mind?" Brett walked over and stood directly in front of him.

Lawrence spoke in a whisper. "Because I've fallen in love with you . . . and I didn't plan to do that."

Brett felt as though she was suspended in that airless, silent void between the first flash of lightning and the clap of thunder that must follow. His words let loose a torrent of emotions that threatened to overwhelm her. "What are you saying?"

"I'm saying that I love you, but it's not as simple as that. I'm saying that I can't control my feelings and it scares me more than anything I can imagine."

"Lawrence, I didn't plan this either . . . but I love you."

They both let the words float in the air and settle softly about them. Then he slid his arms around her and they held each other, rocking gently.

What am I going to do, Lawrence thought.

— *Chapter 11* —

"What do you mean, he didn't *plan* to love you?" Lizzie asked.

"Lizzie, you're reading too much into this. The important thing is that whether he planned it or not, he does love me." Brett was slightly miffed by her friend's reaction. She had barely been able to contain herself until Lawrence and Joe left, and now Lizzie was acting skeptical instead of sharing her happiness.

They had settled on the terrace just beyond Brett's living room. After the eventful day, night, by comparison, had fallen unceremoniously over the Latin Quarter, but warmth from the unusually temperate spring weather still lingered in the air. A candle on the white, lacework-iron table between them glowed steadily, its flame protected by a hurricane glass. Bands of moonlight slipped through the narrow spaces that separated the huddled houses of the tightly clustered neighborhood and created soft shadows that played across the red tile floor and ivy-covered walls of the balcony, obscuring their faces from each other's scrutiny.

"Well, if he didn't plan to love you, what did he plan?" Lizzie, who had showered and changed into pajamas, a daisy-printed cotton campshirt and matching boxer's shorts, scooted her chair forward until she could place her bare feet up on the balcony railing. "Was he just going to sleep with you until he got bored, then go on to the next person he didn't plan to love? A person can't go into a relationship with a master plan for how they're going to feel. Feelings happen all by themselves—they don't come with instructions." Lizzie turned to face her friend.

Brett, veiled in shadows, sat propped against the bright yellow cushions of the white wrought-iron chaise, her knees pulled up to her chest. Her aqua silk trapeze nightgown formed a tent beneath which her toes peeked. "What's wrong with you? He loves me and I love him. Is that so hard for you to understand? Just because you've been in love a hundred times doesn't make you the reigning expert! You were in love with . . . whatever his name was before you came to Paris, and now you're all excited because Joe asked you out."

"I'm not claiming to be an expert, Brett, but what do you know about him? He seems nice enough, but why hasn't he ever been married? He's forty-one. Or doesn't he *plan* to get married?"

"Lizzie, people plan to get married without being in love, so right now, I just want to enjoy being in love." Brett leaned forward slightly. The candle lighted her face enough for Lizzie to see the determination there. "I'll think about what comes next later."

Lizzie lingered on the terrace after Brett, claiming exhaustion from the country air, had gone to bed. *Why can't I ever keep quiet*? Lizzie asked herself. The moon had now risen high and full. She gazed out over the tile rooftops at the steeple of Saint-Germain-des-Prés and tried to put her finger on what bothered her about Lawrence Chapin. Off in the distance she could hear an accordion playing "La Vie en Rose." Maybe there was nothing wrong with him—maybe it was just her. She wondered if she was a tiny bit envious of her best friend. Lizzie loved Brett, but she had always had everything, and now she had a man who loved her.

Lizzie did not give voice to her reservations about Lawrence for the rest of her visit. It was as if the conversation on the balcony never happened. When Brett had to work, Lizzie explored Paris either on her own or with Joe. She found, to her surprise, that she actually enjoyed the galleries and museums. In New York she had always considered them somber and boring, and only went on class trips. She was disappointed that the famed Mona Lisa was not the gigantic canvas she had imagined, and she thought the anachronistic I. M. Pei pyramid at the Louvre strange. But Joe's insights and explanations were more enlightening than a guided tour. There was something about him that was both intense and calming, and Lizzie felt more relaxed around him than she normally did around men.

Joe was inexplicably drawn to the near-frantic energy and boundless curiosity that sometimes led Lizzie to act first and think later. Her spontaneity was engaging and she made him laugh.

Six weeks flew by. Lizzie, having checked her luggage—now five pieces, instead of four—lingered with Brett in the airport lounge. "Joe promised to call me when he's in New York for Clik Claque. Do you think he will?" Lizzie tried to sound nonchalant.

"He's a good guy. I'm sure he will." If Lizzie was going to be enamored of someone, Joe was certainly a good choice. But knowing Lizzie, she would find someone new as soon as she hit Kennedy Airport, Brett thought.

"Why don't you come to New York for a visit this summer? You haven't been home in two years," Lizzie said.

"I can't right now, Lizzie. June and July are the busiest months of the year." Brett explained that although spring was important, it paled in comparison to fall, when the top magazines were so thick they looked like telephone books.

"Oh, Brett, it sounds so exciting! I really love this city! I almost hate to go home."

The two friends hugged warmly. "You'll be back," Brett said.

Not only were magazines brimming with editorial pages in the fall, but advertisers, eager to stoke the fashion fire, produced lavish, multipage spreads, each seeking to be more memorable than the next and to convince women that of all the clothes and accessories they would see, none would suit them more perfectly than theirs.

Brett had already done six ad pages for Martine Gallet, who had produced her first ready-to-wear collection with the backing of a consortium from Bahrain, eager to invest some of their petrodollars.

Most of Brett's time for the remainder of June and all of July had already been booked, and whether she was in Paris or on location, she spent her days behind the camera and her evenings editing film and preparing for the next day. Brett found that she was rapidly outgrowing the studio space in her apartment, and she desperately needed a studio manager, but she did not relish the search for either, so she continued to put them off.

She and Lawrence barely saw each other and had to be satisfied with quick phone calls and an occasional dinner scarfed down before bed.

Often, when Brett lay in bed alone, she thought about Lawrence. She relived the wonderful times they had shared and sometimes she even dared to imagine what the future might be. But she also wondered about the past, and as much as she tried to ignore them, Lizzie's questions nagged her. Lawrence warmed to telling stories about his family and growing up in Buffalo, but when she asked about his life since then, the response was always chilly.

Brett sat cross-legged on the couch in the cluttered living room of Lawrence's apartment on the posh rue Raynouard. They had eaten dinner nearby, since Lawrence was leaving for Italy and Spain the next morning and needed to pack a few things before they returned to Brett's, where he would spend the night.

She removed her necklace, a heavy strand of apple coral, and fingered the thick, smooth disks before laying them in the sling formed by her burnished-orange full-circle skirt. Combing through the fringes of the red-and-gray geometric wool throw that was draped strategically over the black cotton roll-armed sofa to hide the worn spots, she looked around the now-familiar space. It had the same haphazard ambience as his *Voilà!* office—eclectic utilitarian chic, she called it.

Only the row of casement windows, which provided light and a magnificent, unobstructed view of the Eiffel Tower, kept the room from feeling tiny and cramped. The narrow chamber, like so many Parisian apartments, was painted a creamy vanilla that looked time-worn even when fresh. Except for the stone floor—large, gray-veined white hexagons accented with smaller diamonds of coal black—no surface seemed free of objects. In front of her, books and magazines, which showed some evidence of having once been neatly stacked, so completely covered the small coffee table that they appeared to levitate.

Chalky white bookshelves, brimming with volumes and the occasional surprise of a terra-cotta vase or a bronze, lined the long wall opposite the sofa and continued along the adjacent short wall at the far end of the room—the area that Lawrence called his study. A random assortment of pens, pencils, papers, and reading material of all description was scattered across his desk of rough-hewn oak boards supported by slender iron legs. And in the back corner of the desk sat his father's old Remington typewriter.

Lawrence entered the room, heralded by the insistent meows of Monkey, his venerable gray Abyssinian. As soon as he perched on the sofa arm next to Brett and flicked on the lamp, a metal cobra whose coiled body supported a frosted glass cone, the cat marched relentlessly back and forth across his cordovan loafers, leaving a rim of fur at the hem of his tan twill trousers. Monkey was the reason they didn't spend much time in his apartment. She had taken an instant dislike to Brett, and cried almost incessantly whenever she was there. They tried shutting her out of the bedroom, but she had scratched and clawed at the door, making sleep nearly impossible and lovemaking hardly enjoyable.

"You've been awfully quiet. What are you thinking about?" Lawrence asked.

"You."

"What about me?"

"Lawrence, why haven't you ever been married?" she asked.

He stalked over to the window, pushed up the sleeves of his celery-green cotton jersey, then erupted, "Why haven't I ever been pope? Why haven't I ever been the Prince of Wales? I guess the opportunity just never presented itself!"

"If you don't want to answer, then say so, but don't jump down my throat," Brett shot back.

Lawrence settled down. "I'm sorry. I'm a little edgy, I guess. I've been waiting for the right time to tell you this, but there hasn't been one, and I can't wait any longer." Brett looked at him quizzically. "I've got the proverbial good news and bad news. The good news is that I have a location trip to Stockholm the last two weeks in August. I know no one in Paris works in August, but we've booked girls in Sweden and several good hair and makeup people have agreed to do the booking. I'll leave it to the photographer to make the final decision. Brett, I'd like you to shoot it. It's ten pages in the November issue."

"Sweden! That's wonderful! You know I've wanted to go there. The time isn't a problem." Brett was thrilled. She had yet to visit the homeland of her ancestors, and she was already envisioning the fabled gardens and canals of Stockholm when she registered his silence and it occurred to her that this was the good news. "Okay, what's the bad news?" she asked cautiously.

"I've been offered the use of a farm house in Tournon d'Agenais for two weeks. Brett, I haven't had a vacation in over a year, and I'm wiped out. Those two weeks will probably be the only chance I'll have to rest for a while. But they're the same two weeks you'll be in Sweden."

"Oh," she murmured. Brett was happy for the work, but disappointed with the timing. They hadn't discussed vacations, but she had looked forward to relaxing with Lawrence, away from the craziness of the city.

He slipped down next to her on the sofa. "At first I was going to book another photographer, but I thought that would be selfish. You're perfect for this spread." He kneaded the back of her neck as he spoke. "Then I almost turned down the house offer. I still may. It's so beautiful and tranquil there, but I'd really love to share it with you."

"Don't be silly." Brett's eyes shone with affection and understanding. "I know you need the rest. You should go. I *am* tempted to tell you to book someone else, but the logical side of me knows that I'm still growing professionally and I can't turn work away. Life won't always be so difficult, will it?"

"Well, maybe I can make it easier right now. Why don't you join me in Rome this weekend?"

"That's a great idea! I can't leave until Friday night, but I can stay through Monday," Brett said eagerly.

"Good. I'll have Mathilde change my reservations for Madrid to Monday night."

"We'll have the *best* weekend!" Brett threw her arms around his neck. She was in love with a man who understood that she had goals that sometimes interfered with her personal life and gave her room to grow. With that combination, there was no limit to what she could accomplish or how far they could go together.

In mid-August, Lawrence saw Brett and the *Voilà!* crew off to Stockholm, and promised to call Brett every chance he got.

He paid almost no attention to the rolling hills, small vineyards, and ancient churches he passed along the scenic route to Tournon d'Agenais. For the first time in years, he was not looking forward to this visit. The Citroën made its way past chickens and goats, up the steep hill to the four-century-old farmhouse. He parked and retrieved his things from the trunk. As he walked up the stone stairs, he heard a familiar, husky voice singing, "God Bless the Child That's Got His Own" with a decidedly French accent.

"Monkey! Open the door—my hands are full!"

"I still don't know why I answer to that name you call me," she said as she swung open the weather-beaten screen door. But Monique Bachimont had answered to that name for fifteen years.

Monique sensed a tension in Lawrence as soon as he arrived. Their August respite in Tournon d'Agenais had always been a balm for the stress and chaos of their lives in Paris. But now, when they meandered through the countryside, Lawrence was distant and distracted, and their easy rapport was replaced by strained conversation.

On the fifth morning, Monique said, "This girl is different, isn't she?" She methodically tore her croissant to pieces and showered them onto her plate. They had never discussed a woman before—

it had not been necessary. Monique had always closed one eye to Lawrence's dalliances, as is the French way. She had even had one or two of her own. But they were a team, and nothing had ever threatened their union—until now.

"Monique, I don't know what to do anymore. This is torturing me." Lawrence dropped his head into the palms of his hands. "You know I love you. We've been so much to each other, I don't know how I'd make it without you. But she's so . . . I don't know. I can't explain it. I've wanted to let her go. I just can't," Lawrence said ruefully. He had had many pleasant diversions, but like a rich dessert, they tempted the palate but were not substantial enough for a steady diet. Brett was different—the more he was with her, the more irresistible she became. But could he give up the steady, abiding comfort he felt with Monique for Brett's exciting, youthful passion? Could he meet her expectations?

"Even the strongest man cannot keep two arms full forever. He must lighten his load or lose all of it," she said quietly.

In her mind, Monique resolved to give him until December to make his decision. She had many years invested in Lawrence, and felt the wait was justified. Literally, she had pulled him, drunk, from the gutter in front of the little zinc her father owned, and had found the disillusioned young American reporter, fresh from Vietnam, a place to live. She had listened to his disgruntled rumblings and patiently, over time, had urged him back to work and up through the ranks at *Voilà!*.

Monique knew she was the reserve from which Lawrence drew safety and security without the strings of obligation, and she liked it that way. Her own powerful need for self-determination had asserted itself easily in her relationship with him and had given her the freedom to transform the tiny bistro her father had left her into one of the top jazz clubs in Paris. She had a man, but none of the restrictions and duty of marriage—an institution that, from her parents' example, she felt akin to being indentured. Monique and Lawrence lived and socialized in different worlds. She preferred to be the sun in the tiny universe she had created at the club, and not a dim star in the galaxy where Lawrence traveled, yet it was the comfort they found in each other that had sustained their separate lives.

But she was not a fool. And this time, he had to make up his mind. He owed her that.

Lawrence swirled the remains of his morning coffee around the bottom of the earthenware mug, wallowing in his own indecision. Just as he had sat on the curb in his own vomit and waited for Paris to provide a direction, just as *Voilà!* had to teeter on the brink of collapse to shake him from indolence, he would wait, afraid that making a choice between Brett and Monique would leave him with a void he could not fill.

— *Chapter 12* —

"How am I to pin when you keep moving around like a chicken?" Martine asked.

"I'm sorry, Martine, my mind is someplace else," Brett said.

Brett stood on a platform, in front of a three-way mirror, in Martine Gallet's workroom. Bolts of fabric were piled high on shelves, the floor was littered with bits of cloth and thread, and the incessant whir of the sewing machines used by Martine's sample makers made shouting a necessity. Martine tucked and draped yards of emerald-green and royal-purple silk satin, inspired by the luxurious fabric and by Brett's voluptuous curves to create a gown uniquely suited to her. As soon as Martine had learned that in October, she would receive the Alliance du Mode Française's Aiguille D'or, as the most talented new designer, she volunteered to dress Brett for the gala evening. The Golden Needle was the most prestigious award in French fashion, and she felt that Brett's photographs had helped to focus attention on her line. She wanted to show her gratitude, and Brett was also an excellent advertisement for her clothes.

With the affair less than a month away, Martine was anxious to finalize the design. There would be at least three more fittings and she hoped Brett wouldn't be as *nerveux* as she was now.

But Brett's agitation had nothing to do with Martine or the dress. Standing still for the time-consuming process would have been difficult under the best of circumstances, but all Brett could think about now was the meeting she had scheduled with Jeffrey Underwood, chief counsel for Larsen Enterprises, later that afternoon.

Two weeks ago, she had received a letter alerting her to his impending arrival in Paris and his need to meet with her regarding financial matters. The letter was so vague that she couldn't imagine what it meant, and when Jeffrey Underwood's secretary called to confirm an appointment time, he could offer no further details.

Brett arrived at the Crillon twenty minutes early. The habit that served her well in her work now made her lament her promptness. She sat crossing and uncrossing her legs and looking at her watch. The lobby, newly redecorated by Sonia Rykiel, was a quietly sensuous combination of Siena marble, beige velvet, and golden oak, illuminated by glittering crystal chandeliers. Bellmen and porters moved soundlessly across the shining floor, and everyone spoke in discreet whispers. Two minutes before the appointed time, Brett entered the elevator. It was so silent she wasn't sure she was moving.

"Good afternoon, Miss Larsen. Mr. Underwood is expecting you. This way, please." Jeffrey Underwood's secretary, a gray-suited young man, ushered Brett into the suite and toward a closed door which he rapped on twice, then opened. He stepped aside, allowing her to enter the plushly appointed salon. When Brett turned around to thank him, the door behind her was already shut and the young man had withdrawn. Jeffrey Underwood had soundlessly risen from his desk, and when Brett turned back, she was startled to find him standing directly in front of her.

He was much younger than Brett had expected. As chief counsel for Larsen Enterprises, he also served as her grandfather's personal attorney and closest adviser, yet he appeared to be only in his midthirties. He was also the most perfectly tailored man Brett had ever seen. His navy chalkstripe suit was clearly Savile Row, the blindingly white shirt, Turnbull & Asser and his silk foulard tie and matching pocket square, Countess Mara. His handmade Church's oxfords gleamed, his hands were perfectly manicured, nails buffed to a high gloss and every strand of his ash blond hair was where it should be. Even on the set, where there were three or four people whose sole purpose was to create a perfect image, Brett had never seen such faultless attention to detail.

Although she was dressed in the new YSL suit she had decided was appropriate for this meeting, in Jeffrey's presence she suddenly felt self-conscious, as if her slip were showing, or she had lint on her jacket.

"Good of you to come, Miss Larsen. You must be busy, now that your career is doing so well," he said.

"It's very nice to meet you, Mr. Underwood. Grandfather has spoken very highly of you." Brett searched his clear aquamarine eyes for some clue to the business at hand, but she found none.

"Please have a seat," he said, and returned to his position behind the ornate desk.

Brett was struck by the orderliness of his temporary office. A black leather desk blotter framed with telephone lists, charts, and notes lay before him. Situated to his right was a stack of fresh legal pads, a row of sharpened number-two and a half pencils, and an open appointment book, and on his left, color-coded folders overlapped, forming a stripe from the front of the desk to the back.

"I've got to tell you, this is a meeting I haven't looked forward to," Brett began. "I know you're Grandfather's attorney, but he and Aunt Lillian have always handled everything. I thought that would continue until I was twenty-five." Brett still didn't know what this was all about, but she had a feeling she wasn't going to like it. She hated the paperwork and bookkeeping related to her own business; her haphazard filing system reflected that distaste. Now it seemed that her grandfather was generating more paper, and she wanted to avoid it as much as possible.

"Well, they will continue to administer your trust, but this is a matter they can't handle for you." Brett looked puzzled. "You see,

Miss Larsen, the income from your trust account has been quite substantial. You, on the other hand, have chosen to live quite modestly, considering your financial position. You have spent very little of what you have been allowed, so the rest has been invested for you, and the return, as reflected on your quarterly statements, has been excellent. Your current net worth is somewhere between two and three million dollars, not including, of course, your professional income, or what you will receive when you reach your twenty-fifth birthday."

"But I don't have the expertise to manage all of that money, Mr. Underwood. I'm doing quite well on my own—earning a living, I mean—and that takes up all of my time."

"Yes, you are, and your grandfather is proud because you *are* working. We will certainly continue to handle your investments, but there are other things to consider . . . which brings me to the point of this meeting." Jeffrey paused and tapped his fingertips together, considering his words carefully. "Your grandfather is quite fastidious about all of his affairs—both business and personal—and as you have reached your majority, he felt it imperative that the disposition of your assets in the event of . . . there's not really a delicate way to say it . . . in the event of your untimely death, be handled in a legally appropriate manner. You need to draw up a will, Miss Larsen."

"A will? I'm only twenty-one!"

"In your current situation, it will be only a preliminary document. It will undoubtedly be amended as the years go by to reflect changes in your marital status, any children, et cetera."

"That was certainly a mouthful, Mr. Underwood."

"It's not really so overwhelming," Jeffrey reassured her. "Would you like some tea or coffee? We can go through a sample will, point by point, and answer your questions."

"I probably need some coffee to keep me awake through all this." Brett's impatience peeked through. "I'm sorry. That was rude."

"Think nothing of it."

The secretary poured coffee and Brett listened intently while Jeffrey explained the legalese of a will.

"I still don't want to do this, but your explanation has certainly made everything less confusing," Brett said. "I wish I could solve a couple of other problems so efficiently."

"Perhaps there's something we can help you with," Jeffrey offered.

"Oh, no—really. I've been putting off some business decisions that will really make life simpler, but I just hate the process," Brett said.

"Miss Larsen, you have quite a network available to you through Larsen Enterprises, and you mustn't hesitate to make use of it."

"I appreciate that, Mr. Underwood, but what I've got to do is find time to look for separate studio space and a manager to run it."

It was no longer practical for Brett to handle routine matters such as restocking her film supply and sending invoices to clients, and her landlady was losing patience with the constant parade of people who came to see Brett when she was casting a job.

"Have you given some thought to where in Paris you want to relocate?" Jeffrey listened attentively and took notes as Brett outlined her specifications for a studio. "Larsen has a very extensive real estate acquisitions department; they should be able to find some suitable spaces for you to look at. And as for managers, you probably have criteria which involve knowledge of photography and advertising, but we can offer you assistance in evaluating the business acumen of a particular applicant, or in protecting yourself as an employer."

"Mr. Underwood, you don't have to do this. I'm sure you have enough headaches of your own," Brett protested.

"It's no trouble at all, Miss Larsen." He placed the notes he had made inside one of the folders on his desk and added it to the rainbowed stack on his right. "I'll be in touch as soon as Acquisitions has some information," he said as he rose from his seat.

Following his lead, Brett stood and extended her hand. "Thank you for your patience, Mr. Underwood."

She was impressed with Jeffrey Underwood's ability to solve problems. *No wonder Grandfather's corporation runs so smoothly*, Brett thought as she entered the silent elevator once again. The heels of her black eelskin pumps clicked on the gleaming marble floor as she crossed the lobby, now less hushed than upon her arrival. There was a short queue at the registration desk, and bellmen discreetly relieved the late check-ins of their luggage and disappeared toward the service elevators. The cocktail hour had just begun, and businessmen and diplomats who had spent a long day at the nearby British and American Embassies headed for the lobby bar, joined by those who had just completed negotiations of a different sort and were returning from the fashionable rue du Faubourg St. Honoré, laden with glossy shopping bags from Hermes, Lanvin, Gucci and Christofle. The doorman nodded pleasantly as she exited the hotel.

She strolled up the rue Royale past the Egyptian Obelisk from the temple of Ramses II, in the center of the place de la Concorde, feeling not quite depressed, but sobered by the topic of her meeting. When she reached the Champs-Elysées, she paused between Coustou's Marly Horses to look at the swirl of traffic rushing toward the Arc de Triomphe. The broad, tree-lined boulevard at twilight always cast a spell under which she fell willingly, time and again, and when she reached Fouquet's, her mood had already lightened.

It was a warm September evening and the sidewalk cafe was crowded, but she immediately spotted Lawrence waving to her. Brett made her way through the maze of tables, anxious to tell him about her meeting with Jeffrey.

"Don't you look chic!" he said as he kissed her hello.

Brett smiled. "I'm glad you think so, but what's the occasion?" she asked, noticing the sterling champagne cooler beside him.

"It's the anniversary of an invasion. One year ago today, a certain very determined brunette, who shall remain nameless, barged into my office and made me hire her." Lawrence ceremoniously poured the effervescent liquid into their glasses.

"Oh, Lawrence! Is it today?" Thoughts of wills and Jeffrey Underwood disappeared, and her mind flashed back to their rocky beginning. She could never have dreamed it would turn out like this.

"Yes, and here's to one hell of a year!"

"Personally or professionally?" Brett teased, her emerald eyes twinkled with mischief.

"Are you flirting with me?" he asked playfully.

"I most certainly am."

"Speaking of being professional, I want to get your opinion on these." He handed her a yellow slide box.

"The light isn't very good here, but I'll do my best." Brett popped open the lid, and instead of the chromes she expected, found a wad of tissue paper. "What's this?" she asked, looking at Lawrence.

"Keep opening and you'll find out."

Carefully, she unfolded the paper. "Lawrence," she gasped, "I've never seen anything so beautiful!"

Brett was too overwhelmed to speak. Lawrence had given her gifts before—usually something silly that made them both laugh—and when she was in Stockholm, he had wired flowers for her birthday, but he had never given her anything so special.

"Put them on."

She removed her gold knot earrings and replaced them with the luminous mobé pearls, encircled with sparkling diamonds set in platinum.

Brett looked lovingly into Lawrence's eyes for a moment, then leaned over and kissed him. "Thank you," she said. "I'll wear them forever!"

"I had no idea that you would become such an important part of my life." And at that moment, Lawrence could not imagine his future without Brett in it.

Jeffrey Underwood called Brett a week later. He had three loft spaces for her to see at her earliest convenience. Their second stop was the top floor of a factory building on the rue de Mézières. It was within walking distance of her apartment, and only a few short blocks from a Métro station. There was five thousand square feet of open space, with ten-foot windows on all four sides, letting light spill in at all times of day.

"We can direct you to architects who can divide the area to meet your needs and supervise the renovations," Jeffrey said.

"This is amazing." Brett was enthralled with the possibilities the loft offered. "How soon can I move in?"

"You can sign a lease as soon as tomorrow, and work could begin shortly thereafter. I would estimate that basic fixtures can be readied in less than a month, and if you'd like, finishing work can continue after you've moved in," Jeffrey answered in his usual measured tone.

Brett envisioned the Larsen Studio sign on the door and realized that this was the beginning of a new phase in her career. Up until now, she had picked up assistants on a freelance basis, and so had only been responsible for herself, but in this studio, she would need at least one full-time employee, probably two. *I hope I'm ready for this*, she thought.

As they rode down in the elevator, Jeffrey said, "Miss Larsen, this invitation comes rather late, but would you be free for dinner this evening? Your company would be an honor."

Brett had no plans, and although she couldn't imagine what they would find to talk about, she accepted.

They dined at Les Ambassadeurs, the restaurant at the Crillon, and Jeffrey showed a great interest in the intricacies of fashion and photography. Brett hadn't expected him to be so eager to talk about her business, but that was their major topic of conversation during the meal. She found him pleasant and attentive, even if he was terribly formal.

Knowing that parking at the hotel would be impossible, Brett had taken a taxi to dinner, and in spite of her protestations, Jeffrey had insisted upon seeing her to her door, where he bid her a polite good night.

As Brett climbed the stairs to her apartment, she wondered if Jeffrey had a wife or girlfriend. *I can't even imagine him really relaxing*, she mused. *He probably straightens pictures and checks his shoes for scuff marks*, she thought, stifling a giggle as she pictured his sock drawer with perfectly aligned rows of gray, black, and navy, neatly paired, and compared this vision to Lawrence's jumble of solids and argyles that always made him curse before he could extract a matched pair. She usually found it easy to make early perceptions about people—it was necessary for her work—but with Jeffrey Underwood, she found she could go no farther than the obvious.

The backseat of the chauffeur-driven Daimler Lawrence had hired for the evening was as sumptuous as an embrace. Once the solid doors were closed, Brett and Lawrence were sealed in a private cocoon of luxury.

"You look breathtakingly beautiful," he said as they rode along the rue de Rivoli. "I think I'll just stare at you all night."

"Well, you're certainly staring now! Martine really outdid herself, don't you think?" Brett still dismissed compliments on her appearance, and tonight, she felt that if she did indeed look beautiful, it must be Martine's dress. The form-fitting strapless gown accentuated Brett's high, full bust, small waist, and rounded hips, and the rich jewel tones of the lustrous satin seemed to enhance the emerald of her eyes. She wore the earrings Lawrence had given her, and her hair, arranged in a loose topknot, was secured with two gold pins, each with a baroque pearl top.

"It's a nice dress, but Martine gets no credit for what you add to it," Lawrence said. He leaned over and kissed her bare shoulder.

Brett tingled at the touch of his warm lips and nestled back against his chest, her head resting on his outstretched arm.

The ballroom at Maxim's was a kaleidoscopic panorama. The women had abandoned the de rigueur black of daytime in favor of evening splendor in every color of the visible spectrum, complemented elegantly by men in black tie. The crowd seemed imbued with good humor, as though congratulating itself for having rated an invitation—no small feat, as the tickets were scarce and highly prized. Tomorrow the dishing would start, with stories of outlandish costumes, who had been snubbed with seats at the back of the room and who really deserved the awards, flying fast and furious all over town.

A white-jacketed usher escorted Brett and Lawrence through the packed room to a table bordering the long catwalk, where the other *Voilà!* editors were already seated.

The lights dimmed a modest thirty minutes late, and crisp, polite applause greeted Thierry Carbonnier, the president of the Alliance, as he approached the podium for opening remarks. Carbonnier, whose air of sophistication was shattered by a voice as melodious as the nasal quacking of a duck, had the good sense to keep his talk short and get on with the program.

The Golden Needle was presented in the categories of day, evening, and sportswear; career achievement; the most talented new designer; and designer of the year. The recipients were feted with slide presentations documenting their typical workday, accompanied by taped interviews in which they outlined their individual design philosophies. A runway show featuring numbers from the designer's current collection preceded the acceptance of each award.

Brett got a heady rush as her slides of Martine flashed on the twin screens suspended above the stage. She had never seen her pictures larger than life, and now they were being viewed by an exclusive and influential audience. And she was caught completely off guard when Martine included her among those she thanked during her acceptance speech for their help and support.

During the fashion shows this audience, the crème de la crème of the French fashion world, whistled, clapped, and stomped their expensively shod feet like fans at a hockey game, to show their approval of styles and of the models who knew how to strut the runway dripping attitude and confidence. And no one elicited more applause than Randall.

Brett knew Randall was doing well. She was based in New York, where she was constantly in demand for ad campaigns and commercials. It was rumored that she was on the verge of a seven-digit, multiyear, exclusive cosmetics contract, the pinnacle of any model's career. Randall was always in Paris during the collections, and Brett had tried on several occasions to book her, but her agency would consider nothing less than $5,000 a day, and Brett's clients had found that prohibitive. But she had a fondness for Randall. Had Malcolm not discovered the photographs she had taken of Randall, Brett would probably be in her senior year at RISD.

"Brett, honey, come here and let me hug you!" Randall exclaimed as soon as she saw Brett backstage. "I've heard you've been tearing up Paris, and I've seen your pictures everywhere." She had lost none of her Alabama accent. In fact, Brett thought it sounded stronger than she remembered.

"Me? What about you? You've been on the cover of everything, and your bookers won't give me the time of day!" Brett exclaimed.

Randall, her trademark corn-silk hair nearly grazing her waist, looked as young and beautiful as she had the first time Brett had seen her. But now the innocence in her childlike face had been tempered by experience, and she was an intriguing contradiction, with an aura that demanded attention. It was the key to her success.

"Shoot, Brett, you know I'll work for you, no matter what they say. Just let me know first and I'll handle my bookers." Randall slithered into a flesh-tone stretch lace tube.

"I'm shooting a spread for *Voilà!* this Thursday—six pages, one model. Can you do it?" Brett knew there was no time like the present. She'd love to work with Randall again, and although she had another model on hold, there was still time to cancel. Lawrence would be ecstatic, and maybe she could even talk him into a cover try!

Randall pulled a card from her purse and jotted her phone number on it. "Call me tomorrow around noon and I'll take care of it."

"Where did you disappear to?" Lawrence asked when Brett returned to the table.

"You were busy talking and I didn't want to interrupt you, but I saw an old friend." As they made their way through the crowd, Brett told him about her conversation with Randall.

"That's quite a coup," he said as he put his arm tightly around her waist and steered her toward the awaiting car. "But I've got a pressing question."

"About the shoot?" Brett asked.

"No."

"What is it?"

He pulled her closer and whispered, "How fast do you think this guy can drive us home? I'm not sure how much longer I can keep my hands in polite places!"

— *Chapter 13* —

"Dammit! Where is she?" Brett paced the width of her studio. "She's three hours late! Thérèse, call the agency again, then try her home number."

Thérèse, Brett's new studio manager, did as she was told, and returned with the same information she had the other six times she had called. "They said she has the booking time and she must be running a little late."

"A little late!"

"Maybe something has happened . . . like an accident," Thérèse offered.

Just as Brett stopped pacing to consider the possibility that something could be seriously wrong, Randall breezed into the studio.

"Hey, everybody!" she said as if she didn't have a care in the world.

"Randall!! Where the hell have you been?! You were booked for nine, and it's almost one o'clock!" Brett fumed.

"Then I'm on time, honey. Everybody knows I'm always late. Usually later than this!"

"But you kept all these people waiting," Brett said as she directed Randall to the makeup room.

"So they had extra coffee and croissants. What's all the fuss about? We'll still be done by six."

And they were. From makeup and hair to wardrobe and finally the set, Randall was a consummate professional. She was cooperative, quick, and creative. Brett's assistant had put Handel's "Water Music" on the stereo and, inspired by the liquid melodies, Randall instantly transformed each of the six garments she wore into "fashion." She gave mere clothing personality. When Brett last worked with her three years ago, Randall's mesmerizing presence in front of the camera was in its infancy. Now it was all grown up.

When the shoot was over, Brett found Randall in the dressing room. "You were magical out there, but it doesn't make what you did right."

"It's not right and it's not wrong. It's what I do. When I first came to old Paree two years ago, I figured out real quick that I had to do something different—something to let them know I was a mustang, not part of the herd."

"Randall, I could have killed you this morning!"

"Girl, I always knew you needed to relax. Look, on my first trip here, I about made myself crazy trying to find my way around. Everything's spread out like they took a shotgun to a map of Paris and built a studio wherever the buckshot made a hole. I didn't speak two words of French, and Parisians look at you like they've got the Eiffel Tower up their butts if you try to ask 'em anything in English, so I was always late, and it used to make me real nervous. Then one day, I overheard this photographer say he would rather work with me late than ten other girls early, so I figured, let 'em wait! I give 'em a show when I get there, and honey, they love this accent! I'm not spiteful or difficult, like a lot of girls, who act like heaven opened up and spat 'em out perfect. It's the way I deal with men, too."

"What are you talking about?" Brett asked, unintentionally charmed by Randall's philosophical discourse.

"Take Marcel. He's been my man for a year now. He's vice president of this jewelry store. It's a family business that sells diamonds the size of pecans. He booked me for this ad, and I was late, as usual, so afterward, what does he do? Ask me to dinner! Brett, I am forever leaving this man waiting and he loves it." Randall retrieved her clothes, one by one, from the pile on the floor where she had left them, and dressed as they talked.

"I could never do that. It's not fair. I wouldn't like it done to me." Brett leaned against the white formica makeup counter.

"Are you kidding? I have a blue fit if he's late, but it keeps 'em interested if you don't take 'em too seriously. As soon as you do, they think you're supposed to salute or something," Randall said.

"Not if you really care for each other. I've been seeing Lawrence Chapin . . ."

"The editor of *Voilà!*? That's some big fish you reeled in, honey!" Randall patted her on the back.

"But it's not like that. We really tried hard not to get involved. The last thing I wanted was to date a client. But he respects what I do, and the fact that my time is limited and I can't see him every day."

"I'm sure he's a nice guy and all that, but if he's like every man I've met, he probably loves your being busy, since it gives him time to play in the henhouse. I mean, I know as sure as I'm standing here that Marcel will never marry me. His parents have some girl picked out for him. It's supposed to unite their family businesses or some mess. Anyway, he says whatever happens, he'll keep paying for my suites at the Ritz and my apartment in New York, which may be a tub of lard, but it's good while it lasts. When it's over, there'll be somebody else. And I'd bet a great big sack of flour I'm not the only cookie he's got stashed away for a midnight snack, but I don't care. He's already given me jewelry that would make Queen Elizabeth green. I'll look at it and console myself when he's gone."

"But you don't need him to pay your way. You make plenty of money on your own," Brett said.

"And that's the way I want it to stay—my own money! I'm not gonna be the new, hot kid on the block forever, but I plan to have plenty in the bank to comfort me when it's over." Randall leaned close to the mirror and blotted off some of the peony pink lipstick she had worn for the shot. "One day I'd like to settle down with a nice guy. I think about buying a ranch, maybe out in Idaho, where the sky really looks like it goes on forever, but right now, I have to take care of me! My mama gave my daddy her heart and he walked all over it. He didn't even have the decency to hand it back when he was through. I think I'll keep mine under lock and key for a while." Randall turned around and whacked Brett playfully on the leg.

"But how could you go out with someone you don't really care about?" Brett asked incredulously.

"'Cause he's fun, he don't take up much time, and if I didn't go out with him, do you think he'd stay home and watch 'Mr. Ed' reruns? Besides, I'm collecting great stories to tell when I'm old!"

They both laughed. Brett couldn't help liking Randall; her warmth was infectious. *But I'll never be so calculating about men*, Brett thought. She understood that not every man was honorable and, like Randall, she had had a father who had failed her miserably, but she was determined not to blame every man she met for one man's shortcomings. And sometimes she felt that Lawrence had come to her to make up for the hurt and abandonment she had suffered early in her life.

"Are you back there, Brett?" Joe Tate called.

"In the dressing room," Brett replied.

Joe strode in, shouldering a large bundle wrapped in brown paper, which he placed carefully on the counter. "Hello, stranger!" He lifted Brett in a hug and spun her around.

"Hello to you, too! When did you get back?" Joe had been on the road for most of the last two months for Clik Claque.

"Two days ago. It took me that long to figure out what city I was in and what time it was," he answered.

"Well, howdy, sugar! My name is Randall. What do they call you, besides big and handsome?" she asked. Randall had been sizing him up since he had walked in the room, trying to determine if Brett had dibs.

Joe introduced himself and Brett explained that he was a model as well as a sculptor. Randall nodded approvingly.

"Lizzie sends her love," Joe reported. "She met me in New York and we spent a couple of days together. She's quite a fireball. I had a great time!"

"I'm glad you caught up with each other. Lizzie's a lot of fun." Brett made a mental note to call her friend, who was probably beside herself with glee because Joe had called.

"I brought you a little something for the studio, but you can only open it after I get the tour."

Brett showed him around the still-unfinished space. It had been painted sparkling white, and the floors had been sanded and waxed until they gleamed. Just beyond the dressing room, the bars and clamps that supported seamless paper stood like goalposts. Gossamer fabric, draped artfully over thick, pickled oak rods at all of the windows, lent the space an ethereal grace and could be adjusted to filter the light or let it shine clear and true.

A curved wall of glass bricks defined the kitchen, and matte chrome appliances had already been installed, but the red lacquer cabinets, still crated, lay in another part of the studio. An arced counter, which closed the parentheses opened by the glass wall, looked out onto the reception area, as yet decorated only with ficus trees, dueling crimson chesterfield sofas, and a slab of Carrare marble for a table. The corner where walls would be erected for Brett's office was currently occupied by a four-foot light table and a huge, butcher block platform, supported by several file cabinets to make a desk.

"I'm impressed," Joe said approvingly.

"I'm scared, but that's another story," Brett confided.

"So, does she get to open the package now?" Randall asked.

"I'll unveil it for you." Joe knelt by the bundle and loosened the tape as he spoke. "It's something to remind you that there is an ebb and flow to everything in nature and in life. Don't be discouraged by temporary setbacks, because there's a hill opposite the valley." He unwrapped his sand dune sculpture.

Brett thanked him, touched by his gift.

"And now that I've run in, I have to run out again. I'm meeting Gabriel and a client for dinner," Joe explained.

"Are you taking a taxi?" Randall asked.

"Yeah. I'm heading toward Les Halles," he replied.

"Why don't I share a ride with you, then? I'm going in that direction." Randall wanted to get to know Joe a little better. "Brett, I'm sorry if I upset you, but next time you'll know what to expect." She gave Brett a big kiss on the cheek. "Let's get together and hang out soon. I'll call you." And Joe and Randall left the studio, her arm in his.

* * *

"Come on, Brett. It's Friday night and you just said you don't have any plans," Randall cajoled.

"I don't know. I was going to do some work in the darkroom," Brett protested.

"Look, I really want you to meet Marcel so you can see for yourself that he doesn't have two heads! It would have been great if Mr. *Voilà!* could come, too, but just because he has some boring old meeting doesn't mean you should spend your evening in the darkroom. You can go out without him, can't you?" Randall asked.

"Don't be silly, of course I can," Brett said.

"Then, come with us. We'll make a night of it—Marcel's treat, of course."

"Okay, okay. If I don't agree, you'll never let me off the phone. What time should I meet you?"

"Are you crazy?! We'll pick you up, about nine-thirty. Should we come to the studio?"

"Yes, I'll still be here."

"Oh, yeah. We'll be on time, 'cause I told Marcel I'd be ready at eight. He'll wait for an hour, and that'll give us thirty minutes to get to you!"

"Randall, you really are something else! I'll be downstairs. See you later."

Brett went back to the film she had been editing when Randall called. Now that the shower had been installed in the studio, she could bathe and change clothes, then continue to work until they arrived.

When she slipped the last of the edited film into plastic pockets, Brett dialed Lawrence's home number. After the beep tone on his answering machine she said, "Hi, it's me. I'm hanging out with crazy Randall tonight. I'm not sure where we'll end up, but if it's not too late when I'm heading home, I'll call you and maybe stop by. Hope your meeting wasn't too terrible. I love you." Loving Lawrence seemed like such a natural part of her life. *He really makes me happy*, she thought.

On the ride over to the Right Bank, Randall did all of the talking, including a nonstop critique of Marcel's driving, so Brett had ample opportunity to examine the bald spot at the back of his head. She had been so busy watching their interaction that she didn't notice the name of the club they finally entered, but the acrid smell of cigarette smoke hit her as soon as she walked through the doors. The lights shone dimly, with a greenish cast, as though diffused through an old Coke bottle, and scratchy music from a juke-box was barely audible above the muffled hubbub of the crowded room.

The trio was pointed in the direction of their table—actually, the three spots left vacant at a tiny table where five other people huddled.

"How the hell are we supposed to get there?" Randall complained as she looked for a path to their places. Seeing no alternative, she plunged in, squeezing and shimmying among the patrons with a chorus of "'Scuse me sugar," and "I'm sorry honey," Brett and Marcel following in her wake.

Now that they were seated, Brett looked closely at Marcel, attempting to assess his appeal. He was shorter than Randall by almost a head, and slightly built, with hair and eyes almost the same shade of not-quite-brown. He was pleasant and polite, but he lacked the verve and vitality she had expected, given Randall's proclivities. He talked about the weather, soccer, and jewelry—period. Somehow, she had thought that he would be handsome and charming, with a slightly duplicitous patina, but the only word Brett could think of to describe Marcel Duplissey was ordinary.

Just as their drinks were delivered to the table, the spotlight illuminated the tiny stage and a small dark woman stepped up to the microphone. "*Bonsoir, mes amis*: I am Monique. Welcome to Bachimont's. Tonight, for your listening pleasure, I am pleased to present a rising young star on the jazz scene, from New Orleans—Monsieur Wynton Marsalis."

Monique Bachimont disappeared backstage and the young trumpet player took her place, accompanied by modest applause. The audience at Bachimont's was composed of true jazz aficionados, and a performer had to prove himself before the welcoming ovation was more spirited and rousing.

After the first few minutes everyone, including Brett, Randall, and Marcel, was enchanted by his musical sorcery. Brett listened with her eyes closed, floating and drifting on the cascading notes, letting the music flood over her. It both relaxed and energized her, and she was glad she had come.

When Marsalis began his second selection, Brett opened her eyes and found Randall and Marcel closeted in conversation. She glanced around the room, watching people watch the performance. Brett enjoyed observing, and she got some of her best ideas for photographs by simply being attentive to the way people behaved. She zeroed in on the backup musicians, several of whom were playing just as she had listened, with their eyes closed.

Brett then caught sight of Monique standing just inside the narrow passageway that led backstage, looking like it was the one place in the world where she most belonged. She leaned against a tall man who stood behind her, and both swayed slightly to the music. His arms were crossed proprietarily over her chest, his hands rested comfortably on her waist, and he faced away from the audience, rubbing his cheek lightly against her hair. Monique spoke to him and he raised his head to answer.

Suddenly Brett's vision blurred, then went black, except for a dizzying swirl of pin dots in bright red and green, and the sound of the music faded into oblivion. She flushed with fever and trembled with chills and the room fell away like a house of cards. The man was Lawrence.

Brett's hands grasped the edge of the table, and its solidity convinced her that she had not died. She wanted to scream, to run, but she couldn't do either. Her eyes burned with the angry, bitter tears of betrayal, but she could not turn away. She tried to make him someone else—someone who wouldn't look like Lawrence at all—but she knew that face too well to deny it.

"Honey, are you all right? You look terrible." Randall whispered. "Brett? Are you okay?" Randall placed her hand gently on Brett's arm.

Randall's touch felt like a branding iron, marking her as a fool. She looked down at her arm, expecting to see the word burned into her flesh, scarring her for life.

"No . . . Yes . . . I don't feel well. I have to go."

"Honey, if you're sick, we'll take you home."

Brett never heard Randall. She sprang up from the table and pushed her way, unseeing, through the crowd. The room stretched out before her, cruel and labyrinthine, and the exit seemed miles away. She slammed into a waiter balancing a tray of drinks on the tips of his fingers. The crash was a sour note against the plaintive wail of the trumpet, but Brett never stopped. Startled patrons, their musical reverie interrupted, looked up to find the source of the commotion. Lawrence was among them.

He saw her just as she reached the door. He broke into a sweat; his heart pounded in his ears. *It can't be Brett*, he thought, but he had seen the pain and fury in her face and he knew it was her. For a few seconds he stood, rooted to his spot. This wasn't supposed to happen. He had kept his two lives apart almost a year. Now they had collided head-on, and the shock was like shards of glass and metal lacerating his flesh. Instinctively, he shielded his face from the assault.

Monique knew. She had seen his reaction to the young woman rushing from the room, and she said nothing as he brushed past her on his way out the back door. *Now he must make up his mind*, she thought.

Lawrence ignored the two musicians smoking marijuana in the alley and ran around to the front, just in time to see Brett hail a passing taxi.

"Brett, wait!" he shouted.

She didn't need to look over her shoulder—the sound of his voice calling her name pierced the quiet night like a siren and her heart like a dagger. She got into the taxi and slammed the door.

Lawrence chased the car down the street, screaming for the driver to stop. He caught up to them when the taxi paused at a traffic light.

"I need to talk to you!" he yelled, gasping for breath and pounding on the locked doors. Brett refused to look at him, so he darted in front of the cab, blocking its progress on the narrow, one-way street. "I'm not going anywhere until you talk to me!" he shouted.

The driver's irritation and impatience grew as Lawrence continued his one-man blockade. Brett had no alternative but to get out.

"Haven't you done enough? Now you want to cause a scene!" Brett hissed. She had always been humiliated by the scenes Barbara caused. Now she was on the verge of one herself, and that fanned her fury.

"But, I need to talk to you—to explain," he said.

They faced off in the deserted street. Lawrence, his loosened tie flapping in the wind, his shoulders slumped, his arms slack at his sides, looked pitiful and dejected. Brett's pain had temporarily given way to anger. Her eyes blazed with indignation, her feet were planted firmly apart, and her hands were clenched into fists in an effort to contain her rage.

"*You* need? What about what I need? You want to explain—is that it? Why now, Lawrence—because I saw you? You never felt the need to explain anything before! Tell me something—was I the other woman, or was she?"

"It wasn't like that. I never thought of you in that way. I love you, Brett," Lawrence sputtered.

"You bastard! Is that why you didn't *plan* to love me? Was I just supposed to be a little something extra?" Brett felt like she had been beaten by a heavyweight champion, but she would not fall down. This would have to be a win by decision, not by knockout.

"I'll leave her," Lawrence said pathetically.

"Leave her! Is she your wife?"

"No, but Monkey and I—I mean, Monique and I—have been together for a long time. Since I first came to Paris."

"And you'd leave her for me? Then, who will you leave me for? How dare you say such a thing? For almost a year you deceived me—you deceived *her*!" Brett could tell from Lawrence's reaction that Monique knew about her. But then, how could she not? Brett and Lawrence had gone everywhere together; their pictures had been plastered all over the columns. "Okay, you lied to me—or do you think you didn't lie because you never told me there wasn't someone else and I was too naive to ask? I'll tell you something, Lawrence. I may be young, and not worldly and sophisticated enough to play with the big boys, but I'm not stupid, and I won't accept second place. I wouldn't take first place, either, if I knew there was someone else. I bet you think that's corny."

The set at Bachimont's was over and the street filled with pedestrians. They passed Brett and Lawrence without so much as a second glance. After all, lovers' quarrels were as common in Paris as lovers.

"Brett, please give me a chance. I do love you," Lawrence said.

"Lawrence, if you had told me in the beginning, maybe we could have worked this out, maybe not. But now I feel dirty and used and I never want to see you again."

All day Saturday and Sunday the phone rang, but Brett left her answering machine on. She didn't even play back her messages. She knew it was Lawrence and she had no more to say to him. Brett had no idea she could feel so miserable.

Friday night played over and over again. She couldn't sleep and she didn't eat. She racked her brain for clues to Lawrence's deception that she must have missed. His vacation and her trip to Stockholm had been no coincidence, just a well-planned ruse. She shivered at her stupidity as she remembered how overjoyed she had been to spend the weekend in Rome instead. Then she thought about Lawrence's hateful cat, Monkey. She had asked him why he had named the cat after another animal and he had told her it was a long story. But that was what he called Monique on Friday night; obviously, he had named it after her. Brett recalled her conversation with Lizzie and how angry she had become when Lizzie had voiced her mistrust of Lawrence. Maybe Randall was smart to keep her heart out of a relationship. If she didn't feel, it couldn't hurt.

On Sunday night, Brett looked at her appointment book and realized she wasn't ready to face Monday. The thought of listening to the idle, vacuous chatter of models worrying about whether they had gained two pounds over the weekend was more than she could bear in her present state. Brett had never canceled a shooting, but she dialed Thérèse's home number and told her she was sick and would not be in the studio all week.

Brett knew she was lucky to have such a competent studio manager. Jeffrey Underwood's search had turned up several candidates, but Thérèse had shown the most potential, even though she had no photography background. She had trained under the *première vendeuse* for one of Paris's most famed couturiers, but she found life in the showroom too controlled and staid, and was looking for a little adventure. She had plenty of experience with models and clients, so Brett decided to play her hunch. She hadn't been sorry, and she knew that her business was in capable hands.

Tuesday afternoon Brett was awakened by loud pounding on her front door. She dragged herself out of bed and grabbed an old bathrobe before she answered. "What are you doing here?"

"Honey, you look like something the cat dragged in. No, you look worse than that—you look like shit!" Randall exclaimed.

"I'm sick. I told you that Friday night," Brett said.

"Yeah, you're sick of that man. I saw him Friday night, lookin' like he'd seen a haint. He ran out like his tail was on fire, then I put two and two together and got three."

"Randall, I don't want to talk about it."

"I know you don't, honey, but you will, and when you do, give me a call. I'm going to New York for two weeks, but I'll be back. You left this the other night." Randall handed Brett her purse. She had never missed it.

"Thanks," Brett murmured. She clutched her handbag to her chest and the tears spilled down her cheeks.

Randall hugged her. "It gets better, honey. Think of it this way—it sure can't get much worse. I'll call you when I get back!" She disappeared down the stairs.

Brett showered and washed her hair for the first time in four days. She knew she had to pull herself together, and going out, if only for a walk to the Buci market, would be a start.

Over the roar of the blow dryer, she heard knocking once again. Who is it this time? she wondered, annoyed by the intrusion. She opened the door to a uniformed messenger bearing a telegram for her. *Lawrence has really gone too far*, she thought, and tossed the unopened envelope on the hall table. She finished dressing and headed out. Then, as an afterthought, she picked up the telegram. As soon as she unsealed it, she saw that it had been sent from New York. Her hands shook as she read, "Tried to call. Left several messages. Mrs. Cox taken to New York Hospital. Wanted you to know." It was signed by Aunt Lillian's housekeeper, Hilda.

The telegram fluttered to the floor as Brett rushed to the telephone. She called Hilda and discovered that her aunt had been released that morning and was resting. Lillian's condition had been diagnosed as angina, which Brett knew was often the precursor to a heart attack. *She should have stopped smoking those damned cigarettes*, Brett thought as she made reservations on the Concorde for the next morning.

Randall was wrong—things had gotten worse.

— *Chapter 14* —

"You don't look very much like a patient!" Brett shouted over the strains of the Glen Miller Orchestra's rendition of "In the Mood." She had climbed the spiral staircase to the wraparound balcony that housed much of Lillian's collection of twentieth century American art, as well as her studio. She was surprised and pleased to find her aunt seated at an easel, contemplating the still life she was painting.

Lillian smiled warmly. "That's because I'm not. Such fuss and bother over a few chest pains! I'm perfectly fine, although I may be a bit ill-tempered until I adjust to life without cigarettes."

Brett skirted the jumble of canvases and worktables, and the old corduroy sofa, which after years of paint drips and spills, looked decidedly abstract expressionist.

"What am I going to do with you?" Brett laughed as she hugged her aunt.

"Do with me? Nothing, that's what. As you can see, I'm healthy as a horse, and I could have told you that if Hilda had awakened me when you called. There was no reason for you to come home —not that I'm not happy to see you. It's been two years since you've been here. It just wasn't necessary. I'm following the doctor's orders—Hilda has already changed my diet, I've stopped smoking, and next week I start what they call a moderate exercise program. I call it walking. I used to walk all the time, but somehow, it just hasn't been the same since Rush died," Lillian said distractedly.

She looks so vulnerable, Brett thought. In her mind's eye, time had stood still and Lillian looked the same as she always had, but suddenly she appeared so much older. Her hair was far more gray than blonde, and her hands, always so strong, now seemed wrinkled and decidedly smaller.

Before Brett could respond, Lillian's face brightened. "So, tell me all about you and your new studio."

Brett enthusiastically related the details of her work space and the renovations that were underway. When she finished, Lillian went to take a nap before dinner.

Sitting in Lillian's canvas chair, Brett traced the creases in her palm with the bristly tip of one of her aunt's camel-hair brushes. She could not envision what would have become of her if it hadn't been for her aunt. Until this scare, it had never occurred to her that Lillian wouldn't always be there. When Carson had been shot, Brett had witnessed death firsthand, and for years, the mere sight of Turtleback Rock triggered vivid memories of the lurid spectacle. In learning to detach herself from that horror, she had dismissed the possibility of death, never considering that, inevitably, she would have to deal with it again. But Jeffrey Underwood had reminded her of her own mortality, and now Aunt Lillian's illness compounded that awareness. She put down the brush, flipped idly through the pages of a nearby sketch pad, and concluded that as long as she was in New York, she would call Jeffrey and make an appointment to sign the final draft of her will.

Temporarily banishing her own malaise, Brett spent several days engrossed in Lillian's recuperation, pampering her, accompanying her to the hospital's cardiology unit for her stress test, and encouraging her to munch celery sticks when she really wanted to smoke. Shortly after she arrived, Brett had phoned Lizzie and made plans to see her on the weekend. She needed an understanding ear and a chance to let down her guard. The hurt and anger she felt over Lawrence's betrayal was still very close to the surface, and she hoped that talking with Lizzie would be a release.

On Friday, after midnight, the telephone shrieked, startling Brett from a sound sleep. She bolted up and grabbed the receiver. All she could hear was sobbing.

"Hello. Who is this?" she demanded, instantly alarmed by the crying.

"Oh, Brett, it's awful."

"Lizzie, what is it? Where are you?" Brett had never heard her so distressed.

"She's dead!" At the words, Lizzie was overcome by a fit of tears.

"Who's dead?"

Lizzie could hardly utter the name. "It's Kate—Kate and the baby. David just called. He said they drowned this afternoon. Oh, Brett, she can't be gone!"

"Lizzie, where are you?"

"I'm at home. I just drove down from school and the phone rang as soon as I got in. My parents are out for the evening—they don't know yet. How can I tell them?" The sentences came in an anguished stream.

"I'll be there in ten minutes."

When Brett arrived at the Powells' West Eighty-second Street apartment, she managed to calm her friend, and Lizzie told her the sketchy details she knew. Since relocating to Santa Clara, David had become an avid sailor; he and Kate relished the peace and solitude they found on the ocean. They had left San Francisco Friday morning with two of their friends for a leisurely weekend cruise to Monterey Bay. It was the last time they planned to sail the boat until after the baby was born. Late in the day they were caught in an unexpected storm. In the turbulence, Kate was swept overboard and they couldn't get to her until it was too late.

Brett stayed the night, hoping her presence would be a comfort to Lizzie and her family. She booked them on a flight to California leaving in the morning, and had Albert drive them to La Guardia Airport.

The last few days have been a nightmare, Brett thought wearily as her taxi inched through the clogged traffic on Broadway, heading toward the San Remo. If she could just wake up, maybe everything would be all right, she thought, but the obituary in the *Times* she had picked up confirmed that the tragedy was all too real. "Kathryn Hobbs Powell, Pianist, Wife of Hands On Founder," the headline announced solemnly. It went on to detail Kate's musical accomplishments, as well as David's success in skyrocketing his young company to the number-two position in the manufacture of personal computers. Brett's heart went out to David. She could not imagine the depth of his grief or how he would avoid being swallowed by despair.

The results of Lillian's stress test showed that she was well on the road to recovery, and Brett knew that staying in New York any longer meant she was avoiding what she needed to face in Paris. So, promising to return to New York in six short weeks for the Christmas holidays, Brett departed, ironically on the same morning that Kate's funeral was held in California. David had requested that no flowers be sent, so she pledged a perpetual contribution to the music scholarship David had established in Kate's name. On the flight, Brett tried unsuccessfully to keep her mind blank. She felt as if a toxic cloud hung over her and she would suffocate if she didn't get free. *All I can do is take one day at a time*, she thought.

As soon as she was back in the studio, Brett methodically set about getting a handle on her career. Lawrence Chapin was responsible for her first big break, but not for her success. That had come because she had talent, and she was determined to prove that.

Lawrence had called frequently during her absence, as had *Voilà!*'s fashion editor, trying to book Brett for future work, but Thérèse had turned them down, as she had been instructed. Brett intended to sever her professional relationship with Lawrence; she no longer respected him on any level. She needed to mitigate any gossip that would be circulating. A message from Sophie Leclerc, fashion editor of *La Femme Première*, one of *Voilà!*'s hottest competitors, confirmed that the word was already out. Sophie had tried on several occasions to woo Brett away from *Voilà!*. Neither magazine would use a photographer who worked for the rival publication, and defections were seen as coups. Brett arranged to meet

Sophie the next day for lunch, and had a location trip to Venice set up by the time coffee was served. It would be a clear signal that Brett did not need Lawrence as a patron.

Later that afternoon, Brett cloistered herself in her office, poring over the maps of Venice she had picked up on her way back to the studio. Thérèse's voice sounded over the intercom. "Marcel Duplissey on line one."

What on earth does he want, Brett wondered, picking up the receiver. She hadn't thought of him since the fiasco at Bachimont's. After they exchanged pleasantries, Marcel got to the point. He wanted her to shoot a jewelry ad—a last-minute push for holiday business. "I need it by the end of the week. Can you do this?" Brett assured him she could, then questioned him about what he wanted. Marcel replied, "I know gems, you know pictures, but romance always sells, no? Your photos of Randall, they are very contemporary—like the customer we want to attract."

"Are you using her for this?" Brett asked, knowing Randall was featured in many of the Duplissey Frères ads.

"No, she is on location in Australia. I will leave the model selection to you, but whoever you choose should look nothing like Randall, or she will make my life miserable."

After arranging a meeting for the next morning, they hung up. Brett coiled the phone cord around her index finger as she mulled over her new assignment. Her eyes fell on the bright red X she had placed on the map of Venice, marking the Bridge of Sighs—the lovers' bridge. *It's like there's a plot*, she thought. She had planned to keep busy as a defense against the depression that threatened to engulf her every time she thought of Lawrence. But now she had one assignment that would send her to the birthplace of Casanova, and another with the stipulation that her photo conjure up romance. Brett carefully folded the map and put it aside. She had to have a concept for Marcel by morning, and right now, her professional reputation was more important than her personal feelings.

The following morning, promptly at eleven, Thérèse ushered Marcel into Brett's office. He declined the offer of coffee or tea and took a seat at the conference table, but the moment Brett began to explain her ideas, he got up and started to pace. The entire time she spoke he paced, staring at his highly polished wing tip shoes and occasionally stroking the end of his long, thin nose. When she finished, he stopped his circuit around the table but continued to gaze downward, hands clasped behind his back. Brett waited for him to speak. Her idea to use a man instead of a woman in the ad was different, but it was logical. She had rationalized that men bought most of the fine jewelry sold at Christmas and they were notorious last-minute shoppers; therefore an advertisement showing a man making a selection for the woman in his life would be an attention-getter. She had recommended Joe as the model. She knew the approach was novel, but not outrageous enough to warrant silence from Marcel.

Finally he raised his head, causing the track light directly above him to shine through the thinning hair he so painstakingly arranged to cover his balding pate. He looked at her a few seconds longer, cleared his throat, then asked when she could shoot. That was it— no questions, no comments, no suggestions.

She called L'Étoile to check on Joe's availability and booked him for Friday evening, when Duplissey would be closed to the public. After Marcel left, she called Thérèse into her office and reenacted the whole scene. When Brett took the pale pink china saucer from beneath her teacup and placed it on her head to represent Marcel's bald spot, they both exploded with laughter. Suddenly, Brett realized that it had been weeks since she had found humor in anything, and it felt good. *It may take a little time, and it won't be easy, but I'm going to get through this*, she thought.

"These are some pretty ritzy items," Joe commented as he scanned the assortment of diamond and emerald earrings, arranged on a midnight-blue velvet tray, which Marcel had placed on a gilt wood Louis XVI table in front of him. Joe was about to pick one up, when out of the corner of his eye he noticed the guard positioned across the door. His brown plaid jacket revealed the outline of a gun in a hip holster, and Joe decided he could examine them just fine without touching them.

The tiny salon, with its cream and gold flocked walls and Savonnerie carpet, one of several private showrooms upstairs at the flagship location of Duplissey Frères, was barely large enough for the lights and equipment. To get to her camera and tripod without disturbing the reflector cards clamped to metal poles on both sides of Joe, Brett had crawled under the table. Marcel, the guard, Brett's assistant, and the groomer, Mason Pearson brush in hand, now stood with their backs against the wall so they would not be in the frame.

Brett peered through the viewfinder. She had already taken a Polaroid and she liked what she saw. "You look great, Joe. Can you lean in closer to the table?" she asked. Joe scooted to the edge of the pale yellow silk damask fauteil. "That's perfect." She popped her head above the camera and looked straight into Joe's eyes. "I want you to choose an earring—one that you think will really look beautiful on the woman you love. I want you to pick it up, examine it, wonder whether she'll love it as much as you do." Despite the cramped conditions, Brett felt at home. She had been nagged by butterflies all day, but as soon as she had arrived and started supervising the setup, they began to leave her. For a split second, as Joe leaned in and chose a large, pear-shaped emerald, suspended from a cluster of smaller pear-shape diamonds that resembled a snowflake, Brett wondered if Lawrence had looked so lovingly at the earrings he had chosen for her. But the thought vanished as she began shooting with the confidence she was secretly afraid might have deserted her.

Almost overnight, billboards of Joe appeared in prominent spots in the fashionable shopping arenas of Paris. The question, "Will she like it?" that was asked by Joe's expression, was answered by the tag line, "*Mais Oui*. Duplissey."

Brett continued to throw all of her energy into her work, leaving herself no time to dwell on the dull ache in her heart. She went out as much as was necessary to keep her name afloat in fashion circles and to squelch any rumors that she was devastated by the breakup.

On the morning Brett left to return to New York, she received her advance copies of the January issue of *Voilà!*. Randall, a jewel-bedecked black beret tilted saucily on her head, looked confidently back at her. Lawrence had chosen the cover try she had submitted. Brett should have been jubilant; covers were the most visible symbol of having arrived as a fashion photographer, and this was her first, but it also marked the final installment in a bittersweet saga.

Manhattan was spangled with twinkling lights, draped in garlands, and dusted in powdery snow. Leisurely strollers and package-laden shoppers alike were serenaded by resonant trombones played by earnest Salvation Army soldiers, infectious laughter of children awaiting their turn to spin, slip, and slide on the ice beneath the giant spruce at Rockefeller Center; and the always unexpected hollow clip-clop of hansom cab horses trotting through the urban wonderland. The sublime setting did nothing to lift Brett's spirits. She felt empty and incomplete, as if she lacked some vital component in her life.

She went through the motions of shopping, all the while surveying the passersby and trying to sort out her feelings. Even more than lovers, families caught her eye. She saw parents enjoying the animated windows at Lord & Taylor with their excited youngsters. There were fathers obviously proud of the men their sons had become and mothers and daughters hand in hand, talking like the closest of friends, and Brett envied them. She needed that kind of closeness now.

Brett had no trouble convincing Lillian to see the Christmas show at Radio City Music Hall; she anticipated that the pageantry, the wonder of the huge pipe organ rolling out into the ornate Art Deco arena, and the good-natured hijinks of the singers and the Rockettes, would help her recapture some of the awe and wonder she had felt as a child at this time of year. But as they walked along Fifty-second Street after the matinee, Brett found that her mood was much the same.

"I don't know, Aunt Lillian. Somehow, I hoped the show would make me feel like I did when I was a little girl."

"Sounds to me like you're not enjoying the way you feel now," Lillian observed as they rounded the corner and headed up Seventh Avenue.

"Sometimes there's so much pressure. Maybe it goes with being an adult, but it scares me. I've been on my own for the last three years, but I never thought of myself as alone. There was my work, and my friends in Paris. There was even a man, but it didn't work out," Brett said.

"Often it doesn't, child," Lillian said comfortingly, and wisely decided not to press for details. Their leisurely pace was halted by two cellists, instruments in tow, who dashed across their path and into Carnegie Hall.

"But I thought it was so right. Everything was all in sync, and then it just fell apart. But that's not all. I just never thought things could change so quickly. I was going along my merry way, with everything in its place, and wham! I meet Grandfather's lawyer, who has me make out a will. *A will!* I lease a new studio that needs a ton of work. Lawrence and I break up, you get sick, and David's wife is killed in an accident. It's not that I expect things to stay the same forever, but, I don't know, I'm probably not even making sense."

"You had a lot thrown at you at an early age, and that's difficult. I've always been amazed at the way you've handled it all. Sometimes we're given a lot of lessons to learn at the same time, and that makes it even harder," Lillian said sagely.

"The only things I feel connected to are you and my work. Lizzie is like a sister to me, but she has so much to deal with in her own family right now. But through all of it, they have each other. I guess I wish our family was like that, too." They walked the rest of the way in silence.

When they reached the San Remo, Brett wasn't quite ready to go in. "I think I'll walk a while longer," she said.

"Be careful," Lillian called as she waved to her niece.

Brett retraced her steps and turned left onto Central Park South. She walked alongside the park, comforted by the rhythmic crunching of her steps in the ice-crusted snow. Dusk quickly turned to dark and the street lamps came on, casting long shadows through the trees that edged the park. A strong westerly breeze turned the wide street into a wind tunnel, but the frosty air was invigorating. Her dark hair billowed out behind her like a pennant in the wind, and she felt the tingle of tiny crystals of snow on her face just before they melted.

Brett had phoned her grandfather the previous night. She usually spoke with him quarterly, like she received her trust fund statements, but she thought he might be concerned about his sister's condition. The conversation was superficial, as usual. Once they passed the initial pleasantries, there were awkward silences. Sven was more like her business manager than a relative, and he discouraged her attempts to make their conversations more personal. She wondered, once again, why he was so distant.

And then there was her mother. Brett had denied it for years, but she wanted Barbara's approval and love desperately. Barbara had been a beauty, the essence of what a woman could be, to the young Brett. Even now, as Brett photographed models, she found herself looking for the elusive loveliness that memories of Barbara evoked. She had tried to please her mother, but to no avail, and when Barbara gave up custody of her without a fight, Brett was devastated. It was her mother's verdict that she hadn't been worth fighting for.

Deep down, Brett knew she did not deserve such treatment, and that she had every reason to hate Barbara, but it did not negate the fact that sometimes she just wanted her mother to love her, and nothing could take the place of that.

As she passed the Plaza Hotel, the dimly lit windows of the Oak Bar on the first floor revealed patrons who sipped unknown libations in the famed publike watering hole. In front of the hotel, Grand Army Plaza was decorated with a circle of lighted evergreens ringing the dormant fountain. Brett turned left again at Fifth Avenue, and without planning to, found herself standing across the street from Barbara's apartment. Traffic had almost come to a standstill as it approached the magic mile that began under the gigantic Christmas snowflake, suspended above the Fifty-seventh Street intersection, continued past the Cartier building, which was tied with a massive red ribbon like an enormous gift, and ended at Thirty-fourth Street, with a small-town winter festival depicted in the windows of B. Altman's.

Suddenly, she felt cold and buttoned the black shearling jacket she had worn open as she walked. For the last eleven years she had studiously avoided the white brick and limestone midrise she had once called home.

Lights shone from the tenth-floor apartment. *Barbara is probably in the living room*, Brett thought as she turned up her collar to protect her from the chill. But what could she prove by going up there? Their last encounter had been volatile, and she had no reason to believe they could be civil to each other now. She stared at her mother's windows a moment longer, then turned and walked slowly away.

"Brett, it was the hardest thing I've ever done." Lizzie yanked off her cranberry knit beret and ran her fingers through her golden hair. After a suggestion from one of her professors, she had grown her hair to shoulder length and wore it with all but a hint of the curl blown out. The hairstyle lent some age and more authority to her on-camera persona. Lizzie and Brett sat at a back table at Serendipity, the narrow town house cum fun house and restaurant, which brimmed with kitschy objects of all varieties. Some were for sale; others belonged to the permanent collection. Lively patrons, many toting "Big Brown Bags" from Bloomingdale's, had jammed every available table, and the line of those waiting to get in extended out the door and onto Sixtieth Street. Lizzie had spent a week in California with David and their parents, trying to help him through a difficult time.

"The nursery was all ready. It was white with a cute border of geese around the top. Kate had filled the drawers with all the clothes you could imagine—little T-shirts and terry cloth stretches . . . everything." Lizzie's voice cracked as she explained. She sipped some water and continued. "David had given her this big old spindle-back Hitchcock rocker, and she put her favorite teddy bear from when she was little in the chair, with a new one for the baby. It was so sad.

"Mom and I packed all of the clothes and donated them to a children's hospital, along with all the furniture. She and Daddy stayed to make sure the room got painted, but I had to leave. I couldn't look at my brother that unhappy one minute longer."

"How is David holding up?" Brett asked. She had been pushing her chili around the bowl with a sesame breadstick and trying to look stoic for Lizzie's sake, but she had trouble swallowing both her own lunch and the painful details of the accident.

"He's not dealing with it. He leaves for his office, sometimes at six o'clock in the morning, and drags in after midnight. He says there's some project at a critical point. I've tried to talk with him about what he's going through, but he puts his head down, folds his arms, and won't say anything. Then he changes the subject and all's right with the world again."

"Give him time, Lizzie. There are some things you can't say, even to yourself, much less to anyone else for a while." Brett understood his need for silence. "All you can do is be ready to listen when he needs to talk."

"Are ya done, hon?" The would-be actor who was their waiter collected plates from the marble table, took Lizzie's dessert order for a frozen hot chocolate, a Serendipity special, and shimmied off toward the stairs, stopping to wave at another waiter who was sticking his tongue out through the lips of a Betty Boop mask.

A glimmer came to Brett's eyes. "I have an idea. You're out of school now. Do you have any pressing plans?"

"I've got to decide where I want to work. The offer from STM still stands, but I'm not sure I want to keep doing fluff stuff, or if I want to stay in Syracuse."

"Why don't you come back to Paris with me and stay for a while—clear your head a little? It's my graduation present." Brett thought she would enjoy Lizzie's company, as well.

"Do you mean it? That would be too wonderful!" She thanked Brett and began a verbal list of all she would need to do to get ready. "Oh, and I could surprise Joe—spend some more time with him. He's helped me through some rough spots lately. We talk on the phone a lot, and he stopped in New York on his way to Fort Wayne, a few days before you got here. We didn't do much—just went to see some movies—and he let me cry on his shoulder once or twice. I could really get used to him."

I can't handle this, Brett thought. She would be the first person to sing Joe's praises, and she wanted Lizzie to be happy, but she didn't want to think about it today. It only served to reinforce the poor character judgment she had made with Lawrence.

Lizzie decided to do some shopping on her way home, in honor of returning to Paris. "Maybe I'll find something to knock Joe's socks off for New Year's Eve," she said.

Brett begged off, citing store fatigue, so they parted at the steps leading down to the RR train.

Brett continued walking, feeling miserable, but unsure what to do to make it better. In the last few days she had decided to approach her personal life more like she did her career. She would not procrastinate about things that bothered her, but dive in and take care of them. This course of action had worked with the will. She had signed it two days ago, and although it was difficult, it no longer weighed on her mind so heavily.

Brett turned the corner and paused in front of the Pierre Hotel. A long line of shiny black limousines was beginning to form, and uniformed chauffeurs assisted gowned and tuxedoed passengers, obviously headed for a holiday ball, as they alighted and entered the deluxe hostelry. She had convinced herself of the benefits of direct action, and she knew she had to see Barbara. Doubt and fear had forced her to abort the attempt she had made before, and those same reservations were as strong as ever, but she needed to move forward with her life, and in order to do that, she had to try for a reconciliation, or at the very least, some answers. She took a deep breath, continued up Fifth Avenue, and came to a halt outside Barbara's apartment building once again.

"Can I help you?" the tall, brown-coated doorman asked.

"I guess you don't remember me, George. It's been a long time. I'm Brett Larsen, Barbara North's daughter."

"God love you, Miss Brett! You're making me feel my age," he said.

"And you look exactly the same," Brett responded.

"Your mother will be happy to see you. I'll buzz her."

"I want to surprise her, George." If there were going to be fireworks, Brett wanted them face-to-face, not over an intercom.

"Certainly, miss. Go right up."

Brett pushed the elevator call button, then fixed her eyes on the floor indicator. As it inched closer to the lobby, her tension mounted. *Why am I doing this?* she wondered. Brett knew Barbara hadn't changed. She was still selfish and unfeeling, and didn't deserve another chance. Then she realized she didn't care if Barbara had changed. She wanted to let her mother know once and for all how angry she was and how miserably she had failed her. But what if Barbara had faced up to her mistakes during the last three years? Maybe she would be happy that Brett was willing to let her try to be a mother again. Brett ran the gamut of emotions, but realized that she would continue to be plagued by unresolved feelings about Barbara unless she stopped running away and faced her head-on.

She rang the doorbell. After several seconds of silence, she heard Barbara say, "You boys are supposed to use the service entrance, but I don't care, as long as the champagne is chilled." Barbara flung open the door, wearing a red satin surplice wrap top that revealed much of her now-ample bosom, and matching capri pants, both of which were a size too small. Her complexion was mottled, as though she still wore yesterday's makeup, but her hair looked fresh from the salon. "You're not from Sherry Lehmann," Barbara said, disappointed that it was not her regular delivery from the liquor store. She looked at Brett for a moment, as if trying to place her in time. "Was I expecting you?"

"No, Barbara, I just dropped by." She was taken aback by her mother's greeting.

"Never mind. Come in, Brett," Barbara said matter-of-factly, and disappeared into the living room.

Brett closed the door behind her. Everything was in the same place, but it all seemed a little faded. A bedraggled bouquet of sonia roses sat on the chrome-and-glass table in the foyer, and the petals that had not fallen off were tinged with brown.

The living room, half a city block long and furnished all in a white that had been so dazzling that Zachary had nicknamed it the tundra, now seemed gray. Barbara's sweating glass of scotch sat on a worn arm of the suede sofa.

"So you're back from . . . London?" Barbara asked, resuming her seat.

"I've been in Paris. I just came home for the holidays and to check on Aunt Lillian. She's been ill." *What's wrong with her?* Brett wondered as she perched on the edge of a slubbed silk chaise.

"I don't know what you want, but I can't give you any money," Barbara said.

"That's not why I'm here."

Barbara ignored Brett's response and continued. "That bastard Jeremy just cost me a fortune! Worthless little slime. He used me!" Barbara's agitation mounted as she continued. "Spent three hundred thousand dollars of my money renovating that damn junk shop, not to mention stocking it. Antiques and collectibles—hah! As soon as he had what he wanted, he ignored me. Well, I showed him. Cut his accounts right off and divorced him before he knew what happened. And the store won't last two months—none of my friends will go there. He'll have to close, and then he'll come crawling back, but it's too late!" Barbara gulped down the last of her scotch.

"I'm sorry your marriage didn't work out," Brett said quietly. She didn't know what else to say. Barbara seemed to be floating in her own bubble, and she didn't know how to reach her. She wondered if her mother's drinking was causing her confusion.

Barbara wandered over to the rolling bar and poured another drink. "He was young and very good looking, but he was such a drain on me. It was almost like having a child."

Brett recoiled from this last remark, almost as if she had been slapped. "Was having me around really so awful?"

"God, I'm glad to be rid of him," Barbara said, ignoring her daughter's question. She sipped her drink, momentarily lost in thought, then, referring to an earlier statement, said, "I don't know how you do it. I've never been able to stand Europe. Everyone is so . . . foreign."

"I quite like it, especially Paris." Brett felt the need to channel the conversation. "Barbara, I want to talk about us and what happened before I left for Paris. I have a lot of unanswered questions."

"Did I tell you I can't give you any money?" Barbara asked again.

"I have plenty of money. That's not the reason I'm . . ."

"He's giving you money, isn't he? My father sent you here!" Barbara screeched. "It is him, isn't it? You'd better stay away from him—he's an evil man. I know—believe me, I know." Barbara's eyes had become glassy and unfocused, as if she were watching something only she could see.

"Why do you think he's evil, Barbara?" Brett pleaded.

"Leave me alone! Get out and leave me alone!"

"I'm trying to understand, Barbara. I want to make some sense out of what you're saying, but you won't help me!" Brett's throat burned as she tried to keep the anger and hurt she felt out of her voice. She approached Barbara and reached to touch her.

Barbara flinched and turned her back on Brett, like a child who believed that if she couldn't see you, you were gone.

Instantly, something closed inside Brett. She had always been the one to reach out, and Barbara always slapped her away. Now she was through. "Fine, Barbara, I'll go. But also know that I will never bother you again."

— Chapter 15 —

"This is like a movie set!" The first thing Lizzie had wanted to do after they had arrived in Paris was see Brett's studio. Construction had been completed and the finishing touches were in place.

Fluted white Doric columns imparted a classical elegance and were used throughout much of the studio, instead of walls, to divide the space by function.

Poster-sized prints of Brett's work graced the walls.

"I've never seen colors so intense. Are these still wet?" Lizzie asked.

"No. They're Cibachromes. You've seen them as in-store displays. I like the rich colors and the glossy finish," Brett explained. She was happy that Lizzie had decided to come back with her, and after her disastrous visit with Barbara, she was glad to be five thousand miles away from family involvements.

They went back to what Brett called the business end of the studio. A temperature-controlled storeroom housed ample stocks of film, paper, and the chemicals needed to make black-and-white prints, as well as the safe where Brett stored her camera equipment. Next to the storeroom was a state-of-the-art darkroom, and then two offices. Thérèse's center of operations contained the files, records, schedules, and paperwork associated with the business; Brett had relinquished them gladly. Brett's office functioned as both the editing room and a conference room. A light table ran along one end, and in the center stood an imposing burnished-walnut table with a built-in housing for a slide projector.

"I use the projector to present film to clients and prospective clients. The pictures are easier to discuss if everyone can see them in detail," Brett said.

"They must really be impressed," Lizzie said.

Brett ran her hand along the slightly grainy surface of the table. "Sometimes," she said modestly, but she was proud that more and more clients knew who she was and were interested in working with her. She had gotten this far without flaunting her grandfather's name, and had proven she could take care of herself. There was still room to grow and other avenues to explore in photography, but she was pleased with her progress to date.

"I don't know if I'll ever be this successful." Lizzie sighed.

"Are you kidding? I know you'll be a great broadcaster."

"It's not that simple. You and my brother took off like rockets, with a course set for success. I don't feel as sure as you two about which route to take."

"But you were talking last summer about your reel and checking out possibilities for on-air assignments."

Lizzie paced around the table as she spoke. "Yeah, my reel is good if I want to be 'Lizzie Powell, perky reporter of happy news.' That's how everyone sees me. At the station, they think I'm cute and a little ditzy. I'm the one they send to cover the state fair and the citywide spelling bee. I have fun and it comes easily, but I don't think I want to make a career of that." She paused by the window and watched a tricolor above the nearby police station flicker in the wind. "I feel like the first move I make will decide everything else that follows, and I'm afraid I'll make the wrong one. We've come a long way since Mrs. Bennett's first grade class, haven't we?" Lizzie chuckled. "Well, enough melodrama. I came to Paris to be a wild and crazy American girl, so wouldn't you like to call Joe and tell him you're stopping by so we can surprise him!"

"You mean *you* can surprise him!" Brett said. She and Joe had only exchanged snatches of conversation on the phone since October. Their busy schedules had made it impossible for them to get together. She dialed his number.

"What do you think Joe will say?" Lizzie asked excitedly as she and Brett headed down the narrow, dark hall that led to the fifth and final flight of stairs to Joe's garret room.

"Well, I'm certain you're the last person he expects to see," Brett whispered just before she knocked.

"Brett? Is that you?"

"Yes, it's me!" Brett said brightly, winking at Lizzie as he opened the door.

"*And me!*" Lizzie added, popping out from around the corner.

"Lizzie! What are you doing here? This is great!"

"It just kind of happened," Lizzie responded as Joe showed them in.

Although he was in a far better financial position now, Joe steadfastly refused to give up the tiny room he rented. He reasoned that the rent was cheap, he wasn't home much anymore, and he'd never find a studio more conveniently located than six flights down.

Joe's roost was one of four equally small rooms on the top floor of a building near the Sorbonne that housed mostly students. The oblique angles of the sloping mansard roof formed two of the four walls and made the already limited space appear surreal and out of kilter. Joe often joked that he lived in a Salvador Dali painting.

"When did you get here?" he asked.

"Just this morning. We dropped off our stuff, then Brett took me to the new studio, and now, here we are!" Lizzie plopped down on Joe's tattered horsehair sofa, the right front leg of which was missing and had been replaced by a cinder block.

"We thought you might like to go out and get some dinner." Brett's words were accompanied by the creaking of springs as she sat down opposite Lizzie on Joe's serape-covered bed.

"Sounds good." Joe grabbed the rickety wooden chair from the card table in the corner and straddled it backwards.

"So, how would you like two dates for Gabriel's New Year's Eve party?" Brett asked playfully.

"Uh, Gabriel's party? I already have a date—I mean, plans," Joe replied hesitantly.

"But your two best girls are in town." Brett was interrupted by a knock on Joe's door.

"It must be my landlady. She's terminally nosy and I'll bet she saw you two come up here," Joe said, this time grateful for the intrusion.

But before he reached the door he heard, "Joe, honey, are you in there? Open up, it's the 'Belle of Alabama'!" Randall used the nickname Joe had given her.

Joe knew he had to open the door, but he didn't look forward to what might happen next. He'd had enough surprises for one day. "Hi, Randall," he said, but did not move to allow her entry.

"Can't I come in?" Randall asked coyly.

"Sure. Brett's here, and . . ." He stepped aside and Randall was in before he could mention Lizzie.

"Brett, honey! You sure look better than you did the last time I saw you." Randall looked her up and down. Brett, like Lizzie, was dressed casually in jeans and a sweater.

"You look pretty great yourself," Brett responded.

"Santa *was* good to little ol' me this year!" Randall spun around to show off her outfit—a winter-white cashmere turtleneck and matching trousers, topped by a shaggy Tibetan lamb stroller the color of a neon persimmon. "You like?" she asked, now indicating the thick band of gold, studded with Chiclet-size emeralds, around her wrist.

"Yes, I like," Brett said politely, examining the bracelet. "Randall, this is . . ."

Randall ignored Brett and turned to Lizzie, who had not missed one word or gesture of Randall's performance. "Who is this cute little thing?" she asked, molasses dripping from every word.

Lizzie bristled, her hackles raised as much by Randall's presence as by her remark about her size, but Brett intervened before Lizzie let loose her salvo. "This is my best friend, Elizabeth Powell." She purposely used Lizzie's full name. "We grew up together."

"Pleased to meet you, Elizabeth," Randall drawled with a mock curtsy worthy of Scarlett O'Hara. She knew Joe had dated Lizzie, but she wasn't ready to give him up. Unlike Marcel, Joe was young and handsome, and she reveled in the attention they received as a couple. When she and Joe entered a room or strolled down the street together, people often stopped, pointed, and whispered to their companions. Randall and Joe were the glossy pages of a fashion magazine come to life, and she loved it.

"I've seen your pictures. You're very beautiful," Lizzie said flatly. She really wanted to ask why Randall was here, but obviously Randall knew Joe well enough to drop by unannounced, or else she was very rude. Lizzie was convinced both were true.

"Well, like my mama used to say, 'You better make good use of what the Lord gives you.'"

Brett could see that Randall was "on." Her accent was so thick Brett thought that it might congeal, and she sensed that Lizzie was the reason. She didn't know what was going on between Randall and Joe, but Randall had mounted an offensive the moment she targeted Lizzie as a possible rival.

"It's just a shame that beauty doesn't last as long as brains," said Lizzie, unable to stand one more syrupy syllable from Randall.

Joe stood near the door, as if ready to make good his escape, and looked from Randall to Lizzie, and then helplessly at Brett, who pointedly averted her eyes.

Randall sidled up to Joe and languidly smoothed her hand over his chest. "Joe, honey, did you pick up your tuxedo from the tailor's?" she asked, now toying with a button on his shirt.

Joe looked at Lizzie before he replied. "Uh . . . yeah."

"I just can't wait for Gabriel's New Year's Eve party. Le Palace is just too, too bohemian. I met Andy Warhol there. Odd little man. Nice, but he watched everybody like a bird dog." Fabrice Emaer, premier party giver and owner of Le Palace, had transformed the former theater into a bastion of democratic chaos driven by a disco beat. The famous, the profane, the exotic and the hopeful, dressed in couture or cellophane mingled, creating a new brew nightly. "Anyway, I heard Yves might come in from his house in Morocco, and you know he rarely shows up at anything except his collections.

Goodness only knows who else will be there. The invitations said to dress as new as the year or as old as time. Joe refuses to wear a costume, but I might go as Eve. That should be pretty temptin', don't you think? Did Joe tell you we've been invited to Gabriel's private breakfast afterward? That means our boy here is really a star!"

Throughout Randall's monologue, Joe stared at the floor.

Lizzie, realizing the room was no longer big enough for her and Randall, shot out of her seat and stretched up to her full height. In a drawl oozing with sarcasm, she said, "Joe, hush puppy, Brett and I will be leavin'. You all must have a thousand little things to talk about before the New Year's ball." Lizzie bounded from the room before Brett could make her good-byes.

Joe followed her into the hall. "Lizzie, it's not what you think," he began feebly.

"Why, Joe, sugar, whatever would I think?" Lizzie asked, batting her lashes with a vengeance. By this time, Brett had extricated herself from Randall.

"Aren't we going to dinner?" Joe asked.

"Maybe some other time. I think your 'belle' is calling you now. 'Bye!" Lizzie finished, and descended the stairs.

Back outside, she fumed, "It's not that he's seeing someone else. We never even talked about being exclusive, but what could he possibly see in that shallow, conceited, conniving, antebellum she-devil? Why didn't she just strip naked and fling herself on the floor in front of him?"

"I don't know, Lizzie." Brett didn't dislike Randall, but she could not defend her or her actions to Lizzie. It was Joe that Brett wondered about. Was he not to be trusted, either?

They headed toward the Métro station near the Musée de Cluny, but they passed the medieval structure without so much as a glance. Lizzie had hoped to spend New Year's Eve with Joe, and she wore her disappointment all over her face. Brett, on the other hand, was relieved to have a reason not to attend Gabriel Jarré's party. When she had received her invitation, attached to a split of Moet, she had decided to go because it was politically the thing to do, but she did not relish the very real possibility that Lawrence would also be there.

"Well, that's a great start to the new year!" Lizzie said sarcastically as they purchased tickets at the counter.

Brett's decision to take more direct action in her personal life flashed through her mind. She had made a bad choice in starting with her mother, but in spite of that disastrous confrontation, she still believed that acting was better than reacting.

"Lizzie, we're not going to sit at home tomorrow night like two pound puppies waiting to be adopted! There are plenty of things for us to do. After all, this is Paris. In fact, we have all of Europe to choose from!" After her sweeping statement, Brett stopped to consider their options. She thought about the enchanted places she had visited, then, with a start, said, "I know. Let's go to Monte Carlo!"

"Are you crazy? I just got to Paris. Monte Carlo is in another country."

They boarded the train and took the only two seats available. As soon as they sat down, they realized why they were vacant. The woman sitting next to them snored and reeked of fish. Brett surmised that not only must she work in a fish market, but the parcel she carried contained the catch of the day. But she and Lizzie would change trains at the next station, and hopefully, their seatmate would not.

"Maybe it is crazy, but so what? We could fly to Nice in the morning, rent a car, and drive to Monaco."

Lizzie admitted that she found the idea of bringing in the new year in the fabled principality on the Mediterranean beyond her wildest fantasies and by the time they transferred at Odéon, she was thoroughly convinced.

Early the next morning they landed under cloudless blue skies at the Nice airport and picked up the Jaguar Brett had rented. As she nosed the silver bullet onto the Moyenne Corniche and headed toward the tiny sovereign state nestled by the sea in the foothills of the Alps, Brett felt free and unfettered. She rarely made impetuous decisions, but last night, when she had no trouble making last-minute reservations, she knew it was a good omen.

Even though it was only 55 degrees, Lizzie had insisted they put the top down. Brett planned to stop at the picturesque hillside towns of Villefranche and Beaulieu, since Lizzie had never been to the Riviera before. They drove the winding Corniche at a leisurely pace, invigorated by the morning sunshine and salty sea air, and even with their detours, they made excellent time. Brett looked at her watch, turned on to the avenue de la Porte Neuve, and pulled into the first parking area she saw. "If we hurry, we can make it!" she shouted to a puzzled Lizzie, who sprang from the car and followed.

They were breathless when they reached the top of the terraced sidewalk, but they were on time. At precisely 11:55 every day, in front of the main entrance to the seventeenth century royal palace, Monégasques and tourists alike gather for the changing of the guard. Brett and Lizzie watched, fascinated, as the Compagnie des Carbiniers, in full dress black-and-gold winter uniforms, completed their daily ritual. Only when the ceremony was over did they notice the magnificent view from high atop the place du Palais. Monte Carlo lay at their feet and the harbor, which in a few months would be crowded with yachts and sailboats, stretched out beyond it, clear and azure. Brett pointed out Bordighera, Italy to the Northeast and Cap d'Ail to the Southwest, the direction from which they had approached town.

"It's like a fairy tale," Lizzie said, still unable to believe she was actually in Monte Carlo.

"That's what I said the first time I came here."

"This is the hotel?" Lizzie asked incredulously when they arrived at the majestic Hotel de Paris. "It looks like another palace!"

Brett had been a guest at the sprawling Edwardian hotel on her first visit to the Côte d'Azur, and she loved its gracious splendor. The parking valet swept open the car door and a bellman, attired in a crisp navy blue uniform, appeared out of thin air, greeted her by name, and welcomed them. Brett was astounded that they remembered her, then realized that the rental agency must have notified them of her impending arrival, as well as the make and model of the car she would be driving. Their luggage was whisked inside and the Jaguar spirited away by the time they were met by the concierge.

They both marveled at the magnificent frescoes as they walked through the cavernous, vaulted neo-baroque lobby. The hotel was situated on the place du Casino, and their rooms provided a glorious view of the famed Casino de Monte Carlo and the sumptuous formal gardens, which were ablaze with red, white, and green flora.

Their suite was decorated in shades of ivory and pale blue. Brett chose the casual country French bedroom. Lizzie was ecstatic to be ensconced in the more ornate, gilt-trimmed Louis XV chamber. The main salon, in contrast, was distinctly sleek and modern, with low sofas and tables, but both Brett and Lizzie knew they would spend little time in any of the three rooms.

As soon as the maid came and took their dresses to be pressed, Brett called for the car and they went to lunch. They blamed their ravenous appetites on the sea air, and finished their antipasto long before the spaghetti was served. After their meal they drove along Larvotto beach and through Old Monaco before returning to the hotel. By now they were almost giddy with the excitement of their adventure. Lizzie had pushed thoughts of Joe and Randall to the back of her mind, and for the first time in weeks, Brett did not think of Lawrence. They were enveloped by the same carefree spirit that had surrounded them as little girls playing on the beach at Cox Cove.

"We may lose every cent we have, but we look great." Lizzie giggled as they strolled up the walk to the Casino de Monte Carlo. The night air felt charged with energy waiting to power the coming celebration of the new year. Because Brett had been under twenty-one on her last trip, the casino was a new experience for both of them.

"I read all the brochures twice, but I'm still not sure I know baccarat from blackjack!" Brett said as she drew her chiffon stole a bit tighter to ward off the evening chill.

Brett and Lizzie had dined in the grand Empire Room, the legendary dining salon in the Hotel de Paris. Like the magnificent lobby, the ivory room had a high vaulted ceiling that was supported by ornately capitaled triple columns and decorated with elaborate medallions. Their table, directly opposite the Gervais mural that dominated one wall, provided them with a perfect view of the idyllic, delicately erotic depiction of maidens frolicking in the woods. They barely touched the wine they ordered with their côtes de veau aux truffes, knowing they had a long evening ahead of them.

"I've never seen so many limousines! Did you see all those jewels and furs?" Lizzie asked.

"They were all going to the ball at the Sporting Club. When I registered, the concierge asked if we required a car for tonight's gala. I told him no and he said, '*C'est dommage*. You and your friend are so lovely, you would be a very special addition to zee affair.' I almost told him we had no escorts, but he was so serious, I think he would have tried to find us dates!"

Brett and Lizzie entered the casino to the sound of music, laughter, and the clink of glasses. After showing their passports as proof that they were not underage, they stood in the marble-paved atrium surrounded by twenty-eight onyx Ionic columns. The hundred-plus-year-old Casino, a profusion of bas-reliefs, frescoes and statues, was built by Charles Garnier, the architect of the Paris Opera House, and reflected the same splendor. The Salle Garnier, home of the Monte Carlo Opera, and the four towers which housed the gaming rooms were all approached from this richly gilded entry.

All around them was a sea of people in various stages of exuberance and inebriation. "Our reservations for the floor show in the cabaret aren't until ten-thirty. Let's have a glass of champagne while we wait," Brett suggested.

They were shown to a table in the Pink Salon Bar and ordered two glasses of Veuve Clicquot. "Have you looked up there?" Lizzie asked, indicating the ceiling by raising her eyes.

Brett tilted her head back, then looked at Lizzie, and they both began to laugh. The ceiling was painted with naked women smoking cigarettes. "I don't see anyone I recognize. Do you?" Their laughter erupted once again. A waiter appeared, bearing a tray with two more glasses of champagne. "We didn't order that," Brett said.

"Compliments of the gentleman at the bar," he said, nodding toward a tall, well-tailored, thirtyish, dark-haired man who smiled and nodded in return. "He said, there are no strings?" the waiter stated quizzically, obviously unfamiliar with the expression.

"Tell the gentleman thank you," Brett said, placing a twenty-franc note on the tray for the waiter.

"I don't believe you did that! What if he comes over here and wants to . . ."

"To what? Lizzie, he looks perfectly harmless, and if he wanted something, he'd be on his way over here by now. Besides, you're the one who said we look great. How could he resist?" Brett said, laughing.

Brett and Lizzie were indeed a striking pair. Lizzie was a vision of petite chic, in a black velvet strapless floor-length sheath with matching bolero jacket. She had secured her blond curls loosely on top of her head with a faux pavé diamond clip. Delicate drops of jet and crystal dangled from her ears. In contrast, Brett's heels raised her height to an Amazonian six feet. Her long hair, parted on the side, fell in deep, dark waves that all but covered her bare shoulders. She wore a white chiffon, halter-neck gown with a fitted bodice that cascaded into fluid layers of the filmy alabaster fabric. On her ears, almost hidden from view by her hair, were the pearl-and-diamond earrings Lawrence had given her. And when people stared, both were sure it was because they were unescorted, but neither cared. It was New Year's Eve and they were in Monte Carlo.

After two more glasses of champagne during the floor show, which consisted of a dozen feathered dancing girls, a mediocre singer who fancied himself to be Frank Sinatra, and a magician who was quite good, they made their way to the gaming salons. They stopped first in the American room, where they promptly lost three hands of blackjack to the dealer.

"Pardon me, but you don't seem to be having very much luck." They turned to find the man who had sent them champagne. "My name is Schuyler Hunt. My friends call me Sky. I'm from Palm Beach, but don't hold that against me, and I'm not trying to pick you up."

To Brett's surprise, Lizzie spoke up first. "I'm Elizabeth Powell. This is Brett Larsen. And you're right—we're lousy at this game." She extended her hand.

"Have you tried the European Room? I come here a couple of times a year and I always have better luck there."

"But the minimum stake is half a million francs," Brett said. Lizzie gasped.

"You both would be my guests."

"We couldn't do that," Brett protested.

"Think nothing of it. Just consider it money I won't lose!" he chuckled, smoothing his hand over his slicked-back dark brown hair.

Lizzie gazed at him in amazement, as if he were too good to be true, then decided that the idea of spending New Year's Eve in Monte Carlo had also seemed too good to be true. She shrugged her shoulders and tucked her arm through Schuyler Hunt's. "You're on!" she responded, getting into the spirit.

Brett, following Lizzie's lead, took his other arm, and Sky escorted them into the cathedrallike atmosphere of the high-stakes room. Stained glass windows and allegorical paintings were highlighted by brass lamps and looked down on tables where roulette, chemin de fer, baccarat and trente-quarante were played.

"I think I feel lucky at baccarat," Lizzie announced, so they each played and lost. Sky had spotted some old friends across the room, and Lizzie was anxious to try her hand at a different game, but Brett was determined not to give up, and urged them to come back for her later.

Lizzie returned just before midnight with a bottle of Bollinger.

"Where did you get that?" Brett asked.

"Never mind! Come on, have a glass. It's almost next year," Lizzie said, and dragged Brett away from her game. When the new year rang in, they impulsively exchanged kisses with strangers and toasted each other amid the laughter and celebration that surrounded them. The din subsided and a crowd gathered at a roulette wheel where a player had wagered five million francs. Lizzie joined the hushed throng while Brett returned to face the challenge of the baccarat table.

Lawrence had once told her that baccarat was his favorite, and Brett was possessed by the need to master the game. It was as though she thought she could exorcise his spirit once and for all, if only she could win his game. *I have a total of eight*, she thought, looking at her three cards. *I have to win—no one will get nine.* But the player next to her did. "Encore," she said to the dealer.

The man beside Brett turned to her. "Sometimes, the deal makes you a loser. You have to know when you can't win. You have to let it go and move on," he said quietly.

The words hit home, but not the way they were intended. She had to let Lawrence go, or at least start to. "Excuse me," she said as she got up from the table and headed across the crowded room toward the ladies' room.

Brett dampened the towel the attendant gave her with cool water and applied it to the back of her neck. Her earrings glittered in the mirror. When she finished, the attendant held out her hand for the towel. Brett laid the towel on the counter, pulled off the earrings, and placed them in the woman's open hand. "Happy New Year!" she said triumphantly.

"Pardon?"

"Keep them, sell them, do whatever you want. They're yours." Brett sailed from the room feeling as light as a cloud. She had never realized how heavy those earrings had become.

She joined Lizzie at the roulette wheel, just in time to hear her friend say, "I'll bet it all on the same number—red twenty-three."

"Lizzie! What are you doing?" Brett asked incredulously.

"Shh," Lizzie said. "Close your eyes and hold my hand! I think my heart will stop if I watch."

The other players looked on, amused as the two friends clasped their hands tightly together and squeezed their eyes shut. The rattling sound of the little ball seemed as loud as gunfire as it whirled around the polished wooden wheel.

"Rouge vingt-trois! Félicitations, mademoiselle!"

"What did he say?" Lizzie asked.

"You won! You won!" Brett hugged her friend, then together they found Sky to thank him for his hospitality and say good night. They knew little about him, but he had brought them luck, and true to his word, he hadn't tried to pick them up.

After Lizzie collected her thirty thousand francs, she and Brett decided to try Jimmy'z, the discothèque on the other side of the place du Casino, where, if their luck held out, they would dance until sunup.

A strong breeze from the sea blew Brett's hair away from her face and Lizzie noticed her empty lobes. "What happened to your earrings?" she asked.

"I guess I must have lost them," Brett said with a quick toss of her brunette mane.

— *Chapter 16* —

Brett and Lizzie returned to a typically damp, gray Parisian January that seemed even more wintry when compared to the sunny and relatively balmy 50- and 60-degree temperatures they had left in Monte Carlo. Wrapped in good humor and filled with delightful memories of their Mediterranean holiday, Lizzie had decided to give Joe the benefit of the doubt. The phone was ringing when they entered Brett's apartment and she answered before the machine could pick up.

"Hi, Brett. I've been trying to call you two for three days," Joe said on the other end.

"We've been away, but I'll let Lizzie tell you about that," Brett said.

"Wait! Don't give her the phone yet. I want to talk to you. Could I come by the studio in the morning?"

"That sounds fine. Around ten?" Brett suggested. "Hold on a minute," she said, and went to find Lizzie.

"It's Joe, isn't it?" Lizzie asked quietly as she looked up from the suitcase she was unpacking. Brett nodded and Lizzie walked slowly into the living room. She held the receiver for several seconds before she spoke. "Happy New Year, Joe."

"Lizzie, I'm sorry about the other day. I know everyone was

uncomfortable. But let me make it up to you. How about dinner on Friday? You can tell me about your mysterious holiday."

"I'd like that, Joe—and I guess we need to talk about things," Lizzie said. She was nervous, but her clear, calm "on-air" voice revealed nothing to Joe. She hung up feeling hopeful but wary.

"I feel like I should apologize, but I'm not sure what for. I like Lizzie a lot, and I never meant to hurt her feelings, but I didn't know she was coming." Joe perched on the edge of the red chesterfield in Brett's studio.

"Shouldn't you be telling this to Lizzie?" Brett sat on the twin sofa opposite him.

"I will, but you're my friend, too. I felt I owed you an explanation because you two are so close. I guess I should have told you earlier that I've been seeing Randall, but I wasn't sure exactly what to say." He leaned forward, rested his elbows on his knees, and folded his hands.

"Joe, you're a grown man and you can see whomever you please." Brett was having a problem distancing herself from this situation. Memories of Lawrence's deception were still fresh, and even though she knew this was different, and Joe was trying to be honest, she found it hard to be objective. "I just hope that you're fair and make sure everyone knows the rules. You can't assume anything."

"I know you're right. Stop me if you don't want to hear this, but this has never happened to me before. Lizzie is smart, sensitive, and funny, and I find her very attractive. She's a lot of things I enjoy in a woman—in a person. I look forward to the times we can be together, but she lives in New York. It's different with Randall. She's beautiful and unpredictable, and going out with her is like finding yourself in the middle of a movie, except no one gave you the script. Anything can happen! I mean, we're on our way to dinner, and the next thing I know, we're in a hotel suite with Sean Michaels and this model named Adria who's his girlfriend! Hell, I've bought Maelstrom albums since I was a kid. I used to play air guitar and pretend I was Sean, and now he's sitting cross-legged in the middle of a king-size bed, plucking this melody he's working on and asking me if I like it!''

Brett listened attentively. Joe sounded like a child who'd just seen his first circus.

"I can't really talk to Randall about anything important, but that's okay. She likes to go shopping, tell me what clothes I should buy, then take me out and show me off to all of her friends." Joe couldn't tell Brett that Randall also liked to peel those clothes off and do wild things all night long. Sex wasn't a subject he had broached with Lizzie, and he certainly wasn't going to detail his exploits to her best friend. "And I know all about Marcel. But I don't plan to marry her, and she's not looking at me as marriage material either. I just want to have a good time. Is this difficult for you to hear? I don't want to rub salt in any wounds."

"It's okay. Go on," Brett said, although the word *plan* had struck a sore spot.

"There's not really that much else to say. With Randall I've found a world where the people are famous and the deals get made. And sometimes I get a bigger kick out of it than I can explain. Brett, I'm not looking for a response. It's just that your opinion of me is important, and I didn't want you to think I'd gone off the deep end and become a jerk."

"I don't think you're a jerk . . . yet."

"That's fair. I'll take it."

"I'll give it a shot," Lizzie said as the waiter brought the check. Brett had called her from the studio and they had met for lunch at La Procope, a Parisian landmark, which claims to be the oldest restaurant in the world. Brett always enjoyed the sense of continuity and permanence she got from sitting in the vermilion-and-gold dining room, at a table where Napoleon or Victor Hugo might have been enticed by the same hearty aromas that surrounded her now. Brett was glad that they were sitting near the French doors that fronted the café. The cut-glass chandeliers and wall sconces would not have provided enough light to keep drowsiness, the result of all her recent travels, from overpowering her. Over croque monsieur and potage St. Germain, Brett let Lizzie know, without revealing anything that might hurt her feelings, that as far as Joe was concerned, it might be worth hanging in there. Brett wasn't sure why, but she still thought Joe was a good guy, just temporarily enthralled with a world he had only dreamed existed.

Lizzie, too, had seen what could occur when people were thrown into a life-style for which they were not prepared. It had happened to some of her classmates who had nabbed plum anchor positions right after graduation, then found themselves adrift in a sea of money, temptation, and celebrity. She understood what was happening to Joe, but that didn't make it any easier.

Friday night, Lizzie and Joe ambled silently along the Quai des Tuilleries. Other than their footsteps, the gentle lapping of the Seine against the pilings was the only sound they heard.

During dinner, their conversation had been polite and reserved. Joe told Lizzie about Christmas with his family in Indiana, but did not feel comfortable mentioning New Year's Eve. Lizzie told Joe about New Year's Eve in Monaco, but she was reticent about discussing the depressing Christmas she had spent with her brother. Neither had addressed the subject that was on both of their minds.

The air was frosty but still, and when Joe finally spoke, his voice was soft and tranquil, as though his words were cushioned by the misty breath that accompanied them. "I've thought a lot about how to start this conversation, and it always sounds trite and ridiculous. I feel bad that we're having it after you've already seen me with someone else."

"It's not your fault, Joe. I had no right to barge in on you unannounced. It would have been unfair even if I lived across town."

Joe groped for her hand as they walked, but realizing that it was farther down than he could reach casually, he stopped, leaned over, and grasped it, then continued. "Lizzie, I enjoy being with you. I have ever since the beginning. Well, at least since we got beyond sparring in Compiègne."

"Oh, I always feel more comfortable with a man after I fall into a river in front of him," Lizzie kidded, a bit apprehensive about what he would say next.

"I suppose it's very sophisticated to tell people what they want to hear and then cover your tracks so they don't find out the truth. I hope that's not what you want, because I can't do it." He stopped and looked sincerely into her eyes. "I very much want to keep seeing you, but I also know that I'm not ready to say I won't see anyone else, so I'll ask you, what would you like to do?"

Lizzie looked up at him and felt something more tender and real than she had with any of the other men she had loved. "I'd like that a lot, Joe. I realize that the distance we're apart means it may take us longer to figure out what, if anything, comes next, but that's not the important thing now."

"If something should change—if I meet someone who makes me realize that I'd like to share the rest of my life with her—I promise I'll let you know," he declared.

"And I'll do the same, Joe." Joe bent over, and Lizzie, in anticipation of his embrace, stood on her toes. They kissed sweetly, gently, as if to seal their oath. An elderly gentleman wearing a gray overcoat and cap shuffled by and waggled his finger in a good-natured admonition.

"He's right. You'd better behave yourself," Lizzie said. "And promise me one other thing."

"What's that?"

"That you won't fall for some witless bimbo."

Brett, just back from her booking in Venice for *La Femme Première*, knelt on the floor in front of her stereo, trying to decide whether to play Count Basie or Benny Goodman. She had acquired a taste for big band music from Lillian, and she often played it after she'd been away because it made her feel instantly at home.

"You found a job in Paris!" She stopped flipping through albums as soon as Lizzie delivered the news.

In Brett's absence, Lizzie had begun to seriously deliberate her career options. Courtesy of her Monte Carlo windfall, she had the funds to delay taking a job immediately, and she was determined to make the choice that was best in the long run, not necessarily the one that was easiest now.

Donald Greiss, one of Lizzie's former journalism professors at Syracuse, had left the university the previous June to become Paris bureau chief for Global News Service Network, the newest cable television system, whose aim was to provide twenty-four-hour coverage of world events. Hoping to get some sound advice, Lizzie contacted him and he invited her to the network headquarters on the rue de Quatre Septembre, near La Bourse, the Paris stock exchange.

Greiss's office was the largest of those on the perimeter of the sprawling, windowless enclave called "the shop." The room, hushed but for the insistent clicking of computer keyboards, was the hub of GNSN's European news-gathering operation. Some staffers monitored computer readouts from wire services for updates of breaking stories. Others composed news stories to be broadcast from the studio, one floor below. Camera crews were dispatched from a cubicle at the far end of the room, from which the muffled sound of a ringing telephone could occasionally be heard.

Lizzie listened intently as Greiss outlined day-to-day operations. GNSN was one of the pioneers in cable news, and its broadcasts changed constantly as stories developed. The network's dedication to the fast and accurate transmission of information meant that sometimes videotape editing was choppy, and the reporting had some rough edges stylistically, but Lizzie was impressed by the dedication and professionalism she saw around her.

Greiss debated the pros and cons of Lizzie's dilemma, and when he asked her for a copy of her reel and some writing samples, she had assumed it was so he could critique them and get more of a feel for where her strengths and weaknesses were. She had her mother overnight them to her, and two days after she delivered them to his office, Greiss called and offered her a job as a writer. He had an entry-level position to fill. She would be assigned to overnights and weekends. He felt that her on-screen presence was good, as were her writing samples; she had talent that he deemed worth developing. If she was serious about branching into hard news, then the experience there would be invaluable, and he would like to have her aboard.

"I start in a month, so I'm going home to pack and finish some business, then I'll be back to look for an apartment and get settled," Lizzie told Brett.

"This is so sudden. Are you sure it's the best move for you?" Brett asked.

"I think it's the smartest move I can make. An overseas assignment always adds luster to your résumé. My tapes will keep, and if I'm lucky, I can work myself up to correspondent for GNSN, which would make me a hot property when I go back home. And if you hung me by my thumbs, I'd have to admit that being closer to Joe makes the job even more attractive than it is already."

"You know you can stay with me as long as you need to," Brett said. Although she loved her dearly, she hoped that Lizzie would not become a long-term roommate. She didn't want to be privy to the details of whatever evolved between Joe and Lizzie. If it didn't work out, she would be caught in the middle, and if it did, Brett would be happy for them, but she wasn't ready to watch love in bloom.

"Thanks, and I accept, but it shouldn't be long. GNSN has a service called Relocation Assistance that helps find apartments, grocery stores, doctors who speak English, and anything else you might need."

"Welcome to Paris!" Brett said as she hugged Lizzie.

— *Chapter 17* —

Lizzie's transition to life in Paris went smoothly. She stayed with Brett only for the week it took her predecessor, a young man who had been transferred to the network's home base in Dallas, to move out of his rather nondescript one bedroom apartment. Lizzie decided to rent it as soon as she saw it. Located in a well-kept if unremarkable building, it was within walking distance of work, and its windows faced north, which meant the apartment was dark for much of the day—a plus for anyone who worked nights. She made a deal with him to buy his sparse furnishings: a sectional sofa; a mattress and box spring that sprawled on the floor in the bedroom; an oval dining table with a scarred, ink-stained top; and three matching chairs. He thought there had been four chairs, but he couldn't remember what had happened to the missing one. Oddly, there was also a lovely, hand-carved, inlaid chiffonier that she decided would be her start whenever she got around to decorating.

Despite her experience with local television news, Lizzie was severely challenged by her assignment. She worked midnight to eight, which was normally not frantic, so she had time to pick up the network's style and become acquainted with procedures and routines. Even so, she was thrown her share of tests, and often found her stories, which she transferred from her terminal to that of her editor for approval, back in her computer with instructions for rewriting.

Aside from general news duties, she was assigned to write intro pieces for Randolph Peck, the moderator of "Press Conference: Europe," the highly regarded hour-long news-and-views program that placed European leaders in the hot seat, opposite a panel of experts, discussing matters of concern to the United States.

"Randolph is the most pompous ass I've ever met," Lizzie told Brett one morning over the scrambled eggs and toast she had fixed for breakfast. They sat at the table in two of Lizzie's three chairs. The third, like half of the table, was piled high with the research material she had compiled in preparation for Peck's special retrospective for the fortieth anniversary of D day on June 6. "He strides across the shop like the crown prince of newsdom, and whether I'm busy or not, he starts lecturing me in this condescending voice. 'Would you not agree that this passage could be written more succinctly, but with perhaps more eloquence?' Have you ever heard anything so ridiculous? I really believe he wants me to genuflect, but he can forget it. The guy knows his stuff, but only his mother could stand to be around him for more than ten minutes."

Protests not withstanding, Brett could tell that Lizzie really loved her job.

Brett's steady rise among the ranks of young photographers in Paris continued apace, and Lawrence crossed her path repeatedly. The elite society of fashion professionals was a small clan, and avoiding those with whom one had differences was impossible. In fact, the vicious sniping that occurred when enemies collided meant that phones all over Paris, Milan, New York, and Tokyo would light up with a red gossip alert.

Brett had heard several versions of their breakup over the last year, the most elaborate of which had her finding Polaroids of Lawrence in a rather dicey ménage à trois with a certain red-haired model who had the face of an angel and a reputation for promiscuity, and a design assistant from one of the couture houses known for flamboyant, unwearable creations and precarious finances.

Refusing to talk to Lawrence in public would only have given already loose lips something new to flap about, so when Brett could find no graceful way to avoid it, she spoke to him civilly and moved on quickly. Each of these casual contacts was followed by a barrage of calls from Lawrence and his staff, all of which she refused to answer.

Current intelligence held that *Voilà!*'s editorial pages were flat and uninspired since her departure, and that the magazine was again on shaky ground. Whether that was truth or hyperbole, it enhanced Brett's reputation as a strong creative force.

In July, Brett dedicated some of her time taking publicity stills for Live-Aid, the trans-Atlantic benefit concert for famine victims in Ethiopia. When Bob Geldof called she said yes immediately, and in the backstage chaos at Wembley Stadium in London, she got sweat-dripping, hard-rocking shots of Tina Turner, Madonna, Elton John, and lots of the other luminaries.

Finally, in August, Brett followed the tradition of her European home and took a month's vacation, but she spent little time relaxing in the country. Her work at Live-Aid had made her remember how much she enjoyed taking portraits, so she bought a Hasselblad and experimented in the studio. The bigger negatives of the large-format camera meant that her pictures gained in the sharpness and clarity so vital to close-up work.

The new pictures, a hodgepodge of the denizens of Paris that included close friends, proprietors of the stores and cafés she frequented, and even some of the designers, editors, and stylists with whom she worked, revealed her innate ability to capture a glimpse into the heart of her subjects in that fraction of a second when the shutter blinked. This talent was now augmented by her growing maturity as a photographer.

While at Brett's studio, Sophie Leclerc noted the intimacy of Brett's portrayals. She passed the word about the potentially important new resource to the art director of *La Femme Première*, who was responsible for the photo assignments that accompanied all stories in the magazine other than fashion and beauty.

"Portraits are my hobby," Brett protested when he called to inquire about her availability, but she agreed to consider assignments when the subject interested her, and in September, her curiosity was piqued by the opportunity to photograph François Truffaut, the esteemed French movie director. Brett admired the strong visual statements in his films, and he was a lively subject. Ironically, Brett's pictures were the last taken of him before his untimely death the following month.

Joe saw as much of Lizzie as their schedules permitted. With his contractual obligations to Clik Claque drawing to a close, Gabriel filled more of his time with editorial shoots to raise his profile, but after nearly a year of working almost exclusively for one client, Joe disliked the grind and pressure of worrying whether clients liked his look. The novelty of life as a model had worn thin, and frequently he felt like a show horse who was carefully curried, then trotted out and put through his paces. He longed to spend days covered in marble dust, his face unshaven, his hands unmanicured, and his clothes haphazard and distinctly unchic, but he kept telling himself the money was good, and soon he could scale back his modeling and devote more time to his art.

For Joe, the sterling social life of the young and beautiful ones had tarnished, as well. He had seen the traveling carnival too often and realized that the regulars—those characters without whom the games could not begin—had nothing to say. Their main objective was to be seen. So often, when he tried to have conversations that ventured beyond the bounds of clothing, the newest hot spot, or general cattiness, people listened distractedly and looked for the first opportunity to move on.

In July, Randall had arrived in Paris to work the Prêt à Porter, the increasingly significant ready-to-wear shows. Her sassy style, and a presence that *Espion* had dubbed "Randacious," meant that on most days, she showed for three different designers at $5,000 a clip, but despite her rigorous schedule, she still found time to flit about, the lovely social butterfly, with Joe as her preferred escort.

At the end of the first week of shows tout le monde élégant hobnobbed with the fashion press and the all important store buyers, whose open-to-buy dollars were the genesis of the tumultuous hoopla, at the champagne reception hosted by Alliance du Mode Française to fête their thirtieth anniversary. Thierry Carbonnier had overseen the transformation of the stately Louvre courtyard into a horizontal residence de ville, with each room enlivened by a tableau vivant. The actors in each living drama were attired in vintage French designs and guests buzzed about, like flies on so many walls, as the acts unfolded.

"Honey, that happens to me every morning." Randall, looking like a tropical refreshment in a printed silk sarong and bandeau top, entertained Joe and the exceedingly prim gentleman who was the fashion director of an exclusive San Francisco store for whom she worked. "Sometimes I go through ten outfits before I decide which one to wear!" They had stopped in front of a chambre à coucher whose three walls were dressed with shirred ivory damask, to watch a pixie-coiffed brunette with scarlet lips who presently wore only a peach silk teddy and chestnut suede pumps. She pondered wardrobe possibilities in front of a Louis XIV rosewood armoire and finally plucked a cinnamon wool Dior trapeze jacket, circa 1954, from its padded hanger. She donned it, followed by the narrow matching skirt, then floated across the plush rose carpet and pranced before a cheval mirror. Shaking her head in displeasure, she removed the outfit, tossed it atop the sizable pile already on the blush-pink satin duvet covering the canopied bed, and marched back to the wardrobe to make another selection.

Midway through the evening Joe said, "I'm about done in, Randall. Are you ready to leave?"

"Let's take one more swing around. I wouldn't want to miss anyone important," Randall answered as she brushed imaginary lint from his satin lapel. At that moment they noticed a stocky, dour-looking fellow with a ruddy complexion and a stiff, military gait approaching them purposefully.

"Well, if he don't look like a bull with britches on. What do you think he wants?" Randall whispered.

Before Joe could reply, the man had reached them. "Pardon my intrusion, miss," he said to Randall in a clipped, formal voice. "His Highness has asked me to deliver this message." From his breast pocket he removed a creamy vellum envelope.

"Whose Highness are you talking about, sugar?" Randall asked as she ripped open the envelope.

"He requests the favor of your reply," the man said.

The enclosed note card was linen stock embossed with an insignia—a gold crown perched above an intricate script letter *A*. Randall had heard it described by a model she had worked with in London and she recognized it immediately. Written in a loose-fingered script, it read, "Whenever I saw you tonight, I was warmed by your glow. I would be honored if you would join me for a cocktail so I might claim the privilege of knowing you. If you are so inclined, Edmund will escort you to my car. I await your reply." It was signed, "Prince A."

"What is it, Randall?" Joe asked, impatient to leave.

"Joe, honey, it's an invitation," she said, handing him the card. Randall had been fancied by lots of intriguing men, but she had yet to meet a royal, and the prospect made her twitch with excitement. And this one was a bachelor, who was supposed to be fun, too. "Edmund, would you excuse us for one little minute?"

"Certainly, miss." He moved a discreet distance away and turned his back.

Randall purred, "Joe, you know I think you're the sweetest thing in the world . . ."

"But you're going with Edmund. Is that it, Randall?" Joe knew where she was heading as soon as he read the note.

"It's not every day a girl gets to meet a prince. You understand, don't you, sugar?"

"Oh, I understand."

"I'll call you." She kissed his cheek, then turned, smoothed her skirt, and walked toward Edmund.

Joe laughed to himself. *It's perfect*, he thought. In Randall's game it was simple—a prince outranked a model, a wealthy jeweler, or the two combined, any day. As he strolled toward the exit, he decided that it was time to fold his hand with Randall and call it quits.

Once Randall and her indefatigable social energy were removed from his schedule, Joe found himself spending more time sculpting. He also discovered that adapting to Lizzie's crazy hours was no longer as problematic as it had been.

Three weeks after Randall's exit, on Lizzie's Wednesday night off, he cooked dinner in her apartment. With her air conditioner broken, his task was made more arduous by the sweltering August heat. After eating, they escaped to the nearly empty Paris streets in search of a breeze. They wandered through Beaubourg and stopped in a café in Les Halles for a *citron pressé*. The heat was so oppressive that even the ever-present mimes and jugglers had disappeared.

"They've probably gone to the movies. At least they're air-conditioned!" Lizzie said.

"Well, we could do that, or we could ride the Métro until it stops running," Joe teased.

"I'm melting, but there's something really intriguing about Paris as a ghost town," she responded.

They passed the imposing steel-and-glass Centre Pompideau and found themselves on the rue de St. Merri, in front of the whimsical and decidedly odd St. Phalle Fountain.

"Parisians are smart to leave town in August," Joe said.

Lizzie looked furtively over her shoulder, then said, "Why don't you go in the fountain? You'll certainly cool off."

"Because I'm sure it's against the law," Joe replied.

"There's no one here but me, and I won't turn you in. Go ahead," Lizzie said.

"You're nuts!"

"If you go in, I'll go in. I dare you!"

Joe had never been able to resist a dare. He had climbed trees, been chased by a growling Doberman, and even bitten a worm in half, all because he couldn't back away from a challenge. "You're on!" he said, removing his shoes. Moments later, Joe had climbed over the brightly colored serpents and snails that floated on the pool's surface, and stood under the spray from the preposterous creature at the fountain's center. "Come on, Lizzie, this feels great! It's your turn!"

"I changed my mind! Besides, you saw me all wet the first time we met," Lizzie giggled and dashed across the deserted plaza.

Joe, soaking wet, burst into laughter as he watched her run away. "Lizzie! You're the craziest girl I've ever met! And I love you!"

"You what?" Lizzie shouted back, not believing she had heard him correctly.

"You're crazy and I love you!" he repeated.

Joe covered the space between them in long, dripping strides, swept Lizzie into his arms, and whirled her around the square until they were both dizzy and wet.

In October, Lizzie received a promotion at GNSN. She still did the same job, but now she worked Sunday through Thursday nights, giving her weekends off. She and Joe spent as much time together as they could manage, and occasionally they were even able to see Brett, who was pleased that her two friends were so happy.

They continued the habit she and Lizzie had begun of meeting for breakfast. Since it was before Brett and Joe started their day and after Lizzie finished hers, their petit dejeuners required little coordination.

But mostly, Joe and Lizzie used their idle hours to learn about each other. They established an easy rhythm. No one led and no one followed, but their timing was instinctive and they never seemed out of step. When they first made love, Joe had been surprised to learn Lizzie was a virgin. With all of her bravado and saucy repartee, he had never suspected, but Joe was more touched by her innocence than he had dreamed possible, and he vowed to himself that he would never betray the trust that Lizzie had so openly placed in him.

Brett had invited Joe and Lizzie for Thanksgiving dinner. The autumn holiday was not celebrated in France, but the one year she had skipped what marked for her the beginning of the winter holiday season, Brett had felt homesick and out of sorts. This year, Thanksgiving fell on Lawrence's birthday, and even though she had gotten over much of the hurt, she welcomed the timely diversion. Dinner had to be on time because Lizzie, in spite of her promotion, did not have enough seniority at the station to warrant a holiday off if it was her scheduled day to work.

Brett painstakingly prepared all of the traditional dishes and carefully followed the recipes Hilda, Aunt Lillian's housekeeper, had sent. The meal went off without a hitch, and Lizzie made it to GNSN on time.

"You look sad," her supervisor observed when he poked his head into her cubbyhole.

"Oh, it's nothing. I just don't feel like working tonight," Lizzie responded, looking up from the copy she was rewriting for the third time.

Half an hour later, her supervisor summoned her to his office. "Lizzie, I have a story for you to cover—on camera," he said gravely.

"On camera?" Lizzie questioned.

"Hear me out. You may not want this assignment." He explained that Elissa Ysabel, a member of Lifeforce, the radical environmental group, wanted to confess. She ranked high on the most-wanted lists of law enforcement agencies throughout the world. Ysabel was ready to admit to her participation in the kidnapping and murder of the CEO of ANSO Oil in Alaska, the bombing that killed the president of Universal Electric in Denver, and the simultaneous explosions at the Clermont-Ferrand chemical plants in Paris and Marseilles. "She stipulated that the authorities not be notified until after the interview, and that the reporter must be female. She's given us thirty minutes to respond, and you're the only woman on duty tonight with on-camera experience. But I want you to know, you're free to tell me to take a hike. This assignment could be dangerous," he finished.

Lizzie hesitated only briefly. "I'll do it. Who's my cameraman and where am I going?" This was a golden opportunity, and Lizzie knew she couldn't turn it down.

Three hours later, she emerged from an abandoned building in the twentieth arrondissement, near the Père Lachaise Cemetery. She picked up the microphone, took a deep breath, and nodded to her cameraman.

"This is Liz Powell with a GNSN exclusive. Elissa Ysabel is dead. Moments ago, the unrepentant member of Lifeforce confessed to her involvement in violent retaliatory acts against what Ysabel called, and I quote, 'environmental fascists.' But before our crew left the ramshackle interview site here on the rue Ligner, we heard the sound of a muffled gunshot. Her lifeless body was discovered, gun in hand . . ."

One week later, Liz Powell was an official correspondent with GNSN. Again her promotion did not change her hours, but it did come with a healthy raise in salary. As a general assignment reporter, she was not given a regular beat, but dispatched to cover any stories that broke overnight. She received a written commendation from the network's president for her outstanding coverage of the Ysabel story, and even Randolph Peck offered his congratulations, as well as a few tips on how she could improve her style and delivery. Lizzie accepted his comments graciously, because despite all the praise, she knew she still had a lot to learn.

In mid-February, right after Valentine's Day, Joe moved in with Lizzie. He kept his place across town because his landlady would not let him rent the studio in the cellar unless he continued to pay for the attic room. They adjusted easily to cohabitation, and by spring, when Lizzie was bumped to days, the apartment had finally been decorated and Joe had refinished the chiffonier.

In April, Joe was signed to another modeling contract, this time for Monsieur, a men's fragrance line. The exclusive three-year agreement called for Joe to appear in four ads and four commercials per year touting Monsieur products, from cologne and talc to facial cleanser and body bracer. In return, he received an annual six-figure compensation and the rest of his time was his own, as long as he worked for no other client. The arrangement suited him perfectly.

Joe had finally gotten what he wanted: the time and money to sculpt. He completed several pieces that had been unfinished for more than two years, and in June, Brett arranged for his first show with the owner of a small gallery she frequented in Montmartre. She used her clout with the press to get the show reviewed, and the critics who attended the two-day exhibition had written favorably about "a promising new talent." He even made three sales. Joe could hardly believe that someone other than a friend owned a "Joseph Tate."

"We were going to tell you over dinner, but I can't wait," Lizzie beamed. She and Joe, hand in hand, were perched on the wrought-iron settee on Brett's terrace, looking like two cats who had shared a canary. The sun had already dipped below the rooftops and a faint orange glow outlined the horizon.

"What's the scoop?" Brett looked at them expectantly.

"Lizzie's been offered a correspondent's position in New York. What did your bureau chief call it—an opportunity to move into the network's front lines," Joe announced proudly.

"Fantastic! Lizzie, that's great news. You've worked hard. I guess you'll be racking up a lot of air miles, Joe."

"That's the other thing we have to tell you." Lizzie looked at Joe, her eyes full of a love that knew no boundaries. Then she looked warmly at Brett, the friend with whom she had shared all the important moments of her life. "Joe and I—gee, I haven't said this out loud yet. Brett, Joe and I are going to get married."

Brett wasn't surprised. She knew Lizzie and Joe were right for each other. Brett knew firsthand the meanness and trickery that could be committed in the name of love and marriage, but she was sure that no two people could do more justice to the spirit of wedlock. Lizzie was the sister in whose company Brett had found her way to womanhood, and looking at her now, thick tears of joy emerged at the corners of Brett's eyes. "You two . . . this is the best news!" Brett and Lizzie hugged, sharing a moment of pure, untainted happiness.

"You know, this is all your fault," Joe said, looking at Brett.

"And I can't thank you enough!" He put his arms around them both.

"And Brett, you know I can't do this without you as my maid of honor," Lizzie added.

Brett smiled through her tears. "Of course you can't! I wouldn't miss it for the world!"

— *Chapter 18* —

"Aren't you even a little nervous?" Brett asked Lizzie as she straightened the chapel train of her gown one final time, setting it toward its course down the aisle.

"I've never felt calmer or more sure of anything in my life. I just feel elated." Lizzie was radiant. Her gown was a frothy white organdy fantasy, with a décolleté neckline accented by delicate pink rosebuds. Her natural blond ringlets, tamed on all workdays, now framed her face, and the hair at her temples was swept to the top of her head and secured by a cluster of pink rosebuds from which a tulle veil exploded and hung down to her waist.

In the hallway, just outside the Trianon Room at the Waldorf Astoria, Lizzie, Brett, and Lizzie's father, who smoothed his hair and straightened his bow tie nervously, waited for their cue. Joe's brother, Gregory, had just come to seat Mrs. Powell, who made no attempt to stem the stream of quiet, happy tears that had been flowing down her cheeks since she had fastened the twenty-two covered buttons that traced the back of Lizzie's gown. "There were buttons just like this on your christening gown," she reminisced and the first droplet trickled from her eye.

The months since Joe and Lizzie's return to New York had passed in a flurry of job adjustments, apartment hunting, and wedding plans, and no one could believe that the second Saturday in May had actually arrived.

Lizzie arranged a petal of her bouquet—a cascade of white tea roses, sweetheart roses of the palest, gentlest pink, and stephanotis, bordered with graceful tendrils of ivy and lacy baby's breath—then lifted it to enjoy the delicate scent.

When the strains of Chopin's Prelude in E Minor changed to Pachelbel's Canon signaling that the time had come for Brett to proceed down the aisle, she reached for Lizzie's hand, squeezed it, and gave her a final wink. She then finger-combed her wavy ponytail, which was secured with a rose grosgrain bow that matched her gown—a bias-cut slip of silk faille, with a neckline that draped softly from slightly dropped sleeves and scooped dramatically to the center of her back. Clutching the nosegay of Highland heather and irises, she nodded to the wedding coordinator, indicating she was ready. When the door was opened, all heads on both sides of the aisle turned expectantly in her direction, and the first flashbulbs popped before she could step into the room.

This was the part of the ceremony Brett dreaded most. When all was said and done, she still preferred to be out of the limelight—the photographer, not the subject. She breathed deeply, controlling her urge to cover the distance to the arbor in several brisk strides. Instead, she examined the room. Rays of evening sun shone through the ceiling-high windows like spotlights. A sky-blue carpet, criss-crossed by a white trellis pattern festooned with blossoms, marked her path and led to the flower-laden bower under which the white-vested minister waited.

When she proceeded a bit farther, she caught a glimpse of Joe, hands clasped at his back. Looking princely in his tux, black tie, and cummerbund, he waited, unruffled, for his bride.

This is the fairy tale wedding that Lizzie has dreamed about since we were girls, Brett thought, and it seemed fitting. Lizzie's life seemed scripted as a happy-ever-after tale that started with a close and devoted family and proceeded through teen years blessed by good friends and happy times. As an adult, hard work, talent, and the right breaks led to a promising career, and the circle was completed by a wonderful man to share her life with.

Brett found the scales of her own life wildly out of balance. Her career flourished on one side, while a personal life fraught with abandonment, disappointment, and heartache languished on the other. Ever since her childhood, personal happiness had been elusive and ephemeral, and she had convinced herself that it wasn't necessary. Working could provide her with all the fulfillment she needed. But ever since Joe and Lizzie had departed, she had felt insistent pangs of emptiness, and she questioned whether she could continue in such isolation.

At the end of the aisle she shook herself from her depressing thoughts in time to flash Joe a tender smile before reaching her place, where she turned to wait for Lizzie. As she faced about, she caught sight of David, sitting to the left of Mrs. Powell. It had been more than seven years since she had seen him last. His mustache was gone and now he wore tortoiseshell spectacles, but aside from that, he looked the same. It was his demeanor that had changed. David held his weeping mother's hand and stared straight ahead. There was a slight, polite smile on his lips, but his eyes were distant, as though focused on something unseen by anyone else present. She knew he was happy for his sister, but Brett sensed how painful this wedding was for him. She tried to catch his eye, hoping to impart a look that said she understood. He had been so kind to her that night at Cox Cove. Instinctively, he had known there was nothing he could do except be there, and she wanted to do the same for him now, but his gaze remained fixed on the invisible specter.

A jubilant burst from four trumpets sounded the start of Purcell's Trumpet Voluntary. An excited murmur passed through the guests as they stood and craned their necks, anxious for their first view of the bride. After the opening flourish, the back doors were thrown open again and Brett was startled to see that Lizzie's face had become a stony mask. She wore a stiff, enigmatic smile, but in her eyes, Brett could see abject terror. Lizzie held her father's arm tightly, as if only his support kept her from falling, and the bouquet in her other hand shook.

She was fine just a minute ago, Brett thought, watching the slow progress. She hoped Lizzie wouldn't faint before she reached the end of the aisle.

Brett noticed that Joe also watched Lizzie with concern. When she and her father came to a halt, Joe stepped toward her, and as soon as his eyes met hers, the fear and panic drained away. From then on, the ceremony went beautifully.

After the wedding the guests moved on to the reception next door and when Joe and Lizzie entered the pale blue and gold room there was a burst of spontaneous applause, and the ten-piece band switched from "Satin Doll" to "It Had To Be You." The bride and groom led the dance, followed onto the floor by the parents, Brett, and Joe's brother. Waiters hovered about the periphery until the music stopped and then began passing trays of champagne and hors d'oeuvres.

Brett was escorted to the bridal table by Gregory, whom she had discovered to be an excellent dancer. He asked pertinent questions about Brett's photography, and Brett inquired about his wife Helen and their three children, and was promptly regaled with a family anecdote. She could tell that Joe and Lizzie would be a while making it through the throng of well-wishers, so she excused herself to Gregory, grabbed a glass of champagne from a passing server, and began to circulate.

She found Lillian, who was fully recovered, looking splendid in a royal purple tea-length dress. "For a minute there, I thought Lizzie might swoon!" Lillian chuckled.

"I know, I thought the same thing," Brett said.

"The compliments are supposed to go to the bride, but you look lovely, child."

Brett had been at the hotel the entire day, and had dressed there, as well, so this was her aunt's first opportunity to see her in wedding splendor. When she saw Brett appear in the doorway, Lillian had considered for the first time the day her niece would be a bride, and she wondered if there was anyone special in Brett's life.

"Thank you. The great thing about this dress is that I really can wear it again!"

"Mrs. Cox, how nice to see you again," David said cordially as he joined them. "And Brett, I hardly recognized you. Congratulations on your success. Lizzie keeps me informed."

"Well, even if she didn't talk about her big brother all the time, the press would have kept me informed about you. I'm glad Hands On is doing so well." *I feel like I'm talking to a casual acquaintance,* Brett thought. She had known David all her life, had always spoken to him like he was family, but now he seemed detached, isolated by a moat, and she did not know the password that brought down the bridge allowing entry. "Wasn't Lizzie a beautiful bride? She didn't look at all like an inchworm! And I love Joe like a brother—he'll be a great addition to your family." As soon as the words were out of her mouth, David appeared to withdraw. His eyes glazed, and she knew he was thinking about the family he had lost. Brett wanted to say she was sorry, for his tragedy and for her thoughtless remark, but she realized this was not the time or place.

David returned to the present and began to explain in exacting detail the specifics of a new computer he was developing for home use that would respond to voice commands. For ten minutes he maneuvered the subject as far away from family as he could, and Brett could see that for David, talking about work was his means of escape from the anguish he still suffered. "Your glass is empty. Can I get you a refill?" he asked.

Brett wanted to say yes, but the stilted small talk and awkward pauses were too disturbing, and she wanted to get away. She spied a former classmate across the room and decided to relieve them both from courteous social banter. "Thanks, but I see an old friend over there. We worked on the *Daltonian* together, and I'd like to say hello." She placed her hand gently on his arm and said, "See you later."

Brett walked away, remembering the feelings she used to have for David. Yes, they had started as a schoolgirl crush, but more than that, she had always admired him. David always had all the answers, a simple solution to your problem, but now they were all adults. The questions were complex and the answers elusive if there were answers at all.

Lizzie and Joe departed two days after the wedding for their two-week honeymoon in Japan, but before leaving, they called Brett to thank her for the antique Chinese painted leather wedding chest she had given them.

"I was pleased to receive your telex." Phoebe Caswell, still the senior fashion editor of *Vogue*, lifted the ruby glass pitcher from the credenza, poured mint tea into a tumbler, and handed it to Brett.

Two months before leaving for the wedding, Brett had decided it was time to test the waters and see how much leverage her European work would give her in New York, traditionally the toughest market for a photographer to crack. She had a mailer printed showing six of her best tears, and a month before her departure, she sent it to several editors, along with a cover letter highlighting her print credits, and informing them of her upcoming visit and her desire to make an appointment to show her portfolio.

A week before her arrival she telexed, reminding them of the mailing, and as soon as she reached Lillian's apartment, she called their editorial offices.

Of the twenty packets she had mailed, ten editors were not seeing anyone new, but said she could send cards if she liked. Brett could leave her book for three of them, and they would look at it if they got a chance. Three others were on location and would not return until Brett had already gone back to Paris. And one claimed to have received neither the letter nor the telex, but told her that book drop-off was the first Thursday of each month.

Carter Benedict-Howe, the editor and publisher of *CLOZ*, a new quarterly that covered fashion generated "on the street, not in the showroom," agreed to meet Brett at his editorial offices in a storefront on Second Street and Avenue A in the East Village. Benedict-Howe, the son of an investment banker and a Princeton philosophy professor, wore his blond hair shaved from his temples, meeting in a vee at the back of his head. The front was long and flopped over one eye. He dismissed Brett's work as "too focused on grandiose status quo materialism" for his purposes.

Much to Brett's surprise, Phoebe Caswell had also given her an appointment. She had spoken to Phoebe only twice since leaving Malcolm, both times at functions connected with the collections, and both times, she had had the feeling that Phoebe had no idea who she was.

"You're doing very well in Europe," Phoebe intoned in her measured silvery voice. She wore a black linen minidress with bold pewter jewelry and sat with her hands loosely folded on top of the glass-and-black marble pedestal that served as her desk. Aside from the telephone—a red rectangle with forty buttons from which she could summon staff with just a push of her slender, perfectly manicured finger—only a Steuben bud vase, holding a single American Beauty rose, marred the shimmering expanse of glass. The entire office was red and black, Phoebe's favorite colors. Crimson walls lined with photographs of Phoebe with models, movie stars, and heads of state, melded into matching plush carpet. All of the furniture—black, neoteric modular units—was designed for form, not function, and sat low to the floor, save Phoebe's desk chair, an enormous tufted red leather throne salvaged from an about-to-be-razed castle in Scotland. Phoebe's real work space was through the connecting door. A metal desk stacked with galleys and typeset copy, a light table littered with slides, and a wall unit with forty little boxes, each corresponding to the same staff members as on her telephone, remained hidden from public view.

"Yes, I am, thank you. And I'm interested in . . ." Brett began from her seat, which was at least six inches lower than Phoebe's.

"Of course, it's so easy to get work overseas," Phoebe interrupted. "There are so many little magazines that think they're trendy. I even imagine some think they're on the cutting edge. Amusing concept, wouldn't you say?" Phoebe did not give Brett a chance to answer. She leaned back in her chair, crossed her slim legs, and continued. "I remember you scurrying around Malcolm's studio. I always thought you had the potential to be a model. I might even have booked you myself. But when I spoke to Malcolm about it, he told me you were determined to become a photographer and not to bother suggesting a diet or an agency. From the looks of it, he was right."

"Malcolm had me pegged from the beginning. I got my first camera when I was ten, and discovered rather quickly that I wanted to be behind the lens, not in front of it."

"Dear, eccentric Malcolm has always been perceptive. I'm expecting him shortly to discuss our trip to the Maldives." Phoebe rose from her throne, walked around to the front of her desk, and extended her hand. "Thank you for dropping by. It was lovely to see you. By the way, that's a ravishing suit. Armani? Do call when you're in the city again."

Brett took the proffered hand, realizing that her meeting was over. As she walked toward the massive red door, Brett wondered why Phoebe had even bothered to see her, since she hadn't looked at her work. Why should she call when she was in the city again—so they could have tea?

"I'm sorry, excuse me," she said, almost bumping into a man who exited the elevator. "Malcolm!" Brett exclaimed, giving her mentor a bear hug. Malcolm's brown hair was almost completely gray and he appeared thinner than when she had seen him last. Although it was a warm day, he wore a black turtleneck, black trousers, and a black leather bomber jacket.

"Well, this is a surprise. You're the last person I expected to see here. I thought you were the queen of Paris!"

Brett sensed an edge in his voice. "I was going to call you this afternoon. Are you free for drinks later?"

"Sorry, babycakes, I have plans. How long have you been here?" he asked. But what he really wanted to know was, how many of my clients have you seen?

"Almost a week. I came for a wedding and thought I'd combine a little business with pleasure."

Malcolm knew how long she had been in New York. He'd seen her mailer on Phoebe's secretary's desk a week ago and recognized her work immediately. When the secretary went to the ladies' room, he had picked up the folder and examined the contents, including the cover letter. "How about tomorrow night?" he asked, knowing that was impossible.

"I'm leaving tomorrow, but I'll take a rain check. I'm planning to come home more often. Strange as it sounds, I think I miss New York!"

"Well, Phoebe is waiting. Call me." He gave her a hasty double-miss kiss and was gone.

It's not time yet, Malcolm thought as he walked toward Phoebe's office. He had known Brett would be a major talent, but he hadn't expected her to blossom so quickly. Malcolm was still at the zenith of his career, and he did not welcome competition from one so gifted. He had planned the whole scenario in his mind. When he tired of the grind of fashion, Brett would take his place. He could claim credit for discovering and nurturing her, then he would take off to Machu Picchu and photograph the ruins of the ancient Incan city he had read about as a boy, leaving Brett as his legacy to the world of fashion.

"What was that little bitch doing here?" he demanded of Phoebe. "What did you say to her? Did you offer her work?" After their very first meeting, Malcolm never again sat in the chair opposite Phoebe's desk. If they were not meeting in a conference room, he always took a seat that made conversation nearly impossible unless Phoebe joined him or shouted across the room. This time he perched on the edge of a divan across the office from her.

"Malcolm, don't be in such a dither. We had tea and talked a bit. Her work is quite good . . ." Phoebe needled, ". . . but not as good as yours," she offered smoothly and sat down beside him.

"You bet your high-class ass it isn't," he grumbled.

After all these years, Phoebe was used to Malcolm's vulgarities. "You have nothing to be concerned about—there's only one Malcolm Kent. Although she did have four covers last month," Phoebe added. She enjoyed these rare opportunities to put Malcolm off his mark. *He's such a prima donna*, she thought. Malcolm's work was still fabulous, but lately it had shown a static quality. The freshness and innovation that had made every picture new and exciting was waning and he hadn't been looking very well. Phoebe was certain that either his rigorous nightlife or the strain of maintaining two personas was exacting its toll, and she intended to hedge her bets. She had been noncommittal with Brett because she was not ready to act. Brett's tears in *Voilà!* had attracted Phoebe's attention the moment they appeared, and she had made it her business to track her career. Phoebe estimated she had at least fifteen more years as editor of the magazine, but she also knew she couldn't count on Malcolm's continuing inspiration. She needed a reserve, a "photographer in waiting," whose genius and creativity would secure her own undisputed position as a leader in the fickle world of fashion for as long as she wanted it. And Brett Larsen showed the potential to be that photographer.

Brett sat in the back of a taxi that was slowly wending its way through the gridlocked intersection at Madison and Fifty-seventh, still trying to figure out what had happened in Phoebe's office. Phoebe had given her an appointment, then avoided talking about her work. Malcolm had behaved strangely, too. He really didn't look well, she thought—maybe that was it. Then she wondered if he was upset because she hadn't called him. Frustrated, she paid the fare and bolted from the cab at Seventh Avenue, heading uptown on foot, her unopened portfolio tucked under her arm. Before she turned onto Central Park West, the sky filled with threatening thunderclouds and the warm late spring air turned cool. She entered the San Remo lobby just as the first big drops began to pelt the sidewalk.

"You should hurry upstairs, Miss Larsen," the doorman said as one of the other residents approached him with instructions about a package she was expecting.

Brett nodded her thanks. It was nice of him to be concerned that I might be wet, she thought as she rode up to the sixteenth floor.

The door opened before she could put her key in the lock. Hilda stood wringing her hands and looking distraught. "Oh, Miss Brett, we didn't know where you were. It's Mrs. Cox—she's had a heart attack. She was sitting up there, painting away," Hilda pointed to the balcony, "and then I heard a crash. I came running from the kitchen and there she was, passed out cold."

"Where is she?" Brett cried. "She's not . . ."

"No, miss. I called the doctor and 911 and they got here right away and took her to the hospital. The doctor said I should wait for you, because they wouldn't let me see her anyway, me not being family and all." Hilda's tears finally spilled over.

Brett didn't remember how she got to the hospital. She supposed Albert must have driven her, but for two days she waited while Lillian drifted in and out of consciousness. The rules of the cardiac care unit only allowed Brett a ten-minute visit every two hours, but she refused to leave the floor. She catnapped and, when forced to by the nurses, nibbled fruit for sustenance. She had tracked her grandfather down in Sydney, Australia, and while he had registered concern, he made no mention of plans to come see his sister, although he promised to call frequently for updates on her condition.

Family members of other CCU patients struck up brief conversations, but for all of them, talk was a vain attempt to relieve tension.

On the third day, Lillian seemed better, and Brett was allowed twenty minutes with her. She sat at her aunt's side, gently stroking her fingers. Lillian lay in one of eight beds arranged around the circular wall of the CCU. The backs of both her hands were pierced by intravenous catheters. Electrodes on her chest, back, and arms fed a constant stream of data into the electrocardiograph monitor and an oxygen mask covered her face as a machine labored to provide her with air. Lillian was in pain but awake, and she responded to Brett's touch with a slight flutter of her fingertips. Brett looked lovingly at her aunt, wishing she could take some of the pain away. She felt a hand on her shoulder and turned to find Dr. Hathaway, Lillian's cardiologist.

"I'd like to speak with you, Miss Larsen." Brett followed him to the center nurse's station. "Your aunt is recovering nicely, but the tests show that she is suffering from blockage in two of the arteries that lead to the heart. As soon as she has regained some of her strength, we plan to perform double bypass surgery."

"Isn't that dangerous?" Brett asked anxiously.

"Not as dangerous as allowing her condition to remain as is. If we don't operate, she's guaranteed to have another heart attack— one she might not survive. I have informed her of this, and while she is too weak to respond, she does understand the gravity and immediacy of the situation."

Dr. Hathaway explained the procedure and what Brett could expect during Lillian's recuperation. He patiently answered all of her questions, then asked the nurse for her aunt's chart and began making notations.

Brett went over to Lillian, who had drifted off to sleep, and her eyes brimmed with tears. She turned and ran from the unit. Her entire body shook, and she knew it was the preamble to the dam breaking. She shoved open the fire door that led to the stairwell just as she was overcome with racking sobs. Brett had never felt so alone and desolate. When she could weep no more, she just sat on the cold concrete steps and prayed.

That night Brett went home. She sat in the middle of her bed, her back against a mound of pillows, absently stirring the bowl of soup Hilda had prepared. She tried to count the pink stripes on the wallpaper. It was a game she had invented as a child. If she could get to fifty without losing count, she won—only she never figured out the prize. Her room, now occupied only on visits, hadn't changed. Lillian had offered, but Brett was adamant that it remain the same.

She loved this room. It had been decorated to foster creativity in a child. Low bookshelves were still crammed with wondrous tales of mystery, fantasy, and adventure; the small easel and drawing pad stood in the corner; a shadow box held the shells she had collected at Cox Cove; and the dull finish on the table by the window was courtesy of her efforts with modeling clay and plaster of paris. She relished the hours she had spent here. It was so different from her room at Barbara's. Her mother had filled her room with toys and stuffed animals from F.A.O. Schwartz, antique porcelain dolls, and pictures of ballerinas and fairies, and Brett was always confused as to which toys were to play with and which were for show.

Brett put her tray aside, walked over to the phonograph, and played *The Nutcracker*, one of her childhood favorites. Sven had called today and said he would come to New York when Lillian had her surgery. *How considerate of him*, Brett thought. She had asked Hilda to phone Barbara and inform her of Aunt Lillian's status. Her mother had said only, "How unfortunate for her." And that,

Brett realized, covered her family. She had Lizzie and Joe, of course, but they were in Japan on their honeymoon. Fleetingly, she wondered what had become of Brian and Zachary. Surely Zachary was out of prison by now, and late one night in Paris, when she had been unable to sleep, she had been startled to see Brian in reruns of "Hollywood Private Eye" on French television.

Most of the night she slept fitfully, and when the dawn broke and tinted her room with a rosy glow, Brett had been awake for an hour. Thérèse was the first person she informed of her decision. "I know this is sudden, but I have made up my mind and I'd like you to come with me," she had said. She would have preferred to tell her in person, but there were many things that could be done before she returned to Paris. Future bookings had to be canceled, an equipment inventory taken, and estimates of moving expenses ordered. Besides, Brett wanted to give Thérèse plenty of notice and the opportunity to seriously consider moving to the States.

The usually unflappable Thérèse was caught off guard, but she took it in stride. "I will think about it and let you know. It is very complicated, you know, to move to America."

Brett immediately thought of Jeffrey Underwood. If anyone could facilitate this whole process, he could. "I know someone who can take care of everything," she had told Thérèse.

— *Chapter 19* —

"Brett, your great-aunt's illness is most regrettable, but people tell me that Dr. Hathaway is the most distinguished physician in his field. Your grandfather will arrive from Australia tomorrow afternoon and be driven directly to the hospital to meet you." Jeffrey

Underwood rolled a speckled gray Waterman fountain pen between his fingers as he spoke.

Brett, seated near him at the marquetry conference table, nodded her head wearily. Her eyelids felt leaden, so she swiveled her forest-green leather chair from side to side in an effort to stay attentive in the somber quiet of the darkly paneled room at Larsen's New York headquarters. She avoided catching her reflection in the gilt-edged mirror that hung on the wall at Jeffrey's back. Brett needed no reminders of how exhausted she looked.

"You may banish from your mind any worries concerning your relocation. The procedure will be the same as it was in Paris. Acquisitions will schedule viewing as soon as you are ready. It will also locate an apartment for your office manager, Miss Diot, as soon as she arrives.

"Personnel will obtain the necessary documentation for Therésè Diot and channel it through my office to you."

He speaks like he's got a checklist in his head, Brett thought, but she was grateful for Jeffrey's efficiency. "You have no idea what a relief it is not to have this to worry about. With the surgery tomorrow, I only have this afternoon to get a lot of wheels in motion. And that means I should be going. I appreciate your making time to see me today." Brett slipped the strap of her bag over her shoulder and prepared to stand.

"Brett, there is one further matter to discuss."

"What is that?" she asked.

Jeffrey retrieved a blue report binder from a long drawer in the table in front of him and placed it before her. "Your grandfather is aware that this is a stressful time for you, but Mrs. Cox's sudden illness impressed upon him the need to make known to you his plans regarding his estate. He feels that in this way any questions can be answered and oversights addressed, thus averting confusion and misinterpretation."

"Dammit, whatever he wants to do with his money is fine. I don't want to know this!" Brett shoved the folder back at Jeffrey. She was furious. *My grandfather doesn't have a heart, he has a vault*, she thought. *His sister could die, and all he thinks about is his money.*

"Please bear with me a few minutes. We can speak in generalities now and have more specific discussions at another, more convenient time," Jeffrey suggested.

Brett closed her eyes for several seconds and took a deep breath. Jeffrey Underwood had always been helpful and courteous, and he was not responsible for the fact that most of her family was selfish and insensitive. She didn't want to yell at him.

"Can I get you something before we continue? Some water, or a mint, perhaps?" Jeffrey removed a red and white tin of Altoid Mints from his jacket pocket and offered them to her.

Brett exhaled. "Thank you, you're very kind." She placed the white disk on her tongue. Immediately it began to dissolve, dispersing the chalky, strong bitter-mint taste in her mouth. "Please continue."

"As you know from your own recent experience, drafting a will means that you must envision the future in light of the present, become part logician and part clairvoyant, if you will." Jeffrey clasped his hands, laid his forearms on the table, and leaned closer to Brett. "In any case, your grandfather has determined that the future would be best served by leaving the bulk of his holdings to you. Your mother, Mrs. North, will be provided for as part of the document. Mr. Larsen and Mrs. Cox have an earlier agreement that neither will include the other in his will.

"That blue binder is for you. It is an accounting of Mr. Larsen's personal holdings which, as of the latest quarter, total almost two and a half billion dollars."

"What?" Brett asked incredulously.

"The sum sounds a bit overwhelming, but at your convenience, please acquaint yourself with the information in the report. We can go over the holdings at another time," Jeffrey replied.

"Jeffrey, let me be frank with you. I have developed no more of an aptitude for high finances than I had at our first meeting in Paris, and I can't possibly think about it now."

"This isn't the time to concern yourself with these details. For now, just take the binder. When it is appropriate, all of the information it contains will be made clear for you. You've managed your own business admirably, and eventually, you will understand the workings of this one. Your grandfather does not expect you to take a leadership position. He has seen to it that the management of Larsen Enterprises will pass into capable hands, but all of this can wait until another day."

"Sure, fine." Brett gathered her bag and stood to leave. Her head throbbed over her left eye as though a demon pounded from inside with a sharp, metal hammer.

"Don't forget this," Jeffrey said, handing her the blue binder. Brett slipped it under her arm. "Allow me to see you to the elevator." Jeffrey opened the door, which was only distinguishable from the wall by the brass knob, and they left the room.

When Brett had gone, Jeffrey padded down the maroon-carpeted hall toward the conference room, but instead entered the darkened office next door and flicked on the light.

"Turn it off!" Sven Larsen roared, still wedged in the leather desk chair from which he had monitored Jeffrey's meeting with Brett through a two-way mirror.

Jeffrey hit the switch before Sven's words had fully left his lips. A sliver of light cut through the narrow space between drawn draperies and silhouetted the immense, black-clad form.

"Even she behaves as if wealth miraculously rejuvenates itself —as if it is too bothersome to maintain what I am giving her on a velvet pillow!" he fumed, thumping the chair arm rhythmically with his clenched fist.

"Your granddaughter is quite resourceful and industrious, Mr. Larsen. She is doing well in her profession," Jeffrey said, his disembodied voice emerging from the shadowy far side of the room.

"Taking pictures, painting pictures—hah! How can you call those things professions?! Nobody *needs* a picture! There is no *power* in making pictures!" Sven brooded for an instant, then continued, with venom in his voice. "It appears that she is not a spineless, whimpering strumpet like her mother, but I will not see everything I have sweat blood to build crumble and blow away like so much sand! Larsen Enterprises must pass into Larsen hands. Jeffrey, turn on the light."

The fluorescent beams seemed brighter than the sun after the blackness. Sven wheeled his chair around to face Jeffrey, who stood squarely, waiting.

"Jeffrey, I have observed you closely for the last ten years. You are smart, pragmatic, unflinching. You do what is necessary to get the job done. You are very much like me."

"Thank you, Mr. Larsen," Jeffrey said firmly, never breaking the eye contact they had maintained since there was light to see.

In a conspiratorial voice, Sven continued, "My granddaughter will be a very wealthy woman one day. A smart man would make it his business to marry such a woman, to have children. Sons by such a woman would ensure his future." The two Titans, their blue eyes still locked, let a moment pass in silence. "Do I make myself clear?" Sven concluded.

"Quite clear, Mr. Larsen." With a crisp bow of his head, like a knight to his liege, Jeffrey left the room.

When he reached his office suite, two floors above, he conferred with his secretary, signed the letters and documents she had awaiting him, and instructed her to take messages. Then he closed himself in his office.

The cool gray and white of the room created an almost sterile atmosphere. Every legal tome on the two walls of ceiling-high book shelves stood at right angles to the floor. The Scandinavian blond wood desk held only an empty blotter, a white stoneware cup filled with the required number two and a half pencils, and a clear Lucite telephone. The walls were blank, and no photographs or personal mementos were displayed.

Unbuttoning the jacket of his granite gray double-breasted suit, he removed his pen, then flung it carelessly in the seat of his chair. Jeffrey rushed to unlock the bottom drawer of the desk, opening it as far as it would go. He plucked the last, unmarked file, then dug behind the folders to unearth a locked steel box. He brought the folder, the box, and the legal pad from his desk to the charcoal tuxedo sofa across the room. Solemnly, he raised the lid.

Jeffrey fingered the clear plastic encasing each yellowed newspaper clipping that lay atop a stack of folded documents. "I'll get the bastard . . . I'll get them all for you. It won't be long now."

He uncapped his Waterman, dated the top yellow sheet, and began writing notes.

What could be taking so long, Brett thought. Crossword puzzles from each of the city's three daily papers lay at Brett's side, completed. Concentrating on words and tiny squares kept her from imagining the most desperate scenarios. She rose to circle the lobby yet again. She had looked at every item in the hospital gift shop and read all the cards. She had committed to memory the dedications on bronze plaques denoting gifts to the hospital from patrons. Dr. Hathaway had told her the procedure was scheduled for seven o'clock in the morning and should take four to five hours, barring complications, but at quarter to one she had still heard nothing.

Brett had been at the hospital since six o'clock, so she could hold Lillian's hand before she was wheeled off to the operating room. Lillian had looked frail and ashen. "I'll be right here when you wake up," Brett had said, kissing her aunt's forehead. "I know you will, child," Lillian mouthed.

The nurses on duty were courteous, but unable to provide her with any information. Brett tried to remain calm, but as the minutes ticked by, her anxiety mounted.

Shortly after one o'clock, Brett looked up to see Jeffrey Underwood striding into the waiting room.

"What are you doing here? Is something wrong with my grandfather?" Any divergence from the expected now prompted Brett to imagine the worst.

"Nothing serious. Your grandfather phoned to tell me his flight has been detained in Tokyo. Is there anything you need?" he asked, taking the seat next to hers.

"Just to find out how she's doing. The operation is taking so long." Brett's nervousness prompted her to voice the fears she had kept pent up for several days. She needed an ear and Jeffrey listened patiently, offering occasional words of solace. When she was done talking, she lapsed into silence and Jeffrey sat quietly by her side.

At quarter of three, Dr. Hathaway, still dressed in surgical greens, entered the visitors' lounge. Brett sprang from her seat. "How is she?"

The doctor placed a hand on her shoulder. "Your aunt's a real trooper. The procedure went smoothly and she's in recovery. She should be back in her room in two or three hours, and we'll let you come take a peek."

"What took so long?" Brett asked.

"We got an emergency triple bypass in here this morning and our whole schedule was backed up. Mrs. Cox didn't get into the operating room until after ten o'clock."

"Thank you. I'm sorry." Brett tried to blot the tears rolling down her face. Jeffrey handed her his handkerchief.

"It's quite all right, Miss Larsen. Why don't you get a bite to eat?" Dr. Hathaway squeezed her arm. "I've got to get upstairs, but I'll speak with you tomorrow." He hurried down the corridor.

"Oh, Jeffrey—you're still here. I didn't mean to keep you," Brett stammered, only now becoming aware of her surroundings again.

"It's no trouble at all, and it looks like the operation was a success. You must be relieved."

"More than I can explain. I appreciate your company, but I'm fine now. You don't have to stay," she said.

"Would you like some lunch?" Jeffrey asked.

"No, I couldn't eat a thing. I'll just wait here," she replied.

"If the company is no intrusion, please allow me to stay." Their eyes met for a long moment.

"No, I don't mind."

Jeffrey waited with Brett until late in the evening. Shortly after seven o'clock, she was allowed up to the cardiac unit, where Lillian was back in her bed. She was groggy and not yet able to talk, so Brett held one hand and smoothed her hair with the other. Lillian's hospital gown was pulled down low in front, and Brett could see the fine line of the incision, which started below her throat. It was held together on the outside with strips of clear tape.

By the nine o'clock visit, Lillian was sitting up in bed, clutching her pillow. "They want me to cough, but it hurts like the devil," she managed. Then she looked at Brett. "I'll rest better if you go home now, child."

"Okay, but I'll be back early tomorrow."

"You haven't eaten all day, Brett," Jeffrey said as they waited for an elevator. "Let me take you to dinner."

"Not tonight. All I really want to do now is sleep . . . but I'd like to have dinner another time," she replied. She kissed him on the cheek. "Thank you for today. It meant a lot."

Two weeks after Lillian's surgery, Brett left for Paris to close that chapter of her life. Her aunt had protested Brett's decision to return to New York. For Lillian, Brett's move home was a marker. It was a sign that said clearly, in bold print, "you're getting old."

"You don't need to come home to take care of me, child. Your career is just getting started. Besides, I have Hilda and Albert," Lillian had said.

"Listen to me, Aunt Lillian." Brett had taken her aunt's hand, which was still bruised and discolored from the IV, and held it in both of hers. "I know I don't have to do this. My career is portable and I *want* to come home. The Larsens have a pretty bad record for maintaining close family ties, and it has to stop somewhere. I love you—you are my family. I've spent a lot of time envying other people, wishing I had loving parents, and even brothers and sisters. But I can't do anything about that. What I can do is be supportive of the family that's been supportive of me . . . and that's you." It was the first time Brett had seen her aunt cry. They had continued to sit on Lillian's terrace, watching the sun set on the Hudson, holding hands.

Brett went directly from Orly to the studio and was greeted by stacks of neatly labeled boxes. Thérèse had taken the inventory, made a checklist of what items were in the studio and what items had been crated by the moving company. She would use the list to verify that everything had arrived in New York before she signed off on the bill of lading. Since it was more cost-efficient, and Thérèse watched every sou like it was her own, all of the equipment and supplies would be transported by boat, and after clearing customs, would be put in storage until the new studio was ready. Thérèse had coordinated everything with Jeffrey Underwood's office, and one of his staff members would supervise the New York end of the move until Thérèse arrived. She planned to take a month off to spend with her family in Lyon before she departed for the States.

"There's nothing for me to do," Brett said pensively. As she walked through the studio, her footsteps echoed hollowly in the nearly empty space.

"The new tenant moves in next week, and I've hired a crew to clean this place before he moves in." Thérèse had found a photographer who was more than pleased to take over the remainder of Brett's five-year lease.

"Since you have everything under control here, I'm going home. I'm exhausted. And Thérèse, I'm really happy you've decided to give New York a try." Brett took the sheaf of phone messages the young woman handed her and stuffed them into her pocket.

The taxi deposited her on the boulevard St. Germain and she walked the rest of the way. Having left most of the things she had with her in New York, she only had a carry-on bag to manage. As she approached the rue de Bourbon le Château, her pace slowed. For almost six years this had been her home, and she felt a bit melancholy at the thought of leaving. Paris had been an eye-opening experience, and Brett was glad she had taken Malcolm's advice. She *had* learned more than she possibly could have at RISD.

When she opened the door, the Limoges pot swayed gently in the draft and sprinkled its bright red geranium petals on the floor. Once inside her apartment, Brett threw open the balcony doors and raised all the windows. The late morning sun was bright, and a warm breeze billowed the white lace curtains like sails. She had stopped at Boudin on the rue de Buci on her way home. Claude, the owner, had just taken freshly baked loaves of fougasse out of the oven. She had chatted with the baker and his wife and after telling them she was leaving Paris she had jokingly asked, if they shipped the delectable puff pastry bread to her in New York, could they guarantee it would arrive still warm. They had laughed and promised to try.

She put on a pot of coffee and began returning phone calls. From the messages that Thérèse had given her, Brett believed that everyone she had ever met in Paris knew of her impending departure.

By midafternoon, most of the calls had been made and her calendar was filled with lunches and dinners for the week she would be in Paris. Brett kicked off her espadrilles and put her feet up on the hassock in front of her chair. Friends and colleagues were anxious to bid her a personal farewell, even though most of them would be at the party Gabriel was giving on Saturday. Brett was touched by his gesture. Gabriel was known for lavish and outrageous gatherings at the latest Paris hot spots, but this morning he had said, "No, no, this party will be at my home. You are my friend—a real person, not a fashion freak—and I want to give you a proper send-off."

Brett dozed off, feeling warm and contented, and thinking of all the good times she had had since she had come to Europe. Half an hour later she awoke, startled and gasping for air. Her dream had been too real. The movers had come, but they had not seen her sleeping in the chair. They crated and loaded it onto the truck before she woke up. She screamed and banged, but no one could hear her. Just as the huge wooden box was about to be carried into the ship's hold, she heard the lid being pried open. The glaring sunlight flooded her prison and temporarily blinded her. When her vision cleared, there was Jeffrey Underwood.

What a strange dream, Brett thought as she surveyed the room. All of her possessions were in place. *Of course they are*, she thought. She had not wanted to witness the dismembering of her home, and since she paid her rent yearly and had a month left on her lease, Thérèse would supervise the packing here, just as she had done at the studio, but not until Brett was gone.

She padded barefoot into the kitchen and poured herself a glass of mineral water. Glancing at the clock above the stove, she realized that she would have to hurry if she was going to be on time for her dinner with Sophie Leclerc. *Jeffrey Underwood, my rescuer. How odd*, Brett thought as she headed for the shower.

The week sped by in a flurry of activity. Time was distinguished only by what restaurant she was in with whom. On Thursday she returned from drinks with Georges, her favorite makeup artist, and sitting by her door was a long, white florist's box. Inside were two dozen long-stemmed yellow roses and a card that read, "Good Luck, Lawrence." She had almost tossed them in the trash, but decided that the flowers were lovely and she had every right to enjoy them.

For the party, Brett selected an outfit from Martine's spring collection—a midcalf circle skirt and matching sleeveless shell in a silk voile the same color as her emerald eyes. Simple gold hoops adorned her ears, and on her feet she wore snakeskin sandals with green ribbons that tied around her ankles. Gabriel had suggested that she arrive at least an hour late for the party, but she had insisted that she wanted to welcome everyone who came. Brett had plaited her hair down her back, and just before she left she made a final inspection in the hall mirror. A sweet scent, pleasant and unobtrusive as a fleeting memory, emanated from the roses she had arranged in a blue-and-white-porcelain urn and placed there. In the early evening light they gave a golden cast to her reflection. Thoughtfully, she took one of the delicate yellow blossoms that hadn't fully opened and held it for a moment. Brett had spent months regretting her involvement with Lawrence, but over time, the bitter taste of betrayal had taken on the bittersweet flavor of experience. Lawrence had taught her a great deal, personally and professionally, and she knew that wherever she went, whatever the future held, a small part of him would always be with her. She slipped the flower into the top of her braid and walked out the door.

The house on the avenue Marceau was a classical sandstone structure with a wide pilastered portico. Brett had been here only once before, and she had been surprised that Gabriel's private life was so very different from his public one. He was the heir to one of the best known wine fortunes in France. His parents had insisted that he learn the family business literally from the ground up, and until they had died, fashion had only been a hobby. Once the international enterprise was his, he promptly hired someone to run it and opened up L'Étoile. Gabriel Jarré's luxurious life-style did not depend on the commission he received from his models, and his home reflected his wealth.

The door was opened by Gabriel's houseman, who showed Brett through the terra-cotta-tiled foyer, down a long hall carpeted with an Aubusson runner. To her left was the spacious living room, furnished with modern and contemporary classics, and several pieces of primitive sculpture. The hallway, like every room in the house, served as a place to display one of the most envied art collections in the world. She passed Picasso, Utrillo, Manet, and Degas on her way to the garden, where Gabriel waited by a scale replica of the fountain in the square des Innocents. He kissed her on both cheeks and offered her a glass of champagne. "It's not Jarré, I'm afraid, but we only produce lowly burgundy," he said in jest. "And everyone knows you cannot say bon voyage—and that's what I'm saying, Brett, not *adieu*—without bubbly."

Almost immediately, guests began arriving. Brett took their promptness as a tribute to her. It meant that they were not coming just to be seen, and therefore, making an entrance didn't matter. Dinner was a buffet and guests dined either in the garden or whichever room of the house suited them, and were entertained by a strolling classical guitarist. Brett's glass seemed to fill itself, and taking Gabriel's cue, she said no good-byes. Conversation was light and casual, and it was one of the best parties she had attended since she had been in Paris. When everyone had gone, she and Gabriel sat once again by the fountain and talked until well past midnight.

"I should be going," Brett said as she rose from the marble bench. "It was really lovely. Thank you."

Gabriel walked her down the long hall to the front door. He kissed her on both cheeks. "You'll take New York by storm."

Brett nodded silently, sensing that her voice would activate her tears, and departed.

As she drove across to the Left Bank, she could see the incandescent spire of the Eiffel Tower. The City of Lights had been a proving ground for her. It had been her decision to move here, and it had been a right one. Some of her choices since then had not been so right, but Paris had opened windows through which she could observe and doors through which she could pass, and she had made memories and friends that would last a lifetime. *Every ending is a beginning*, she thought, and as she turned onto the boulevard Saint Germain, Brett knew it was time to go home.

— *Chapter 20* —

Brett removed her thick white terry robe, hung it on the back of the door, and stepped gingerly into the steaming water. Her own bathroom at the San Remo was fine for the showers she usually took, but for lounging in a bath, she loved the huge white porcelain clawfoot tub in Lillian's bathroom.

She had spent most of her summer at Cox Cove, where her aunt was now recuperating. When Brett returned from Paris, she found that Lillian was up and about and walking a few blocks every day, but her doctors agreed that the tranquility of Cox Cove would provide a wider range of activities for her. The property had almost a mile of beachfront, as well as four wooded acres to walk, and that, combined with tending her garden and painting to her heart's content, would surely speed her recovery.

Glad she had brought a supply of Roger & Gallet with her from Paris, Brett slid down in the tub until the sandalwood-scented bubbles reached her chin. She had come into the city early in the day to meet with the contractors who were adapting the town house she had purchased on Gramercy Park to serve as both studio and residence. Now she had almost two hours until she met Jeffrey for dinner, and the quiet comfort of a bath was just what she needed after an afternoon spent making nitty-gritty decisions about the project.

Brett stretched out fully and tried to reach the hot water tap with her foot, but it was too far away. Aunt Lillian's tub, like all the fixtures in the white-and-black-tiled room, was custom designed to be comfortable for someone tall. In addition to the six-foot tub, the glass-encased shower stall was six feet square and the pedestal sink was three inches higher than standard. Brett scooted to the end of the tub, added water until the bath was just shy of cauldron hot again, then leaned back, resting her neck against the inflatable pillow on its rim.

Beads of perspiration dotted her forehead, but the silken water felt good. She closed her eyes and a sigh escaped from her lips as the tension flowed out of her limbs. The decision to buy the five-story house had been a hasty one, but after Jeffrey had explained the tax advantages of owning rather than leasing the property, it certainly seemed to be a sound investment. Her biggest problem had been accepting the idea that she could afford the nearly two and a half million dollar purchase price. In spite of all the information Jeffrey had given her about her finances, Brett had trouble thinking of herself as a millionaire, much less the billionaire she would become when her grandfather died.

She squeezed the natural sea sponge and tiny rivulets of water parted the bubbles as they streamed down her breasts. Warmth from the water suffused through her, making her body pliant and receptive. Suddenly Brett was overcome with a feeling of longing, of needing to be touched in a way that hadn't been really meaningful to her since Lawrence. She was young and vital, and her body wanted to respond to a man's touch. Putting down the sponge, Brett grabbed the loofah and vigorously rubbed her arms and legs, trying to dismiss the fluttery ripplings of arousal, but she couldn't help remembering the passion she had known with Lawrence and wondering if it could be that way again.

The difficulty was that there was no man in her life now. Well, no one except for Jeffrey Underwood. For some reason, she didn't think of him as a suitor, although Jeffrey had become more than a business associate since the day of Lillian's surgery. He phoned regularly to inquire about Lillian's condition and her own. When Sven had finally arrived from Australia, Jeffrey had accompanied him to the hospital, and had waited with Brett while he visited his sister. The three of them had dined at Smith & Wollensky, the East Side steak house. Sven had eaten his meal sequentially, progressing from tossed salad to a baked potato, which he buttered and ate in quarters, finishing with a porterhouse steak, well done. He spoke only when absolutely necessary, and when Brett offered him the guest room at the San Remo, he informed her that since Lillian was all right, he would fly back to Racine that night. Her grandfather seemed even less approachable in person than he had during their phone conversations, and Brett was glad for Jeffrey's presence.

She and Jeffrey had been out twice since then—once to dinner and a performance of Manon Lescaut at the Met, and once to lunch. He had been attentive and pleasant, but he did not strike Brett as touchable. His precise speech always sounded as if he were reading a legal brief aloud, and his attire and grooming were so perfect that sometimes Brett wondered if he ever relaxed and went without a tie. But in spite of his reserved manner, Jeffrey seemed genuinely interested in her. He had obviously learned about how her business worked and now, as in Paris, the value of his help and advice was incalculable. Brett felt no pressure from him, and that alone made him a good companion.

The bath had become tepid—the bubbles had all but disappeared. Brett drummed her fingers on the water's surface, splashing it gently, deciding whether she should freshen it or end her ablutions. Opting for the latter, she got out of the tub and wrapped herself in a gigantic black-and-white-striped towel. Hilda and Albert were at Cox Cove with Lillian, so the apartment was empty. She walked down the hall toward her own room, listening to the silence.

When Brett knew she was going to see Jeffrey, she paid meticulous attention to what she wore. It was not to impress him, but rather that she always felt slightly disheveled in light of his extraordinary ability to look perfect. *He's almost too perfect*, she thought, but tonight they were meeting Joe and Lizzie at a restaurant down in Soho, and she wanted to be relaxed and comfortable, not confined by the heels and hose she usually wore with Jeffrey.

Lizzie and Joe are really the ideal couple, Brett thought as she stared in her closet, waiting for inspiration. They had come out to Cox Cove the Saturday after Brett had returned from Paris. Joe had mixed frozen margaritas and they had lain in the shadow of the great oak that shaded one end of the pool area. They laughed and talked so much that the potency of the icy, refreshing drinks hit them too late, and Joe and Lizzie had stayed the night, rather than make the long drive back to the city in their tipsy condition. They were right for each other and with each other, and that day they seemed even more in tune than Brett had remembered, if that was possible.

Lizzie had been Lizzie. She was not Liz Powell, hot shot reporter, nor was she insecure or trying to impress. She was alternately hilarious or serious, and wise observations were found right on the surface of her seemingly inane remarks. Brett was glad her friend had finally become so comfortable with herself.

Joe was warm, funny, and loving. With Lizzie he displayed openness and honesty, as well as the confidence that she would not betray his trust. He had tested himself with all that could tempt a man: beautiful women, money, and fame, but his real values had served him well and proven true in the end. Brett knew they were lucky to have found each other.

As she pulled a black gauze Norma Kamali dress from its padded hanger, she remembered that she had had first crack at Joe, but she hadn't been interested. Deciding that she didn't feel that way about Joe might have cost her the happiness that Lizzie was experiencing now. Brett fastened her wide black leather belt, centering the silver buckle at the back of her waist. *It should be clear to me that I don't have good judgment where men are concerned*, Brett thought as she applied mascara and sheer red lipstick, and brushed her hair until her shiny waves hung loose and free. She held up a squash blossom necklace, then decided that the turquoise and silver earrings and matching bracelet were enough. She surveyed the whole effect in the mirror and was tickled by what she saw. *All I need is a crystal ball*, she thought. "You will meet a tall, dark, handsome stranger," she said to her reflection. *But maybe not. Maybe he's tall and blond, and I just need to look at him differently*. Perhaps this time she should go against her own initial perceptions and really try to consider Jeffrey as a romantic possibility.

Just as she slipped her feet into silver sandals, the intercom buzzed. Brett checked her watch. *Jeffrey's right on time*, she thought as she went to answer it.

"You look very lovely this evening," Jeffrey said.

"Well, thank you. Come in." She moved aside to let him enter, turning her head slightly to hide a growing smirk. *This is certainly different*, she thought. Not only had he never commented on her appearance, but Jeffrey Underwood, the personification of formality, was not wearing a tie. She had told him the evening would be casual, assuming he would take that to mean he could wear a blue shirt instead of a white one with his suit. She never expected the khaki twill trousers, white polo shirt, navy blazer, and brown loafers, worn with pale blue-and-yellow-argyle socks. Without his usual padded shoulders and rigid tailoring, Jeffrey was more slender than Brett remembered. *He almost seems fragile*, she thought fleetingly.

Jeffrey settled on a nubby, fawn-colored sofa in the living room. He held out a shiny brown box, the size and shape of a one quart Chinese take-out container, which had been hidden behind his back. "These are for you," he said.

The heady, sweet aroma of chocolate greeted her before she opened the package. "Mmmm . . . these smell heavenly!" she exclaimed, examining the top layer of the assorted, hand-dipped confections, each nestled in brown fluted paper. "I've got to have one, even if it's before dinner. One truffle couldn't hurt. Thank you. This is very sweet . . . pardon the pun." She smiled and bit into the dusty chocolate morsel. "Would you like one?" she offered.

"Choose one for me," he replied, the hint of a smile playing at the corners of his thin lips.

"Hmmm . . . you look like a chocolate and hazelnut kind of man," she said holding out her choice. "Am I right?" She searched Jeffrey's face for a clue to what he was like beneath the polite exterior, but she found none. His eyebrows, as pale as his fine blond hair, were invisible at a distance, and the absence made his face seem blank, expressionless.

He placed the candy in his mouth. "This is delicious," he reported.

"Chuck Hitchcock from Brandenberg, Weiss had some really good plans worked up for me this afternoon. I can go forward on the house, and he said it should be ready for me to move in by the end of September. That's only six weeks," Brett told Jeffrey as she took a seat on a green brocade ottoman.

"They're an innovative architectural firm and their work is first-rate. They've done work at the Larsen offices, and on my apartment, as well," he replied.

"Where is your apartment, Jeffrey?" Brett asked.

He sat forward on the sofa. "On sixty-eighth and Third. Really quite convenient. Walking to the office from there is enjoyable."

"Do you have a home in Racine, too?" Brett realized how little she knew about Jeffrey that was not connected to Larsen Enterprises.

He shifted in his seat. "No. Not any longer. Most of my time is spent in New York now, so when business takes me to Racine, a hotel is sufficient."

"It's funny. I guess you could say I'm from there, since that's where I was born, but I can't really say I've been there since my mother and I left when I was small. I should go back one day, to see where the business started and grandfather's house. Where are you from, Jeffrey?" Brett asked.

"Warren's Corners, Minnesota. It's a small place, known for sunflower farming, if you can believe that. I haven't been there in many, many years." Jeffrey glanced at his watch. "What time are we supposed to meet your friends?" he asked.

"Joe and Lizzie live on Seventy-fifth and Columbus, so they're going to walk over here to meet us. We can all take a taxi together. They should be here any minute, so why don't we head downstairs?"

"Certainly. I look forward to meeting them," Jeffrey replied.

Brett looked forward to the meeting, as well. None of her friends had met Jeffrey yet, and she was anxious for Lizzie and Joe's opinions.

"The place used to be a saloon, and it's not much to look at, but the food is really good," Joe said as the taxi stopped on Prince Street in front of Raoul's. The four entered and were shown past the bar, where the tweedy stood elbow to elbow with the denim clad and the bejeweled and sequined, all engaged in friendly conversation.

Brett and Jeffrey sat on one side of the dark wood booth at the back of the restaurant, Lizzie and Joe on the other.

"Brett tells me that you were recently married. Congratulations and best wishes to you both."

"We appreciate it. We spent our honeymoon in Japan, and I think Lizzie's ready to move there permanently," Joe said.

"I am not!" Lizzie said, playfully swatting Joe on the arm. "He kept teasing me that I must feel right at home since everything there was my size. It was kind of neat, though, not being at armpit level for a change!"

"Larsen business has afforded me the opportunity to visit Japan several times. It is a fascinating country," Jeffrey said.

Their waitress, a birdlike young woman whose hair was arranged atop her head like a doorknob, took drink orders.

"So, where did you go to law school, Jeff?" Lizzie asked.

"That's Jeffrey. Yale is my alma mater," he answered.

"Oh, when did you graduate? I think one of my brother's friends went to Yale Law School," Lizzie continued.

"Surely it was a lifetime ago. Your brother's friend's father's class would be more like it. But the best thing about law school is graduation." Turning to Joe, he asked, "Is learning to sculpt as torturous a process?"

"Actually, I've been chipping shapes out of blocks of anything I could find since I was a kid. My mother kept waiting for me to outgrow it. When I finally studied art, I loved every minute of it. I still can't believe I'm lucky enough to work at something that makes me so happy." Joe described a work in progress, sketching it on the white paper that covered the table.

They interrupted the conversation only long enough to make dinner selections from the chalkboard above them. Brett tried to goad one of her companions into ordering the sweetbreads with Calvados cream sauce, but she found no takers.

After the meal, Brett and Lizzie excused themselves to go to the ladies' room.

"Well?" Brett asked, once inside the makeshift conference room.

"Well, Jeffrey is a bit hard to figure. He's very attentive, though. He watches you all the time," Lizzie said.

"Does he really? I don't know what to make of him yet either.

He seems interested in everything I do, and he's very helpful. Mostly, he's good company. That's enough for right now."

"You do like them mature," Lizzie noted.

"Oh, come on, it's purely a coincidence," Brett said.

"It's just an observation. He's the one who made a comment about his age. But I'm going to keep my mouth shut this time. I'm only glad to see you're going out again." She applied a dab of peach parfait lipstick to the center of her bottom lip. "You had the red snapper, too. Are you feeling queasy at all?"

"No. I was just thinking about the strawberry mousse I'm going to order for dessert," Brett said.

"It's probably just my stomach's reaction to eating a whole meal sitting down. It's so busy at the station that I barely have time to chew. Let's go. That mousse could be really tempting."

After the meal, the quartet joined the strollers ambling along the narrow, gritty streets of Soho. They paused at the corner of Prince and Mercer, in front of Clayton Gallery. *Trajectory*, one of Joe's recent works, was on display.

"Larsen buys a fair amount of art on a corporate level. Gretchen Pauling, our consultant for art acquisition, should see your work," Jeffrey said.

"I'd like that a lot. I've been told there's a healthy business in institutional purchases," Joe replied. Lizzie, her arm draped around his waist, looked up at him proudly, but with eyes clearly at half mast. "You look wiped out, Lizlet. Are you ready to call it a day?" Joe asked.

"I think so," she said.

"I feel like walking some more, Jeffrey. How about you?" Brett asked.

"The night is young," Jeffrey replied with a smile.

When Joe and Lizzie had departed, Brett and Jeffrey continued along Prince. While stopped at a corner, waiting for traffic to pass, Jeffrey offered Brett his arm. She smiled and grasped it, thinking that he really was from a different time.

At Mercer they stopped at A Photographer's Place, one of Brett's favorite haunts when she was in high school. The bookstore brimmed with books on every aspect of photography, and she was glad to find it as cluttered as ever. She became engrossed in browsing, nearly forgetting she was not alone. When they left the store, Jeffrey presented her with a book of the works of Henri Cartier-Bresson, the French photojournalist.

"It was the one you seemed to enjoy the most," he said.

"Jeffrey, you really shouldn't have bought this," she protested.

"Please accept it. It would make me happy," he countered. "You don't even have to carry it until you get home," he said, taking the book back and placing it under his arm.

"Thank you. I hope I didn't sound ungrateful. It's just that you didn't have to do that." Brett took his hand as they continued their walk, trying not to admit to herself that she enjoyed the attention he paid to what she liked.

At Broome Street they turned west, deciding to look for a café where they could have a nightcap before bringing the evening to a close. When they reached Wooster Street, Brett noticed a yellow pennant attached to a grimy building, which in another era would have housed a factory. It billowed lazily in the light breeze, and she had almost passed by when she saw the name Zachary Yarrow.

"Wait a minute," she said, stopping to read the sign.

"The Loading Zone Theater presents *Time Off for Good Behavior*, by Zachary Yarrow," it proclaimed.

"Someone you know?" Jeffrey asked.

"I think so, and I haven't seen him in a long time." There were so few people with whom Brett could reminisce. No long threads ran through the fabric of her life. The characters came and went, like patches in a crazy quilt, some big, some small, some jagged, some smooth. She felt drawn to touch this part of her past—a person of whom she had been fond and had lost, through no fault of her own.

Brett and Jeffrey entered the lobby through a black steel door that was propped open with a fire extinguisher, and were stopped by the stifling heat. Jeffrey hung back near the entrance while Brett continued inside. She asked a woman who was busily collating programs at a folding card table if Zachary was in the house. Removing her wire-rimmed glasses, the woman thought for a few seconds, then excused herself and disappeared up a flight of stairs.

In a minute she heard footsteps, then Zachary was standing before her. He was dressed in faded jeans and a denim work shirt, and clenched a meerschaum pipe, brown with age, in his teeth. He was leaner than Brett remembered, and somehow shorter, but his eyes twinkled, and she instantly remembered the way he had looked when she was a child and he was enthusiastic about a project.

"I saw the sign . . ." she began cautiously. Brett knew she must be tied to a tragic episode in his life, and she was unsure of the welcome she would receive.

"Brett . . . I've often wondered what became of you," Zachary said in a whisper.

"You've written a play," she said. It was hard finding words. The last time she had seen him he had been cuffed and manacled and was being led away by a court officer after being found guilty of manslaughter.

"Yeah. I've done a lot of writing in the last few years. It's a fluke that I'm in the city now. Mostly I've worked at regional theaters—for a while in Connecticut, then Vermont. I've been in Minneapolis for the last two years. That's where *Time Off* was first produced. It's running here through the end of the month, but I'm leaving day after tomorrow. These days I get restless when I'm in New York for too long." He had not taken his eyes off Brett as he spoke. "You're out of school?"

"For a long time. I lived in Paris for six years. I've just moved back here," she said, not knowing what details to fill in.

"That's great, kid. You look like the first day of spring—fresh and promising. I'm glad. I wished that for you." He took a long drag on his pipe, releasing the smoke slowly so it hung in the air like thunderheads. "I'm glad you stopped here, Brett. You were a delightful, special child, and it looks as though you've stayed that way. But I have to go now. To start my life again, I had to take some memories and lock them away in a box. I can unlock it every now and again to ramble around inside, but mostly I keep it closed." Zachary shoved his pipe in his back pocket and moved across the room to stand in front of her. He took both of her hands, then kissed her on the forehead. "You stay well . . . always," he said, then turned and disappeared slowly up the stairs.

Jeffrey, who had been watching from his vantage point near the door, appeared at her side just as the first tear trickled down her cheek.

"Would you like to go home?" he asked, taking her hand.

"Yes," she said weakly.

Brett stared out the cab window in silence during the ride. She suffered the desperate ache of aloneness, like a howl from her heart. She needed someone to whom she was more than extra baggage to be shed when the going got rough—someone who could help her heal the fragile, battered places she kept hidden deep inside.

As soon as they arrived back at the apartment, Jeffrey asked, "Would you like me to stay, or do you need to be alone?"

"I'm sorry. This is not the way I'd planned the night to end, but I wouldn't be very good company right now," she said.

"You don't have to explain." Jeffrey placed one hand on her shoulder and kissed her lips quickly, as if embarrassed by his forwardness. "Good night, Brett."

"Good night, Jeffrey. I hope I haven't scared you. I'm not usually so distracted," she said.

"Don't worry. You'll hear from me," Jeffrey replied.

— *Chapter 21* —

"So, how did you hear I'd moved to New York, Todd? We mailed announcements day before yesterday, but I know your name wasn't on the list." Brett was seated in the middle of one of the ruby chesterfields, which was now at home in the parlor-reception room of Larsen Studios' new Gramercy Park location. She had been confounded by his phone call that morning, but had agreed to meet with him in the afternoon. If nothing else, she would get a lesson on the pathways of information in New York.

"I've got feelers everywhere. It's one of the things that makes me such a good rep," Todd Banks answered with no pretense of modesty. Banks, a photo rep, slouched gape-legged in the petit-point Louis XV bergère. His keen-featured, steel-jawed handsomeness hinted at his former incarnation as a model, a career cut short by a hairline that had receded prematurely to midscalp. After he married a photographer with whom he had worked frequently, she fired her rep, accusing him of preferential treatment toward another photographer he represented. Todd took over the job of managing her career, learning the business as he went along. When the marriage ended, he lost his ex-wife as a client, but had developed a healthy business representing other photographers, hair and makeup people, and fashion stylists. He had a lot of good contacts, was aggressive, and was exceedingly good at turning nos and maybes into yeses.

"Now, if I were a mean guy, I wouldn't tell you and you would be tormented by the mystery," he began, obviously enjoying the intrigue. "But since I'm not like that, I'll clue you in. You've worked with Frederica Badescu in Paris . . ."

"Sure. She does good, clean makeup. I haven't seen her in a long time," Brett interjected.

"She moved back to the States a year and a half ago. I rep her, too. Anyway, I got her booked on a cosmetics ad for Revlon—fabulous new campaign, you'll see it everywhere. Well, Toji, the stylist, worked that job with her. I don't know why anyone still books him. He hasn't done any interesting work in years, probably because he's coked out every brain cell in his head." Todd spoke in a rapid-fire barrage, stopping only for air. Brett leaned back on the sofa, crossed her legs, and took in the performance. "Toji was going on about some job he did for Saatchi & Saatchi, and he mentioned that the art director had gotten your card and asked him if he had ever worked with you. Freddy told me about it since she thinks working with you is a blast, and she wanted me to show you her book, with all her new tears."

"That was complicated," Brett remarked.

"Everything is complicated in the Big Apple. That's why you need me. My ear is always to the ground and I know how people in this business think." Todd flipped one leg over the chair arm, then continued. "For instance, if I were you and you were me and I called this morning to make an appointment and got in this afternoon, you would think that I must not be very busy, since I had time to see you. That's death in this town. You've got to make everybody think that a herd of wild art directors and editors is beating down your door."

"Frankly, I've always preferred to make contacts with clients myself. I worked that way for several years in Europe," Brett explained.

"Clients in Europe are different. They make time to see everybody. It's all very Old World and polite. You visit, show your book, have a glass of wine and a little chit-chat—it's nice and social. Here, you'll find out that everybody works at warp speed. Their phone is ringing, they've got pressure to finish the project by yesterday, so they need a shortcut. That's where I come in. I give them the supermarket approach to booking talent. Why should an art director make separate calls to book everyone he needs for a shoot when he can call me? I can book hair, makeup, photographers, and stylists with one phone call. No muss, no fuss, life's a beach!" Todd finished with a flourish of his hand.

Brett asked Todd who he represented, what kind of bookings he had been getting, and how his billing system worked. She was reluctant to hand the responsibility of invoicing and collections over to an outside party, which she knew was necessary if she took on a rep. She had heard too many horror stories of reps going bankrupt, owing those they represented thousands of dollars that were seldom, if ever, recovered. She had also been selective in shaping her career and did not want to risk signing on with someone who was in it for the fast money and not the long term. Being a canned photographer on the shelf in Todd's market did not sound to Brett like the way to go.

"I appreciate your visit, Todd, but I'm going to handle my own career for the time being," she said, then added, "Of course, if you're as nice a guy as you say, you'll tell me which A.D. asked about me."

"You know, I was just trying to remember who it was, but there are so many that I can never keep them straight," he answered coyly. "Brett, it's really good to meet you. I know your work and you take good pictures. I could save you a lot of time and trouble, but give it a shot on your own. You've got my number if you change your mind. I just hope I haven't taken on another photographer when you call me. I can really only handle one more person, and I'll hate like hell to have to turn you down. And remember Freddy if you've got anything coming up!"

After Brett showed Todd out, Thérèse, who had been working at her desk in the adjoining room, said, "Who does that man think he is that you should worry about him turning you down? I have never heard such arrogance!"

"It's nothing. People here are a bit more direct than they are in France. You'll get used to it."

"I will never get used to rudeness," Thérèse muttered as she pulled a folder from her files. "I have for you the list with names, addresses, and telephone numbers of all the people who were sent your card."

"Great. Tomorrow I'll start making phone calls. Leave it in my office." Brett looked out the window at the street. A teenage boy wearing a gray Shetland sweater and blue jeans struggled to walk two dachshunds, a German shepherd, a standard poodle and a Dalmatian. Hopelessly entwined in a tangle of leashes, he seemed resigned to follow where the pack led him. Brett left the window and wandered aimlessly through her new work space.

The Paris studio had been sprawling in its spaciousness—a tabula rasa to which stylistic elements, dictated by both form and function, had been added. This time, the task had been different. The dignified Federal-style town house bore the unmistakable stamp of an epoch, and Brett wanted the renovations to preserve the charm and elegance, while carving out a functional work environment and living space.

Starting with the cellar—which, in addition to housing the guts of the structure, now contained supply cabinets and the darkroom

—Brandenberg, Weiss had reshaped each floor. Many of the fixtures and much of the furniture used throughout had been transported from Paris, and while the setting was different, it provided Brett with a sense of continuity.

The ground floor was bisected by a center hall. To the right, through sliding doors that disappeared into the walls when open, was the reception area and Thérèse's office. On the left was a casual dining room with an exposed-beam ceiling, scrubbed oak farmhouse table, and Shaker chairs that invited lingering. Brett recalled relaxed, happy moments during meal breaks at her shoots in Paris. She believed, as did many photographers who had worked in Europe, that the half hour or so spent allowing the crew to enjoy a good meal, instead of eating sandwiches on the run, was time well spent, as it fostered good morale and creativity. She worked those breaks into her shooting schedule whenever possible.

A galley kitchen and a bath were behind the dining room, and across the back of the house, looking out on a rose garden that she had been told would offer a glorious view come spring, was Brett's office, furnished with a walnut conference table and the necessary light tables. An informal sitting area, defined by a cubist-inspired Ferdinand Léger rug, was situated by the glass double doors that led to the garden. Bay windows, on either side of the doors, were mounted with flower boxes on the exterior and curved, citron leather-cushioned window seats inside.

Brett climbed the stairs to the second floor and entered the rear studio. She would use this space for daylight shooting, so the three towering windows were left unobstructed. Chalk-white walls, white oak wainscoting, and gleaming parquet floors would be the constants, and the room could be decorated with whatever furnishings her clients required, courtesy of the furniture rental businesses that thrive in New York, to create the desired atmosphere for her photographs.

The other studio, which occupied the front of the second story, was designed for her work against seamless. Wall brackets held the ten-foot rolls of paper in a spectrum of colors, with extra rolls of white, black, and gray, the colors she used most frequently. The huge black safe, which held cameras and other valuable equipment, stood in a corner, and lights, reflectors, and umbrellas were suspended from the ceiling, to be raised and lowered as needed by an automated pulley system.

The two studios were separated by a makeup room to the right of the stairs and a dressing room to the left. In the dressing room, dozens of padded hangers dangled from the two stainless steel rolling racks. Brett poked her head into the makeup room and was struck by its immaculate condition. She flicked on the light switch that illuminated the room-wide mirror, bordered by daylight-tinted bulbs. The back of the black polished granite counter was lined with clear lucite containers, filled with cotton balls, swabs, tissues, scissors, pins, tape, and other necessities, all unused. *I haven't worked in four months*, she thought, realizing how much she missed the organized chaos of a shoot and the sense of fulfillment she got from her work. Her unplanned hiatus could not have been prevented, but Lillian was fine, the move and renovations completed, and she was ready to pick up her camera and take on New York. It couldn't be as difficult as Todd Banks had intimated.

The next day, Brett sat across from Lizzie at a back corner table in Sal Anthony's on Irving Place. Frustrated after completing her thirtieth call of the morning and netting only four appointments to show her book, Brett was glad when Lizzie had called and asked her to lunch. They had tried on several occasions in the last month to meet for one of their breakfasts, but each time Lizzie had called at the last minute to cancel. Today she was investigating the effects of a recent pesticide scare on the retail sale of produce, and had found herself at the Union Square Farmers' Market, within walking distance of Brett's house. Brett had suggested a restaurant located conveniently for them both.

"Are you ready to order?" asked the waiter.

Brett was about to say yes when Lizzie interrupted. "Not yet. Give us a few more minutes, please," she said. Then, turning to Brett, she said, "Guess what!"

"You're going to be the first reporter on the moon? Lizzie, do you realize how many conversations we've started exactly this way over the years?" Brett asked, laughing.

"Lots, I suppose, but this is different," Lizzie said. "Do you remember the night at Raoul's when I felt sick after dinner? And all those breakfast dates I called off? I was sick then, too!"

Brett couldn't understand why her friend was so pleased about being sick, and then it dawned on her. "Lizzie, you're not . . ."

"Yes—I'm going to have a baby!" she said exuberantly. "Joe and I talked about it often before we got married. We both knew that we wanted a family, and we really couldn't see a reason to wait."

"Oh, Lizzie, I don't know what to say. I'm so happy for you," Brett said as tears welled up in her eyes.

Lizzie reached for Brett's hands. "Don't cry, because then I'll start, too, and we'll need a mop back here! I've been crying at the drop of a hat. My doctor says it's raging hormones, but I just think I'm happy. We have it all planned. These days, a lot of reporters work while they're pregnant, so I can stay on the job almost up to the time I deliver. Joe and I decided that I should take most of my maternity leave after the baby comes, and his schedule is really flexible, so I'll have lots of help. My mother is beside herself. This baby really means so much to her—I mean, after David and all."

When the waiter reappeared, Brett ordered the salad niçoise and Lizzie requested lobster bisque, a house salad with extra Russian dressing, and a rare steak with all the trimmings. "I'm eating for two, you know!" She winked at Brett.

Brett recalled how strange it had seemed to think of Lizzie as an aunt, but now her best friend was going to be a mother. "Lizzie and Joe become Ma and Pa Tate. It has a certain ring, don't you think?" Brett teased.

"I know it's not going to be easy. Our lives will change completely—probably more than I can even imagine. But Joe's contract with Monsieur was renewed. They want the same commitment from him and they're paying even more. And as far as my career is concerned, there's no better time. I'm on solid ground at GNSN, my work is respected, and I'm based primarily in the city. But with the track I'm on, things are likely to get more demanding. I'm afraid that if I wait, I'll keep putting it off until I finish this report, that investigation, or a two-month trip up the Amazon."

"You'll be a wonderful mother, Lizzie. You're kind and patient, and you always see straight through to the heart of the matter.

Besides, you have a great sense of humor, and I think you're going to need it."

After finishing their meal—Brett with coffee and Lizzie with double chocolate cheesecake and milk—Lizzie grabbed a cab to take her back uptown to the station and Brett walked the two short blocks home.

It was a clear October day, more reminiscent of summer than indicative of autumn, and Brett savored the sunshine as she turned onto Gramercy Park. *I'm really happy for her, for them*, she thought, but an insistent voice inside her chanted, "Lizzie has it all—a great career and a great marriage. Lizzie has it all."

On her way in she met Thérèse, who was on her way out. "I'll see you in the morning," her studio manager said. Noting Brett's puzzled expression, she added, "Remember, I'm having a furniture delivery this afternoon." Larsen's Acquisitions Department had found Thérèse an apartment on a lovely tree-lined block in Chelsea, and she had settled happily into life in New York.

"Oh yes, of course! Have a nice evening." Lizzie's news had been so unexpected that it had pushed everything else to the back of her mind. Instead of resuming the task of making follow-up calls, Brett leafed through invoices that the always frugal Thérèse was planning to rebill. It appeared that several of her French clients were not concerned about prompt remittance now that she was no longer in Paris, but she couldn't concentrate. Her thoughts returned to Lizzie and Joe. They had a perfect marriage, and now they were going to have a perfect baby and become the perfect family. She snatched her sweater from the back of the chair and took her keys to the park from her desk drawer.

The four blocks that comprise Gramercy Park surround a private square whose wrought-iron fence denies access to nonresidents. Brett unlocked the gate, closed it behind her, and wandered over to a bench near the birdbath. She had only been sitting a few moments when a young woman entered with her two toddlers in tow. Brett guessed that the little boy was about four years old and his sister, two. Dressed in brightly striped sweaters and denim overalls, they chased birds and squirrels and tossed handfuls of yellow and red leaves into the air. Their mother played right along with them.

I can't ever remember having fun with my mother, Brett thought. And as she continued to observe, she realized that Lizzie and David had grown up with a mother who allowed them to be children, and loved and accepted them because they were her flesh and blood. Joe probably had a similar upbringing, maybe even Jeffrey. But she had no such memories. She was grateful to Lillian for giving her the only real childhood she had had, but it did not replace what her mother had withheld from her.

Now Lizzie and Joe would continue the kind of nurturing love they had experienced in their own families, and once again she would watch and wonder why it couldn't be that way for her. Brett gently rolled the red-and-white-swirled ball that landed at her feet back to the children, nodding in response to their mother's thank-you.

If Joe and Lizzie become the kind of parents their parents were, does that mean that I'm destined to be like my mother? The thought was such an anathema to her, she shuddered and bolted from the bench. "It's not possible," she muttered to herself. "I won't let it happen."

She headed across the park toward the exit. The little boy shouted, "Bye-bye!" and waved vigorously. His little sister mimicked her brother's wave. "Bye-bye," Brett called. *Dammit, I have my career. The rest will come later*, she thought. She just had to be patient. Closing the iron gate with a clank, she hurried across the street to change for her dinner with Lillian.

Brett called her aunt every day and they had lunch or dinner at least once a week. Tonight, Lillian had cooked the meal herself. "Are you sure there's nothing I can do to help?" Brett asked as she took her seat at the dining room table.

"Not a thing. This has been quite enjoyable. I had forgotten how much I like cooking. Besides, Hilda hasn't taken a day off since I had my heart attack." Lillian placed a plate in front of her niece.

As they ate, Brett told Lillian about her surprise encounter with Zachary. It was the first time she had spoken of it since that night, and time had helped put the traumatic meeting in proper perspective. She also told her aunt that she was "kind of dating" Jeffrey Underwood and that he was picking her up later that evening. Lillian was delighted when Brett informed her of Lizzie and Joe's impending arrival, and immediately planned a shopping expedition to her favorite toy store.

"You know, that's one of the reasons I agreed not to redecorate your room, here and at Cox Cove," Lillian said.

"Pardon me?" Brett asked, not seeing a correlation between her announcement and the decor of her room.

"Well, I thought if they stayed the same, one day your child could enjoy them, too."

"That's a lovely thought, Aunt Lillian, but I'm afraid you'll have to hold on to it for a while!" Brett tried to sound cheerful, but she was not able to see the day her aunt so clearly envisioned.

Brett was having imported Swedish coffee in the living room with Lillian when Jeffrey arrived—as usual, right on time. "Good evening, Mrs. Cox. It's good to see you up and about. You don't look like you've been at all ill." Jeffrey, according to proper etiquette, waited for Lillian to offer her hand, which she did without rising. Then he kissed Brett lightly on the cheek and took a seat across from them.

"I'm pleased to meet you, Mr. Underwood. I understand that you're the young man who keeps my brother out of trouble. Brett has told me quite a bit about you."

Jeffrey stiffened imperceptibly, then relaxed, realizing that Brett couldn't have told her much because she only knew what he wanted her to know about him. "I'm hardly young, Mrs. Cox, and the fact that Mr. Larsen is rarely in trouble has less to do with me than with his superior business sense. By the way, please call me Jeffrey."

"So, how was your meeting?" Brett asked him.

And as they discussed their days, Lillian observed Jeffrey Underwood. There was something familiar and vaguely disturbing about him. He was more flawlessly attired than anyone she had ever seen. His navy suit, white shirt, and silver-blue tie looked morning fresh, even though he had worked in them all day. But it was more than that. His pale blue eyes appeared to see everything, but revealed nothing in exchange. Then it hit her. In spite of his slight build, Jeffrey Underwood reminded her of Sven. It was not really his appearance, so much as his mannerisms, that caused her pause. *Leave it to my brother to hire people just like himself*, she thought. He was never much on variety. But unlike Sven, Jeffrey seemed to be actually friendly, and he was obviously taken with Brett, so Lillian put aside her doubts.

Brett and Jeffrey rose to leave. "Dinner at my place next week, Aunt Lillian. I can't promise that the meal will be as good as your poached salmon—I'm still a pretty lousy cook. But I'll think of something."

Lillian was glad that Brett was in such good spirits. *Maybe this young man is good for her*, she thought.

"Again, it was a pleasure to finally meet you, Mrs. Cox." Jeffrey smiled, but Lillian noticed that his eyes did not.

— *Chapter 22* —

By January Brett had barely cracked the glossy, nearly impenetrable shell that protected New York's fashion fortress from invasion by outsiders. Admittance was by invitation only. Brett had hoped to make some headway with Phoebe Caswell, but just as in the spring, Phoebe was pleasant, even friendly, but noncommittal. And on several occasions she had tried to phone Malcolm, but he hadn't returned her calls. Since she had seen him last, Brett had been somewhat concerned about his health, but his photo credit line appeared regularly in all the usual places, and rumors of his outlandish escapades were in steady circulation. Brett couldn't believe that he was still angry that she hadn't called when she had come home for Lizzie's wedding, and attributed Malcolm's behavior to his well-known peculiarity.

Her portfolio, now filled with tearsheets, had made the rounds.

So far she had only shot fashion for *Glamour* and *Self*, but both had assigned her pages in the front of the book, not the highly coveted feature pages. She had managed to snag a press kit representing several lower-echelon designers who were all handled by the same P.R. company. That led to a regional advertising campaign for Alexa Starr, the best financed of the group.

Brett had tried in vain to convince Alexa that her concept of "Put on a Starr and Make a Wish," with a model standing in an open field gazing at a star-filled sky, was ill-suited to the classic career clothes she designed. But Alexa had the whole scenario firmly etched in her mind, so off they went to her house in Southampton on a cold, damp November night.

Reality fell far short of Alexa's expectations, and she made everyone involved miserable. She herself had chosen the model—a willowy girl with furious curly red hair—but when the model was made up and dressed, Alexa complained, "Her hair is covering too much of the dress. And it's so . . . wiry. Can't you do something with it?"

After spending an hour straightening the model's hair with a hot iron, the crew proceeded to the location—a nearby field with dune grass that stood almost waist high. Brett and an assistant had metered and set lights beforehand so they would be ready to shoot immediately. Brett was uncomfortably cold in her parka and boots, so she knew the model, wearing only a silk dress, would be freezing.

Alexa didn't care if the model was cold. After all, she was being paid. "There aren't enough stars. And I want one big one, way up high," Alexa snapped when she saw the Polaroids, as if she could order up the Star of the Magi.

To get the sky full of stars, the field, and the model all in the same frame, Brett had to shoot with a long lens. "I can hardly see the dress! It could be a sack, for all I can tell!" Alexa's tirade continued. "I drew exactly what I wanted. Why can't you just do it?"

Because it's impossible, you silly bitch, was what crossed Brett's mind, but she held her tongue and continued to make adjustments until Alexa was satisfied, if not happy.

Brett could afford the luxury of picking and choosing only work that suited her personal tastes. She did not need the Alexa Starrs of the world. What she did need, more than anything, was the reassuring, hands-on involvement in her craft.

To her surprise, it was her portraits and character studies that initially generated the most interest. Brett photographed a variety of people, from astronauts and evangelists to zoologists, for news and popular culture magazines around the country. It was not where she wanted to make her mark. She had to break through to the American fashion journals to prove, if only to herself, that her Parisian apprenticeship had been well served, but she was proud of the work, and it paid Thérèse's salary. Brett had supported herself on her earnings for several years, and continuing to do so was a matter of pride.

New York Style, a trendy start-up publication tirelessly dedicated to the task of promulgating the best, the newest, and the costliest finds in Gotham, had hired Brett to photograph five entrepreneurs for a piece entitled "Sweat Equity." It would profile the strategies of five New Yorkers who had parlayed a unique skill, insight into the needs of a particular sector of the market, and creative financing into million-dollar businesses. Brett had started reading the bios her editor had sent over, but stopped after the first one, deciding that she did not want preconceived notions about their personalities to interfere with the process of capturing a spontaneous moment on film.

Brett had found that people who did not have their picture taken for a living usually viewed the camera with a degree of trepidation, from slight tension to panic, so she conducted her portrait sessions differently from her fashion shoots. While controlling the technical aspects of the sitting, Brett let her subjects dictate much of the studio atmosphere. She had found that music helped set the mood, so she kept a stock of tapes that ranged from classical to bluegrass, and encouraged each subject to make selections.

She also made the matter of appearance an individual choice, and instructed people to wear or bring whatever made them feel best. Hair and makeup assistance were always available for women, and on hand for men was a groomer. Some people bristled at the ministrations and needed to be coaxed into allowing even a touch of loose powder to combat a shiny face, while others indulged completely, treating the session as a private image consultation.

Brett's day had started at five-thirty in the morning to accommodate the founder of the New York Fitness Exchange, a network of twenty-four-hour health clubs, who had requested a six-thirty sitting. Despite the snow that commenced just after the morning rush hour and drifted in downy, slow-motion flakes throughout the day, each of her subjects had been prompt and, for the most part, less egocentric than she had expected.

Margaret Beale, the president and CEO of I'll Do It, Inc., Brett's three o'clock subject, had proven the most challenging. The personal service business that Beale had started to make money during high school summers had burgeoned into a national chain, and she was consumed by her success. She had arrived a half hour early with two assistants, a cellular phone, a microcassette recorder, and a laptop computer, and had turned the reception area into her office outpost. When Thérèse showed her upstairs to the makeup room, the equipment-laden entourage followed and continued with their tasks. Beale rebuffed Brett's attempts at conversation. "If I'm not minding my business, then someone else will be," she said, and dictated a memo to her Denver branch manager while Brett checked the lighting.

By the middle of the second roll, Brett still felt she had not taken a picture worth printing, and the cellular phone sounded yet again. At first Brett was livid when one of the assistants informed her that Beale had to stop and conduct a five-minute telephone interview with a radio station in Seattle, the site of I'll Do It's newest branch. Beale had the phone brought to her on the set and launched into a vivacious recitation of the company's history. Brett, realizing that she was being given a glimpse of the essential Margaret Beale, went to work and took two rolls of film by the interview's conclusion. She snapped another roll to cover herself in case the editor wanted a more formal portrait, but Brett knew that she had gotten the shot during that phone call.

"I'm glad the day is almost over. Who's next?" Brett asked Thérèse, who had come up to bring Brett the coffee she had requested.

"He's not due for another few minutes or so, but his name is David Powell," Thérèse said, reading from the Lucite clipboard she always carried. "His company . . ."

"David Powell? It can't be the same person. Let me see his bio." Brett read the first two lines. "It's him! I don't believe it! This is Lizzie's brother. She told me that Hands On was moving its executive offices to New York, but I never expected him to be included in this piece."

"It says that the company opens here in March. This is for the March issue of the magazine, isn't it? Very good publicity, I think. He sounds like a smart man," Thérèse said.

"Yes, he is. I know Lizzie would have told me he was coming today if she had been here." Lizzie had been in San Juan, Puerto Rico, for GNSN since the second of January, covering the aftermath of a tragic hotel fire that killed ninety-six people.

At five-fifteen, when the buzzer sounded, Thérèse answered the intercom and confirmed that it was David Powell before she released the door. "I will go down and escort your friend upstairs," she said.

Conscious of her appearance for the first time all day, Brett ducked into the makeup room, reapplied her carnelian-red lipstick, and secured her hair with black silk cord in a thick, wavy ponytail. Checking herself in the mirror, she smoothed her tailored amethyst flannel jumpsuit and adjusted her red cashmere cardigan. *Lizzie's been saying he seems more like himself again*, she thought. She hoped so, or the sitting would be very difficult. Brett emerged just as Thérèse and David appeared at the top of the stairs.

"David! I see you, but I still don't believe you're here!" Brett started to hug him, caught herself, and took both of his cold hands in hers. At the age of eleven, when her crush on him had blossomed fully, she had eliminated hugs and most physical contact from her interactions with him. She had been confused by the unaccustomed fluttery feeling in her stomach whenever David was near, and even though she could not explain her butterflies, she instinctively knew they would become more active at his touch. That feeling was only a memory, but Brett felt self-conscious, as though David might somehow be privy to her thoughts.

"I'm as surprised as you are, but it's good to see you, Brett. You look like you're the one who should have a picture taken. I could be a double for the abominable snowman." He dusted snow from the shoulders of his distressed leather Eisenhower jacket, and the flakes in his hair rapidly turned to tiny glistening beads of water.

"Don't worry, we can take care of that," she said. She helped him out of his coat and caught the musky, damp smell of leather, mingled with the woodsy aroma of aftershave, as she draped it on a padded hanger. "When did you get into town?"

"Last night. I never looked at the slip of paper my assistant handed me when I left California until after lunch today. And there you were, right in my pocket!"

David seemed more relaxed than he had at Lizzie's wedding, and Brett hoped that time was doing its job and healing in the way that only its passage can. Brett still did not know the exact circumstances of the accident, but she did know firsthand how devastated and helpless one feels witnessing an untimely and tragic end to someone's life. "Let me hang this up and we can talk while you get ready."

"It'll take some effort to get used to this weather again. California spoiled me."

"Your bio says Hands On opens here in March, and the worst of it will be over by then," Brett said.

"Yeah, but I'm here for the duration. I'm staying with my folks until I find a place of my own."

Brett introduced him to Rocky, the groomer, and they all chatted while Rocky dried David's hair and dusted translucent powder on his nose and forehead. "The instructions said wear what makes you feel good. I hope this is all right." David was dressed in well-worn denim jeans and a blue chambray shirt, open at the collar. "It's not regulation dress for success, but I only wear a coat and tie when it's absolutely necessary. That used to be for meetings with bankers, but now that Hands On provides them with such a tidy return on their investments, they don't care what I wear!" he said jokingly.

"I think what you have on is great. You're the first person today who didn't look like he would bronze a key to the executive washroom!"

Brett showed him to the set and asked if he preferred a chair or stool. He selected the latter and sat with one leg up on the second rung, watching Brett as she adjusted lights and reflectors. She hadn't hired a full-time assistant. Her workload didn't warrant more than a freelancer for complicated assignments, and relatively speaking, this was an easy day. "I'll be with you in half a second," she said, changing the angle slightly on the gold foil reflector at his feet. "I'm making sure I'll be able to see your eyes through your glasses."

"If it makes life easier, I can take them off. They're really a prop. When I shaved off the mustache you and Lizzie used to think was so funny, I still needed something to make me look older, and more like I really could own a computer company. I've gotten so accustomed to wearing them that I reach for them first thing in the morning, just like I really need them to see."

"Great, we'll do some with and some without."

"Pardon," Thérèse interrupted. "If you don't need me for anything else, I will leave now. The weather has really become quite unfriendly, and I'd like to get home before it turns, as you say, nasty. The radio is nothing but reports about warnings and watches and something they call chill factors. Every few minutes they announce a cancellation of some event. It sounds the way my mother described broadcasts during the war, only there are no bombs!" Thérèse said, shrugging her shoulders.

"No problem, Thérèse, and if we survive the blitz, I'll see you in the morning," Brett said.

"She's really very funny," David said after Thérèse had gone. "I loved the unfriendly weather! Where did you find her?"

"She was my studio manager in Paris. Thank goodness she decided to come to New York with me. Otherwise, I would have had to learn what's in all her files, and I really don't want to know! I hope our scare tactic weather reports don't make her change her mind!"

Brett shot while they talked, carefully guiding the conversation to allow David ample opportunity to expound about Hands On. She captured the animation and excitement in his face as he told her about bytes and density and interfacing, but her progress was more leisurely than usual because she often found herself listening with interest to his replies, not just using them to trigger an expression.

"You can take off your glasses now," Brett said. Rocky stepped in and applied a dab of concealer, followed by some loose powder, to the bridge of David's nose, hiding the slight indentation left by his glasses.

"Rocky, I think we have everything under control now. You can pack up and leave," Brett said.

As Brett continued shooting, she constantly shifted her sights through the viewfinder, monitoring the little details that would show up as glaring errors in a print, but her gaze always returned to his brown eyes. They were alive with the passion and wonder he seemed to feel about his work. "If I didn't know better, I'd think you were talking about a game or a hobby, not some semiconductors!" Brett commented as she moved in for a closer shot.

"Acting the executive is a necessary evil, but the dividend is that I can close myself in the lab and fiddle to my heart's content. The world thinks it's hard work, when it really makes me as happy as a kid with a new toy." David grinned, adjusting his position on the stool, and Brett was struck by how handsome he was. He wasn't model handsome, which worked for Brett on film, but usually implied a certain haughtiness and hands-off detachment. He possessed a good-humored, intelligent attractiveness with tawny, sun-warmed skin, lips that could smile even when his face was at rest, a strong, distinctive chin, and tousled brown hair that seemed to welcome rearranging by the wind . . . or roving fingers. Perhaps it was the denim and chambray, but his broad shoulders and erect carriage reminded Brett of a cowboy sitting high in his saddle.

"In the not-too-distant future, everyone will need to be computer literate, and it's my dream that Hands On will make that seem less frightening," David said.

"*C'est tout!*" she said as she clicked off the last frame on the roll.

"Say what?" David asked, smiling.

"Sorry, it's a habit. We're done. Come on, I'm dying to look outside."

David followed her to the front windows. Two stories below them, a feathery blanket of snow covered everything. The spiky black wrought-iron fence around the park looked as if it were floating in a cloud, and the snow continued to fall, not in single delicate flakes, but in lacy clusters that swirled, airborne, in eddies around the nimbus of the street lamp before landing silently on the softly cushioned ground below.

"I was going to offer to buy you dinner, but from the looks of the weather, that might not be such a good idea. Nothing is moving out there—not even pedestrians. Look, no footprints!" David said, pointing to the far east end of the block.

"It is pretty desolate, but it's really beautiful," Brett said, looking in the direction he indicated. She turned back just in time to see Rocky, watch cap almost covering his eyes and backpack thrown over one shoulder, trudging through the knee-deep drifts. "Well, so much for untrod snow! I am hungry, though. We could have dinner here. Well, not here—upstairs."

"Upstairs?" David asked.

"I have the whole house. I live on the top three floors."

"Now, that's really living. I guess your commute to work is a breeze," David said.

"Look who's talking. I've heard about your sprawling compound—complete with tennis court and swimming pool, I believe."

"No, I sold that house a few years back."

"Oh, I'm sorry. I didn't mean to . . ."

"It's okay. I don't expect people to walk on eggshells around me. I've gotten much better at talking about Kate's death. And if that was an invitation, I accept—on one condition. That you let me cook."

"Has Lizzie been telling you disaster stories about my culinary skills?" Brett teased.

"I can't reveal my sources!" David said, playfully holding up both hands to deflect further questions.

After David helped her secure the equipment in the safe, they headed up to Brett's apartment. On the upper floors, the original staircase, with its polished mahogany balustrade and intricately carved newel posts, had been left intact. Lighted, recessed niches on either side of the door held lush plants in gleaming copper pots.

"This is very nice. Nineteenth century, isn't it?" David said, running his hand along the top of the cherry console table in the entry hall. "Don't look so surprised. Kate was into antiques, so I learned by osmosis."

"Yes, it's Empire—or at least that's what Claudio said. I'm not really much on periods or styles. I know what I like, and when I told the architect that, he suggested a designer who would help me find it instead of imposing his tastes on me." Brett flicked the switch by the door, bringing to life the two Italian brass torchieres, which cast a rosy glow as they stood at attention in opposite corners of the living room.

"I'd like his name and number. When I find a place, I'm going to need all the help I can get." David laughed.

"Claudio Briondi, and I'll give you his number later. Would you like a glass of wine before we tackle dinner?"

David sank down on the camel-back sofa and crossed his legs while Brett opened the japanned cabinet that concealed a temperature-controlled wine cellar. "Do you have a preference?" she asked, surveying the contents.

"Surprise me. I trust you," David said. "I almost feel like I'm in the country, not in the middle of Manhattan."

The living room had been furnished in colors that made it warm, cozy, and inviting in winter, and as cool and airy as a gazebo in summer. Gauzy white sheers framed the multipaned, double-hung windows, and on the forest green stippled and glazed wall behind the leaf-patterned sofa, one of Lillian's seascapes added the misty feel of the ocean at dawn to the room. The other walls, covered in celadon linen, held more of Lillian's work, as well as pieces Brett had purchased from young artists in Paris. Both Joe and Lillian had given her an appreciation of the vast talent many unknown artists possessed, and she was determined to support their struggle. Sand, rose, and apricot accents were reflected in the other furniture, the silk Besserabian carpet, and the Tiffany lamp, set on a satinwood table. A thicket of leafy plants and ferns, including a miniature tangerine tree, whose delicate blossoms lightly perfumed the air, added a natural tranquility. All of it was repeated endlessly in the two sets of mirrored French doors.

"That's what I wanted—an oasis." Brett set two stemmed glasses on the coffee table, handed David the bottle of Chardonnay and the corkscrew, and relaxed into one of the two apricot velvet wing chairs facing him.

After several sips of wine, David said, "This is going straight to my head. You'd better show me the kitchen before I forget how to scramble an egg."

"Well, I know I have eggs, but I can't vouch for much else," she said, leading David to the kitchen.

"Okay, I give up. Where's the refrigerator?" he asked.

"Right here!" Brett opened a door that was finished in the same pale chestnut as the cabinets in the English country kitchen.

He rummaged inside and emerged with full hands. "I think we have the makings of a pretty good omelet and a salad," he said as he laid eggs, a tiny wedge of Gruyère, chives, half a container of sour cream, a small head of Kentucky oak leaf lettuce, and the only four mushrooms that did not resemble shrunken heads, on the counter.

"I'll go get the wine," Brett said as the telephone rang. "Hi, Jeffrey," she said when she picked up the receiver. "Yes, I'm fine. The weather hasn't been a problem at all. Can I call you tomorrow? I've got company. Lizzie's brother, David, is moving back from California. He turned out to be my last subject today and he's still here. . . . All right, I'll talk to you then. 'Bye." She replaced the receiver. "I'll be right back with the wine." *I can hardly imagine Jeffrey cooking*, she thought as she strolled to the living room. In all the time they had dated, Jeffrey had never even been in her kitchen. On several occasions she had considered preparing an impromptu meal for him, but had thought better of it. She didn't think he would enjoy the simple dishes she usually made. Yet it had never occurred to her that David might object.

When she returned, David was at the cerulean blue restaurant style stove, pouring his concoction into an enamel-clad cast-iron omelet pan that he had removed from the iron rack above the chopping block. "That smells delicious," she said.

"We'll soon find out!"

David cut the omelet down the center and deftly slid the halves onto plates whose grapevine borders were painted to resemble mosaic tiles. "So tell me about Paris," he said as they sat at the blue and white speckled enamel-topped refectory table.

"I loved it, right from the beginning. I had really wonderful experiences. I started my career there, and honestly, I miss it." She leaned forward, folding her arms on the table. "I'll always think of Paris as the place I grew up. There's a vitality and style that's distinctly French. Some people think the French are snobs, with an exaggerated view of their own superiority, but actually, they're just supremely confident. And I guess that's easy when you come from a country that has set standards for design, fashion, architecture, and perfume, that the world uses as a benchmark. I traveled all over Europe and discovered something new wherever I visited, but Paris seems to be the place where people flock to learn about life and about themselves," Brett said thoughtfully. She hadn't really expressed her sentiments about her time in Europe to anyone, but David made her feel as comfortable as he always had.

"So, I guess you didn't like Paris much," David said, laughing. "You should eat before it gets cold."

Brett looked at his almost empty plate. "I guess I got carried away." Brett ate the savory omelet with gusto, and when she finished, she offered to make cappuccino. "Don't worry, it's my specialty," she said, pointing to the espresso pot and milk steamer on the tile counter.

They took their coffee back to the living room, where they talked about the present and the future, including Joe and Lizzie's baby, but neither drifted back to the past. They were enjoying themselves too much to risk broaching history. Brett felt as though an old friend had come back into her life, and she welcomed his return.

"I can't remember when I've had such a good time," David said. "I don't think I realized how much I missed my friends and family."

"I know. Even with all I said earlier about Paris, I'm glad to be home, too."

"I wonder if it's still snowing." David walked over to the front windows. "Well, I think the storm is over. I should really be leaving, Brett. It's late and I've got a wicked tomorrow."

"Your jacket is still in the studio. We can get it on the way down."

"Today has been a lovely surprise, considering I was going to grab some dinner alone this evening and look over apartment floor plans my realtor sent me. Thank you," David said warmly as they made their way downstairs. When they got to the studio and Brett handed David his jacket, he took it in both his hands and looked down at it a moment, as though studying the collar. When he looked up, he said, "I'd like to call you—to see you again, take you out."

Brett was caught off guard. She had assumed she would see him from time to time at Lizzie's, but his words and his tone suggested something more than an outing with his little sister's friend. *I can't read too much into this*, she thought. "Sure. I'd like that, David. We native New Yorkers can get reacquainted with the city together."

They made their way down to the front door and stood close to each other in the foyer, not quite touching. David shifted his weight, seeming ill at ease for the first time that day. "Have you ever considered a computer for your business? There are so many applications, from accounting to keeping track of mailing lists. There are also some computer-generated graphics being developed that look so real you'd swear they were photographs. Not that they're anything like what you do with a camera, but they're pretty amazing. I'll be glad to show you." The relaxed tenor of his voice had become a disembodied patter. He zipped his jacket and pulled the collar up around his neck.

"You may have to tunnel your way out," Brett said, fiddling with the locks. When she swung the door open, the snow that had drifted against it fell in a heap on the floor. Rocky's footprints had been virtually obscured, and not even tire tracks marred the plush carpet of untainted snow. "Will you be warm enough? I can get you a muffler or a sweater. I have big, bulky ones," Brett said.

"No. I'll be fine. It's only a block to Third Avenue. I should be able to catch a cab there." David let himself look into Brett's eyes, and he slowly extended his hand. She grasped it gently but firmly, squeezed it for a moment, then let go. "Good night, David."

"You should go inside. You're not dressed for this," David said.

"Good night," she said again, then quietly shut the door and leaned her back against it. She stared into the velvety darkness, a contented smile on her face. She felt giddy, like she did when she drove a winding road on a sunny afternoon in May, her favorite music playing and the wind bewitching her hair. *Get hold of yourself*, she thought as she made her way upstairs. Suddenly, each step seemed three feet tall, as she realized that it had been a very long day and she was tired.

She got through her bedtime preparations by rote and donned a filmy white batiste poet's shirt. She climbed the two steps into her rice-carved mahogany four-poster and was asleep as soon as her head hit the pillow. She felt like she had been sleeping for hours when she became aware of an urgent ringing that at first sounded miles away, then progressed closer and seemed to come from within her. With a start she awoke, realizing it was the doorbell, and bounded barefoot to the window. She could make out curly hair and shoulders hunched over in a brown leather jacket. Snatching her white terry robe from the footboard, Brett raced downstairs, not bothering to stop for the intercom, and threw open the door.

"David, what happened?" she asked.

David was shivering noticeably. Trying to control the quiver in his voice, he said, "I don't know how I could have been so stupid. I should have known that getting a cab would be impossible. I'm sorry, Brett. I didn't want to wake you, but nothing is moving out there. I waited forty-five minutes, then started walking. I got as far as Thirty-fourth Street, realized I wasn't going to make it to the Upper West Side, and headed back here."

"You must be freezing," Brett said, cupping her hands over his reddened ears.

"I deserve it. I'm an adult. I'm supposed to think ahead, not walk around with my head in my pocket."

"Don't be so hard on yourself. You could have gotten frostbite.

I'll yell at you in the morning for waiting so long to come back. Right now, let's get you warm."

Brett shepherded him to her living quarters, gave him her navy cashmere robe, an oversized white T-shirt, emblazoned with the Zoom Models logo, and a pair of the thermal socks she used for skiing, and pointed him toward the guest bathroom. While he changed from his cold, wet clothes, she warmed a snifter of Armagnac and pulled an alpaca throw from the Chippendale highboy where she stored bed linen. After he used the phone in the hall to let his parents know he would not be home, Brett escorted David to the guest room and made him get into bed, then surrounded him with the eiderdown comforter, wrapped the throw around his shoulders, and sat on a tailored white slipper chair while he sipped the warm potion.

David had his knees pulled to his chest and under the mountain of covers he looked like a crouching bedouin, idly tending his flock. "I feel remarkable silly," David said. "This is not exactly the image of me I'd like you to remember, but you've saved my skin. Thank you."

Brett came and tucked the comforter more tightly around him. "You're very welcome," she responded, and turned off the lamp before she left the room.

David had gone when Brett rose the next morning. She found the bed made and her robe and other gear neatly draped on the chair. She dressed hurriedly and gathered the film she needed to take to the lab. If she got it in by eight, she would have it back by one.

When she swept open the front door she stopped short, flung her head back, and burst into laughter. A snowman, squat and rotund, with the cork from last night's bottle of wine for a nose and two shriveled mushrooms for eyes, sat in the middle of the walkway. Attached to a yardstick skewered through the center of his body to make arms dangled a sign, which read, "David says thanks."

— *Chapter 23* —

"It's so big!" Brett exclaimed, eyeing the oval of smoked glass, still swaddled in plastic bubble packing and balanced on two cylindrical, black steel helixes, that formed David's desk. It was the only piece of furniture in his enormous private office. "The coils look like giant Slinkies." As she walked farther into the room, her footsteps crackled on the padded brown paper that covered the newly installed black granite floor.

When David had called the night before to ask if she was free for dinner, he explained that he was spending the day at his new headquarters, checking on the progress of the construction underway.

"Why don't I meet you there? I'd love to take a peek," Brett had said. So he sent a private taxi to transport her to the elliptical skyscraper on Third Avenue and Fifty-second Street where his new offices were. The unusual lines made the building resemble a giant tube of lipstick. The thirty-fifth through thirty-eighth floors were being renovated for Hands On.

"As soon as we settled on the building, I had the idea for the desk. I thought it was kind of funny," he said, following her to the windows. The outer walls arched in a slow curve, and the inner walls of the room had been constructed to complete the orbit. A view of the East River and Queens stretched out below them, and a string of angry red brake lights extended across the Fifty-ninth Street Bridge, from the Second Avenue entry ramp out of sight.

"I'm usually in the office by seven in the morning, and I liked this location because it faces east, so it gets the early light," David explained.

"From what I've heard, you're in the office late at night, too," Brett said. She admired David's accomplishments. He had built the Fortune 500 company on his own, and that took a special kind of person, yet he still seemed so . . . regular.

"Yeah, sometimes I get carried away. I'll be sitting at a terminal working, and one thing leads to another. I just forget the time." He showed Brett where his computer workstation would be installed and talked about some of the new systems in production. "We've just installed our first air traffic control computers in a small airport in Arizona. They're programmed to simplify the job of monitoring arriving and departing aircraft, and the early word is that they're a great improvement on the old equipment." He paused, and they followed the progress of the tram suspended high above the river as it moved almost imperceptibly from Roosevelt Island to Manhattan. "And I promise I won't say another word about computers for the rest of the evening. I really do think about other things." He looked over at Brett. "I must say, you're a natural in a hard hat." Much of the four floors was still a network of ducts and risers, so they had been issued yellow helmets on the way in.

Brett smiled and rapped hers with her fist. "If work stays as slow as it's been, maybe I should take up construction," she said. She had not admitted to anyone her disappointment about the sluggish pace of her career progress, but she recognized David as someone who would empathize. "But let's not talk about that now. I want to see the rest of the place."

The tour was cursory, at best. So much of the space was still raw that it required almost all of Brett's imagination to see the offices as David envisioned them.

When they exited through the revolving doors, they were assaulted by a gust of wind and the rush of pedestrians zig-zagging impatiently along the sidewalk. "I'd almost forgotten how intensely New Yorkers walk. If you don't keep up, you can get trampled," David commented as he steered her to the hired car. "There's one stop I'd like to make before we go to dinner, if that's all right with you."

"I'm game," Brett said brightly as she ducked into the car.

The driver picked his way painstakingly through the tangle of crosstown traffic and stopped in front of the Steinway & Sons showroom on West Fifty-seventh Street.

"I donated Kate's concert grand to our local music society after she died," David explained. A distant look flashed across his face, but he quickly recovered. "I just settled on an apartment, and the first piece of furniture I want is a piano."

"I didn't know you played," Brett commented as she passed through the doors.

"I learned pretty late. I wanted piano lessons in the worst way when I was a kid, but my parents worked hard to come up with whatever tuition wasn't covered by scholarships for Lizzie and me, so I didn't bug them about it. When the business started doing well, I treated myself to lessons. It relaxes me to sit in a room by myself and play. I can forget whatever ails me."

They were met by a gracious receptionist, who told them to feel free to test the pianos. The dark-paneled room, two stories high and wrapped by an ornately carved gallery, was scattered with oriental carpets and empire settees, and looked more like the music room of a manor house than a store. A youngster dressed in green woolen trousers and a red-and-green-plaid jacket perched on the edge of a piano stool, his feet dangling in the air. He played scales tentatively, dwarfed by the massive walnut grand, as his parents watched eagerly and spoke in whispers to one of the salesmen.

"Which one do you like?" David asked.

"The black one," she announced.

"Excellent choice," David declared as they approached the classic baby grand. He dropped his jet suede duffel coat next to him on the bench and spread his fingers over the keys. The delicate opening strains of "Clair de Lune" floated on the air. David, his eyes closed, seemed mesmerized by the melody. Brett rested lightly against the piano, enchanted by the expressive music. She could feel the vibrations of the tiny felt hammers striking the fragile strings, and it was as if the rhapsody played through her.

"That was beautiful," Brett said when the final note had faded.

"Thank you," David said when he opened his eyes. He had a slight frown, as though he was trying to ignore a persistent headache.

"It's nothing like the way Kate played, though. Her playing was woven magic."

They were interrupted by a saleswoman, who also complimented David, then answered his questions.

He's still not over Kate, Brett thought. The accident had been so tragic. She tried to imagine the torment he must have felt as he fought to save her. Now he seemed to be trying to get his life in order and to live again.

David noodled on several other pianos, then announced, "I think you picked the best one right off the bat, Brett. I'm going to take it." He completed the necessary paperwork and they left. "It will really feel like home. If I only have a mattress on the floor and a piano, I'll be happy!"

They reentered the waiting car. "So, I know you can cook and play the piano. What other hidden talents do you have?" Brett asked.

"Let's see . . . I can tie a mean square knot, ice skate forward and backward . . ."

"Wait a minute. You can skate?"

"Sure. I wanted to be a speed skater when I was growing up."

"I love ice skating! It's so graceful and fluid."

"We'll have to go sometime," David said.

"The Rockefeller Center rink is only a couple of blocks away. Let's go now," Brett said impulsively. The impatient sunset of February had left a clear night, and the air was crisp and invigorating, not cold. Brett's face was alive with the spontaneity of the moment and her eyes twinkled with mischievous excitement. She wasn't sure what had motivated her impromptu suggestion. It seemed silly and frivolous, but it was exactly what she wanted to do right now, and she sensed that David would be game.

"Okay, let's head for the ice."

At the rink they checked their coats and laced into rented skates. Brett looked as if she had dressed for the occasion. Her black leggings fit neatly into her skates, and the teal jersey peplum top she wore resembled a skater's short, flirty dress. She wrapped her scarf, a field of poppies and peonies painted on a long rectangle of silk, loosely around her neck.

David looked sporty in his charcoal corduroy trousers and a bulky, Aztec-inspired hand-knit pullover. "Don't laugh. I haven't skated in a long time, and I may be a little rusty," he said as he glided onto the ice.

"Wait, don't leave me!" Brett squealed as she grabbed the railing, tiptoed gingerly onto the rink, slipped, and found herself seated on the cold surface. She giggled as she tried to stand, and two rink guards descended on her, stopping in a hail of ice shavings. By the time they helped her up, David had made his way over and, looking ever so slightly disappointed, they delivered her into his care.

"I thought you could skate," David remarked, an amused grin on his face. He held her firmly around the waist and she clutched his other arm tightly.

"I said I *like* skating! I'd do anything to learn how to skate, but up 'til now I've been a total failure at it. I *am* a willing pupil, though," she said sheepishly.

By this time David had begun to move her around the rink. "The first lesson is you can't skate in steps. You've got to let go and glide."

"But I can't!" she said, eyes glued to her feet.

"There's nothing to it. I've got you. Just relax your body, shift your weight from side to side, and hold on." With that he set off in long, smooth strokes, in time to Liza Minelli's rousing version of "New York, New York".

Brett squeaked as she slipped and stumbled on the ice, but David held her firm. After several turns around the rink, her awkward stumbling looked more like gliding. She stopped fighting the flow and let herself join in his rhythm, enjoying the giddy sensation of speed and the whoosh of other skaters passing quickly by them. Her body was pressed close to David's, and his arm felt strong holding her waist. Occasionally she looked up at the crowd of spectators leaning over the brass railings. The colorful blur of their clothes looked like confetti, tossed to celebrate her accomplishment on the ice.

"So, are you ready to go solo?" David asked brightly.

"Don't go far!" Brett said.

First he let go of her waist, and after a few strokes, her hand, and Brett continued to glide on her own. She laughed and clapped her hands, captivated by the rush of freedom. Then, like a child who takes his first steps and panics when he realizes he's walking, she slipped to the ice once again. They continued around the rink, Brett taking her share of spills but gamely getting up and starting over. David stayed with her, giving her encouragement and pointers.

"I probably won't be able to move tomorrow," Brett said when they had finally turned in their skates and headed back to the car.

"But you looked great. Keep up the good work—the Olympics are coming soon."

"I had no idea I was so wet until we sat down in the car," Brett said as she unlocked her front door. "Make yourself a drink or whatever. You know where everything is. I'll be down as soon as I change."

David removed his coat and busied himself at the bar cart while Brett ran upstairs to her bedroom. She was happy. Her afternoon with David had been easy and unconstrained by dating anxiety. And even though neither one of them had referred to their outing as a date, in Brett's mind, that's what it was.

When she had been younger, she had dreamed this scenario so often that the loosely woven homespun of her reveries had been worn thin by overuse and she had patched it with carefully placed 'maybes' and 'what ifs'. Now Brett was at the spinning wheel again, imagining David in her life on a regular basis. *You have to stop this. You have no reason to think he's anything more than a friend*, she told herself as she stepped out of her sodden leggings and socks.

Leaving them in a heap on the floor, she padded into the arched passageway between the bedroom and the bathroom. Two walls of mirrors slid back to reveal closets that had been adapted with shelves, drawers, and multilevel rods to hold gowns, dresses, skirts, slacks, sweaters, blouses, lingerie, and shoes. She grabbed a pair of panty hose from a drawer and sat on the tufted bench that occupied the space in the center of her dressing room. Standing again, she smoothed her hose and pulled a form-fitting black knit dress from its hanger, then decided that it was too suggestive for a first date

—especially one that wasn't really a date. She explored several options, and finally selected a sapphire-blue lambswool and angora sweater and skirt.

At the pink marble vanity in her bathroom, she hastily applied makeup, freed her hair from its ponytail, and brushed it. As she passed through the dressing room, she took a pair of fuchsia suede boots from a shelf. When she walked into the bedroom, she saw the message light blinking on her answering machine. She perched on the edge of the bed, pushed the play button, and tugged on her boots as she listened.

"Brett, it's me. Call me the minute you get in—I mean, the very minute. Have I got news for you! Call me!" Lizzie's message ended.

By the excited tone of her voice, Brett could tell that something major was up. *Maybe she's being transferred to Katmandu*, Brett thought as she dialed her friend's number. Lizzie picked up on the first ring.

"Hi! I just got your message, and don't say guess what," Brett said.

"Okay, I won't—I'll tell you straight out. But I hope you're sitting down," Lizzie said.

"I'm sitting. What is it?"

"You know that baby I'm having? Well, it seems that he or she is going to have a sister or a brother, too!" Lizzie said.

It took Brett a few seconds for Lizzie's convoluted revelation to sink in. "You're having twins?" Brett said. "You and Joe wanted a family, and I guess two babies is a good start. This changes everything. Now you have to buy baby things in pairs. Are you going to have enough room?"

"It'll be fine in the beginning, but we'll have to find a bigger place once they're older." Joe and Lizzie's West Seventy-fifth Street apartment was spacious by New York City standards, but even it would become cramped with two little ones on the loose.

"Your parents must be wearing ear-to-ear grins," Brett said.

"I think they've called everyone they've ever known to brag," Lizzie said proudly. "But no one can find David."

"Lizzie, I'm on my way out to dinner, so I'll call you tomorrow, but could you hold on just a second?" Brett asked, and without waiting for her reply, bounded down the stairs.

David was sitting in one of the apricot velvet wing chairs, his feet propped up on the needlepoint tabouret in front of him, holding his drink in one hand and conducting Duke Ellington's "A Train," which played on the stereo, with the other.

Brett grabbed the telephone from the writing table by the window and handed it to him. "Someone wants to speak to you," she said mysteriously.

"To me? I never even heard the phone ring," David said, puzzled. "Hello?"

"David! What are you doing there?" Lizzie asked. "Brett said she was going out to dinner. You're her date? Who would've guessed, after all these years?"

"I'm not sure that's any of your business, but I don't think that's why you wanted to speak to me," David teased. "Are you all right? Is everything okay with the baby?"

"The babies are fine," Lizzie said.

"I know you're my baby sister, but that's not what I meant," David said.

"It's not what I meant, either. I'm going to have twins, David! I had a sonogram this afternoon, and the doctor confirmed it—two babies!"

Brett chattered about the babies on the way to the restaurant. She was bursting with excitement. David made no effort to change the subject, but Brett noted that as she continued, he seemed more taciturn. *He's probably thinking about Kate and the baby*, she thought, and tactfully changed the subject.

Seated side by side over their late supper at Positano, they conferred about everything from Brett's work to David's decorating. When they finally returned to Gramercy Park, David escorted Brett to the house.

"Can I get you a nightcap?" she offered, once inside the foyer. She was not anxious for the evening to end. She felt more lighthearted and happy than she had in months—since Paris, and Lawrence.

"I've got to pass this time," David said. He leaned against the doorjamb and removed his tortoiseshell glasses deliberately, stuffing them in his coat pocket. The intensity of his unencumbered gaze seemed magnified tenfold. "You're quite something, Miss Brett Larsen. Why do I have such a good time when I'm with you?" he asked, a hint of bemusement in his voice. He put his hands around her arms and moved them slowly up and down. "It's getting redundant to say I had a good time, but I did, Brett."

She edged closer, straightening the horn toggle on his coat. "It's only redundant when you're bored. Are you?" she asked. Her heart seemed to beat to the rhythm of his gentle massage.

"Somehow, I think I'd rarely be bored with you." For a moment they stood in silence, their faces illuminated by a moonbeam shining through the three glass panes in the door. "Good night, Brett," he finally uttered, then his lips met hers in a kiss as clear and full of hope as the trill of a violin. "I'll call you tomorrow."

Brett was so transfixed by the kiss that she could only nod her head. David's lips were the first ones she had ever imagined kissing, but that fantasy did nothing to tarnish the reality.

As soon as he stepped back into the night, he said, "Lock the door. I wouldn't want anyone out here to hurt you." When he'd heard the snap of the dead bolt, he returned to the car.

Slumping in the backseat, he pressed his palms to his temples, as if to squeeze unwanted thoughts out of his head by sheer force. He rolled the window down midway so the cold air slapped his face. *You like her. She makes you see the world in color again. Don't fight it*, David admonished himself. After Kate had died he had remained outwardly strong, but silently wore a hair shirt of blame. Despite the assurances of the couple who were on the boat with them, and his family and friends, that he had done all he could to save her, he held himself responsible. He should never have let her go out on the boat. He should have foreseen the shift in weather and sought a haven. In his mind, he had paid for his recklessness with the life of his wife and child. He had been granted the happiness that some people seek in vain for their whole lives, yet he had lost it, and he felt unworthy of another chance.

With time, he had partially raised his impenetrable curtain of solitude, allowing himself to respond to those around him, but not enough to permit the possibility of loving another woman.

When he had realized that Brett would be taking the photographs for his magazine profile, he had thought it was a pleasant coincidence, like finding himself seated at a dinner party next to a classmate he hadn't seen since graduation. He expected they would make small talk about the past, touch briefly in the present, and shake hands until the next time. But from the first evening he had spent with Brett, he had felt powerless to curb the sprouting of emotions, like new green seedlings, relentlessly pushing upward through charred earth and ash after a forest fire.

Dammit, I didn't kill Kate, and giving up my life won't bring her back, he thought, slamming the car door resolutely once it stopped in front of his parents' home. He didn't know if seeing Brett would lead him to happiness, but he would at least take the chance.

— *Chapter 24* —

Jeffrey pushed the brass handle on the etched glass door and ushered Brett into the red and pink gilded opulence of the Russian Tea Room. Brett was not particularly fond of the posh restaurant, but it was one of Jeffrey's favorites and they dined there often. After checking their coats, the maître d' greeted them warmly, as usual. "So nice to see you again, Mr. Underwood. Your table is ready," he said, and smoothly palmed the money Jeffrey handed him as he slid into the curved, red leather banquette. Brett had figured that if only half the restaurant's patrons were as generous as Jeffrey, the maître d' could make anywhere from five hundred to a thousand dollars a day in tips alone from people who were gratified by the recognition and elitism that set them apart from even those with reservations, who had to wait for a table. She also surmised that Jeffrey liked the deferential treatment he received, and she knew he enjoyed being seated in the bustling, slightly noisy, eminently desirable, highly visible, front of the restaurant.

To their left, a corpulent, world-renowned tenor who was in rehearsal for *Rigoletto* at the Met added a dollop of sour cream to his chilled borscht, and on their right, a national network anchorwoman who had just been given her own prime-time interview show shared a plate of pirozhki with her third husband. Directly opposite them a balding Arab, reported to be the wealthiest man in the world, washed down his kirsch-soaked baba with gulps of steaming dark Russian tea from a cup that was instantly refilled by the tunic-clad waiter who anxiously hovered nearby.

Jeffrey had ordered appetizers, and almost before the heavy white linen napkins were in their laps, a waiter appeared, balancing a tray that he placed on a folding stand beside the table. He set the dishes before them, one by one, and without so much as a ping, removed the domed silver lids with a flourish, then disappeared. He had waited on Mr. Underwood before and knew that prompt, silent service ensured that a healthy tip would be added to the bill.

Brett dipped her palette into the mound of shimmering, black Beluga cradled in a snowy bed of crushed ice and savored the pungent, salty flavor.

Dislodging a frosty crystal flacon of Stolichnaya from its arctic home and ignoring the bits of ice that clung to its sides and base, Jeffrey filled two pony glasses nestled in the same silver server as the vodka. He handed one of the tiny flutes to Brett. "Skoal!" he said, and finished his drink in one swallow.

"You're not Swedish," Brett said playfully. "Although you certainly have the coloring."

"That's true," Jeffrey said hastily. "But my mother was part Dane, and spending so many years around Mr. Larsen has influenced me in many ways," he added.

Brett knew that Jeffrey was probably closer to her grandfather than anyone, and since their first meeting in Paris two and a half years ago, she had tried to glean information from him about the enigmatic Sven Larsen. But Jeffrey's accounts of her grandfather were not insightful or enlightening. They were as clinical and sterile as those she had read in various business journals, so she gave up asking.

Brett had been given the regulation computer-dating bio on Jeffrey. He had grown up an only child in Minnesota. His parents had been killed in an auto accident when he had been a sophomore at Northwestern, and he had attended Yale Law on a partial scholarship and the insurance money he received from his parents, but Brett still felt as if she didn't know much about him. At first she had thought he was detached, but she had come to realize that he was unattached—not connected to anyone or anything—and in light of her own feelings of displacement, she could understand his deliberate creation of a space around him.

Jeffrey was kind, attentive, and stabilizing. Chaos was as foreign to him as riding the subway. But there was something studied about the order in his life. He didn't seem to really want what he wanted. Rather, he appeared to want what he thought he should want, such as a prime table in the Russian Tea Room, and Savile Row suits.

Brett had been seeing a lot of David, but there was something calm and reassuring about Jeffrey, and she wanted to know him better. She hadn't slept with either of them, and after Lawrence, she was not ready to put all her eggs in one basket.

Brett took a blini from the platter, laid it on her plate, scooped caviar onto the center of the small yeast pancake, and dribbled juice from a lemon wedge over the pearly black roe. "I'm really glad we're having dinner tonight, Jeffrey. I know I've been tied up a lot lately. It's harder to get started in this town than I thought. But enough excuses. There's something I want you to do for me."

"Brett, all you need do is ask," Jeffrey said.

"I want to buy an apartment—not for me or as an investment. It's to be a gift," Brett said, for once enormously pleased that money was at her disposal.

"Granted, there might be some tax advantages, but why would you want to make a gift of that size?"

"It's for Lizzie and Joe. Jeffrey, they're having twins. I didn't have a chance to tell you before, but isn't it wonderful? Lizzie mentioned the other day that the owner of the condo directly below hers was being transferred and she's putting her unit on the market. Don't you see? It's the best gift I could give them. Of course, I also want to pay for the conversion to a duplex, but they'll have so much room, and heaven knows they're going to need it."

"That is good news, and the purchase should be no problem. The present owner would probably enjoy a direct cash sale. If you can get me her name and number, you can consider it done. When do you want Elizabeth to know?"

"As soon as the offer is accepted. Then she and Joe can meet with the architects. I've already spoken to Chuck Hitchcock. He knows the building, and he's anxious to take on the project."

Jeffrey methodically cut a blini with his knife and fork and took a mouthful.

"You have sour cream right there," Brett said, pointing to a spot above his upper lip. Jeffrey instantly dabbed the place she indicated before the white blob could be noticed by someone else.

"When is Elizabeth planning to leave her job at GNSN?" he asked.

"She'll work as long as possible and return a few months after the babies are born. Now that they don't have to worry about buying a larger place, they can afford to hire full-time help."

"She will certainly need help, but don't you think she should be a full-time mother? It's very important, you know." He refilled his tiny glass.

"This is the twentieth century, Jeffrey. Women work *and* raise children all the time!"

"Some women have to work; your friend does not. Her husband's income from his so-called profession is quite substantial, according to you."

"So-called? What's that—his modeling or his sculpting? Yes, Joe makes enough money to support his family, even if it's not what you'd consider a profession, but that's not the point," Brett said, pushing her plate away.

"That *is* the point," Jeffrey said sternly. "A man has a responsibility to provide for his wife and children."

"Let's talk about something else," Brett suggested before she gave the waiter her order for green schi, a light creamy spinach soup.

"Is that all you're having?" Jeffrey asked, then selected the grilled rack of lamb with eggplant à la Russe.

Brett nodded and Jeffrey dismissed the waiter. The blinis had partially slaked her hunger, and Jeffrey's strong opinions had taken care of the rest.

"What was it you were saying earlier about this being a difficult town?" Jeffrey asked solicitously.

"I'm not sure you can understand, but I can't seem to get anywhere, and it's frustrating. I know I could attend the right parties and play the 'if I do something for you, what can you do for me' game, but I don't want my future based on something so inane."

"It's not so unusual. It happens in every profession." Jeffrey paused, adjusting a moonstone cuff link. "You know, Larsen controls a lot of advertising dollars. We could arrange an introduction to our account exec."

"That's not what I want! I don't want the doors to fly open because I'm a Larsen. I'm a damn good photographer, and I'll work as hard as I have to, but obviously, the dues I paid in Paris don't cover me here," Brett said, exasperation evident in her voice.

"You really shouldn't be so upset. You have no need to earn a living," Jeffrey said.

"You sound just like my mother did when I told her I was going to be a photographer. This is my career. You chose the law, I chose something else, but that doesn't make it any less important. It's what I do."

"You can take photographs any time and place you wish. You don't need to do it under the aegis of a well-lifted spinster who's dedicated her life to fashion, or some blatantly fey homosexual who really wishes he were a woman."

"Jeffrey! How can you say such things? Talent and passion for one's work don't apply just to lawyers and doctors. They apply to anyone who cares about what they do."

"It was just an observation. You mustn't infer an insult that wasn't intended. Your work is very good," he said, retreating slightly from his stance.

Brett looked down at the pale green soup, which had become cold and congealed. "I have a headache, Jeffrey. I'm going home. Thank you for dinner. I'll call you tomorrow about the apartment." She slid out of the banquette. "Good night," she said, and headed toward the coat check.

Jeffrey was incensed and embarrassed. No one had ever walked out on him before, and the specter of public humiliation made him cringe. The congested room suddenly annoyed him, and he wanted to flee the restaurant, but he could not. The only way he could save face and deflect the attention of the prying eyes he imagined were on him was to finish his meal unhurriedly.

He looked around him. The tenor, now gone, had been replaced by a divorce attorney known for his flamboyant style and the seven- or even eight-figure settlements he routinely attained for his clients, usually women. The anchorwoman and her husband were deep in discussion, and seated where the Saudi billionaire had been were an actress whose poignant portrayals of troubled women had won her several Oscars, and the dark-haired, chevron-eyebrowed, quixotic actor who had been her co-star in a recently released film. The waiters and waitresses were busy with the demands of their duties. No one paid him any attention.

But now he was annoyed at being ignored. He knew he was not as famous or rich as most of the celebrated diners, though his lifestyle indicated otherwise.

Business affiliations allowed Jeffrey to live as though he were a very wealthy man. His six-figure salary package included perquisites such as club memberships and a car and driver at his disposal. So Jeffrey salted away most of his income in very safe investments and offshore bank accounts, except for what he spent on clothing, which was considerable, and the mortgage on his Upper East Side apartment. Season tickets to the ballet, opera, and symphony, and box seats at all the major sporting events, were gifts from those thankful for the opportunity to do business with Larsen Enterprises. And his expense account, which often totaled as much as fifteen thousand dollars a month, was justified to his parsimonious employer as part of the cost of doing business internationally.

So with his splendid custom-made wardrobe, and refined manner and speech, and regular tables at "21", The Jockey Club and The Four Seasons, Jeffrey Underwood moved about freely in the world of wealth and power.

He waited impatiently for his check to come; then, as he retrieved his dove-gray vicuna topcoat, the maître d' said, "I hope your companion is all right. She left in quite a hurry."

"She had another appointment," Jeffrey lied.

A cold blast of wintry air greeted him as he made his way through the crowd leaving a concert at Carnegie Hall and into his car, which was double-parked just beyond the restaurant. By the time the driver had turned left on Third Avenue and headed uptown, Brett had taken two aspirin and gone to bed, wondering if she and Jeffrey could ever get beyond such basic differences in their views.

Jeffrey realized that the predawn phone call from Sven's secretary, instructing him to appear at the LARSair terminal at quarter past nine that morning, did not bode well. Sven Larsen deviated from schedule only for matters of the utmost importance, and his itinerary did not call for him to be in New York for another two weeks.

Jeffrey awakened his secretary and dispatched him to the office to retrieve several files on projects of immediate concern to Sven. He alerted his driver to pick up the files and be in front of the building at quarter past eight to take him to Kennedy Airport. A sharp, icy rain had rendered the Grand Central Parkway a twisted maze, littered regularly with tangled wrecks, still smoking and tended by police officers and ambulances.

"Don't you know an alternate route? We could walk faster," Jeffrey had carped. He did not want whatever was bothering Sven to be compounded by his lateness.

Jeffrey skittered through the terminal, dodging slow-moving travelers wheeling bulging satchels on folding metal carts and backpack-laden students posed like statues with eyes upturned to the departure board. He flashed his ID badge at the security officers and continued past the metal detectors without breaking stride, finally coming to a halt in front of an unassuming door painted the same industrial shade of nonwhite as the rest of the corridor. It was the entrance to the Viking Club, LARSair's VIP lounge. He stopped just outside to mop sweat from his face, adjust his clothing, and smooth his hair, long strands of which drooped in his face, revealing the thinness normally hidden by his careful combing. As soon as he entered the lounge, a woman uniformed in a crimson LARSair coatdress with gold trim ushered him through the somber room. Its only occupant, an elderly gentleman in a glen-plaid suit, sat on the far side of the lounge in a club chair, chuckling at the salmon pink pages of the *Financial Times*. She stopped in front of the larger-than-life oil portrait of Sven Larsen that guarded the room, flipped a latch hidden behind the gilt frame, and pulled open the door concealed by the painting.

Sven sat with his back to Jeffrey. Hands clasped in his lap, he peered through the windows at airplanes taxiing in slow motion along the runway. Abrupt gusts of wind battered the glass panes with icy pellets.

"Mr. Larsen, your visit is most unexpected. Hopefully, nothing untoward has occurred," Jeffrey said.

Without appearing to move a muscle, Sven wheeled the chair around. "Mr. Underwood, you have proven in the past to be an able facilitator, and I have had no reason to look over your shoulder to ensure that a job is being handled to my specifications." Sven took a silver cigar bullet from his breast pocket, removed the thick rod of tobacco, bit off the tip, and spit it on the floor. He balanced it unlit, in his left hand, between his middle finger and the stump of his index finger, then continued. "I arrived yesterday, telephoned my granddaughter, and invited her to dinner. I asked her to bring the guest of her choosing, fully expecting to find you at my dinner table. Imagine my surprise when she showed up with another gentleman." Dressed in black, Sven looked like an unmerciful judge.

Every muscle in Jeffrey's body tightened in response to the news, as though girding for the worst possible verdict. "Brett has been my frequent companion for several months," he began feebly. He was mortified and furious, but he was careful to mask his emotions. After years of working himself into a position of power and influence, he was now reduced to defending the progress and effectiveness of his courting techniques.

"That may well be. It seems to me the question is whether you are her companion of *choice*." Sven fished a wooden matchstick from his pocket, flicked the head with his thumbnail, and lit his cigar, sucking on it until a steady ember glowed at the end and the pungent aroma permeated the room. "Women desire what you teach them they can't live without, Mr. Underwood. I suggest you keep that in mind." Sven's piercing blue eyes bored into Jeffrey, emphasizing his words. "That is all." Sven rotated his chair back toward the window.

Jeffrey spun on his heels and left the room. His white-hot rage short-circuited his senses. He neither saw nor heard the hostess who said good-bye to him as he left the lounge. Like a zombie, he put one foot in front of the other until he passed from the LARSair terminal and came upon a bank of telephones. Each was currently occupied. Jeffrey paced like an animal.

When he noticed a young woman peeking at him, then quickly averting her eyes when he looked at her, he realized that his agitation was apparent and he had to get control of himself. Jeffrey stopped pacing and leaned against the plate glass window of the gift shop across from the phones. He pressed his arm across his body, propped the other elbow on his clenched fist, appearing to rest his head in his hand, but with the nail of his thumb he gouged the back of his ear lobe. The force of his anger seemed to dissipate as the stabbing pain increased. When an army sergeant wearing dress greens and carrying a black briefcase left one of the phones, Jeffrey hurriedly took his place. As he entered the string of calling card numbers on the phone, he noticed blood under his nail and a thin trickle down his thumb. He reached for a handkerchief to wipe it away.

"Explain to me why I'm paying you for information about Brett Larsen when I just found out that she went to dinner last night with someone else!" Jeffrey said angrily into the receiver. "I don't care what you think is or is not important—I want to know *everything*! I want to know if she has a cold. I want to know if the same messenger delivers packages two days in a row. Do you hear me? Or else you will find yourself in more trouble than your feeble brain can comprehend!" With that, he hung up the phone.

* * *

For the last three months, rumors of *Voilà!* starting an American edition had been rampant in the fashion and magazine industries. Word was that based on the phenomenal success of *Elle*'s transmigration, *Voilà!* planned to challenge the brash new interloper for a slice of the American pie. Brett had heard many versions of the story. One had the entire staff of the Paris office setting up shop in New York. Another held that the American magazine would duplicate exactly the fashion pages of the French edition, and only the articles would be geared to the new *Voilà!* readers. With one phone call, Brett knew she could get the whole story, but she wasn't willing to ask Lawrence for information that might imply she was hungry for work.

At the end of February, work was still scarce, and Brett decided to call Nathalie Corbet, the fashion editor of *Voilà!*. After her initial reservations about Brett's inexperience, she had become an ally. Even after her break-up with Lawrence, Nathalie had kept in touch until Brett had left Paris. In Brett's estimation, Nathalie would be close enough to have answers, and she trusted her not to tell Lawrence about her inquiry.

When Brett went down to her office at six-thirty, it was still dark outside, but it was six hours later in Paris, and she wanted to place her call before Nathalie left for lunch. Her lunches were notoriously long when she didn't have a shoot scheduled, and now that Brett had made up her mind, she didn't want to wait.

She dialed the country and city code, then the number she still knew by heart, and was immediately put through to the fashion editor. After a surprised but happy hello, Nathalie launched into an abbreviated version of the latest Paris gossip before telling Brett that she had saved her a call. *Voilà! was* starting up in New York. She would be named editorial director, and she emphasized that Lawrence Chapin had no involvement in the New York operation. The premiere issue was slated for September and she planned to assign a minimum of fifteen editorial pages and a cover try to Brett. Work on the fat fall edition would not begin for another three months, but she wanted Brett to take all the photos necessary for their promotional materials. Press kits and ads had to be shot, as well as several dummy covers to show advertisers. She dropped the entire package in Brett's lap and scheduled a meeting for the day of her arrival in New York the following week.

How ironic, Brett thought. It was once again *Voilà!* that would provide her with the leg up she needed to climb the fashion ladder. *I don't care*, she said to herself as she penciled her meeting with Nathalie on her calendar. This time there are no tricks and there is no Lawrence. This was an editorial decision based solely on the strength of her work. New York was a mecca for fashion photographers, and any of them would consider themselves fortunate to have been given this assignment. But Nathalie had selected her, and Brett felt a surge of confidence she had almost forgotten.

Excited to share her good news, Brett looked at the digital clock on her desk. Although she and Nathalie had talked almost an hour, she decided to wait until at least nine o'clock before calling anyone. She sorted through some prints that had come in yesterday from the laminator, then put coffee on to brew in the studio kitchen. As the brown liquid dripped into the glass carafe, she flipped mentally through the pages of agency books, thinking of which portfolios she wanted to call in for her meeting with Nathalie. With a steaming mug in her hand, she returned to her office and curled up on the window seat.

Hazy, early morning light poked through the darkness and she could see several pigeons scrounging for their breakfast. She hoped the day would be bright and sunny—a rarity in New York this time of year—but only the warmth of the sun could melt the icy gray crust that coated the garden.

When she checked her watch again, it was finally nine o'clock. She returned to her desk, picked up the phone, and automatically dialed David's number, but hung up before the connection was made. She picked up her loupe and absently rolled it between her fingers.

Brett knew that David's reaction would be as natural and spontaneous as her own, because that's the way it was when they were together. Their dates were random and unplanned, but eager and full of promise, and when she was with him, Brett felt carefree and girlish. She could say what was on her mind without worrying whether he would agree. David didn't seem to want or expect anything from her. They just had a good time. But Brett wasn't sure yet if she was attracted to him for the David he was now, or if she was drawn by the possible realization of her childhood fantasies. She had already concluded that it didn't matter because she enjoyed his company, and she was bursting to tell him about *Voilà!*.

On the other hand, maybe I should tell Jeffrey first, she thought as she replaced the loupe in its appointed spot. The day after their dinner at the Russian Tea Room, Brett had called and left information about the apartment with his secretary. Jeffrey had surprised her two days later by sending flowers and calling to apologize for his behavior. Somehow, she felt that Jeffrey had been there from the beginning. Without his help, it would have taken months for her to find and renovate a studio in Paris. He had also been supportive when Lillian had been ill, and he had made her move to New York painless. *And what would I have done if he hadn't found Thérèse?* she wondered.

In spite of his remarks at dinner, Brett knew that Jeffrey cared about her, and he obviously cared about her career. Why else would he put himself out? Her grandfather certainly had enough work to keep him busy, and she was aware that Sven viewed her career as a temporary fancy, an indulgence. So Jeffrey's actions on her behalf had to be motivated by his personal interest in her life and work. And because she liked him, Brett wanted to see Jeffrey enjoy himself, live a little, and lately, he seemed to do that more easily than he had in the past. But she knew that he was only that way with her. *I really am fond of him*, she thought. *He's done so much for me*.

She continued to stare at the telephone, weighing her options. Then, making her decision, she punched out a number.

"This is Brett Larsen. Liz Powell, please."

— *Chapter 25* —

Brett dropped the ticket she was given in exchange for her coat into her rhinestone and brass minaudière.

"Pardon me, I didn't get that," said a short, bearded man whose black eye patch added a hint of mystery to his otherwise ordinary appearance.

She looked across the reception area, which looked like a cobalt and silver space capsule. It was so sleek that she imagined it could take her into the twenty-first century. Seeing no one else in the room, she replied, "I didn't say anything."

Then the silky alto voice repeated, "We're glad you could join us this evening. I am Lottie, the Hands On reception module. What is your name?"

"It's the machine," Brett said, indicating the VDT unit, encased in brushed steel, to the left of the doors that led into the corporate reception center and executive offices.

The gentleman looked at Brett, then chuckled. "What on earth has David dreamed up this time?" he said and approached the terminal. He searched the keyboard to find out how to respond.

"Do not be shy. I am voice activated. Please tell me your name," Lottie intoned pleasantly.

"Well, I'll be. Richard Harrison," he replied.

By this time, Brett had joined him at the machine. As Lottie spoke, her words appeared in bright blue on the black screen.

"Professor Harrison, I hope your journey from Sacramento was pleasant, and congratulations on the publication of your new textbook. Please enter and enjoy the party." With a pneumatic pshhhhh, the glass doors that completed the circle of the walls slid open.

A smiling Richard Harrison disappeared inside and the doors closed behind him.

David didn't tell me about this, Brett thought, but Lottie interrupted her. "Thank you for waiting," she began, then continued her greeting. When Brett said her name, Lottie replied, "Your picture of David Powell in *New York Style* is excellent. David is looking forward to your arrival. Please enter and enjoy the party."

Only David could make a computer that I actually like, Brett mused as she joined the guests who had been invited to celebrate the official opening of the New York office. She was amazed that the space, which had been so rudimentary when she had seen it a short time before, was now the office of tomorrow. On both sides of the entrance, the walls peeled back in spectacular parabolas, and the dramatic curves were repeated in all the walls that circumscribed the spacious center core and formed the corridors that radiated out like spokes, leading to the offices of the corporate chieftains. All the surfaces in the room had a luster. The cobalt-blue floor shone like deep, still water under a full moon, and the color flowed seamlessly into the walls, where it gradually paled into a lighter, silvery hue that drifted into white at the ceiling. The work of contemporary American artists was exhibited on the walls and on chromium-plated cubes situated throughout the room.

"Brett—over here," she heard, and saw Joe waving at her.

"We'd about given you up for lost," he said, kissing her in greeting. "Brett, I'd like you to meet Enid Walker Sinclair. She's a corporate curator, and she oversaw the acquisition of the pieces in this collection."

"Pleased to meet you, Enid," she said, shaking hands with the tall, angular woman whose spiky, blue-black hair had been styled to resemble the prickly bur of a chestnut. "I haven't made my way around the room yet, so I haven't seen many of the pieces. Are they a permanent collection?"

"Actually, this is designed to be a revolving exhibit, with installations that change about every four months. Some of the pieces are for sale, some are on loan, but I've found that it's an ideal situation for many institutions and artists," Enid answered.

"Well, if it isn't the duchess of Gramercy Park. How's tricks, babycakes?'' Malcolm Kent, conservatively attired in a traditionally cut, notched-lapel tuxedo, crafted in black leather with suede trim paired with a collarless black linen shirt and steel-tipped ostrich leather cowboy boots, joined the circle.

"You're about the last person I expected to see here," Brett said, trying to keep the edge out of her voice for Joe and Enid's sake. She had given up looking for reasons why Malcolm might be miffed at her and had become annoyed at his outright snubbing.

"I'm like the timber wolf. I have a far-reaching natural habitat," he said.

"Aren't they nearly extinct?" Brett quipped. Malcolm's skin was the color of toast, courtesy of a trip to Rio for carnival, and Brett thought he looked more robust than he had the last time she had seen him, but she was hardly going to stand still for the verbal assault she could feel coming.

"I asked Malcolm to come as my escort, although I'm never sure I can handle him for a whole evening," Enid remarked. "We've known each other since I curated a show of his many years ago. How do you two know each other?"

"I saved Brett here from the throes of privilege by hiring her and giving her a trade. Tell me, darling, have you been working under an assumed name since you've come back? I've hardly seen your credit line," he said, twisting the knife.

"No, Malcolm. The name's the same, but keep looking. You'll find it." Brett's tone was gelid.

"That's right, I heard that Parisian rag you worked for is coming to New York. Just what this town needs—another magazine," Malcolm said.

Brett knew if she said one more word to him, the exchange would deteriorate into one of the bitch fights he so loved, and Brett wanted no part of it. "Joe, where's Lizzie?" she asked.

"She was sitting over near the windows a few minutes ago. Her mom and dad were over there, too," he replied.

"Enid, it was good to meet you. Joe, I think I'm going to find your wife . . . Malcolm." She nodded her head in his direction, but said nothing more to him before she strode off.

The lilting sound of an electronic harp was the perfect accompaniment to the tinkling chatter of the guests. People hovered near the display at the center of the room that featured Hands On models, from the new Fingertips-II PC to the more sophisticated and powerful Outreach office systems and computer aviation equipment. *There are at least two hundred people here*, she thought. *David must be so pleased*. She still hadn't seen any sign of him, but she knew he would be tied up tending to his guests.

Brett whisked a glass of champagne from the tray carried by a server dressed in a form-fitting jumpsuit of cobalt and silver—the Hands On corporate colors. She noticed a commotion, followed by laughter, coming from a cluster of people standing to her right. From the group emerged a five-foot robot with a computer monitor for a head and a barrel-shaped blue steel midsection, mounted on a rubber caterpillar tread. In its arms—black rubber bellows that ended in movable metal pincers—it held a tray of artfully displayed delicacies. It rolled over to Brett and stopped, and again a crowd of interested onlookers gathered.

"Would you like an hors d'oeuvre? We have crab in puff pastry, vegetable paté, and my favorite, the rumaki," the automaton offered solicitously in a nasal tenor voice.

Taking the computer's word, Brett chose the liver wrapped in bacon, took a napkin, and moved aside to allow others to make their selections. Suddenly she felt an arm around her waist.

"Brett, I'm so glad to see you." David looked dashing in his tuxedo and blue paisley bow tie. He kissed Brett on the cheek, then held her at arm's length. "You look sensational."

Brett beamed. Getting dressed had not been the leisurely process she had envisioned. Her power pack had malfunctioned during a test and the shooting had run late. Luckily, Frederica, the hair and makeup artist, had had time to stick around while Brett showered, and had swept her shiny, dark hair into a sleek topknot and applied her makeup. Brett loved the dress she had found for the evening, and secretly hoped that David would like it, too. The form-fitting raw silk dress, the vibrant pink of a tourmaline, had a wide vee neckline that began at her shoulders and pointed to the alluring roundness of her bust. The gently curving tulip skirt ended above her knee and revealed long, shapely legs. Her feet were encased in suede pumps that matched her dress exactly. The heels towered to an uncharacteristic four-inch height, and a suede bow flirted at the back of the ankle. Brett had chosen diamond drop earrings, a gift from her grandfather, to complete the ensemble.

"You must be on cloud nine. This is quite a party, and the place looks exactly the way you said it would."

"I wish I could take the credit, but the architects and designers are really the ones responsible for this," David responded modestly, indicating the dynamic, hi-tech space around him. "And one of my vice presidents handled the party plans." He didn't take his eyes off Brett. "I missed you," he said quietly. The final details of readying the office for occupancy had taken up most of his time, and David had been to California three times. Then he added, "I know I haven't seen you in two weeks, but did you grow?"

"It's the shoes." Brett extended her foot and rotated her ankle. "I don't know what possessed me. I missed you too," she added honestly. "Tell me about Lottie. I know I shouldn't be jealous, because she probably can't ice skate or play the piano either. Or can she?" Brett teased.

"Lottie's been my girl for a long time. I'll tell you all about her . . . later. There's someone I need to speak to. Promise not to leave? I'd hate for you to give Lottie an edge." David squeezed her hand, then melted into the crowd.

Brett spied Lizzie across the room, seated on one of the few pieces of furniture that had both a back and arms. Against the panoramic backdrop of the windowed wall she looked like a very petite, very pregnant Guinevere on the throne of a lofty, space age Camelot. The black and gold brocade cocktail dress Lizzie wore crisscrossed her bosom with gilded braid and her black velvet Louis heeled slippers with gold soutache truly gave her the appearance of a medieval lady-in-waiting.

"You look positively radiant. And I can't believe how long your hair is," Brett said, sitting on the bench opposite her friend.

"Thanks, you're no slouch yourself. My hair has grown like crazy since I've been pregnant. The doctor says it's not unusual." Lizzie's blond hair was piled high on her head, and individual ringlets had sought their own random position around her face.

"So, are you feeling okay?"

"I feel great, but I have orders to spend as much time off my feet as possible. It's working out fine at the station. When we're on location, I hang out in the van until the last possible moment. But I had no intention of missing this party, even if it means I have to sit through most of it," Lizzie said.

"I almost envy your excuse—these shoes are torture. I haven't seen your parents. Are they still here?"

"Oh, they're here, all right! My mother hasn't been so teary since my wedding, and by now, Daddy has probably popped all the studs off his shirt."

"I see you found her," Joe said as he joined them. "Brett, what was all that back there? I've never seen you like that before."

"Malcolm Kent has always been difficult, but now he's impossible. It's a long story, Joe, better left to another time." Changing the subject, Brett said, "David has really outdone himself."

"It's really something, isn't it?" Lizzie said fondly. "Have you had your horoscope done yet?"

"My what?"

"There's a computer that predicts your future according to the stars. It's right by the man with the eye patch. Maybe it can give you the scoop on you and David," Lizzie said.

"There is no scoop, Lizzie, and if there were, I'm sure you'd be the first to know. But I think I'll try it anyway. See you later." Brett rose and sailed off in the direction of the electronic astrologer.

"There are so many toys! David was always interested in the fun he could have with computers," Professor Harrison said when he noticed Brett standing beside him. "Give it a try. The stars have unlocked many secrets of the universe, you know."

Brett entered August 26, 1962, 7:06 A.M., Racine, Wisconsin—the date, time and location of her birth. The information appeared briefly on the screen, then was replaced by the greeting, "Hello, Virgo." Suddenly, the display filled with data about her astrological sign and characteristics that were supposedly unique to her. Her eyes moved down the screen until they became riveted on the lines that began, "You have chosen an unlikely career, but events in the immediate future will provide the impetus you are seeking. The men in your life have disappointed you and caused you pain. This will change, and you will find the answers you seek, but avoid the man with the Greek name. Future travel will be problematic."

At first she was intrigued by the readout, but by the time she read about mysterious Greeks and a trip she had not planned, she decided that this was just a New Age version of the circus fortune-teller. Nevertheless, she pushed the print button and slipped the perforated paper into her bag.

When she turned around, the crowd had thinned noticeably, and she was just in time to say good-bye to Lizzie and Joe before they departed. David was still schmoozing so she sat in the chair Lizzie had vacated and discreetly slipped off her shoes. On the other side of the room, the robot stood immobile, like a futuristic sentinel, guarding the corridor that led to David's office. Brett adjusted her position so that she could see out the window and stared into the inky darkness at a plane descending for its landing at La Guardia. She briefly wondered if it was a LARSair flight, and thought about her grandfather. He had seemed agitated and distracted the night she and David had had dinner with him. *Maybe he didn't expect me to bring a man.* It had never happened before, and they certainly hadn't discussed the details of her social life. *He's probably one even the computer can't figure*, Brett thought.

"Even barefoot you look great," David said as he came over to her.

"My feet really are killing me. I don't know if I can bear to put those wicked shoes back on," Brett said.

"No reason to. I have a car downstairs and it will deliver you right to your door—under my direct supervision, of course. Let's get out of here."

When the limo pulled up in front of her house, Brett held a pink pump in each hand. "How will I ever get these back on?" she declared. "Maybe I can attach them to my knees and crawl."

David motioned to her. "Here, give them to me."

"Gladly. Do you have something else in a nine medium, low heel? Sneakers might be nice," she said, laughing.

David stuffed the shoes into the pockets of his overcoat and stepped out of the car. He tossed a tan lap throw that was folded on the seat out to the ground. "Step on this."

Standing in the center of the folded wool square, she said, "Now we only have about twenty feet to go."

"That's easy." He scooped Brett off her feet and over his shoulder in a fireman's carry.

"You can't do this, you crazy man—you'll hurt yourself!" Brett squealed, pummeling his back with playful blows.

He held her thighs tightly and headed for the door. "No problem at all, ma'am. Now, where do you want this?"

Brett hung upside down laughing. She craned her neck in time to see a young woman wearing running shoes and socks with her business suit, carrying a bag from the all-night deli in one hand, and a briefcase in the other. She monitored their progress with interest. When the woman caught Brett's eye, she called out, "Enjoy it now. My husband used to carry me, too, but not anymore!"

"How am I going to unlock the door?" Brett asked, once David came to a stop in front of it.

"With your key, my dear," David replied, and turned so that Brett faced the door.

Brett fumbled in her purse for her keys, and when they finally stood inside, David reversed the procedure so she could lock the door. "You can put me down now, Superman. I walk around barefoot all the time."

"Those feet are probably still pretty tender. I don't think they're ready to handle two flights of stairs," he said as he approached the steps.

Brett turned on lights as they made their way upstairs. David set her back on her feet in the middle of the living room carpet.

"If you're in traction tomorrow, don't say I didn't warn you," Brett said as she flung her coat on the tufted ottoman.

"Nonsense, dear lady. Tonight I think I could leap tall buildings and swim the English Channel. Then maybe I'd stop for breakfast and run the marathon." David peeled out of his coat and tuxedo jacket, and threw them on top of Brett's.

"What can I get you?" Brett asked.

"Not a thing that isn't already here," he replied, pulling her down on the sofa next to him.

"Your parents were so proud of you tonight. And your sister can't stop smiling."

"That means the world to me," David said. "My family has been there for me since the beginning, urging me on. Do you know this company was born over cheeseburgers in the Stanford cafeteria? When I'd call home and babble about what I was going to do, my folks never told me I was crazy. They said to go for it." David leaned forward, his elbows on his knees. "Sometimes you dig a hole so deep and work harder than you thought you could and you just know you'll never find your way out. But it's all been worth it, Brett—all the hard work." He turned to face her. "And I'm really glad you were there tonight."

"Where else could I possibly have been? I've known you almost my whole life, David. You're like . . ."

"Don't say I'm like a brother, because I'm not feeling very fraternal right now."

"I'm happy to hear it."

"I watched you all night, and I kept telling myself that I shouldn't be thinking what I've been thinking, but it didn't do any good. In fact, it's gotten stronger."

This was the moment Brett had dreamed about. She parted her lips to speak, but let them close. Instead, she looked straight into his eyes, conveying wordlessly that he was not alone in his longing.

David lifted his hand and removed the pins from her chignon. A cascade of hair tumbled to her shoulders, and he combed his fingers through it. Brett closed her eyes, basking in the tingling that started at her scalp and washed over her like a warm spring rain.

He sighed, suddenly overwhelmed by the desire he had cloistered since tragedy had wrapped him in a shroud of mourning. And in an instant, he relinquished the past and succumbed to the renaissance of sensation.

"I don't think you need these now," she murmured as she lifted his glasses off and laid them on the coffee table.

David caught her hand, but held it only briefly before he turned her palm up and kissed its soft, delicately scented center. It was as if his lips completed a circuit long left broken and a charge too powerful to control surged through Brett, magnetizing her. David was helpless to resist.

"Brett," he said in a voice full of desire and need. He drew her to him and kissed her—deeply, fully. Only their lips touched, until Brett could no longer suppress the tug of her own feelings. She slipped her arms under his and let her hands wander freely, feeling the strong, sinewy muscles under the crisp starched cotton of his shirt. They did not speak. It was as if they both knew that words were not necessary. Only their breathing, rapid with anticipation, could be heard.

He slipped his hand under the curtain of hair and lifted it, baring her neck. Starting at her nape, he trailed sweet kisses down to her shoulder until he was stopped by her dress. His strong fingers held the back of her head and drew her to him until their lips met again. This time his tongue explored relentlessly, only deviating from its course when it met hers and sent tremulous waves of yearning through them both.

Brett tucked her legs under her and knelt, her body pressed close to David's. His hand found her zipper and pulled it down past her waist. She got to her feet and shrugged her shoulders, letting the dress fall in a puddle of pink silk around her ankles, then kicked it aside. "Now it's your turn."

David rose and undid his bow tie, then Brett reached out and removed his cuff links and studs. She slipped her hands inside his open shirt front and ran them languidly up his chest, watching her fingers thread through the thatch of dark hair. She tugged the shirt down from his shoulders and tossed it on top of her dress. The small space between them closed of its own accord as their bodies overruled any questions or doubts they might have and sought their own fulfillment. They were both propelled by the same urgency to satisfy a hunger that bordered on starvation. He slipped his arms between them, unhooked the front closure of her lacy bra, and added it to the mounting pile of clothing casualties.

In seconds they lay naked on the carpet. David covered her lips with a kiss so profound and soulful that Brett sensed it came from a place she did not know. Lawrence had shown her firecrackers, but David was reaching into the core of her, and she trembled in anticipation of what was to come. He lifted his weight from her and inched down until he could rub his cheek against the softness of her breasts. Then, turning his head, he suckled one rosy, erect nipple, then the other. Brett rubbed her hips against him, driven as much by her own need as by his demanding hardness.

Unable to hold back any longer, David raised his hips and entered her. Their bodies fit together like cast to mold and they both gasped in response to the rightness of their union. Brett arched her back and dug her fingers into the silken nap of the rug as she pushed up to take in all of him. Her warm wetness welcomed his swollen penis and she met his lunges with ardent abandon. Shock waves foreshadowed by her earlier tremors radiated from her now molten center and intensified with each thrust, until she shook from the awesome power of a quake that shattered her into fragments which knit together again only at the moment David exploded in his own breathless climax. Limp with release, they lay side by side and silently shared the wonder of their newfound intimacy.

Time passed unnoticed, until David rolled over to glance at the carriage clock on the mantel. "I guess I should call the driver and tell him he can go." He smiled at her. "I'm really glad tomorrow is Saturday."

They made their way upstairs and climbed into bed, where they lay quietly, holding each other until their arousal again demanded satisfaction. This time, their lovemaking was slow and leisurely. Knowing they had all the time in the world, their earlier frenzy gave way to tenderness and exploration ending in a tumultuous tidal wave that had begun its rush to shore long before their first kiss.

Brett awoke the next morning to find David propped up on his elbow, staring at her. "You really are a great sleeper. Your face kind of twitches and you smile. It made me wonder what you were dreaming about."

"How good you make me feel," she replied sleepily. Her bare shoulders peeked above the coverlet, and her tousled hair was fanned over the shell-pink Pratesi pillowcase like a veil of dark, shiny ribbons.

"I bet you say that to all the boys," David teased. "Would you like coffee? I made it already."

"There aren't any other boys." *Except Jeffrey*, she thought. But as she gazed at David's morning stubble and twinkling brown eyes, she suddenly realized that this was the face she wanted to wake up to every day of her life, and that somehow she had always known that. Jeffrey was nice, and she knew that he was interested in her romantically, but in spite of her best efforts, she had never really been able to think of him as more than a very good friend. She hadn't even imagined what making love to him would be like. "How long have you been awake?" she asked.

"A couple of hours. It's a habit. Besides, it gave me the chance to stare at you as long as I wanted." He got up and bowed formally from the waist. "I'll be back straight away with your coffee, madam."

Brett watched his broad shoulders and strong back disappear down the hall toward the stairs. She stacked pillows behind her head and stared at the bundles of rice grass carved into the bedposts. The morning was gray and cloudy, and light struggled to filter through the curtains into the room, but to Brett, the day was beautiful. She glowed with happiness that made sunshine unnecessary. But there was a nagging question she had not asked David, and she knew she had to before this went any further.

He entered the room, ceremoniously placed a white wicker bed tray over her legs, and climbed back into bed. "Coffee is served," he said as he poured the steaming elixir into the delicate Sevres cups she had bought in Paris.

"Umm . . . this is wonderful," Brett said after she took a sip and was surprised by the flavor of cinnamon. "David, there's something I have to ask you," she said tentatively.

"So ask," David responded.

"I know about Lottie, your computer girlfriend, but is there anyone else? I'm sorry, but I need to know." Her green gaze did not waver as she met his liquid brown eyes.

"That's an easy one. No. There hasn't been since . . ."

Brett interrupted. "You've told me all I needed to know. You don't have to explain anything more. Thank you for being honest with me." She leaned over and kissed him gently on the cheek. David was what she wanted. She loved him, she always had, but she knew it was too soon to tell him that.

"I really care about you, Brett. I had forgotten how good it feels to care. What would you like to do today? Lady's choice—except maybe for ice skating."

Brett thought for a minute as ideas flashed through her mind. She wanted to be alone with David today. She had no wish to share their time with strangers on the streets of New York, his family, or the telephone. "I'd really like to get out of the city. Spring isn't quite here yet, but I'd like to see something besides tall buildings."

"My car is garaged uptown. I never drive in the city because it's such a nuisance, but we could pick it up and head for Connecticut."

"That sounds perfect. I'll jump in the shower and we can stop for breakfast on the way." Suddenly modest and, unlike David, acutely aware of her nakedness, Brett grabbed her robe from the chair by the bed and slipped it on before heading to the bathroom.

"That's not fair," David said.

"I know." Brett winked and disappeared into the passage that led to the bathroom.

She had just reached for her favorite sandalwood soap when the door to the shower stall opened and David joined her. He took the bar from her hand and slowly began to bathe her. Starting with her back, he rubbed in lazy circles, then progressed down her arms. Turning her around, he bent over and skipping to her feet and ankles, worked his way up her calves to her thighs. Then, rubbing the soap in his hands until he had a foamy lather, he put the bar down and gently massaged her breasts and belly. When he parted her thighs and slipped his hand between her legs, Brett gasped and felt her knees weaken. He slowly edged her to the wall, draped her arms around his shoulders, and lifted her as she wrapped her legs around his waist. With the next move he was inside her, and again they experienced the completeness of their union and under the torrent of water, they confidently continued their odyssey of discovery.

* * *

"Here are the keys. You can tell Elizabeth and Joe that they should receive the deed within the month." Jeffrey leaned across his desk and handed the keys to Brett.

"I can surprise them tonight at dinner," Brett replied, accepting the small white envelope. *This is the easy part*, she thought. Jeffrey had offered to drop the keys off at her apartment, but Brett had volunteered to come and get them. She felt it was only fair to tell Jeffrey that her relationship with someone else was no longer casual, but although she had rehearsed the scene all morning, she still didn't know where to begin.

Jeffrey came and perched on a corner of the desk, closer to Brett. He paged through his desk diary as he spoke. "I think we can leave for lunch now. We have one-thirty reservations at the Four Seasons, and we should just about make it. Oh, before I forget," he said, looking up from the diary, "there's a reception at the Santa Verdian consulate a week from Saturday. Would you like to attend with me?" Larsen had started courting the emerging Central American nation after the recent discovery of a major gold lode had made it cash rich. The small country was eager to develop its white sand beaches into the next major vacation resort. LARSair saw the tiny country as a way to expand into the lucrative Caribbean routes.

Brett took a breath. "I can't go, Jeffrey—and there's something I have to tell you." He looked at her intently. "You've become a special friend to me since I got back from Paris. There were some pretty rocky times that you helped me through, and I'll always be grateful for that."

"Getting to know you has been one of the greatest pleasures in my life, Brett," Jeffrey said.

Brett toyed with the gold clasp of her shoulder bag, but consciously made herself stop and settled her hands in her lap. "Jeffrey, I always want to be honest with you, so I want to let you know that there is a man who has become very important to me. We've known each other for a long time—since we were children, in fact—but we've only recently become reacquainted." Brett noticed the dismayed look on Jeffrey's face. "You probably don't want to know this. Anyway, I'd like it if we could remain friends. That would mean a lot to me."

Jeffrey walked toward the window and smoothed a hand over his hair. "I appreciate your candor, Brett. It just comes as a bit of a shock," he said, turning to her, his hands locked tightly behind his back. "I think of you so often, so warmly . . . but I guess I've never said that, have I? You would think that I would have learned how to make my feelings known, but I suppose it would be unmanly to burden you with that now."

Unable to think of anything she could say to make the conversation any less painful, Brett remained silent.

Jeffrey sat on the desk again and looked at her earnestly with his piercing blue eyes. "Always know that I am here for you, that you can call on me for anything—anything at all. That will never change."

"Thank you," Brett said.

Jeffrey looked away for a moment, then said, "Would it be rude of me to bow out of lunch? I'm not sure I . . ."

"I understand." She kissed him on the cheek and left the office.

Jeffrey was rooted to the corner of the desk. After several minutes, he stood, opened the Waterman fountain pen that lay on his desk, and plunged the tip into a legal pad, creating a violent inkblot and showering the desk with tiny blue speckles.

You idiot. You damned idiot, he thought, still clenching the dripping pen in his fist. His slow, deliberate courtship had backfired and left him at a temporary disadvantage with Brett, but he had to keep his head. There was a lot to do. He needed to stay in Brett's good graces and become even more indispensable to her. He would also need to monitor the course of her affair closely, but he would take care of that phone call later.

He unlocked his file drawer and pulled out two folders. He tossed his file on Brett aside and opened the other. On top was a yellowed newspaper clipping announcing the marriage of Barbara Larsen to Brian North. It was time to investigate other possibilities.

— *Chapter 26* —

"Sixty-third and Fifth," Jeffrey announced as he banged the cab door shut. He winced at the thick smell of garlic that permeated the taxi, but taking his own car and driver had been out of the question.

Rush hour clogged even the wide, sedate boulevard that marked the enclave of Manhattan's rich and powerful. White tulips and pale yellow jonquils dotted the grassy center median. They bobbed their heads in the spring breeze like traffic police, signaling cars to move along. Jeffrey lowered the window, but the cacophony of horns and engines was as unpleasant as the malodorous driver, so he cranked it up again.

The taxi screeched to a halt just as it passed St. Bartholomew's, allowing a jaywalker to cross the busy street unharmed. Jeffrey lurched forward in his seat, but he paid no attention. The driver could have hit the defiant pedestrian for all he cared. Barbara Larsen North had finally agreed to see him, and that alone occupied his mind.

For years Jeffrey had pieced together bits of information about the Larsens, and even though Barbara had been the most public member of the family, she had also been the most difficult to get a handle on. Like a shadow, her existence could only be inferred from her reflection and, based on the source of light illuminating her, the image Barbara projected varied wildly.

Although reports of Brett's activities still came to Jeffrey regularly, and he spoke with her at least once a week, he had put her on the back burner for the time being. He had been consumed by anger for days after she had informed him of her intentions. At first he directed it at Brett, then he began to berate himself for his stupidity where she was concerned. He had spent many years hatching his plan for revenge, and Sven, the object of Jeffrey's rancor, had unwittingly given him the window of opportunity he sought so obsessively. He had blown it, and that's when Barbara became the second pawn in his game.

Barbara and her daughter didn't speak, so there was little chance of either finding out about his dealings with the other. Jeffrey knew little about Barbara's early years growing up with his widowed employer, and it was as if she had fallen off the face of the earth from the time she left Racine to attend Barnard College in New York, until shortly after Brett was born. Then commenced a series of events that Jeffrey was convinced were not coincidental.

In Sven's personal files, Jeffrey had discovered a canceled check in the amount of four million dollars that had been paid to Barbara when Brett had been four weeks old. Starting later that year, she also began to receive an allotment of $250,000 annually. Jeffrey sensed that there was something unusual about the arrangement, since no similar one had been made for Brett, and it seemed to correspond neatly with the beginning of Barbara's estrangement from her father.

The rift was not a secret. There had been no attempt at joint appearances or family gatherings to quiet wagging tongues. Jeffrey's endeavors to ascertain what had precipitated their fallout had been thwarted thus far because Sven adamantly refused to speak about his daughter.

Seven months after Brett was born, Barbara had married Brian North. It was the first concrete evidence of a man in her life, other than the one listed as "unknown" on Brett's birth certificate.

For the next two decades Barbara's trail was relatively easy to follow, since her splashy life was routinely covered in the gossip columns, but five years ago, around the time when Jeffrey estimated the four million dollars had evaporated, her name also disappeared from print.

Jeffrey had used Brett to confirm much of the information he had gathered about her mother. In addition, he had learned from her that Barbara seemed to be losing her long battle with alcohol and prescription drugs.

Aware that Barbara was struggling to maintain her extraordinary spending habits and a life-style to which she had grown accustomed, Jeffrey had called two weeks ago to offer help, advice, and his best efforts to increase her yearly allowance. In the process, he intended to fill in the gaps in her dossier and formulate an alternate plan of attack.

Barbara had reacted with rage and paranoia. She had screeched into the telephone, "You and that bastard had better keep out of my life!" and hung up.

After this dismissal, he had tried to contact Brian North, hoping that the reclusive actor might be able to shed some light on Barbara's past and her financial arrangements with her father. Jeffrey knew that their divorce had been sudden and unpleasant, and that rumors of Brian in a homosexual dalliance—a situation that Jeffrey thought repulsive and aberrant—had been abundant. But the potential for information overrode his personal distaste. Brian North, however, turned out to be a dead end. He had been in a nursing home in Pasadena for the past five years, incapacitated by Alzheimer's disease.

When Barbara had called this morning and asked him to come to her apartment at six, Jeffrey had felt the window slide open again, and this time it would not close on his fingers. There would be no mistakes. He had faxed his bank in the Bahamas and requested a wire transfer of fifty thousand dollars to his personal checking account. Then he had gone, in person, to Bergdorf's, Saks, Bonwit's, Martha, and Tiffany's and paid the balance on each of the accounts that prior digging had uncovered were overdue. Jeffrey knew that he needed a good-faith gesture, and this was certainly little enough, considering the potential payoff.

As the fetid taxi neared his destination, Jeffrey resolved to do whatever he had to in order to win Barbara's confidence.

Jeffrey was admitted to the apartment by the housekeeper and escorted to the library to wait. He took the opportunity to snoop around. He didn't know exactly what he was looking for, or where he would find it, so he had fine-tuned all his senses to detect the minutest details. They might prove useful later.

He flipped on the microcassette recorder in his breast pocket. The microphone, a tiny metal disk, was concealed behind the burgundy foulard square that peeked from the pocket of his navy blazer. Then he took in the darkly paneled room, observing that its somber, heavy decor showed little sign of wear and contrasted greatly with the lightness of the foyer and the long hall, which led to other rooms and a staircase.

He wandered to a bookshelf near the doorway and randomly plucked a leather-bound volume. He blew the fine layer of dust from its top and opened the book, but looked beyond it to the living room. Even from that distance he could see that the carpet in the entrance had been worn flat and that the white suede sofa was badly in need of replacement. A highball glass containing what appeared to be the caramel-colored remains of scotch on the rocks had been left on the white-marble coffee table.

When Jeffrey heard the deliberate, slightly halting click of a woman's shoes descending the stairs, he hurriedly replaced the book and took a seat at the wide mahogany table in the center of the room.

"I didn't keep you waiting long, did I, Mr. Underwood?"

"No. Not at all." He stood to greet Barbara, who posed in front of the door. She grasped the knob behind her back, hooked a heel of her white kid pumps on the lowest strip of door molding, and swung ever so slightly back and forth, like a child on a wooden gate.

"Under . . . wood. It makes me think of a big stack of oak logs that some poor sap has to load one by one onto a truck. Is it a heavy name, Mr. Underwood?" Barbara asked in a provocative opening maneuver. Her blue eyes, accentuated by theatrical wings of black eyeliner, focused on Jeffrey. She took in the stylishness and refinement of his clothes, his stark, angular features and pale blond hair. He impressed her as capable, strong willed, maybe even more so than her father. Since her phone call to Jeffrey that morning, she had spent the day preparing for this meeting.

She had dismissed him out of hand at his first call, but his words repeated in her head like a round. "I think your father has cheated you. I can help you," he had said. He could help her get back at her father. Her anger at Sven had had years to feed on itself, and as she drifted further into solitude, she had fewer allies and more time alone to stoke the angry fires. But alone, she had no way to make him feel the flames.

"It's no heavier than any other name," Jeffrey replied.

So this is the elusive Barbara Larsen North. She looks like a prize sow dressed for the fair, he thought. Barbara was much shorter than he had expected, and her narrow shoulders and small wrists were overwhelmed by doughy flesh. The silk dress she wore—swatches of red, yellow, green, and blue on a white background—had a bubble-shaped top that ended midhip and a straight skirt. She looked to him like an abstract Easter egg.

Barbara positioned herself in a chair opposite Jeffrey. He resumed his seat, clasped his hands, and leaned his forearms on the table. "Mrs. North, I'm sure my phone call must have seemed highly irregular."

"Irregular—to hear from a man who works for my father? It sounds insane. It sounds like a setup. I'm still not sure you should be here."

"I have worked for Larsen Enterprises for fourteen years, and have been chief counsel for the last seven. More to the point, I have been Sven Larsen's personal counsel for those seven years, as well." Jeffrey paused and looked down at his hands. Then he raised his head and continued in a voice calculated to sound heavy with regret. "Let me be honest with you, Mrs. North. I'm doing this more for myself than I am for you. A man must be able to live with himself, and over the last several years, Mr. Larsen's handling of certain financial situations with regard to you has troubled me deeply." Jeffrey had a look of utter sincerity on his face.

Barbara had become noticeably upset as Jeffrey spoke. She got up from her seat and hastily closed the door, then said, "We have no financial dealings. I've had nothing to do with him for more than twenty years. He uses people, then rolls over them when they get in his way."

"Yes, he can be ruthless," Jeffrey agreed solemnly. "Mrs. North, I don't know if you're aware of this, but your daughter, Brett, stands to inherit the bulk of his estate. That's roughly two and a half billion dollars."

"I knew she was in with him, and it's all her fault. I tried to protect her from him, and I've paid for it ever since. That ungrateful little bitch!" Barbara's fists were clenched at her sides and her eyes bored a hole in the parquet floor. She stared, frozen, as if oblivious to Jeffrey's presence.

Deciding to probe deeper, Jeffrey asked, "Mrs. North, what were you protecting her from?"

"What?" Barbara asked, awakening from her trance.

"What were you protecting her from?" Jeffrey repeated.

"I can't tell you that," Barbara said quickly, her anger now tinged with fear. "How do I know this is not a trick? How do I know you won't tell him every word I say?" She edged closer to the door, as if she planned to flee from the room.

"Wait. Mrs. North, I didn't have to start any of this. I'm putting myself in jeopardy even being here. I have no reason to deceive you." Barbara stopped, drawn in by Jeffrey's earnest gaze. "I understand your caution. Sven Larsen is not a man to be trifled with. Just hear me out." Opening his attaché, he began, "In checking through the files, I stumbled on a 1962 check paid to you in the amount of four million dollars."

"So, what about it? He gave it to me; I spent it. It was easy to find people to help me do that. Does he want it back—is that it?" she said defensively.

"No. Not at all. But in light of his current position, it's a paltry sum to give his only child."

"You're damned right. I should have made him give me more. He owes me."

Jeffrey's assumption that she would be hungry for money had been correct. He pressed on. "I don't know the nature of your disagreement with your father, but do you think that the two of you could reach an amicable resolution of your differences?"

"No, I couldn't. I don't ever want to see him again. You won't make me see him, will you?" Barbara asked, almost pleading.

"By all means not." Jeffrey noted the apprehension in her voice every time he mentioned Sven. What was she afraid of? "Mrs. North, I think I can help you, but first, I wanted to find some way to show you that I am sincerely on your side." From his attaché he pulled a manila envelope and emptied out a stack of receipts. "While doing some preliminary investigating on your behalf, I discovered that many of your charge accounts around the city are, well, in arrears."

Barbara bristled. "How dare you pry into my business? What gives you the right . . ."

"Please don't take this the wrong way. I wanted to show you that I really am concerned about your well-being. I've paid all these debts in full, in cash, so there are no canceled checks. There's no evidence that you're indebted to me." He handed the stack of papers to Barbara.

Her eyes shifted between Jeffrey and the handful of papers, as if she could not believe either one existed.

"Please, Mrs. North." Jeffrey laid them on the table and inched them toward her.

Sidling closer, Barbara touched the first page gingerly, as if she expected it to disintegrate in her fingers. In slow motion she picked up each receipt, one at a time. When she had them all, she pressed them to her chest. "You did this for me? But, why?"

"Let's just say that someone once did something for me and my family, and it changed my life. I want to return the favor. I know that Sven Larsen takes advantage of people who can't defend themselves, and I think he's taking advantage of you. I won't kid you. This won't be easy, and it's going to take some time. If you let me, I can help you get what's yours, but you have to help me," Jeffrey said.

Barbara tilted her head to the side, and in a kittenish voice, she said, "I don't know what to say. It's been a long time since a gentleman has offered to help me."

Jeffrey picked up the cue. "If you'll pardon my saying so, I find that hard to believe."

"Mr. Underwood, I know this is a business meeting, but it's cocktail hour. Can I interest you in a drink?"

They proceeded into the living room, and Jeffrey watched as Barbara tossed down three glasses of scotch in half an hour. He told her that he would work on getting her yearly allotment increased first, and assured her that he could accomplish that without Sven's knowledge. But the more she drank, the less she cared about her father. She hoisted herself on the rolled arm of the sofa, crossed her legs, and dangled one shoe off the end of her foot as she spoke.

She actually thinks this is appealing, Jeffrey thought, astounded. But he had determined that Barbara was easily manipulated, that her sense of reality was decidedly askew, and that letting their dealings progress to a more social level might be the quickest avenue to the information he was seeking.

"What do you think?" David asked.

"I love it, but how will you decide which way to put it together?" Brett asked.

They stood in the sleek Roche-Bobois showroom on Madison Avenue in front of an enormous black ash wall unit that was arranged in one of its infinite combinations. This incarnation was a large, complex, bridgelike room divider.

"That's Claudio's department. It's part of our agreement. I told him that there were some things I wanted to select myself, and I asked if he had any problems with that. He said if I bought it, he would find a place for it, so I'm taking him at his word." In keeping with his profession and his workplace, David's taste was hi-tech contemporary with an emphasis on the *fun* in function. David turned to the salesman and asked, "When can you deliver it?"

"That depends on where you live, sir," said the clerk, who was thrilled to have made a sale with so little effort.

"Across the street," David replied.

He had seen dozens of apartments and had finally settled on Morgan Court. The newly completed condominium building was located on Madison near Thirty-fifth, right next door to the historic Church of the Incarnation. David liked the plans the realtor had shown him, and when he saw the apartment, he made his decision almost instantly. The thirty-two-story obelisk was not a skyscraper when compared to some New York City high-rises, and although the street was fairly noisy during the day, it was almost a dead zone at night, when he expected to be at home. The sand-colored tower was not fully occupied, so he had a choice of units. He selected a two bedroom apartment with a river view on the thirty-first floor.

True to his word, David moved in as soon as the plush, charcoal-gray carpeting had been laid in the bedroom. He slept with his king-size mattress and box springs on the floor until his black leather sleigh bed arrived from Italy. The living room currently contained only his piano and a hand-carved, eight-foot-tall, Wendell Castle grandfather clock that looked more like an intergalactic sculpture than a timepiece. But Claudio was hard at work, and assured David that the rest of the apartment would be ready soon.

David signed the sales slip and confirmed the delivery date, then he and Brett exited onto Madison Avenue.

"Let's stop for a drink before we go to Aunt Lillian's," Brett suggested. One of her girlhood fantasies had become a reality, and she wanted to mark the occasion.

"Sure thing," David replied.

As they stood on the bustling sidewalk, trying to think of a place nearby, Brett realized that everything with David was just as she had imagined it would be.

She felt a deep, serene happiness that surrounded her wherever she went, whatever she was doing. Even her professional life had taken a turn for the better, and she had already done three additional jobs for the ad agency that was handling the American *Voilà!* account. *Yes, I do want to celebrate*, she said to herself.

"The Judge's Chamber is just a couple of blocks from here. Do you know it?"

"No, but it gets fifty points for proximity." She laughed as David grabbed her hand and they dashed across the street on the last four flashes of the 'Don't Walk' sign. As soon as they reached the other side, the sign glowed a steady red warning to pedestrians and a rush of uptown traffic, led by a caravan of commuter buses transporting city workers to their suburban dwellings, barreled by them.

David gave a 'thumbs up' sign to his startled doorman, who watched their perilous sprint from the brass and glass cage in the front courtyard of David's new residence.

A few minutes later, they entered the Sheraton Park Avenue by the side door, ducked into the paneled bar, and were shown to a corner banquette in the rear of the busy room.

"Let's have champagne," Brett said, and ordered before David could object to her suggestion.

"Are we celebrating something I don't know about?" he asked.

"Well, I'm celebrating, and I thought I'd let you join me," Brett teased.

"I see, but do I get to know what the occasion is?"

"You might think it's silly, but I want to commemorate a daydream fulfilled. I won't say don't laugh, because you're going to anyway."

"Who, me?" David asked in mock seriousness. As the waitress poured their champagne, he settled back against the upholstered cushion.

As Brett spoke, the pianist began to play "If I Loved You", a lilting ballad from *Carousel*. "When I was a little girl, I used to make up stories about you, and one of my favorites was that you had finished school and come back to New York, and I helped you decorate your new apartment. In a way, shopping for furniture with you today was like having that daydream come true. I know you're probably cracking up inside, which is a lot better than Lizzie used to do. She would laugh out loud and say, 'David? You're crazy! He's a brainhead—he'll only need a cot, a computer, and a can opener.'"

David smiled and lifted his glass in salute. "So much for my sister's clairvoyant powers. I hope I can make all your dreams come true so easily."

"David, when I first met you, I wished you were my brother. Then, as I got a little older, my feelings grew into a full-fledged crush. But you knew that, didn't you?"

"I guess you could say I knew, but you were so sweet about it. I felt sorry for you—no, maybe that wasn't it. I think I felt sad for you. Your life seemed so lonely, and you tried so hard to please. But that all changed when you moved in with your aunt. You became a different girl."

David's sincerity was compelling, and Brett felt safe. He wasn't going to laugh at her or hurt her. "You're right. The person I really wanted to please was my mother, but I've found out that's impossible, so we each live our own lives. It's still sad, in a way. David, I've never thanked you for being there the night of the shooting. I couldn't then, and by the time I was able to talk about it, you were living in California. But I remember that I kicked and screamed and scratched, and you just held me as tight as you could. You didn't have to do that."

"It was the only thing I could do."

"Thank you," Brett said quietly.

A faraway look clouded her green eyes, and David could see that tears were not far away. "You see—I didn't laugh once. What time is Aunt Lillian expecting us?" he said, lightening the conversation.

"Eight, so we have plenty of time."

"Good, it's a perfect evening for a walk. What do you say?"

"Great," Brett said.

David placed a twenty-dollar bill in the brandy snifter on top of the piano. The young man tinkling the ivories nodded his appreciation and winked at them as they departed. Hand in hand, they floated out into the balmy April night on the chords of Billy Joel's "I Love You Just the Way You Are."

Brett turned to David and said, "I do, you know."

He squeezed her hand a little tighter, but did not respond.

— Chapter 27 —

After their first meeting, Jeffrey sent Barbara flowers, with a note thanking her for her time and charming company.

Barbara hadn't received so much as a posy from a man in years, and she had been thrilled by his gesture. When she called to thank him, he suggested that, because discretion was of the utmost importance, it would be better if he called her in the future. Then he asked her to dinner the next day at a restaurant of her choosing. She had been so impressed with his manners and style that she wanted to show him off to her friends, so she suggested Le Cirque. Jeffrey was relieved at the choice because it was not a restaurant he frequented where he would have been embarrassed to be seen dining with a woman of Barbara's ilk.

The excitement and anticipation of a real date had sent Barbara into the throes of preparation. Having noticed that Jeffrey's taste was simple and classic, she charged several basic silk dresses on her newly cleared charge account at Martha and spent the day at Elizabeth Arden, allowing herself a full beauty treatment. She arrived at eight and was waxed, massaged, manicured, pedicured, facialed, and coiffed. When she emerged at three, she felt better than she had in years.

Since their first outing, Jeffrey had called every day and taken her out three or four times a week. Barbara reveled in his attention. She even went on a diet and stuck to it.

Tonight they were going to Mortimer's, Barbara's favorite dining spot. She usually preferred lunch there—the crowd was more to her liking, even though they hardly noticed her anymore—but Jeffrey was so seldom free in the middle of the day that she was grateful for dinner in the Upper East Side bistro. She dressed carefully in a new navy-blue silk sheath and added a double strand of opera-length pearls to keep her look elegant and understated. She surveyed the results in the mirror and liked what she saw. The ten pounds she had lost was finally noticeable, and she wanted to look good for Jeffrey. Barbara realized that she was drawn to him because he was patient and kind. He wanted to help her. *This is a man who wants to take care of* me, she thought.

Jeffrey arrived and complimented her on her appearance, but inside, he was sickened by the sight of her. Although she had dropped some of her avoirdupois, he was repelled by her pale, sallow skin. He knew that it was probably the result of her pill habit, but for him, that only increased his intolerance for her weakness and stupidity. How could she have given birth to Brett, who was so beautiful and vibrant? But Jeffrey had seen pictures of the young Barbara, and she had been quite beautiful in her time.

Not that looks or carnal matters appealed to Jeffrey on any level other than as a means to an end. He could not even remember the last time he had looked at his own body unclothed. He had no physical desire for Barbara, or any other woman, if the truth be known—not even Brett. He never had—not even when he was coming into his manhood, and all around him, boys at the military academy were lusting after women. After he had had to leave the school, all his time and energy had been spent lusting after revenge. It would have been much easier to have sex with Brett than with this sack of spineless flesh, but he suspected he would have to make love to Barbara if he wanted more information from her.

The miniature tape recorder was his constant companion on his evenings with Barbara, and he knew that he was getting closer to what lay hidden under the surface of her loathing for her father. Gently he prodded and coaxed, fueling her scathing assessments with his own acid comments about the malevolent Sven. This maneuvering netted him bits and pieces of information, but Jeffrey knew there was more.

Last night, after dinner at Barbara's, she had begun to reveal details about her childhood under her father's oppressive hand. She had told him how lonely it was growing up in the rambling but isolated Victorian house on the outskirts of Racine. Almost everything in the house that was not darkly stained wood had been painted brown, and the heavy velvet drapes were opened only when Sven was not in the house.

"He never told me anything about my mother," Barbara had said. "Except sometimes, he would look at me like I was a ghost and call me by her name. Then he'd catch himself and ask me if I had washed my hands before dinner. You see, that was the only time I was allowed to talk to him. He took me to school every morning and picked me up every afternoon exactly at three, so I could never play in the schoolyard with the other kids. He drove a big black Packard, and the other kids teased me. They said I had to ride in a hearse and my father was an undertaker. I think they were afraid of him . . . a lot of people were. But he wouldn't let me talk. I couldn't even ask questions about my homework. He'd say, 'I'm thinking about our business. Whatever it is can wait until five-thirty.' And he'd drive the rest of the way with this stony look on his face. We ate dinner every day of the year at five-thirty."

She paused, wandered over to the front windows, and stared silently at the park for a few minutes. Jeffrey, fearing she would reveal no more, went to the bar and made her another scotch. He strode over to where she stood, handed her the drink, then gently massaged her neck.

Barbara had stiffened at first, as though his hands were too hot or too cold, then relaxed, lolled her head to the side, and kissed his hand. Jeffrey was prepared to go as far as he had to, but he was relieved when she began to talk once again.

"I couldn't have friends over—or go to their houses, either. He said they were riffraff. He had this friend, or I thought it was his friend, who had a new baby, and I couldn't even play with her— or was it him? I don't remember. I must have been five or six then. I would ask Karl—my father's friend—about the baby, but I never saw it."

Barbara had joined Jeffrey on the love seat and he took her hand. "It must have been awful. That's no way for a little girl to grow up," he said, encouraging her to continue.

"When I got to high school, I would go downtown to the soda fountain and watch the boys play baseball because he couldn't stop me. I just wouldn't be there at three o'clock. Finally, he stopped coming to get me. He would be angry, but—oh, never mind. This was all such a long, long time ago," she said.

"Yes, it was, but although time passes, it never leaves us," Jeffrey had responded. He knew that he would get nothing more. Whenever she brought herself back to the present, the past was temporarily shelved once again. "I really should be going," he said.

"Do you have to?" Barbara asked, suggestively rubbing his thigh. "We could pass some time that I'm sure we'll both remember fondly."

Jeffrey had gotten close enough to what festered inside her to smell it, and so he asked her out again, hoping to break through the top layer of fill and filth and expose the putrid carrion long buried underneath. "How about tomorrow? Do you have plans?" he asked, knowing she didn't.

"None I wouldn't change for the right man. Are you the right man, Jeffrey?" she flirted as she walked him to the door. She stood on her toes and kissed him fully on the mouth, forcing his lips open with her tongue.

"I may not be the best judge of that," Jeffrey said, trying to regain his composure. "Good night, Barbara." As soon as the elevators closed, he snatched his linen handkerchief from his jacket pocket and wiped his mouth, inside and out. He replaced it and turned off the recorder. *Maybe I won't have to*, and Jeffrey had shuddered at the thought.

But now, as they sat in Mortimer's, Barbara was playing footsie with him under the table, and he was afraid that tonight he might have to give in to her other appetites.

He was right.

As soon as they returned to her apartment, Barbara threw her arms around his waist and rubbed her body against his like a bitch in season. "Jeffrey, how long are you going to make me wait?" she asked.

Having exhausted all but this last effort, Jeffrey summoned up a smile. "Not another second," he said, and he followed her upstairs to her bedroom. He was startled by the frilly white room. With its canopied bed, ruffled spread, skirted boudoir chairs, and chaises, the doilied, beribboned room appeared to belong to a very privileged fifteen-year-old girl. There were dolls and stuffed toys everywhere, and stacks of movie fan magazines on the eyelet draped table by the bed.

Barbara excused herself and Jeffrey removed his clothes. He arranged them neatly on a nearby chair so that the microphone under his pocket square faced the bed, and quickly jumped under the covers. When she quietly emerged from the bathroom, she was wearing a white, lace-collared nightgown straight out of the nineteenth century. She had scrubbed her face and tied a silk cord in a bow at the top of her head. *Why, she almost looks young*, he thought.

"Please be patient with me," she said as she climbed tentatively onto the bed in an almost trancelike state.

What kind of sick game is this? Jeffrey wondered. He had heard about people who created elaborate sexual fantasies, then acted them out, but he had never experienced such a thing. "Of course I will," he said. He wondered if this was her usual act, or if he had triggered something inside that made her behave this way.

"I know you won't hurt me. I trust you." Her voice had lost its usual husky, throaty timbre, and she kissed him, this time with sweet, almost virginal innocence.

Jeffrey untied the neck of her gown and undid the tiny mother-of-pearl buttons. Then he proceeded as though following carefully detailed directions. Lips, breasts, pubis—he did everything he was supposed to do, and even brought Barbara to climax, or at least thought he had. Jeffrey, however, did not have an orgasm.

Barbara looked up at him and said, "Thank you, it was really lovely, Michael," and promptly fell asleep.

Who the hell is Michael? Jeffrey wondered as he lay beside her, watching her breasts rise and fall under the sheer white cotton lawn of her gown.

When Barbara awoke twenty minutes later, she looked calm, almost serene, as she gazed at Jeffrey. "I really like you, Jeffrey, and I trust you. I haven't had much luck with men, but I can tell that you're different. You don't want me because you think I'm rich. You *know* I'm almost broke." She reached out and covered his hand with hers.

"I'm sure many men have wanted you because they cared for you—you're a beautiful woman," Jeffrey said.

"I was. Not anymore. And . . . there was a man who loved me once, but my father took him away from me."

This is it. I have to be careful not to push too hard, Jeffrey said to himself. "How could Sven take someone away from you?" he asked, his face full of concern.

"He killed him. Or, to be more exact, he had him killed."

"You can't be serious," Jeffrey said. This was better than he had thought possible. Now he'd have Sven Larsen exactly where he wanted him. "Excuse me," he said as he reached across to pull his jacket to him. "I think I feel a sneeze coming on." He pretended to dig in his pocket for a handkerchief while he checked to make sure the recorder was on, then extracted the white square and replaced the jacket on the chair.

"Of course I'm serious. He had my husband killed." Barbara lay quietly. She looked more tranquil than Jeffrey had ever seen her.

"That's a lot to carry around for almost twenty-five years," he said, thinking of the load he had shouldered for the same length of time.

"I'm tired of it." She gazed into Jeffrey's blue eyes. "But I thought you wanted to help me carry it."

"Of course I do," Jeffrey said with sincerity.

She stared at the underside of the canopy, as if the whole story were written there.

Sven had been possessive of his only daughter. He had treated her as his rightful replacement for the wife he had lost, and Barbara had received permission to go away to college only by promising to return home after graduation. But in her junior year at Barnard, she had met and fallen in love with Michael Flynn, a bright, idealistic organizer for the Peace Corps. Michael was poor, his earnings were meager, and although Barbara had plenty of money, he wouldn't take any from her. Sven had made her move out of the dorms and into an apartment on Sutton Place because he didn't think university housing was safe, or good enough for his daughter, and she and Michael had spent many idyllic hours together there. Barbara would do his laundry and cook meals—Michael didn't mind that. When they finally decided to get married, she knew her father would be furious. And he was. He threatened to cut her off without a cent if she didn't come home immediately. But she and Michael got married anyway.

Barbara and Michael returned to the Sutton Place apartment one evening and found the locks changed. Undaunted, they moved into a tiny fifth-floor walk-up on One Hundred Fourteenth Street, near Broadway. Their two rooms, with the bathtub in the kitchen, was a far cry from their luxurious former abode, but it was close to campus and the storefront where Michael recruited the young, able, and altruistic to join the war on ignorance and poverty.

Right after Valentine's Day, Barbara found out she was pregnant. Convincing herself that a grandchild might make her father relent and become less hostile, she called him in Wisconsin with the news.

Sven was enraged and told her that as long as she was married to a bum, she didn't exist for him. Barbara was nearly inconsolable. In spite of everything, she loved her father and wanted to share her happiness with him. Michael, who was compassionate and understanding, told her that he was certain Sven would change his mind once the baby was born.

In late July, Barbara came home from her weekly pottery class, eager to show Michael the tiny cereal bowl she had crafted for the baby. Her climb to the fifth floor was exhausting because she was in her seventh month and the heat was oppressive, but her excitement sustained her ascent. She found the door ajar and pushed it open. The baby dish slipped from her hands and crashed to the floor. The place was a shambles, and Michael lay in a pool of blood in the middle of the kitchen. Her screams summoned a neighbor, then she fainted. When Barbara awoke in the apartment next door, she was in shock. The police questioned her, but she could provide no useful information.

The official investigation turned up no clues so, grief-stricken, widowed, pregnant, and broke, Barbara called her father. He sent his private plane and welcomed her home with open arms. Sven was sympathetic and considerate, even indulgent. He immediately had one of the bedrooms converted to a nursery, and sat with Barbara in the evenings, planning their future together.

The stress Barbara had endured in the wake of her tragedy had taken a greater toll than she had thought, and she went into labor a month early. When she brought Brett home from the hospital, Sven was like a new man. He had gotten a second chance at a family, and he worshipped his baby granddaughter.

His behavior awakened in Barbara thoughts of her mother for the first time in years. She was afraid that if she asked him questions, he would revert to his old taciturn self, so she decided to go through her mother's things and piece together her own memories. In the room off Sven's study where they were stored, Barbara discovered an old photo album, and in it, a picture of her mother on her wedding day. Lost in thought as she gazed at the photograph, she did not realize her father had come home until she heard him light into someone about some plans he had taken from Holmlund Metal

Works, the company owned by her father's friend, Karl. When she had returned to Racine, she had found out that the metal works had closed and the Holmlunds had left town. Unable to make sense of the conversation, she dismissed it, removed her mother's jewelry box from the chest in which it was stored, and took the leather box up to her room.

Later that night, after she had put the baby to sleep, Barbara opened the satin-lined treasure trove. The cameo her mother had worn in her wedding portrait lay on top, next to several strands of pearls in varying lengths. She moved on to the compartment that held rings and slipped on a large, single-cut ruby ringed with diamonds.

Sven had given the ring to Ingrid when she had finally agreed to marry him. He had told her that it was the only thing he could find as fiery as she was. He had been smitten the first time he had seen the young, beautiful actress. He had followed her to every theater in the Midwest, and regularly appeared in her dressing room after a performance with flowers and a proposal of marriage. The burly young man's tenacity and utter devotion won Ingrid's heart, and against the wishes of his stern, conservative father, they had wed.

Barbara looked at the sparkling stone a while longer, then returned it to the box and continued to rummage. On the bottom layer were bracelets, and as she took a gold circlet set with cabochon sapphires and emeralds from its place, she felt a lump under the satin. She lifted the faded cloth and found a signet ring that she recognized instantly. It had belonged to Michael. In a flash of horror, she put the whole story together. She took a nail file from her dressing table, pried Brett's sterling silver rattle open, and placed the ring inside. Then she coated the edges with clear nail polish, resealed it, and replaced it in Brett's bassinet.

She raced down the hall and burst into her father's room—a gloomy sanctuary to which no one was admitted save the maid. At first Sven denied Barbara's allegations, claiming she was hysterical and deluded. He threatened to take Brett from her and send her to a home for the insane. When Barbara told him she had hidden the ring and he would never find it, Sven went crazy. He raged through the house, turning over furniture, tossing the contents of drawers on the floor—even lifting the floorboards in Barbara's room. Barbara grabbed her baby, ran downstairs, and huddled in a corner of the dining room, clutching the whimpering infant to her breast.

Calmed down after his tirade, shirttail out, trousers twisted and dusty, Sven loomed over her. Barbara thought he would strike her, but instead, he began a halfhearted confession. His only admission was that Michael's death had been an accident—no one was supposed to get hurt. It was supposed to be a burglary designed to frighten Barbara into leaving Michael and the hovel where they lived. But Michael had come home, surprised the hired intruders, and been stabbed in the struggle.

Barbara didn't believe him and, remembering the conversation she had overheard, told him she knew he had done something wrong to Karl, and that she would reveal that, too, unless he left her alone.

Sven, grasping for straws, reminded Barbara that she and her baby were alone, and if something happened to him, there would be no one to take care of them. Outraged, Barbara reminded her father that he had never taken care of her, except with money. Desperate and frightened, she wanted to turn him over to the police, but Barbara, who had believed since she was a child that her original sin was causing her mother's death with her own birth, reasoned that in some perverse way, her silence might finally take care of that debt to her father. But she didn't tell him that. Instead, she demanded what she thought was enough money to last a lifetime, and extracted his promise to stay out of her life and her daughter's forever.

But when she was ready to leave with the baby, Sven tried to stop her. His eyes blazing like blue fire, he shoved her against the wall and, transported to a time twenty-one years ago, he released the anger he had repressed toward his beloved Ingrid for leaving him so soon. He railed, saying she had left him the last time she had had a baby and it wasn't going to happen again.

Barbara was terrified. She struggled mightily and, freeing herself from his iron grasp, she searched desperately for a way to defend herself. Using a pewter candlestick, she broke the glass encasing Sven's collection of antique knives and grabbed a pearl-handled dirk. When he lunged past her and blocked the door, she stabbed at him wildly. He held his ground, but finally, she plunged the knife into his hand, once and then again—so hard that it pierced his flesh and the tip became embedded in the wainscoting.

That's what happened to his fingers, Jeffrey thought as Barbara's recitation ended and she turned to look at him.

"I did that for Michael, but I did it for me, too. I still have the ring." Barbara toyed with the ribbons on her nightgown. "You know, Brett looked just like Michael. I guess she still does," she added quietly.

What do I do now? Jeffrey wondered. He wanted to leave, to replay the tape that would help him bring Larsen down. He looked over at her, and was surprised to find that she had fallen asleep again, so soundly that she snored slightly.

He waited a few minutes, then crept out of bed and took his things into the bathroom. Not willing to taint his clothing with the scent of fornication, he showered thoroughly before getting dressed.

At the bottom of the stairs, he put on his shoes and let himself out. Now he had proof—evidence enough to nail Sven Larsen. But Jeffrey wanted more. *He killed my father and took away my legacy. He owes me his fortune—all of it*, he thought. And as he walked the few blocks to his apartment, his thoughts turned to Brett.

"Some of them are extraordinary and some are just ordinary," Nathalie Corbet said to Brett.

"It makes you wonder, especially when they come from the same agency," Brett responded.

They sat in Brett's studio, exhausted after their third day of go-sees. The last model had just left and a stack of composite cards, almost six inches high, sat on the table before them. Brett and Nathalie had met many times during the last two months to discuss the promotional photos Brett was taking for American *Voilà!*. Nathalie decided that she wanted the premiere issue of the magazine to use only unknowns. She knew that it might have been a safer bet to use the hot girls everyone recognized, but for the new magazine, she wanted new faces.

Starting a publication in New York was difficult enough, even with the healthy reserve coffers Nathalie had at her disposal from the French publisher, and she could easily have taken the tried-and-true path. But Nathalie wanted to make her mark, and this was her chance. Experience had taught her that a magazine bears its editor's fingerprints, clearly identifying the guiding force behind it, and she wanted to come out of the gate fast, and with something nobody had yet seen. Since fashion hopelessly repeats itself, she could not rely on it for the freshness she sought. She and Brett had come up with the idea of using new models late one night after shooting the cover for the press packet.

All the agencies in New York had a new-face division—girls who had yet to be discovered and who were gloriously underexposed. Some would be duds, of course, but they could cull the best from the lot and start their own stable of American *Voilà!* girls. The only catch was that they had to see all of them, in person.

They had scheduled four days of go-sees and were thrilled to have only one more day to go. They estimated that they had seen almost six hundred girls.

"What did you think of Tonya?" Brett asked.

"Which one was she?" Nathalie hadn't even tried to remember names, but she had set apart the comps of those girls she really liked.

"The black girl from IMG Models. Here," Brett said, withdrawing the card from Nathalie's pile.

"Ah, yes, she's one of the extraordinary ones. She'll be fabulous in Azzadine Alaia or Patrick Kelly. We might even give her a cover try."

"I think she's special, too. I'm glad you like her."

Their conversation was interrupted by Thérèse, who told Brett she had an urgent phone call. Brett tried to calm herself as she reached for the wall phone next to her. "This is Brett Larsen. How can I help you?"

"It's Auntie Brett now," Joe said. "They're here—a boy and a girl. Isn't that great—we got one of each!"

— *Chapter 28* —

At last, Brett was caught in the swirl of activity that she had flourished on in Paris, and Larsen Studios was again a bustling nucleus that attracted a corps of talented, creative fashion innovators. Brett worked harder on the debut issue of American *Voilà!* than she had on any project before.

Nathalie Corbet felt enormous pressure from her publisher to stop traffic from the first issue—no small feat in a marketplace crowded with publications targeted for every group of females from pre-teen to post-menopausal. She called on Brett to be unrestrained by available notions of what a fashion magazine had to be and to experiment with what it could be. Brett accepted the responsibility and pressure of the task, excited by the prospect of a landscape unmarked by prior exploration.

Brett and Nathalie had chosen models who ran the gamut of age and race, and even trod upon the hallowed ground of size, choosing a model who was beautiful, fit, and fuller than the traditional size eight. Their primary criterion was that the women exude the spirit of unlimited possibilities that Nathalie believed to be the essence of the American woman. The hours were long and the tension ran high, but for Brett, the satisfaction was immense.

She found that David was astonished and impressed by the tempo of her life once she hit her stride. "I had no idea it got so intense," he had said. "It's like starting from square one every day, and you can never predict exactly what will happen."

Late one night, while Brett was still plowing through boxes of chromes, David had arrived with homemade raspberry ice cream and a stack of boxes it took him two trips to his Saab to unload. He served up dessert, then busied himself setting up Brett's new Fingertips-II, complete with all the accessories. "I know you won't use it," he told Brett, so he made a point of coming back to the studio and instructing Thérèse in all its office applications and as soon as she learned to move the cursor, she was in love.

Brett spent as much time as possible with Lizzie, Joe, and the babies. From the time Emma Brett and Cameron Powell arrived, it was like they had been a part of the Tate household forever.

Renovations on the apartment Brett had bought for them were not yet complete, so Emma and Cameron were rooming with their parents. Brett would stare at them in their white wicker bassinets, mesmerized.

"Go ahead, you can pick them up," Lizzie had coaxed.

For a long time, Brett demurred. They seemed so small and fragile, she was afraid she might do something wrong and hurt one of them. But after Emma squeezed her finger so hard that it actually hurt, she realized that babies were pretty strong and not easily broken.

From then on, Brett availed herself of every opportunity to hold them. She would sit in the bentwood rocker in Lizzie and Joe's bedroom, cradling one or the other of them. "Babies smell so fresh and sweet you just have to hug them," she said, enjoying the concentrated warmth they seemed to generate and the blond peach fuzz of their hair against her cheek.

And David played the quintessential uncle. He routinely arrived with an armload of toys, and he teased Joe and his sister about how much fun the children would have with their Uncle David when they got older, and how they were going to cry when they had to go home.

"Brett, line one is for you. It's Todd Banks," Thérèse said over the intercom.

"What's doing, Todd?" Brett actually looked forward to his periodic calls. He was a good source of industry dirt, and quite entertaining once you got past the bombast.

"Who's doin' is usually more to the point, but I've heard you did some most righteous work for *Voilà!*. Can't wait to see it," he said.

They discussed the IRS seizure of the assets of one of the most venerable Seventh Avenue houses. Then he told her about the lawsuit filed by four models against a certain hair care line. Each model had been given one of the company's home perms prior to shooting a commercial, and within a week, they all had begun to lose their hair.

"Frederica worked with one of them. She said it was coming out in handfuls."

In answer to the question that Brett knew was coming, she replied, "It was touch and go for a while, Todd, but work is picking up, and I'm still going to go it without a rep."

Todd was winding the conversation to a close when he said, "On a serious note, it looks like we're going to lose another star in this business. I hear the watch is on for Malcolm Kent. They don't expect . . ."

"Todd, no!" Brett said in horror.

"Yeah, he's kept it quiet for a long time. I heard he tried all the treatments available here. He even went down to Mexico for some new therapy, but he collapsed day before yesterday in the studio, and it doesn't look good."

Brett had heard the rumors that Malcolm had AIDS, but she had heard the same rumor about nearly every gay male in the business at one time or another. Suddenly, the air-conditioned cool of the office seemed clammy and unnatural. She unlocked the doors to the garden and climbed into the hammock that stretched between a hickory and a maple. Outside, the atmosphere was so dense and humid it seemed to have texture, and a thin film of sweat coated her skin almost immediately. A squirrel leapt from the stockade fence onto a low limb of the maple, disturbing the wind chimes that dangled there. The discordant clanging jarred her.

Malcolm conjured up feelings for Brett as disparate as pleasure and pain—he always had. When she had worked for him, he could make a day so hellish that when she lay in her bed at night in the darkness, she heard his shrill, relentless harangue ricochet off the walls of her room. But then he would also take her into his office, close the door, and spend hours going over her film, giving her suggestions and praise. It was Malcolm who had goaded her into going to Europe, who had given her the confidence to call herself a photographer and believe it.

And that was why it had hurt so profoundly when she had returned to New York and he had shunned her. When they met by chance, he either snubbed her or hurled darts tipped in acid innuendo. But she could not accept that he was dying.

Brett stood outside Malcolm's hospital room in the putty-colored corridor, bathed by the sickly fluorescent haze. She was preparing herself for what she would find inside. She had been ready to see him until she had reached his door and had seen the laminated warning sign, printed in red block letters. She read the instructions, which prescribed the wearing of rubber gloves whenever there was the possibility of contact with bodily fluid. It advised that oxygen was in use and all combustible materials were prohibited, and that hospital staff must dispose of syringes and other medical waste properly.

Brett opened the door. She heard the congested wheezing first, then was met by the strong, sweet smell of gardenias. Malcolm had never been a big man, but lying in the middle of the bed, the covers pulled up to his chin, he looked tiny and frail. He was asleep, so she shut the door silently and stood by his bed. The railings on both sides were raised, and it looked like an oversized crib. One of his arms lay outside the covers, and an IV tube taped to the middle of his forearm led to bottles of glucose and saline suspended from a battered metal pole. Someone had tied a fluffy, pink grosgrain ribbon at the center of his headboard, the ends of which trailed to the floor on either side, and the three gardenias, floating on the water in a crystal bowl on his bedside table, were the only flowers in the private room.

Brett felt it was eerie, seeing him so still and quiet. Her memories were always of Malcolm in motion. As if he divined her thoughts, his eyes fluttered open. He focused for a long moment, then was racked by a fit of violent coughing. Brett felt her own chest constrict with his spasm. Finally, he settled back on the pillow.

"Babycakes?" he asked in a raspy voice.

"Yes, Malcolm, it's me," Brett said.

"My mouth feels like the desert. Would you get me a cup of water? And be sure to put on gloves—they're in the drawer," he said haltingly, then closed his eyes.

Holding back her tears, Brett slid her hands into the latex gloves, poured a cup of water, and unpeeled one of the straws fanned out in a plastic cup on his bed table. Brett held the cup until he finished sipping.

"I've been a prick to you for a while," he said.

"Malcolm, it doesn't matter."

"It does, Brett . . . I've been angry." Coughing interrupted him momentarily, then he continued. "Angry at the world, angry at myself—angry at you for being so good and so young."

Brett leaned on the railing, removed her gloves, and smoothed his hair.

"Phoebe thinks you're good. Go give her a swift kick in the ass. She'll give you some work," he said, smiling weakly.

"Sure, and I'll tell her you sent me," Brett said, in as light a voice as she could muster.

"Good." He rested for a moment. "Brett . . . I'm scared. It's not time for it to be over."

"I know," was all she could say. She reached for his hand and held it tightly, and they were quiet for a while.

"I have to go to sleep now," Malcolm whispered, and his eyelids gently shut.

Brett held his hand until it went slack in hers. She backed away from the bed, deposited her gloves in the receptacle by the door, and left.

She was waiting for a red light to change when the tears began to fall.

"Miss, are you all right?" asked a mail carrier who had stopped her cart beside Brett.

Brett nodded her head yes, wiping her tears on the backs of her hands.

The woman dug in the pocket of her uniform shorts. "Here, take these," she said, handing Brett a packet of tissues before she headed across the street.

"They were so good during the whole service," Lizzie bragged.
"That's because they slept through it," Joe countered.
"It doesn't matter. They were quiet because my godchildren are excellent babies," Brett called as she shook Tabasco into the Bloody Mary she was mixing.

The Powell and Tate clans were now gathered in Brett's living room. That morning, Emma, dressed in the white batiste gown with tucks down the bodice, pink flowers embroidered at the neck, and a matching bonnet that had belonged to her mother, and Cameron, in white linen trimmed in Battenberg lace that had been his father's, were christened and Brett and David were the new godparents.

Everyone had come to Brett's house for brunch, and she had performed her first official godmotherly duty—changing the children from their delicate white christening costumes into more casual attire.

The last five days had been a whirlwind. To celebrate Brett's completion of work on the first two issues of *AV!*, the nickname for American *Voilà!*, David had taken her to a villa in Jamaica for a four-day getaway. They had no people to see and no schedules to keep. A delicate white gazebo overlooking the sea was the setting for their leisurely breakfasts, and in the afternoons they talked, read, or napped on the terrace, where the bougainvillea ensured their privacy. It was an idyllic vacation, and it confirmed for Brett that her love for David was not a fantasy.

Brett had made some of the preparations for the christening celebration before her trip to Jamaica, and had completed them by phone. On Sunday, she had been so preoccupied with babies and brunch that she had not noticed how withdrawn and quiet David had been all morning. He had picked through the meal and struggled to hold up his end of conversations, but his thoughts were elsewhere.

"Brett, I need to make a phone call. Do you mind if I go down to your office where it's quiet?" he asked her when she had settled on the couch with her Bloody Mary.

"Sure, go ahead. You know where everything is."

David lumbered down the stairs as though his shoes were leaden. He slumped in one of the Barcelona chairs that faced the window seat, his hands limp in his lap.

He had tried with all his heart to believe that he was not to blame for the accident. But in church that morning, holding little Cameron Powell in his arms and listening as the minister outlined his duties as a godfather, he wanted to yell, "I am not worthy!" How could Joe and Lizzie entrust him with such responsibility for their children when he felt the blame for Kate's death and their baby's rested squarely on his shoulders, and the weight would be his to bear forever?

He had asked himself the same questions thousands of times. Why had he taken her out on the boat? Why hadn't he insisted that she wear her life vest? She had complained it was hot and uncomfortable, but he should have been adamant. Why hadn't he headed for shore at the first report of squalls?

He had no answers that would absolve him of the burden of their lives, and in his mind, he did not deserve to enjoy his own.

Through all of it David had not cried, feeling that so public a show of grief was only a plea for sympathy and that he deserved none. But now his oppressive guilt, coupled with an overwhelming sadness, washed over him and unleashed desolate, mournful sobs. His shoulders quaked and heavy, hot tears coursed down his face. He made no attempt to stop the deluge. The storm had to run its course.

When he had composed himself and sat, red-eyed and limp, he thought of Brett. It had all been under control until she had come into his life. She had allowed him to feel happiness again, but he could not stand the sorrow that came in tandem. Knowing he could not go back and join the others, he picked up the phone. "Brett, it's me. Yes, I'm calling from downstairs. We've run into a problem at the Sunnyvale facility and I need to go to the office for a while. Yeah, it's a pain. I don't want to come upstairs—Mom and Lizzie will make such a fuss about my leaving. Will you tell everybody good-bye for me? Tell them I'll see them later. Thanks."

Brett sensed a change in David immediately. When he came over for dinner two days after the christening, she thought that he was quieter than usual, almost sullen. When she asked if anything was wrong, he told her that the problem in Sunnyvale was more serious than first suspected, and that he would be going out to California to evaluate matters. Understanding that the pressure of a burgeoning company could sometimes be all consuming, she tried to be comforting, but nothing she did seemed right.

She had asked if he wanted to talk about it, but he said no. When she changed the subject, telling him that pictures she had taken at the gathering on Sunday were back from the lab, he said he'd rather look at them another time. So she decided that he just needed to be left to his thoughts.

In the den—the room that housed the stereo, TV, VCR, and a deluxe Tarzan pinball machine—David flipped cable channels restlessly for half an hour, then told her he had to leave. He would have gone without even a kiss if Brett had not positioned herself between him and the door. After a peck, he disappeared.

He spent the next ten days in California, then flew to South Korea for a week to begin negotiations on a joint computer venture. After the first five days, Brett realized that she had called him on several occasions, but he had never initiated a call. She decided to wait and let him phone her. But she didn't hear from him until he returned to New York.

Brett casually asked Lizzie whether something was bothering her brother, but her friend could offer no help.

When David returned, matters worsened. He stayed in the office late most nights, and even worked weekends. Brett offered to bring him meals, or to come and keep him company, but he always declined.

It was like someone was slowly closing the valve, shutting off her supply of oxygen, like she was being gradually smothered.

"Brett, I have to talk to you," David said when his secretary put him through to her.

"You can come by tonight," she replied. Maybe she would find out what was going on.

"I'll be at your place about nine, if that's all right with you," he said.

"It's fine, David. Would you like a late dinner?"

"No," he answered.

What was the matter with him? Why was he behaving so strangely? Brett asked herself those questions for the rest of the afternoon. She purposely kept herself busy in the darkroom until eight-thirty and then went upstairs to wait. Nine-thirty melted into ten, but her doorbell didn't ring until nearly eleven o'clock.

"Where were you?" she blurted.

"Working," David said.

"You don't have a phone?"

"I didn't have time to call."

"It takes ten seconds."

"I don't have to account my time to you," David said.

Brett couldn't believe what she was hearing. She turned on the light in the reception area, not wanting to wait until they climbed the stairs to get to the bottom of this.

"I won't take up much of your time since it's late," he said. "We've seen a lot of each other in the last few months. It's been enjoyable. But all of a sudden I'm feeling boxed in, and I don't want to anymore."

"Boxed in? That's all you feel. We've gone through months of sharing the most intimate times together, and now you stand here and tell me all you feel is boxed in!" Brett was dumbfounded.

David winced and swallowed hard, but continued. "Look, you want me to be up-front with you. I'm being up-front. I'm not going to apologize for the way I feel."

"So you're saying it's been fun, but you've gotta run—is that it?"

"Call it what you want. I had to tell you," David said.

Brett's total disbelief had made her momentarily calm. She looked at David evenly. "Get out of here. Just go. I can't look at you anymore." Brett turned her back until she heard the door close.

"How could I have been so *wrong!*" Her voice echoed in the empty house. She walked in frantic circles around the room. She had done it again—been burned by a man who had turned out not to be what she had thought he was. *I won't cry! He can't make me cry!* she thought to herself. She dashed up to her bathroom, ripped off her clothes, and stood beneath a frigid blast of water in the shower. When she emerged she was shivering, but she wasn't crying.

The next day she had several clients to see and she returned to the studio in the afternoon with a four-day trip to Nova Scotia booked for *Seventeen*. She was just about to tell Thérèse when she saw the concerned look on her face and stopped.

"I am afraid I have sad news for you. Todd Banks called about an hour ago—Malcolm Kent died early this morning."

Brett clutched her portfolio to her chest. "He had gotten worse last week when I saw him," she said, almost to herself. "But he made me swear on a stack of fashion magazines that I still wouldn't tell anyone his name is Earl Cooley. Malcolm is a funny man." And then it sank in that he wasn't anymore, and the tears rolled one by one down her face.

Thérèse stood and hugged her.

"Why is it so awful sometimes . . . all at once? Last night, the man I thought was the most wonderful, sensitive, and honest person ever born announced to me that he was feeling boxed in and had to go. Thérèse, I was so happy with him, and poof, it's over. And today Malcolm is gone," Brett said through her tears.

"My grandmother used to say that misery comes in a long season," Thérèse said, comforting her.

Brett left Thérèse and went upstairs. Thérèse cleared some papers from her desk, then dialed the phone. "Jeffrey Underwood, please," she said, and then waited. "Mr. Underwood. Last night Brett and the man she has been seeing—yes, David Powell. They had some kind of disagreement. They are no longer together."

— *Chapter 29* —

Brett was determined not to succumb to the depression and desolation she had felt after her breakup with Lawrence. *If David wants to shut himself away and be a jerk, then let him*, she thought. Not that his unexplained departure from her life didn't hurt—it did—and Malcolm's untimely death only increased her suffering. But she had no intention of wasting the summer wallowing in self-pity.

Brett had expected Jeffrey to have some resentment when she and David became a couple, but he surprised her by being even more patient and comforting than he had before. He did not press, but let her know in his own subtle way that, true to his word, he *was* there for her. He quietly resumed his courtship, availing himself of every opportunity to make his intentions known. He called her two or three times a day, and Brett was amazed at how he seemed to intuitively know when she wasn't busy and had time to talk. "I was just thinking of you, so I thought I'd call," he would say. And by the time the heat of summer cooled into a crisp fall, Jeffrey was her most frequent companion.

Remembering how her spontaneous decision to go to Monte Carlo had helped to free her from her tailspin of depression after Lawrence, and the exhilaration she had felt driving the Corniches with the wind in her hair and the sun warming her face, Brett called Jeffrey to ask for his help in selecting a car. She had sold her Peugeot before she had left Paris and hadn't purchased another car since her return to the States. Jeffrey had been delighted to assist her, and they had spent two days looking at various makes and models before Brett decided on a silver Jaguar convertible, just like the one she had rented in Nice. She wanted something fast and sleek, somehow expecting that the powerful, smooth ride would speed her escape from the hurt she felt. Jeffrey had agreed with her choice, but when he suggested that the Jaguar was not the most practical vehicle for her line of work, Brett knew he was right, so she bought a Range Rover, as well.

Every weekend, and sometimes on free days during the week, Brett would retrieve her car from the garage on Lexington and head out of the city. Often she would pick up Lillian and they would explore the upper Hudson Valley or the winding country roads of central New Jersey. They stopped at roadside diners for lunch, and would return to the city laden with farm-fresh eggs and bundles of homegrown produce.

On those occasions when Lizzie was free, Brett took the Rover and they would strap Emma and Cameron into their car seats and set off on an adventure.

Lizzie sensed Brett's restlessness, but could not offer the explanation she knew Brett needed because David had withdrawn from her, as well. He still visited his niece and nephew, but always on occasions when she and Joe were not in and the twins were in the care of their nanny. She knew he had resumed his sixteen-hour workdays, just as he had done after Kate's death. She had tried to broach the subject of David's relationship with Brett only once, and had been met with almost venomous hostility. He had been unable to talk about Kate for almost a year after the accident, and Lizzie only hoped that he would not keep whatever was eating at him now locked away that long. She wasn't particularly thrilled that Brett was seeing so much of Jeffrey Underwood, but she had butted in on Brett's romantic life once too often, so she remained silent.

"You can't do that to me! I thought you loved me!" Barbara cried. Black shadows—a combination of mascara and tears—marked her pale white skin and gave her the appearance of an albino raccoon.

They had just finished one of the by-the-book lovemaking sessions that Barbara didn't seem to mind and were ensconced in the white cocoon of her bedroom.

"But I'm doing it for you—for us," Jeffrey said, sitting up under the frothy meringue of covers. "I've exhausted every other avenue. Brett is our only answer. She's the key to the money. Sure, I've been able to increase your allowance without your father's knowledge, and I've even set up a dummy corporation that Larsen Enterprises supposedly does business with. I can funnel larger sums through B & N Consultants, though not nearly what you deserve. But Brett is going to get it all, and her financial savvy is almost nil. If I marry her, I can control what assets she has now, as well as her inheritance. Her own personal portfolio has almost tripled in the last two years, and she doesn't even know it."

"But that could take forever. I don't think my father will ever die. He's too evil! Even the devil doesn't want him. Besides, if you marry her, you'll have to . . . sleep with her. I couldn't bear the thought of that, Jeffrey," Barbara said. She removed a tissue from the lace-covered box on her bedside table and wiped her eyes, smearing her mask further.

Jeffrey knew he had to convince Barbara that this was the only way. He had used her to get the information he now had on Sven, but although he was certain of her stupidity, he needed her cooperation in his plan to marry Brett, or everything he had worked for could backfire. He took her hand and held it as he spoke. "Listen, Barbara, if we keep going as we are, we're bound to get caught. I can bury things it would take the auditors years to find, but eventually they'll catch on. I'll be fired *and* disbarred, and we won't have anything."

"But we'd have each other," Barbara said pitifully, staring down at the blackened tissue.

"How long do you think we'd last with no money, Barbara? We've gotten used to a certain standard of living, and my idea is to elevate that standard, not lower it."

Barbara looked thoughtful for a moment as she considered Jeffrey's rationale. "But I love you. If you marry her, we couldn't see each other anymore and . . . I think I'd die!"

Well, that would take you off my hands, Jeffrey thought. He had to marry Brett. Sven had made it clear that as a son-in-law, he would be next in line to head the company. Sven was old and, unlike Barbara, Jeffrey did not believe in his immortality. Sooner or later

Sven would die, and if Jeffrey and Brett produced a child, it would ensure Jeffrey's own ties to the Larsen fortune. Nothing could dissuade him from getting back what he saw as rightfully his. "I love you, too, Barbara," he lied. "And having to make love to your daughter will hurt me as much as it hurts you, but it's what I have to do. It's what I'm supposed to do. A man has to make sacrifices for the woman he loves." Jeffrey paused to allow his words to sink in. "I didn't want to have to tell you this." He looked down at the floor, then back at Barbara. "I had hoped you would understand, but . . . your father is dying," Jeffrey lied once again. "This is top secret. If word of his ill health got out, it could affect not only the future of Larsen Enterprises and our own financial security, but the economy, as well. Larsen is a privately held company, but most of its competitors are not. If this information got into the wrong hands, it could cause a flurry of activity in the stock market. Acquisitions and mergers would take place left and right, and the financial stability of the whole transportation industry would be threatened. The doctors have given him less than a year. He's seen specialists all over the world and the prognosis is the same. So you see, I wouldn't have to stay with Brett long. When he dies, I'd take over the company, and I could easily maneuver transactions that would give us more money than we could spend in a lifetime."

"Is he really dying? Serves the bastard right," she said. "You promise it won't take long?"

"I promise, darling."

"I had a lovely day, Jeffrey. Would you like to come in for a while?" Brett asked.

"I can't think of anything I'd like better," Jeffrey said. "Besides, I think you could use some help with those."

Brett had placed the three gallon jugs of apple cider by the door while she found her keys. Jeffrey had met her early that morning at her garage and they had driven to Pennsylvania. The rich amber, golden yellow, and vibrant reds of the autumn foliage had turned the countryside into a landscape created by the brush stroke of a master. Pastures were dotted with Guernseys and Holsteins idly grazing and chewing their cud, and fields of late corn waved their tassels in greeting to the city slickers who had come to get a taste of another way of life. Farmers on tractors or loading hay onto ancient trucks nodded as the silver Jaguar meandered along winding country roads.

They got lost twice. Brett was not as able a navigator as she was a photographer, but they finally made it to New Hope. Tucked about halfway between New York and Philadelphia, the quaint but sophisticated little town is populated by refugees from both cities who want to escape the hectic urban grind and live in a place that offers the hope of a simpler existence. Visitors sought that same release, but only on a temporary basis. Galleries, craft shops, candlemakers, bakeries, and bookstores lined the main street, and Brett and Jeffrey had browsed a good part of the day.

Brett found an eighteenth century stained-glass lamp shade that she decided she couldn't live without and Jeffrey bought it. Jeffrey found two Hepplewhite chairs that he said would look perfect in his foyer, so Brett bought them and arranged for their shipment to New York. On the outskirts of town they ate pork chops, potato pancakes, and applesauce washed down with cider that was so good, Jeffrey convinced the owner to sell them two gallons to take home. The restaurateur thought they were in love, so he accommodated the young man's desire to impress his lady and gave him an extra gallon.

When they returned to Brett's house after their outing, Jeffrey laid a fire while Brett heated the cider and carried it back to the living room in tall pewter tankards, then joined him on the sofa. "You always know exactly the right thing to do, Jeffrey. How do you know me so well?" she asked.

"Because I care about you, darling. No, it's more than that. I waited too long to say it the last time, and I won't let that happen again. I love you, Brett, and I want to spend my life taking care of you."

These were the words she wanted to hear. She had wanted to hear them from Lawrence. She had wanted to hear them from David. But now, they came from Jeffrey, the man who had always been there, quietly waiting his turn. *He has to mean it*, Brett thought. *He's spent years holding my life together. I could learn to love him. I know I could.*

"Jeffrey, are you saying . . ."

He reached out and took her by the shoulders. "I'm saying I want to marry you, Brett. Will you be my wife?"

Brett didn't have to ask herself many questions. Jeffrey wanted her. Not like Lawrence, who had wanted her and someone else. Not like David, who didn't appear to know what he wanted. More than anything, Brett wanted to be wanted. Deep down she longed to have a public acknowledgement that someone had chosen to love her. Her father had abandoned her before she was born. Barbara had given up custody without a struggle. Lawrence had ridiculed her love with his deception, and David had just deserted her without a word of explanation.

"Yes. I'll marry you, Jeffrey."

They sat for a moment in silence, neither looking at the other. Jeffrey couldn't believe she had said yes so easily, and Brett, who was unprepared for his proposal, wondered at her immediate acceptance.

"Let's do it right away," he suggested. "I have an acquaintance who's a judge, unless you'd prefer a religious ceremony, and he can marry us in chambers. You're still going to Paris next week, aren't you? We could make it a honeymoon."

Martine Gallet was being honored by the Alliance du Mode as designer of the year, and Brett had promised that she would be there. "But I'm only going for the weekend. I have a shoot scheduled the Tuesday after I get back. I've already confirmed the job and booked the Concorde," Brett said.

"That doesn't matter. We'll spend our first weekend as man and wife in the city where we first met."

"That sounds wonderful and romantic, Jeffrey. Are you sure you won't be bored at the awards?"

"Not with you at my side." Jeffrey leaned over and kissed her gently on the mouth. "Then, it's all set."

"Would you like to . . . stay tonight?" Brett asked. She and Jeffrey had never gotten to this point before, but now that they were getting married, it seemed natural that he would spend the night.

"Yes, I would," Jeffrey answered. "But I'm going to wait. I

want to reserve that privilege for the time when it's rightfully mine and you are Mrs. Jeffrey Underwood."

He departed with another chaste kiss, elated that Brett had accepted so readily. At the corner of Seventeenth Street and Park Avenue South, he stopped at a phone booth and dialed Thérèse's number. "We're getting married, so I won't need as much on her as I did before. Still, keep an eye on her and inform me of anything you deem important that I might not be aware of." No sooner had he extended his hand than a cab pulled over to the curb. *This is really my night. They'll all be under my control*, he thought and gave the driver his address.

The moment he arrived home, he made another call—this time, one he did not mind showing up on his phone company record. "She said yes, sir. We're getting married next week."

"Fine," Sven Larsen replied. He hung up and wrote them a check for five million dollars—a wedding present.

"Granddaughter of Transportation Czar Secretly Wed," the headline read. He had told her it would be soon, but by the time Barbara saw the announcement, Brett and Jeffrey were midway over the Atlantic.

She tossed the offending newspaper to the floor, reached for the bottle of Valium in the drawer of her dressing table, and swallowed two, along with a glass of Cristal. Then she lit a cigarette, and another, and another. . . .

Mr. and Mrs. Underwood were registered at the Crillon, where she had first met Jeffrey. Brett felt a little strange staying at a hotel in a city she had once called home, but after all, it was her honeymoon. Their first night together was tepid, at best, but Brett attributed Jeffrey's lack of ardor to his very old-fashioned notions. He had been gentle, and had done everything she had come to expect. *It just lacks fire*, she thought. *A little time will take care of that. I'll try harder and love will make it better*, she convinced herself.

The abbreviated trip was a whirlwind of activity. Martine was delighted that Brett really had come, and the awards ceremony on Saturday night was exactly as it had been for years. Only the recipients changed. Thierry Carbonnier was as boring as usual, and she had even spied Lawrence across the room, but did not have a chance to speak before she and Jeffrey left for the party Martine was throwing at Castel's.

On Sunday they had lunch with Gabriel and dinner with one of Jeffrey's business associates. Monday morning, before they departed, she made a few phone calls while Jeffrey was out. He returned with a four-carat emerald cut diamond ring from Cartier. "I wanted it to be special and to come from the place where it all began," he said as he slipped the ring on her finger.

He really is very sweet, Brett thought as they boarded the jet for their three-hour flight home.

— *Chapter 30* —

"Of course I miss you, darling," Jeffrey said.

"I was just making sure," Barbara responded coyly. "It's just that this is all so hard. I didn't realize that we couldn't go out anymore, and I only see you once a week, if that." Barbara toyed with the frog closure of her flowing black-and-gold caftan. Its generous dimensions hid her diminishing girth. She had cut her hair short for the first time in her life. It framed her face in soft waves, and she now wore so little makeup that it no longer collected in the fine lines under her eyes and in the creases on either side of her mouth. For Jeffrey she had shed almost twenty of the thirty pounds she planned to lose. But in place of food, Barbara had substituted another habit. She reached for the slim gold case on the coffee table, removed a cigarette, and waited for Jeffrey to light it.

"I know. It's difficult for me, as well, but I look forward to the time we spend alone." He picked up the Baccarat table lighter and held the flame to the cigarette until the tip glowed red-orange and wisps of smoke floated in the air. Looking around the apartment, Jeffrey was struck by how much he hated this dingy place and this slatternly woman. But he couldn't risk alienating her, until he and Brett had a child. Convincing Brett to become pregnant had proved trickier than he had expected. He had hoped that her attachment to her godchildren would ignite a maternal fever in her, but each time he mentioned having a baby she would say she wasn't ready.

"Can you stay longer this time?" Barbara asked hopefully.

"I'm afraid not. We have tickets to the symphony tonight."

"You're always going someplace with her!" Barbara said petulantly.

"This is business. A client is in town with his wife, and it would be highly irregular if my wife did not attend the concert, as well."

"I guess so," Barbara muttered, lighting another cigarette.

"Must you do that?" Jeffrey said, more forcefully than he intended. He found this addiction vile, dirty, and disgusting, and he hated the smell of smoke that clung to his fine custom-tailored clothing when he left her.

"You wouldn't want me to get fat again, would you?" she asked sweetly.

"You were never fat, darling. You're just womanly," Jeffrey lied as he remembered the first time he had seen her naked. Cellulite dimpled her blue-veined flesh, and aside from her breasts, the curves he imagined were once there had settled into amorphous androgyny, and he had been repulsed. "It's just not good for you, that's all. I want you to be as concerned about your health as I am."

"As soon as all the weight is gone, I'll quit. I promise."

"I really should be going soon, but before I leave, there's been a new development. Brett changed her will, initially to include her friend Elizabeth's children, but she also made me the main beneficiary."

"So what—she's twenty-five years old. I'll be dead before you get your hands on that money. And, by the way, could you take care of Sherry Lehman and Elizabeth Arden for me? I'd hate not being able to look good for you, and a girl needs her champagne, you know."

She couldn't have spent the fifty thousand I got for her, Jeffrey thought. Then he realized it was a test. Barbara was looking for additional proof that his loyalties hadn't changed. "Certainly, first thing tomorrow. About Brett's will, of course I can't touch that now, but don't you see? It means she trusts me, and by the time she inherits Larsen, getting what I want . . . for us will be like taking candy from a baby."

"Oh, I see what you mean." But she didn't. All she knew was that she didn't have enough money and the man she loved was married to her daughter.

Jeffrey put on his beaver-collared navy polo coat in front of the mirror in the hall. He watched Barbara in the reflection as she slipped her hand into her pocket, then put it to her mouth, and took two good belts of scotch.

He strolled out into the cold, dry air of December and breathed deeply, as though for the first time in hours. Deciding that walking a few blocks might remove some of the foul stench of cigarettes that lingered in his nostrils and sullied his clothes, Jeffrey headed down Fifth Avenue on foot. He had moved into the Gramercy Park house. It was too airy and botanical for his tastes, so he retained his apartment. Its dark rooms, heavy with tapestries and Biedermier furniture, served as a sanctuary where he could worship the god of revenge in private.

It was the day after Christmas, and Brett and Lillian sat in the solarium at Cox Cove over a late breakfast. There had been no snow this year, but the temperature hovered in the single digits. Outside, the bitter cold made everything appear frozen in time. The sun shone with a glinty brightness and gave the false impression of affable warmth, but nothing moved. Not even a sparrow perched on a limb of the massive oak tree, looming like a skeleton of its former lush self over the covered pool. The garden lay barren, its soil so hard that the colorful profusion of spring and summer could barely be recalled. But inside it was cozy and the festive enamel pots of poinsettias and hanging evergreen boughs centered with pine cones tied with red ribbons provided an air of conviviality.

Jeffrey had returned to the city before sunrise, claiming an overload of paperwork resulting from the new tax laws that would take effect January 1. They had come out on Christmas Eve for Lillian's annual open house, and Cox Cove had been a bustling outpost of chatter and merriment from four o'clock to well after midnight. North Shore regulars mixed with friends from the city who had braved the Long Island Expressway—the road to mall heaven—on the last shopping day of the season. Brett acted as co-hostess, and had invited friends and associates from her circle as well as Jeffrey's, so the crowd was even more eclectic than usual.

The tranquility of Christmas Day had been a welcome relief. Hilda had prepared a small but traditional dinner for the three of them. After the meal they had retired to the living room for eggnog in front of the fire. Conversation was low-key. Lillian politely asked Jeffrey about her brother and the state of his health, and Jeffrey reported that Sven was as robust and fit as ever, and still working like a steam engine.

When Brett and Lillian began to reminisce about Christmases past, Jeffrey lapsed into uncharacteristic silence. Instead of joining in with stories of his own boyhood and teen years, he had wandered over to the ten-foot blue spruce and fingered the hand-crafted Swedish ornaments almost reverently. Then he excused himself, saying he had a headache and needed to lie down. He didn't return, and Brett and Lillian continued their retrospective until they had both grown sleepy. Lillian went to bed troubled by her niece's husband. He gave every appearance of loving Brett, but the feeling she had had when she had first met him hadn't left her. There was something about his eyes—they always had a detached look, as if he had long been haunted by ghosts he couldn't identify, but whose presence he took for granted.

"Of course I'm happy. Jeffrey loves me," Brett responded to her aunt's question.

"I know that, child. You've said it before . . . but do you love him?" Lillian had observed her niece over the course of her ten-week marriage, and although things appeared to be fine, she sensed an undercurrent. Brett talked about him often, and always in glowing terms. "He's so kind." "He's really very sweet and old-fashioned." And, of course, "He really loves me." Lillian was aware that Brett had almost no examples of a loving relationship between a man and a woman in her life. There had been no marriages in her family she could look to because Brett hadn't known Nigel. And Lillian fervently wished that she had been able to see what a marriage was like when it works.

"He's a very special man," Brett finally replied.

Lillian had her answer. She fingered the two gold rings she still wore on her left hand. She had hoped this wouldn't happen. Lillian had seen Brett bravely accept rejection by her mother and had suspected then that her life would have to include the search for a love to replace the one Barbara could not give—the natural, unconditional love of a parent for a child. She had witnessed the dejection Brett had tried to hide when she had come home after her relationship in Paris ended, and then there had been David. She had no idea what had happened between them—just that what was once so right had suddenly been wrong. She wanted Brett to wait for the love she deserved—a mutual, abiding love that would transcend time and adversity. But she had settled for the first man who was willing to make a commitment, thereby giving her a badge of honor that would show the world that she was worthy of someone's voluntary affection.

They finished their coffee in a vacuum of unspoken acceptance of the invisible sign that read, "No Trespassing". Then Brett had gone upstairs and prepared to leave.

Lillian stood in the doorway, the icy cold filling the foyer with a speed that implied it too sought refuge from itself. "Just know that I love you, child," she called, then waved at Brett's departing back.

Brett arrived at home and found that Jeffrey had sequestered himself in the room on the fifth floor he had converted to an office. She went down to the studio, collected the stack of European fashion magazines that had piled up during the busy holiday season, and carried them back upstairs to the living room. The afternoon had already begun to grow dark, so she turned on the lights and curled up on the sofa to tackle her homework.

She leafed through the magazines, making notes for future reference, but thoughts of Jeffrey nagged at her. *We haven't been married three months yet. This must be the period of adjustment everyone talks about.*

During the first two weeks after their return from Paris, Jeffrey had been warm, loving, and romantic. He had surprised her by purchasing a lens she had mentioned she was considering. One day early in November a bouquet of tropical flowers as large as the delivery man had arrived for her in the middle of a shoot. He had her most recent painting from Aunt Lillian beautifully framed and hung on the wall of their bedroom so that the pastoral country landscape was the first thing she saw when she awakened each morning. His lovemaking was hesitant, almost insecure, and she decided that he was just trying to learn what pleased her.

But lately, he seemed distant and withdrawn. She had tried to probe, to ask questions that showed she was genuinely concerned and wanted to know what was bothering him. He told her simply that he was under a lot of pressure at work. "Larsen Enterprises is a huge company. You should know that, since it will all belong to you one day. I'm taking care of your business," he had said.

I want to love you, I really do, Brett thought as Jeffrey strode into the living room.

"Shouldn't you be getting ready? We have reservations for eight o'clock." Jeffrey had showered and changed from his country clothes—corduroys and a tweed hacking jacket—into a gray and black houndstooth blazer, charcoal cashmere turtleneck, and flannel slacks.

"Oh, the time just got away from me. I'll be ready in fifteen minutes," Brett said as she dashed up the stairs.

They dined out almost every night. Jeffrey didn't cook, and although Brett's skills in the kitchen had improved greatly, thanks to David, Jeffrey complained that he didn't like the smell of food in the house to remind him all night of what he had eaten for dinner. Jeffrey hadn't even been in the kitchen more than half a dozen times, and then only for a glass of water.

When Brett came downstairs she was wearing a red wool Donna Karan dress and black suede boots. Her hair was neatly fastened in a low ponytail with a black velvet bow and diamond studs, and her wedding rings were her only jewelry.

"You look lovely, darling," Jeffrey said, and kissed her lightly on the cheek as he helped her into her coat.

The car and driver waited at the curb, and as they rode uptown to the Manhattan Café on First Avenue, Brett thought to herself, *so this is what it's like to be rich*. Not that she had ever considered herself to be without resources; she just had never taken full advantage of the world of privilege into which she had been born and on which Jeffrey seemed to thrive.

Jeffrey had suggested they get live-in help the moment he moved in. He insisted that the cleaning woman who came in twice a week was insufficient. They had compromised on a maid who came daily, but Jeffrey always found something she hadn't done to his satisfaction, and voiced his aggravation so often that the woman finally quit and had to be replaced.

Seated in the center of the spacious, mahogany-paneled dining room, at a table laid with heavy starched white linen, Jeffrey nodded at regular intervals to those he knew who were also "power" dining. A polite banter accompanied their steaks and, mission accomplished, they returned to their chauffeured car and were duly deposited in front of their door.

Once inside they had cognac in the living room, discussed who they had seen at dinner, and what their days were like tomorrow, then retired to their separate bathrooms to get ready for bed. Jeffrey used the guest bathroom down the hall, saying that Brett's pink marble bath, filled with scented soaps and perfume bottles, distracted him and precluded his use of the room for its intended purpose.

When he returned to their bedroom in his navy silk pajamas, he sat on the side of the bed where Brett already lay and took her hand. "Darling," he began. "I really wish you would reconsider. Think of how much joy children have brought to your friends Joe and Elizabeth."

"Jeffrey, do we have to have this conversation every time we go to bed?" Brett asked wearily. The spaghetti strap of her nightgown slipped from her shoulder and she pulled it back up.

"It's just that I'm not getting any younger, Brett, and a man wants to leave something of himself in this world."

"Jeffrey, you sound like you have one foot in the grave. You're only forty-one and I'm only twenty-five. I think we both have a little time left. Let's give it a couple of years. My career has just taken off again, and I don't want to lose any momentum—not now."

"But Elizabeth had children right away. It doesn't seem to have hurt her career. She's just been promoted to weekend anchor."

"Lizzie's career is different. She doesn't climb ladders, carry heavy equipment, or crawl around on the floor."

"You don't have to do that, either, you know."

"Is this the beginning of lecture number two? The one where you remind me how rich I am and that I don't have to work at all?" Brett's annoyance was mounting.

"Well, it's true."

"Can't we just go to bed, make love, and fall asleep in each other's arms?" Brett asked. She smiled at Jeffrey and held out her arms. *Practice, that's what he needs*, she thought.

"People have sex so they can have children. That's its purpose —reproduction!" Jeffrey got up and walked to the foot of the bed.

"What?" Brett asked incredulously. She stared at him, her mouth agape.

"Men and women couple to create children. It's pleasurable in order to ensure the survival of the species."

He's serious, Brett said to herself, amazed by his premise. "I always knew you were old-fashioned, Jeffrey, but that is the craziest thing I've ever heard!" She sat completely up in bed. Her pink nightgown clung to her bosom, revealing the fullness of her breasts.

"Don't think you can tempt me with a wanton display of your body," Jeffrey said, his voice full of agitation.

"What are you talking about?" Brett felt her anger and resentment boil over. "You've seen my body plenty of times and it didn't tempt you to wild displays of passion! Why should tonight be different? I'm going to sleep. We can talk about this another time." Brett had learned from their first disagreement in the Russian Tea Room that when Jeffrey was trying to make a point, he acted like he was arguing a case in front of the United States Supreme Court. He needed time to cool down before he could listen to a dissenting opinion.

"I'll sleep in the other room," he said, a suspicious calm in his voice. He padded noiselessly out of the room and down the hall. *They're both the same*, he thought. *She and her mother. All they want is sex. Well, let's see how long she can do without it. She won't divorce me. It's too great an admission of failure, and she doesn't want to repeat her mother's mistakes. She'll come around to my way of thinking.*

When Brett heard the soft click of the guest room door closing, she rolled over on her stomach, clutching her pillow. *What can I do to make it better?* Tears began to soak the pillowcase. *I can't have a baby now—I just can't. He has to give me time to learn to love him. I know I can do it. Maybe next year. I'll tell him that tomorrow.* Still the tears came and the nagging little voice returned. What have you done? What have you gotten yourself into?

Jeffrey had gone to the office when she awakened the next morning, and he slept in the guest room again that night. And the next night, and the next.

— *Chapter 31* —

"I confirmed Rachel Gibson for this booking two weeks ago. What do you mean, she's been released?" Brett yelled into the receiver.

Brett had been confident that beginning the new year with a shoot for a new client was a good omen. Her personal life was in disarray, but professionally, she was on the upswing. Tyler and Hackford, the East Side clothier, was known for providing the executive woman with the exquisitely tailored clothing that men who have achieved a certain level of success in the business world have always taken for granted. They produced sleek, quarterly catalogs that were sent to professional women of the highest echelon across the country.

Several photographers had been submitted by their ad agency, but Melissa Tyler and Merriweather Hackford had been impressed not only by the caliber of Brett's work, but by her professional demeanor, and they were also eager to give their support to another working woman.

Brett had gone to great lengths to ensure that the job went off without a hitch. The clients were very particular about which models were used. They had painstakingly examined models' portfolios and had chosen women with the classic looks, understated elegance, and self-assurance that they felt would best speak to their clientele. As soon as the book was cast, Brett had called to hold time on the models while she worked out a shooting schedule.

They would shoot twelve shots a day on four successive days. She had scouted spots around the city, paid the necessary fees, and obtained permits. It was a tight schedule with little margin for error, but Brett knew she had laid the groundwork well and that everything should have run smoothly.

Except that her first model was an hour and a half late. Brett had booked Rachel to arrive at the studio at seven o'clock. Her hair and makeup would be done there while the stylist and Brett's assistant loaded clothes, accessories, jewelry, and photo equipment into the location van, one of the beige and brown RV's that were rented by photographers and film makers to serve as a base of operations when they worked outside the studio. All the gear was stowed and they were ready to proceed to the World Trade Center, their site for the morning, but the model still had not shown up.

Brett was fuming by eight-thirty when Zoom Models opened and she could finally call to find out why there was a holdup. They were already behind schedule and it would be difficult to recover by the end of the day.

Brett reached D. V. Woods, head of the women's division at Zoom, who was less than thrilled to have a screaming photographer on the phone first thing in the morning. She pulled Rachel's chart and informed Brett of the release.

"Who called to release her?" Brett asked, astounded.

"It says here that your office manager, Claude Sanders . . ."

"I don't have an office manager named Claude. You know that, D. V.!" Brett could feel the blood vessels in her neck pulsing.

"Honey, you can't possibly expect me to keep up with the studio managers floating around this town," D. V. said.

Brett knew that the most important thing to do right now was to salvage the day. She would have to get to the root of the problem later.

"Fine. Can you get Rachel over to the World Trade Center by nine-thirty? She can meet the van."

"Brett, honey, Rachel is booked all day today and tomorrow. I can't give you a minute on her until Wednesday, and then she only has the afternoon open."

Brett used every ounce of control she possessed to stifle the panic that threatened to strangle her. Tyler and Hackford had been very particular about which models wore which outfits, and about where each garment was to be shot. Brett looked at her watch. The two women were planning to meet the van at ten o'clock to see how the shoot was progressing. How could she tell them they didn't have a model?

"D. V., let's shelve this for a minute. I booked Grace Bianco for one o'clock today. Make sure she's not canceled." Brett had to be certain the rest of the day would not go awry. She would figure out how to reschedule Rachel later. While Brett waited for D. V. to pull the chart, she buzzed Thérèse on the intercom. "You've got this week's shooting schedule on the computer. Call every agency whose models I've booked for this job and make sure they're still booked."

Brett chewed on her bottom lip and rocked back and forth in her chair, waiting for D. V. to return to the phone.

"Sorry, honey, Grace was canceled, too. You can have her tomorrow."

"Fine. Put her on hold. I'll get right back to you. And, D. V., make a note, *do not* take any changes on model status unless they're called in by me or Thérèse Diot."

Brett dropped the receiver into the cradle and paced the floor.

This isn't real, screamed the voice in her head. *I've got to stay calm. This can't get out of hand.* She took a deep breath and went out to Thérèse's desk, hoping that the news was not as grim.

By now the crew had gathered in the reception area, talking, drinking coffee, eating doughnuts, and waiting for instructions. When Brett emerged, a hush fell over the group.

"This is unbelievable! All of your girls have been released, by this same Claude." Thérèse's voice shook.

"Shit!" Brett exclaimed, before she could hold it in. All eyes were riveted on her, but she didn't care. This was a nightmare, except she was awake.

She felt like her brain was approaching meltdown and she had to cool it quickly so, slamming the door to her office, she headed out to the garden. She braced herself against the cold stone of the building and breathed deeply. This had the potential to be the worst day of her professional life and she had no choice but to go through it.

After a minute she went back in, explained to the crew that there was a scheduling problem and that she would get back to them. Brett knew that whether or not she took one picture, she would have to pay all the staff and rental fees associated with the day, as well as any cost overruns caused by the scheduling problems.

She returned to her office to make the hardest call. She had to catch Tyler and Hackford before they left the store to meet the van that wasn't there. While she dialed the number, she wondered who had done this to her, and why?

The conversation was as bad as she had expected. The retailers were adamant about schedules and order. They were appalled by the situation Brett outlined and placed the blame squarely on her head. Brett assured them that they would have a catalog shot to their specifications, as close to schedule as she could manage, even if that meant she had to work the weekend. In addition, she assured them she would assume any expenses brought on by the delay.

Now she had to begin the task of reworking the schedule. She sat with the list of models and locations and began the arduous task of getting the pieces of the puzzle to fit again.

After two hours of phone calls, she had wrenched order out of the confusion. The Upper West Side town house she had booked for the third day of shooting was available this afternoon, and so was the model scheduled to work that day. Brett would have to pay the $1,500 location rental fee twice, since it was too late to cancel the day she had originally scheduled, but at least she would have some film today and a sense that she was digging her way out.

Brett left instructions with Thérèse to reconfirm every model, hair, and makeup person—anybody she had scheduled, for any reason, for the next month.

On the way up the West Side Highway she rode in the seat next to the driver, her eyes closed, telling herself the nightmare would be over soon.

The afternoon passed without further incident. Periodically, Brett would catch people whispering, but they either became silent or started talking about the weather when they caught sight of her. *Terrific. This little fiasco will be all over the city by lunchtime tomorrow*, she thought. So far, there had only been good press on her. She had never shown up for a booking unwashed or high, and she didn't sleep with teenage motorcycle gang members or have any other unusual quirks, so she knew this episode would make the rounds.

When she returned to the office, Thérèse informed her that her fears had been well-founded. Every model she had either confirmed or put on hold had been released. Thérèse was able to salvage time on all but two models, and she had put tentatives on people to replace them.

"Thanks, Thérèse. I couldn't have gotten through this without you." She hugged her assistant and headed up the stairs. Every cell in her body ached. The apartment was dark, but Brett didn't need the light. She headed straight for her bedroom and threw herself facedown on the duvet.

The panic and disbelief she had experienced earlier had ripened into bloodcurdling rage. Someone had maliciously and intentionally set out to sabotage her. None of it made any sense. Only she and Thérèse had access to that scheduling information. Thérèse kept hers on computer disks, but Brett always kept paper copies, since she still had not mastered the computer. Brett never locked her office, and she often had papers strewn across the table. Perhaps someone had stolen a copy of the schedule. But why? Was this an attempt to stifle competition, or some kind of perverse warning? She felt eyes spying on her and had no clue to where they were or how to cover herself.

When the front door opened and closed she had no idea how long she had been lying in the dark. She listened as Jeffrey's measured footsteps approached and stopped outside her door. He rapped softly.

"Come in," she called.

"I wasn't sure you were home," he began as he flipped on the ginger jar lamp on the dresser. "Are you all right?" he asked with alarm in his voice when he saw Brett sprawled on the bed.

She did not relish the thought of explaining her plight to Jeffrey. She was expecting one of the lectures he had delivered so deftly of late. To her surprise, he listened compassionately, expressing his dismay at each distressing development.

"This is very serious. Your business is obviously as cutthroat as any other. Do you know what photographer worked for these people before you?" he asked.

"You don't think . . ."

"I don't know what to think, but anything is possible," he replied. "It may be hard for you to imagine, but some people will stop at nothing to get what they want. You've got to start locking your files. I know this is a possibility you don't want to imagine, but how much do you trust Thérèse?"

"Jeffrey, really!"

"I know you think I'm being an alarmist, but she bears watching. If you'd like, I'll hire someone to investigate further," he offered.

"No. I don't think it's reached that point yet," she said, dropping her face back into the pillow.

Jeffrey sat lightly on the bed and massaged her shoulders. "Would you like to join me for dinner?" he asked.

Brett turned and looked at her husband. Jeffrey was like two people. Sometimes he was the soul of concern, caring and understanding, but then he would become obstinate, opinionated, and glacial. *I don't want to give up on this—not yet*, she thought. "I'm not really hungry. I think I'll stay here. Stop in when you get back," she said tenderly.

That worked as well as Thérèse had said it would, Jeffrey thought as he stripped to shower before going out to dinner. A few more days like this one, and Brett would be sorry she had ever seen a camera. And then she would be his.

Upon his return, Jeffrey visited Brett's room. She had readied herself for bed, and when he knocked, she put on a lavender kimono before asking him to come in. He only stayed long enough to ascertain that she was all right and give her encouragement to get through the coming day. When he left he ran his hand over her hair and kissed her lightly. Brett tried to imagine that she felt some sense of longing, some urgency for their differences to be settled, but when he closed the door, all she could honestly say was that she was relieved to be alone.

Despite the disastrous start, she completed the job, using the prescribed models at the agreed-upon locations, by working two extra days. She presented film to the clients on the following Monday, the day it was due. If nothing else, she felt the work was good and bore no evidence of the distractions. Both Tyler and Hackford were pleased, as well, and told Brett they respected her integrity in handling the emergency, but she left their office not knowing whether they would work with her in the future.

Brett had letters sent to all the major model agencies in the city, advising them to accept bookings or cancellations only from herself or Thérèse until further notice. She forced herself to learn enough about the computer to input and recall scheduling information, and she had a dead bolt lock installed on her office door. She endured the flurry of gossip, but felt she had prevented any lasting repercussions.

With increasing frequency, Jeffrey retired to his East Sixty-eighth Street lair to relieve his mounting fatigue, the result of the unceasing pressure of living multiple lies. For decades he had plodded along, steadily, patiently, the prospect of retribution his only fuel. Now he was so close that, like a shark, he could smell the blood of his victim. He had to struggle to control the frenzy it incited in him.

Jeffrey had removed his files and the locked box, which now contained the precious tapes of Barbara's damning tale, to his apartment. Collapsed on the maroon brocade divan in his living room, he listened over and over again to Barbara saying, "He had my husband killed," and "I knew he had done something awful to Karl."

I have you, you self-serving, greedy bastard, he would gloat, reveling in the fantasy of Sven Larsen in prison, publicly debased. But that was not enough. Vivid memories of the humiliation, indignity, and loss he had suffered because of Sven would grip him, but he would only be satisfied when he had control of everything Sven had ever owned or loved.

But Jeffrey had not counted on either Brett or Barbara to waylay him so completely. He was weary of his role as selfless, attentive caretaker; it was time for them to do his bidding, but they were both unresponsive to his timetable.

Thinking of his latest custodial visit to Barbara made his flesh crawl. When she wasn't professing her devotion or groping for his zipper, she whined because everything was taking so long.

"Isn't he even in the hospital yet? You said he was going to die soon," Barbara had said.

Jeffrey concocted stories of the caravan of doctors parading to Racine, attempting to prolong the inevitable.

"He's desperate," Barbara responded. "Let him see what it feels like to die!"

And Brett was proving more willful and resourceful than he had given her credit for. With no help from him, she had extricated herself from the mishap he had engineered. He had thought leaving her bed would hasten her acquiescence to his need to have a child, but while she expressed concern and a willingness to work at their marriage, her suggestion was that they seek counseling.

Jeffrey felt like a juggler, balancing spinning plates atop slender rods. The trick required total concentration, and while he tended one, the others would list precariously, threatening to crash to the ground. For now, all the plates were spinning, but he didn't know how long he could keep it up.

It was time to give the screw another turn.

* * *

Brett had gone to see Phoebe Caswell, just as Malcolm had suggested. At least once a month for the last six months they had touched base. Initially, the visits had been the same as before—cordial. Nothing concrete transpired until March.

When Phoebe called and asked if she could come by the studio the next day, Brett knew something was up. Like a visiting head of state, Phoebe was afforded the VIP treatment, and after a tour of the studio, they settled in her office, by the bay window, and Thérèse brought them tea. Then Phoebe got right to the point.

She described the trend toward flowing dresses and gowns, draped in sheer fabrics to accentuate the curves and contours of the body. "I've seen the most astounding colors, Brett. Aquamarine, crocus, sea foam, mango, all so dense, yet transparent. Oh, and the fabrics! Yards and yards of glorious chiffons, organzas, mousseline de soie . . . I haven't seen gowns so utterly breathtaking since I don't know when!" Phoebe raved. "How would you conceptualize a layout featuring these clothes?" Phoebe held the delicate lavender and yellow Sevres cup and inhaled the aroma of the full-bodied Darjeeling before she took a sip.

Phoebe was testing her. Brett's mind raced. Not wanting to appear hesitant, she said the first thing that came to her mind. "Your description conjures up images of classical Greek draping. I see clothes with a timeless elegance and respect for the exquisite lines of the body. They don't try to alter it or improve on it, just celebrate it." Brett suggested that they shoot against the uncontrived background of white seamless, using a fan and the models' movements to exploit the sensual quality of the clothing. She proceeded as though the job was already hers, pulling chromes from her file to illustrate the kind of lighting she believed would be most effective and suggesting models who possessed beauty strong enough not to be overwhelmed by the clothes.

Phoebe listened with rapt attention, pursing her lips, nodding her assent, then unclipping her Mont Blanc from the jewel neck of her black and white tick check jacket, she jotted notes on one of the newsprint scratch pads that she carried with her everywhere.

When Brett was done, Phoebe took her time rereading the notes she had taken, then said, "You know, dear, I love clothes. When I was a child, my mother used to think it quite aberrant that when we went to a store I wanted to examine every dress, blouse—any piece of clothing that was within my reach. I would feel the fabric, finger the buttons, and look at the stitching. She would ask if I wanted it, and mostly I said no. It was only the really special ones that would tempt me." Phoebe took a sip of tea, then continued. "And wearing new clothes always makes me nervous. Sometimes I buy an outfit and leave it in my closet for a year or two before I actually put it on, and then I try to wear it with something I've had for a very long time so it feels more familiar. Now, that was a long way around the block to say that I feel very much the same about the people I choose to work with. I always examine them carefully, and spend a lot of time getting to know them before we work together. After all this time, you probably thought I was just lonely or sadistic to have you come to my office so often, seemingly for nothing, but there's really a method to my madness. I like your ideas on this piece. My assistant will be in touch to schedule the editorial meeting and tentative time for the shoot. I think it's time for you to come out of the closet."

Brett was elated. This job would mark an important milestone in her career.

It was dreary and raining on the day of the shoot, but inside, the atmosphere was convivial. By eleven o'clock one model was in the makeup room, with patches of concealer under her eyes and in a mustache above her lips, waiting for foundation. The other was already dressed and on the set, totally engrossed in exploring the folds of her strapless apricot chiffon dress, whose flowing skirt was slit up the left side to her waist. Brett had just snapped a Polaroid, which her assistant held while looking at his watch, counting the seconds until it was ready.

Phoebe sat in a director's chair just to the right of Brett and the camera, so that her view of the action was close to the one Brett was shooting. She exhibited none of the nervousness of working with a new photographer that she had alluded to, and waited patiently for the proceedings to get underway.

Brett's assistant ripped the black backing from the instant film and handed it to her. She grabbed a loupe that sat on the equipment cart to her left and looked at the print, then, holding her breath, passed it Phoebe.

"Stupendous!" she exclaimed, and after everyone else took a look to see if any last-minute adjustments were needed, Brett started.

In the middle of the second roll, everything in the studio went black. The CD player stopped midnote, the blades on the fan spun in slow motion, then stopped, and almost in unison, a surprised cry rose from the group. Brett, completely baffled, ran downstairs, but was met halfway by Thérèse.

"What has happened? All the lights just went out," Thérèse called.

"They're out upstairs, too. I'm going to the cellar to check the circuit breakers." Every one of them was in the on position, but there was no electricity anywhere in the house.

Brett explained the situation to Phoebe, who suggested an early lunch to give Brett time to straighten out the problem.

While the others ate in the kitchen, with only candles to light their meal, Brett and Thérèse frantically phoned electrical contractors, and finally found someone who could come immediately.

"There's a cutoff timer back here," the electrician informed her after a careful examination of the wiring.

"You can't be serious," Brett replied in disbelief.

"Look for yourself." He held the lantern while Brett peered over his shoulder. She saw some kind of digital device set for the time when the lights went out.

She felt fingers of panic grip her neck. Someone had been in her house and planned for the lights to go out in the middle of her booking.

"What do you want me to do?" he asked.

"Take it off and get the lights back on, but don't destroy it," she answered.

When Brett questioned Thérèse, she found that someone claiming to be a meter reader had been downstairs the day before.

"Did he have identification?" Brett asked.

"I didn't look—I never look. He had a blue uniform and a flashlight so I let him in. *Mon dieu*, he was in the house and he did this!" Thérèse began to cry.

Brett comforted her, but instructed her to call the police. This was clearly a crime, and it was aimed at her.

Shortly after three o'clock the lights were on again, and she resumed shooting. At five-thirty, a squad car showed up, and Brett had to excuse herself to explain the situation to the officers. They took notes, examined the cellar, and said a detective would contact her. Nothing escaped the crew and models, and as bits and pieces of the story leaked out, the general consensus was that somebody was out to get Brett Larsen.

Everyone was understanding and sympathetic, and they worked until nine, finishing the shots that were scheduled. Phoebe held Brett's hand as she walked to the door. "You be careful, dear. Something very irregular happened here today, and you must definitely take it seriously."

Brett dragged herself upstairs, to find Jeffrey waiting anxiously. "Thérèse told me what happened. This is very alarming. There was someone in our house, Brett."

"Jeffrey, I was here. I know what happened." She was too upset to sit still for a repetition of the facts. She pulled a bottle of wine from the cellar and began to peel the seal from around the neck.

"Well, aren't you concerned?" he asked, coming to join her at the bar.

"Of course I'm concerned, but what would you like me to do about it?" Brett slammed the bottle down.

"I'd like you to consider not taking pictures for a while," Jeffrey replied.

"Dammit, is that your answer to everything? You actually sound like you're happy for the opportunity to say it again!" Brett glared at him. "I'm going upstairs."

Brett curled up in the mauve easy chair in the corner, feeling trapped and alone. She had wanted to keep everyone calm this afternoon, so she hadn't dared admit how frightened she really was. As much as she wanted to believe that this was not connected to her troubles in January, she knew in her heart it was. What she didn't know was why it was happening.

And right now, she wanted to talk to someone who would not use her fears and doubts against her. While completing the job today, she had had serious thoughts about taking a break, at least until she could find some shred of sense in these attacks, but she knew that to admit that to Jeffrey was to hand him the ammunition he needed, and that he would not be satisfied until the battle was won. *How strange to think of being at war with your husband*, she thought as she heard the knocking at the door.

"I'm sorry I lost my head out there. I just get so upset when you don't take these things seriously." Jeffrey came and sat on the ottoman in front of her. "I know we've had our differences these last few months, but it's only because you mean so much to me."

Brett wondered what exactly she did mean to him, and what he meant to her, but tonight she had no answer for those questions, either.

"I'm half expecting to hear there's a contract out on my life," Brett said to Lizzie and Joe. She had come over for the evening, ostensibly to visit her two godchildren. But before long, she had told them the story of her mishaps.

"What have you done about it, Brett?" Joe asked.

She told them about the police reports, detectives dusting for fingerprints, and Thérèse's trip down to headquarters to look through mug books in an attempt to find the mysterious meter man—all to no avail. After the second incident, Jeffrey had hired a private investigator, but so far, he had unearthed nothing. And this time, the news had made the fashion rounds and seemed to stick. Although Brett had finished the job and Phoebe adored the pictures, the word was out that Brett Larsen was having a run of bad luck and that someone seemed determined for her to have more.

"What does Jeffrey have to say about all this?" Lizzie asked.

Brett hadn't even told Lizzie about the turmoil in her marriage. She had wanted to work out the glitches on her own. But Lizzie looked at her now with those inquiring eyes that had always made keeping secrets from her difficult. Joe, sensing that the two women wanted to be alone, excused himself and left the room.

"Lizzie, I've tried," Brett began.

— *Chapter 32* —

"She's so miserable, David." Lizzie had stopped by her brother's office on her way home from GNSN.

David pushed back his chair from the oval glass desk, got up, and walked over to the corner, where an enormous Calder mobile hovered. It was suspended from the ceiling by nearly invisible wires and it shimmied, almost imperceptibly lulled into motion by the natural air currents in the room. With his fingertips he gave the section shaped like Saturn a slight push and the entire animated sculpture was called to action. Some of the spheres revolved clockwise, while others rotated in their own orbit, and boomeranglike elbows moved up and down like pump handles. David watched intently for a few seconds.

He turned to his sister. "I didn't know, Lizzie. I had no idea—none at all. I thought she had finally found the happiness that she deserves."

It was almost May, and Lizzie hadn't seen David since Christmas dinner. He had lost several pounds. The frown lines on his brow had deepened, and the twinkle was missing from his usually merry brown eyes. He had spent most of January in California, and then had gone on to Korea to finalize the start-up of operations over there. When he had returned, he phoned regularly and dropped by to see Emma and Cameron, but still, only when she and Joe weren't at home.

Lizzie knew David was going through a rough time with the

business, and she also knew he hadn't been the same since his breakup with Brett. David had refused to discuss the end of their affair, and for once, Lizzie resolved to stay out of the whole mess. She sensed that her brother was suffering from some unknown torment. She hadn't seen him so miserable since Kate died, but she had allowed him to dismiss her offers of help and a friendly ear. Today she decided that she wouldn't give him the chance to put her off or claim he was too busy for a chat. If he didn't want to talk to her, she would talk to him.

Brett had been heartbroken after David had stopped seeing her, but her recovery had been quick—too quick for Lizzie—and the next thing she knew, Brett had married Jeffrey Underwood. She felt Brett had made a horrible mistake when she married Jeffrey, but she had said nothing. Now, after her friend's confession that all was not right in her marriage, Lizzie had to know what had precipitated all that had happened between Brett and David. And since Brett didn't know, she hoped that hearing about Brett's troubles would prompt David to tell her something. Lizzie wasn't naive enough to believe it would change anything—she just wanted to know and maybe find a shred of redeeming evidence to take back to Brett.

One of the things that worried Lizzie most about Brett was her willingness to shoulder the blame for things that went wrong in her life. When they were little, she remembered trying to convince Brett that it was Barbara who was wrong because she didn't act like a mother. Then she watched Brett berate herself for not catching on to Lawrence, and it seemed that David had finally convinced her that she was just unlovable, until Jeffrey came along and picked up the pieces.

David walked around to where Lizzie sat in one of the black leather and steel Wassily chairs facing his desk. "Let's sit over there. It's more comfortable," he said, pointing to the sleek sofa, upholstered in black silk parachute fabric.

Today Lizzie's cool, unruffled appearance was that of a television journalist, not a harried mother of eleven month old twins. Her hair was tamed smoothly away from her face and she wore a royal blue, silk shantung suit with a mandarin neckline. She looked like a news professional in search of a story. Because she was. Using the time-honored technique of giving information in order to get some, she continued. "And not only is her marriage to Jeffrey awful, her work life is a shambles, too." She told him about the two unexplained episodes at the studio. "The police can't turn up anything—no fingerprints, nothing! She's worried sick, and can't figure who would be out to get her."

"You're right. That is awful. I'm sorry," David said.

"You're sorry? Is that all you have to say?" Lizzie edged forward on the sofa and swiveled to face her brother.

"What do you want me to say?" he asked quietly.

"I want to know how this happened." Lizzie rose and stood in front of her brother.

"I don't know who's out to get Brett."

"That's not what I mean! I want you to tell me what sent her straight into the arms of that cold, self-righteous creep." David started to get up. "No! You stay right where you are, David Powell! I'm not going to have you towering over me while I talk to your chin. You're my brother and I love you, but I love Brett, too, and you have to tell me what went wrong." By now Lizzie was shouting and David was glad his office was soundproof.

"I can't, Lizzie—I just can't." He stared down at the Hands On logo woven into the cobalt-blue carpet. The two hands holding a geodesic globe emblazoned with a computer terminal and keyboard seemed to mock him. He had not held on to what had been so trustingly placed in his hands.

"You mean you *won't*." Lizzie stood, arms akimbo, and announced, "Well, I'm not leaving until you tell me *something*!"

David had never seen his sister so vehemently defiant, and he knew from her stance that he would have to bodily remove her or tell her what she wanted to know. But he had never given voice to his grief, his guilt, or his feelings of unworthiness. And even now that he had finally found the places where those feelings fit into the matrix of his life, he didn't know if he could tell anyone about them. He looked at Lizzie's face and could see the jut of her jawbone as she clenched her teeth tightly together, waiting for him to speak.

"I don't know where to begin, Lizzie. But it would be a lot easier if you sat down."

She dropped her arms and sat on the sofa next to him again. But once she had settled herself, she folded her arms across her chest, her body language clearly letting David know that just because she had sat down didn't mean she had weakened her position.

"I still love her, Lizzie. But . . ." He paused.

"Then, why did you drop her cold? That's not the way a person treats someone he loves."

"I did it because I loved her and she deserved a better man than me."

"For a genius, you certainly are stupid! You're a fine man, David. You're sweet and honest and . . ."

"Don't start a list of my exemplary qualities. Yeah, I know, good old David, he's really a great guy. Well, he's a great guy who's had a lot of problems he couldn't handle. I've gotten over most of that now, though. For years I blamed myself for Kate's death. But what I found out was that it was easier to make myself feel guilty than to admit the hurt and pain that was tearing me apart. I never let myself mourn for her because I didn't think I had the right to indulge my own sorrow for something I made happen." He crossed his leg over his knee and began to fiddle with the lace of his wing tip shoe.

"How could you blame yourself? It was an accident." Lizzie unfolded her arms and reached out to still David's fidgety hand.

"I thought I should have been able to *make* her wear the life vest. But I finally realized that Kate was a seasoned sailor, and she was at least as responsible for her own safety as I was. By the time Brett and I . . . well, you know . . . I thought I was pretty much over it. Then Emma and Cameron came along, and at the christening, I realized how much you trusted me by having me as their godfather. All the uncertainties came rushing back in a flood. I loved Brett, but I couldn't saddle her with my baggage, especially when the contents were spilling out all over the place, so I walked out of her life."

"And you never told her any of this?" Lizzie asked, astonished by her brother's story.

"No, and by the time I figured out I was a jerk, and that life did give you second chances, it was too late—she had married Underwood. I don't know about you, but I could use a beer." David got up and walked over to the gleaming chrome cube that sat between the chairs in front of his desk. He pressed a small button on the side and the front swung open, revealing a small refrigerator.

"I never would have guessed," Lizzie said, and smiled for the first time since she had arrived.

"I got the idea from Brett's kitchen. You know how her refrigerator looks just like the cabinets? So I had this one designed." He removed two bottles. "Glass?" he asked his sister. She shook her head and reached for the frosty bottle. "I'm actually glad you made me talk. I can feel the spring inside me unwinding."

"Good, then I'm glad, too. But what are we going to do about Brett?"

"Do? We can't do anything about her marriage. That's between her and Jeffrey." David thought for a moment. "But maybe I can help with the business end of her problems."

"How?" Lizzie asked hopefully.

"Well, her computer may have some answers she hasn't known how to look for. It has a built-in modem that's linked directly to her phone system. Maybe somebody has been pirating information."

"Yeah, like that weird husband of hers."

"Don't be silly, Lizzie. He's her husband. Just because they aren't getting along right now doesn't mean he's sabotaging her career. He's a lawyer, not James Bond. Besides, you told me yourself that he's trying to help her, and he even hired an investigator."

"Maybe I've seen too many late movies. I just don't like him—I never have. But it would be wonderful if you could do something, David. You can still be friends. She'll understand, I know she will. She's going crazy getting ready for a trip to Tahiti right now. Why don't you call when she gets back?" Lizzie stood and gave her brother a hug. "So, why don't you come home with me? We could have dinner. You look like you could use a good meal, and you could change a few diapers, maybe give your niece and nephew lessons on that crazy computer you gave them, and find out if they're geniuses, too."

"Sure, Lizzie, I'd like that."

American *Voilà!* had captured the hearts of American women, just as Nathalie planned, from the first issue, and each subsequent edition of the innovative magazine continued to embrace more readers. Nathalie borrowed French *Voilà!*'s location scout, intending to send him on a quest for the ultimate paradise in which to shoot the summer swimsuit issue. But the instant he heard her request, he said, "French Polynesia—the Society Islands, to be exact." He told her that of all the places he had been in the world, the archipelagoes of the South Pacific were the lushest and most beautiful.

After an eight-hour flight from Los Angeles, Nathalie, Brett, two assistants, two stylists, two hair and makeup artists, five models, and *AV!*'s travel editor, Marie Reynard, landed at Tahiti-Faa'a Airport in Papeete. There they would transfer to Air Tahiti and continue on to Bora Bora, a fifty-minute plane ride from Tahiti and the first stop on the three-island, five-day junket. The trip had been coordinated by Marie, so transportation, lodging, and meals were all comped for mentions in the magazine. Only *AV!* would contain the swimsuit layout, but both the French and American editions would run a vacationer's guide to the South Pacific, written by Marie.

They had a breathtaking view of the majestic peaks of Bora Bora, which soared more than twenty-five hundred feet above a large multiblued lagoon. The island itself was too small for an airstrip so they landed offshore on a coral islet, and a launch took them to their final destination. The crew was overwhelmed by the glorious mountains, green with dense tropical vegetation, and the clear water, inhabited by fish of every color in the visible spectrum.

Work began the next morning at dawn. Brett was energized by the beauty around her. They started the day with two models on the slopes of Otemanu, the island's highest peak. The girls, in gauzy white sundresses, looked like two long-stemmed calla lilies as they cavorted in the midst of a green so dark and intense that it was almost black. The wind blew in the right direction, and the sun reached its zenith at just the right moment to make shadows that were interesting, not intrusive. Brett worked her assistants and the models hard—the morning's shots had to be completed before the sun became too glaring and harsh.

They toured the island in the afternoon, had lunch at Bloody Mary's, a Bora Bora institution, and resumed work at sunset. The models, standing ankle deep in a lagoon dressed in floral sarongs, were the subject of the photograph, but the spindly coconut palms and orange-purple sky peeking through low-hanging cotton candy clouds provided an awesome background. Brett knew it was one of the best photographs she had ever taken. If she had been in New York, the clip tests would have proven her intuition right in a matter of hours.

Exhausted by the day's efforts and needing to go over Marie's notes before their flight to Huahine at seven the next morning, Brett left the others in the hotel lounge. As she passed by the desk, the clerk handed her a message slip. Jeffrey had called. Realizing that it was four in the morning in New York, Brett decided to wait and call him tomorrow. They didn't talk at home, so she couldn't imagine what he wanted to talk about now that she was halfway around the world. But there was no time the next morning, either.

Tonya, one of the models, awakened with a fever, and they had to find a doctor before they could leave for Huahine. The doctor couldn't pinpoint the girl's malady, but gave her antibiotics and pronounced her well enough to travel. According to Brett's schedule, they should have completed at least two shots on Huahine by the time they left Bora Bora, but when they arrived, it was midday, and the strong light made it impossible to photograph the girls. So as not to waste time, Brett and Marie set out on bicycles to photograph the extensive open-air museum that housed ancient Polynesian maraes. Pictures of the shrines, grouped along the shore of Lake Fuana, would accompany the travel article.

By the time they returned around four, Nathalie had all the models, including the girl who had been ill, ready for their short jaunt across the bridge to Huahine Iti, the miniature sister island known for its beaches. The five girls frolicked in the gentle surf. White flecks of sand and glistening beads of water dotted their lithe, shimmering, oiled bodies. As an apparently recovered Tonya, clad in a sun yellow maillot, sailed off a rocky embankment, Brett captured her perfect swan dive midair. The girl was happy to repeat the dive but Brett knew she had gotten it with the first shot.

Like most of the natives and visitors, Brett had taken to wearing pareus when she wasn't in her safari shorts and tank tops, and when she joined the others for dinner that night, she wore the brilliantly hand-painted turquoise and shocking pink cloth as a dress, draped over one shoulder, then wrapped tightly about her waist. Her hair was adorned with a single tiare, its blossoms emitting the same sweet fragrance as its cousin, the gardenia. As soon as she sat, she was called to the phone. She knew it was Jeffrey. She hadn't returned his call from yesterday.

"Yes, I'm fine, Jeffrey." She waited for the echoed delay before she spoke again. "No, there are no problems at all on this trip." "I didn't mean to have worried you—we've just been really busy." "Yes, it's beautiful here." But when Jeffrey suggested they might vacation there, she tried with all her might to imagine him lying on the sand or swimming in the sea, and couldn't. *We'd probably have separate rooms in the most romantic place in the world, and be chauffeured to the beach*, she thought as she listened to him. "All right. I'll see you soon. 'Bye."

Their relationship hadn't improved, and as much as she hated to admit it, she now didn't believe her marriage would ever work out. When she rejoined the others, they were consuming tall pink drinks called Erupting Volcanoes and thoroughly enjoying their working vacation.

They landed on Moorea the next day, and Brett was convinced she had died and gone to heaven. Her *fare*—a mat-walled, thatched-roof bungalow built over a lagoon—had a lanai deck with a ladder that led directly to the sea. She wanted to stay there forever. There had been little time for fun in the sun on this trip, but after witnessing a spellbinding sunrise on the second day, she vowed to return.

The Tiare Moorea was a new hotel, anxious for publicity, and its staff had gone to great lengths to ensure that the American magazine crew had whatever it needed. The hotel arranged for the crew to use a three-masted ship to sail around the Sea of the Moon, the stretch of water between Moorea and the big island of Tahiti, provided air-conditioned Land Rovers for exploring and shooting in the back country, and guides to show them the best lagoons on Cook's and Opunohu bays.

They were three perfect days, and Brett finished the layout with an extraordinary sense of confidence and accomplishment. She felt she had done some of her best work, and everything had gone without incident. So, worries behind her, she boarded the plane home, ready to take on her problem marriage.

"There has to be a mistake—that's not possible!" Brett's hands shook as she held the phone and blind rage overshadowed reason. "Well, you'd better do something!"

She had just checked the lab to find out when the *AV!* film would be sent over, and had been informed that all one hundred twenty rolls were streaked and splotchy, as though exposed to excessive radiation. Leaving the phone dangling from the set on the wall, Brett walked into the reception room and sat, staring into space.

This can't be happening to me. It can't! she thought. But she knew Duggal was reliable. Somebody had deliberately destroyed her film. She had randomly shot rolls from each brick, or thirty-six rolls, of film, and had had the photos developed before the trip to make sure the film was fresh and the proper emulsion. At airport security checkpoints she had the film hand searched, so someone had tampered with it after she had tested it. Who would do such a vicious thing?

She got up from the chair and began to pace. Her palms were clammy and coated with sweat, and a dewy film covered her brow and upper lip. *I have to call Nathalie*, she thought in horror. *A reshoot is impossible . . . but they can't lose fifteen editorial pages.* After the Tyler and Hackford debacle and the nearly disastrous *Vogue* booking, this was the final nail in the coffin someone had been so painstakingly building.

Panic mounted, then receded. The good news was that they wouldn't shoot her—but that was also the bad news, she thought.

Brett wanted to talk to someone, anyone. She needed to vent her fear and frustration, but Jeffrey had already gone to the office, and she wasn't in the mood for his "you should quit this silly business" speech. Thérèse was coming in late. *Why me?* she asked herself as the studio buzzer sounded.

It's Duggal, Brett thought as she ran to answer it. *They made a mistake before and now they've found my film.* But when she threw open the door, it was not a messenger standing there, but David.

"What are you doing here?" Brett snapped. She felt like a metal band encircling her head was being pulled tighter and tighter and she gripped the doorknob with such force that her arm quaked.

All of David's rehearsals for this meeting had still left him unprepared for the torrent of feelings unleashed by the sight of her. The back of his neck tingled, and for an instant, his voice hung in his throat. He wanted to hold her, to feel the warmth and softness of her body, and to hear joy and laughter in her voice again. But what he wanted had nothing to do with what he could have or what he must do. Finding his tongue, he said, "I've wanted to talk to you for some time now, and I hoped you would hear me out."

"So you just appear and I'm supposed to drop everything and listen to you!" She stood squarely in the entryway, as though blocking the path of an intruder.

"Please . . . this won't take long, and you deserve an explanation." *She has every right to slam the door in my face*, he thought. That was what he had done to her, but he hoped she would let him set the record straight. It was too late to change anything, but at least she would know what had happened.

"Honestly, you couldn't have picked a worse time," she said, trying to control the trembling in her voice. "I've got a really big problem on my hands at the moment."

"I know you just got back from Tahiti. Did something go wrong over there?" Noting the look of surprise on her face, he added, "Lizzie told me what's been going on. Could I come in?"

She looked past him, focusing on two boys racing along the sidewalk. Their arms, pumping rhythmically, helped to propel them faster, and their whoops and laughter lingered after they disappeared around the corner. She should just tell him no. She had enough problems, and nothing he had to say could make a difference now anyway. Without knowing why, she said, "Okay. Come in," and walked abruptly away, leaving him to close the door and follow her into the dining room.

"Brett, what happened?"

She ached to tell him. Unburdening herself to David used to be so natural. But he had abandoned her without whys or goodbyes. Now her marriage was a sham and her career was unraveling right in front of her eyes. Why should she expose her failures to the light of his scrutiny? She wheeled around and leaned against the cold brick. "You came here to talk to me, so why don't you tell me what happened?" Her hostility showed, but she didn't care.

David made no attempt to deflect her scorn. He pulled one of the Shaker chairs from the table and sat down heavily, bracing his elbows on his knees. He sighed deeply, then said, "I made a mistake, a stupid mistake—one that I'll probably regret for the rest of my life." He hung his head, as though exhausted by the weight of his load.

Brett, fighting the impulse to come to his side and comfort him, kept her post at the fireplace. She listened without interruption as he revealed the same things he had told his sister. Each detail brought her sadness and understanding in equal measure.

"I'm really sorry, Brett. I blew it, and there's no way I can make it up to you," he finished quietly.

As if released from a spell, Brett finally sat down beside him. "I don't know what to say. David, if only you had told me . . . well, I guess you're right. It happened and it's over." They were the right words to say, but deep inside she felt heavy with sorrow, like a sponge filled to saturation with spilled hopes and wasted longing.

"Okay, case closed," David said firmly. "Would you like to talk about whatever happened this morning?"

Jarred back to the situation at hand, Brett started with the news from the lab and, over coffee, backtracked to the first incident, with the canceled models. When she finished, David agreed with her assessment that someone had done these things deliberately.

"Maybe I can help you get to the bottom of this," he said.

"You couldn't possibly make it any worse."

"Let's start with the computer." They headed for Thérèse's office. First, he duplicated Brett's entire mailing list of clients, colleagues, friends, and acquaintances onto a blank disk. As he worked, Brett came and perched on the desk beside him. The crisp, delicate scent of sandalwood, her favorite soap, surprised him and triggered a flood of memories of their time together. He forced them from his mind. "I'll take this with me and have it printed at the office. Our machines are much faster than this one. Then we'll go over the names, one by one. You'll have to remember as much as you can about every one of them—anything at all that might make a person a potential enemy," David said, slipping the disk in his pocket. "Someone may be pirating information, so I'm going to change the access code for your modem. No one except me, you, and Thérèse will be able to get into your system—at least, not for a while. If that's what's happening, whoever's doing it will eventually figure out the new code, but it will give us some time."

"Can someone really do that? Break into my computer, I mean?"

"If they know what they're doing, it's easy."

They were so absorbed, they didn't hear Thérèse come in. "Good morning, Brett. Mr. Powell, what a surprise to see you here. It has been quite a long time," she said pleasantly.

"How are you, Thérèse? We'll be out of your way in a second," David said.

"Are we through?" Brett asked.

"That's about it, for now. I have to get going. Walk me to the door?" Once they reached the hall, he whispered, "It may be better if no one knows what I'm doing. You have no idea who it may be. There is something else I'm going to do. I have a buddy from Stanford who's a computer specialist with the phone company. He can get a printout of all the calls made from your phone—even the local ones. I'll ask him to go back as far as November, since the first incident happened in January. It's not exactly aboveboard, but he owes me a couple of favors. The only problem is that he's on vacation, but as soon as he's back I'll get him started. It may take some time, even then."

"You sound like one of those spy novels. But call me when

you're ready to go over my mailing list. And David, thank you. Jeffrey hired an investigator, but he didn't turn up anything. I'm not even sure what he did. I really appreciate this."

They looked at each other, and suddenly the foyer seemed tiny. Their closeness made them uneasy. David opened the door and nodded. "I'll call you soon," he said. Brett closed the door behind him and went back to Thérèse's office.

"This person is probably mad. It sounds to me as if you should be very careful," Thérèse said after Brett told her what happened to her *AV!* film.

"I know, it all seems so cloak-and-dagger that it's hard to believe it's real. I'm going back to my office. I have to call Nathalie. Don't put through anyone until I let you know. I feel like shit, Thérèse."

"Merde!" Nathalie shouted when she heard the news. "I can't believe it! A reshoot is impossible, Brett—you know that." Brett tried to explain, but there was nothing she could offer that would make the situation better. Even if she could gather all the personnel and make the trip again, it would be too late to meet *AV!*'s deadline. "This is going to cost me more than half a million dollars in ad money!" In her heart, Nathalie believed that someone was out to get Brett, but that would not be a satisfactory explanation to her publishers. She hung up, dreading the transatlantic call she would have to make.

As soon as she saw the light on Brett's line, Thérèse called Jeffrey and told him that David had been there when she arrived but that she did not know what they had been talking about.

Jeffrey stalked the perimeter of his seventeenth-floor office at Larsen Enterprises like a caged lion. His quarry was within his grasp but out of his reach. He had returned to his wife's bed, finally realizing that he could not make her want to get pregnant if he did not make an attempt to appear loving. But it wasn't working. She either was asleep when he came to bed, or stayed up until she thought he was. This was his third attempt at sabotaging a job, in hopes that she would quit and that the resulting idle hours would inch her toward the decision he required. But now David Powell was back in the picture, and Jeffrey didn't know why.

He stopped his trek around the office and stared out the window at the Pan Am Building down the block. He really had to watch her. Why had David been at the studio? he wondered as the intercom sounded.

"I told you I was not to be disturbed," Jeffrey shouted at his secretary.

"She insists that you will see her, Mr. Underwood. It's a Mrs. North."

Barbara floated into the room in one of the vivid floral dresses Jeffrey hated. "What in the hell are you doing here?" he growled as she closed the door behind her.

"You haven't been to see me in three weeks. I can't call you at home, I can't call you at the office, so I decided to drop by. I miss you, darling. I know you've been busy, but I just couldn't stand it anymore. Aren't you even going to kiss me hello?"

"Here? Of course not. This is my office. There are people in the other room. You have to leave. What if your father found out you'd been here?" Jeffrey said.

"How could he find out? I haven't seen anyone but you and your secretary, and she has no idea who I am." Barbara flounced over to the charcoal-gray sofa, sat down, and crossed her legs, revealing more of her than Jeffrey wanted to see. "Should I have told her that I'm your mother-in-law?" she asked, smiling at him.

"That's not funny, Barbara. Coming here was insane!"

"I'm tired of waiting, Jeffrey. This is taking much longer than you promised. My father still isn't dead and you're still married to Brett. I need you, Jeffrey. If you divorce her, can't you get half of her money? My husbands always tried to, and you're a lawyer. We could live on that."

"I've told you before, Barbara, it isn't enough. You deserve more than that. But we shouldn't be talking about this here. You have to go. *Now!*"

"You can't throw me out, Jeffrey. You wouldn't dare! How would you like your wife to know you're sleeping with her mother?" she asked.

He had to get rid of her. He was infuriated by her effrontery. Barbara was no longer merely a loathsome presence in his life—she had just become a red flag, and he wanted to charge at her.

Trying to suppress his wrath, he said, with all the control he could muster, "I'll come by your place tomorrow and we can talk then."

"Don't disappoint me, Jeffrey," she said and sailed from the room.

He stood stock still for a moment, then his heart began to pound in a thunderous rhythm. His eyes burned with hate, that like a laser, bored through the air seeking a target. Slowly, as though moved by marionette strings, he walked over to the credenza, picked up a lead crystal tumbler and squeezed it until it shattered in his hand. Oblivious to the blood dripping onto the carpet he continued to stare into the raging abyss of his own personal hell.

— *Chapter 33* —

Brett Larsen stories and jokes ran rampant in the fashion industry. She had become known as a jinx, a moniker that was taken very seriously in a business where almost everybody's time was booked by the hour and paid at rates that could take a healthy chunk out of the national debt. As a result, Brett's work had virtually come to a stop. She gave Thérèse the summer off with pay and encouraged her to travel and see something of America. Thérèse protested, saying there must be some work for her to do, but Brett insisted.

Jeffrey wasn't pleased when Brett told him that she had seen David, even though she explained that he was only being friendly and helpful. In order not to make her home life any more stressful than it already was, she and David worked mostly at the Hands On office or his apartment.

They combed through her mailing list, but found no one with an obvious motive for trying to ruin her career. There were several photographers with whom she had competed for jobs, but their reputations were solid and Brett assured David that their competitive edge was a friendly one. He was inclined to trust her judgment. His friend at the phone company had proven helpful and supplied the necessary records of outgoing calls, but before David could tackle the pages and pages of computer printouts and feed the data into his own Outreach system, he had to make another trip to the Sunnyvale plant in California.

When David returned, he asked Brett to photocopy her appointment calendar so that it could be input and merged with the phone company list to find possibly correlated information. She left the copies at his office on her way out of the city. David hadn't been there and she was glad. Brett didn't want to talk about lists and data retrieval—she needed time to think.

When she had awakened that morning, she had decided to go out to Cox Cove. Lillian was in England visiting friends, so Brett could have some time alone. Suddenly, her whole world had become an unfamiliar place, as if she were living someone else's life. To get through all this, she had to get her bearings, and no one could help her do that. Jeffrey agreed with her decision, saying she should take all the time she needed, and that he would feel more at ease if she were safe in the country.

Brett stopped the car and inserted her key into the box in the red brick post. The massive wrought-iron gates swung open with only the slight creaking that always welcomed arrivals at Cox Cove. She drove through, repeated the process, and continued up the wooded drive. The paved expanse was lined with stately poplars and bordered with beds of zinnias, petunias, cock's comb and impatiens that Lillian lovingly tended. A groundsman came only to mow the lawn, prune trees when necessary, and trim the privet hedge that camouflaged the fence that surrounded the property.

The atmosphere was close and humid in the sprawling Georgian manor. Everything was pristine and spotless, but the house was badly in need of fresh air. She put down her overnight bag and began to open windows.

Retrieving her bag from the foyer, Brett smiled as she remembered how Rush used to laze on the cool black and white tiles in the summer. It all seemed a lifetime ago.

She changed into cutoff jeans and a bright red T-shirt, took a peach from the refrigerator, and headed for the beach. The noontime sun was high in the sky and as she passed the tennis courts she could hear Aunt Lillian admonishing her as a child for playing in the hottest part of the day. "Only mad dogs and Englishmen . . ."

Just as she reached the plank steps that led to the ocean, a tiger swallowtail landed on the railing. For a moment she watched the butterfly. It perched tentatively, its yellow-and-black-striped wings opening and closing, then glided effortlessly away. *That's what I want to do,* Brett thought. She wanted to fly away and leave this whole mess behind her. But as she padded barefoot down the stairs, she considered that the butterfly's carefree existence, feeding on nectar and following the wind, was its trade-off for so brief a life.

She shuffled her feet through the sun-warmed sand, thinking. It might take some time to find out who was trying to ruin her professionally. But she was responsible for her own personal happiness and she had known for a long time that she had married Jeffrey for the wrong reasons. He had always been there for her; he was kind and helpful, and he loved her, or so she thought. Now she wasn't sure if Jeffrey knew what love was. Brett had also discovered that she would never learn to love him—not in the way that a woman should love her husband. She hated the surge of relief she felt when he was not around.

By now she had reached Turtleback Rock, the place that had been her childhood favorite at Cox Cove, and the place to which she had been unable to return for years after Carson Gallagher's shooting. The route to the top was natural and familiar, as though she had climbed the huge boulder only yesterday. Her feet instinctively knew the right nooks and her hands the right crevices to ease her ascent.

She sat with her knees pulled to her chest, and the breeze from the sea cooled and evaporated the perspiration generated by the heat of the sun. Peach juice dribbled down her chin as she took a bite and she wiped it away with the back of her hand. For a while she was transfixed by the gentle lapping of the surf and calmed by the assured constancy of the ebb and flow of the ocean. Then she spotted a lone sea gull hovering gracefully above the water. Suddenly it dove into the sea, emerging with a fish wriggling in its bill. The bird flapped its great wings and disappeared in the distance. And Brett realized that her life had veered too far off course and that she too would disappear in the distance if she allowed things to continue as they were. When she finished the peach she clambered to her feet and tossed the pit as far as she could. It didn't even make a splash in the ocean. She knew what she had to do.

That night she made a ham and Swiss sandwich for dinner and sat on the fieldstone terrace, sipping lemonade and listening to the insistent chirp of crickets until the sky was black as pitch and spangled with winking stars. Relieved by her decision and certain that Jeffrey would agree, she slept soundly for the first time in months.

For the next two days she did laps in the pool, practiced her tennis serve, and lay in the sun, evening out the tan she had inadvertently begun on Turtleback Rock. By the end of the week she felt rejuvenated and ready to talk to Jeffrey. The only thing she hadn't figured out was what to do about what was left of her career. But before she reached Manhattan, she had an answer for that, too.

When Jeffrey arrived home from work, she had showered and changed into white linen slacks and matching shirt. "I'm in here," she called. He walked into the living room, leaving his briefcase on the console table in the hall. "I've mixed martinis. Would you like one?"

Jeffrey was surprised by her radiant glow, and he sensed the calm confidence that Brett used to exude. "Yes, thank you." He took the frosty stemmed glass and sat in a velvet wing chair. "Are you going to join me?"

"I have a glass of wine," she said, indicating the goblet on the coffee table as she took a seat opposite him on the sofa. "We have to talk, Jeffrey. I want a divorce. I'm sorry—truly, I am—but I'm not in love with you. I never have been. Somehow I thought I could learn—that with time, I would grow to care for you in that way—but it hasn't happened."

Jeffrey put the martini glass to his lips and downed it in one swallow. He continued to hold the glass with one hand, but the other gripped the arm of the chair so tightly his knuckles whitened. "But we . . ."

"Let me finish, please. I was wrong and unfair. I had just come out of a relationship that ended badly, and I wanted someone to want me. You were that person. It was a terrible thing to do, but I want to make it right. I know you aren't happy, either. We don't have many common interests, and a family is more important to you than it is to me right now. You should have that. I also think you should have grandfather's wedding present—all of it—and if I know you, and I think I do, you've probably invested it so that it's well on its way to doubling." She smiled. "I really am sorry, Jeffrey, but it's what I have to do."

"This is quite a shock," Jeffrey said. The sweat rolled down the center of his back. He felt dazed as though he had run headlong into a brick wall. "Is it David Powell?" he asked as he placed his empty glass on the table.

"No, Jeffrey, it's me. David has nothing to do with it. I just can't go on like this. Polite conversation, polite dinners, and good manners don't make a marriage."

Jeffrey's brain slipped into overdrive. "But, what will you do? These incidents have put a damper on your career, and it doesn't look like it's going to change any time soon." Now both his hands were free to grip the chair arms.

"No, it's not going to change by itself. I'm going to change it. I'm going to start doing work on spec."

"Isn't that what photographers do when they're trying to get started? You have a reputation to consider." His fingers started to numb from the pressure he applied to the chair.

"Not anymore, I don't. Things are so bad that I may as well be starting from scratch. But I can do it. I'm going to scout a few locations—really interesting places—then pick out the clothes, models, and crew. We shoot, and once I have the film edited I send the chromes, along with my story ideas, to the magazine. If they like the shots, they buy them. I get a credit line and the opportunity to start building again. Spanish and Brazilian *Vogue* get about half of their editorials that way."

"Well, it sounds as if you have it all planned. I can't get you to change your mind?" Jeffrey wondered if the perspiration would stain his clothes as it continued its steady stream down his back.

"It's best this way."

"When would you like me to move out?" His head began to pound.

"As soon as it's convenient. And you can have this back." She slipped the huge diamond ring off her finger.

"Oh, no, I couldn't consider it. It was a gift." He had just refused almost half a million dollars. Jeffrey felt his lungs constrict as he struggled to breathe normally. "We can still be friends, can't we?"

"I hoped you would feel that way. It's the way we started . . . and probably should have remained."

"I could help you with finding locations for your spec shoots." The hammering in his head wouldn't stop. "Larsen has some interests in a small Central American country on the Caribbean called Santa Verde. It's a brand new resort area that would probably welcome publicity."

"Jeffrey, you've already done more than enough to help me. I couldn't possibly ask for anything more."

"You didn't ask—I volunteered. I'm still employed by you, or I will be one day. Consider it a favor for the boss." He forced a smile and wondered how long it would take Sven to find out. "It's no problem. I can take care of everything you would need in a phone call. When would you like to go?"

"The sooner the better, but I'll let you know."

"I'll just pack a bag and go. I'll send for the rest of my things." Jeffrey got up and headed for the stairs. He packed without regard to neatness or order and went back downstairs to the living room. Brett had refilled her glass and sat on the sofa with her hands calmly folded in her lap. *She's tougher than I thought. It's probably the Sven in her.* "I'll be going now, but will you allow me to tell your grandfather?"

Brett nodded. She had no desire to have a conversation about her marriage with Sven.

"Call me as soon as you decide when you want to go to Santa Verde." He closed the door, trying to suppress the bile rising in his throat.

Jeffrey approached the familiar phone booth at Seventeenth and Park Avenue South and, hands trembling, searched frantically for a quarter. Finding none he pushed aside the two people at the fruit cart on the corner and demanded to know the price of an apple. He handed the vendor a twenty dollar bill and when he received two quarters back in change he ran back to the phone booth, leaving the apple and nineteen dollars and fifty cents.

"Señor Cissaro, we met at the Santa Verdian Consulate several months ago. I think we might be able to do some business."

"It must take a long time to count to a million on one of these," Brett called as she moved the top row of smooth ivory beads from left to right on the antique abacus. Next to it, on the black ash wall unit in David's apartment, sat the multicolored wooden abacus with chipped paint and tooth marks that had helped David learn to count.

"Yeah, and by the time you finished counting whatever it was, there probably weren't a million of them anymore," David answered, entering the room and handing Brett the seltzer and orange juice she had requested.

The bridge divided the arena of the living room, with its charcoal gray glazed walls and ebony stained wood floors, into a main seating area and a smaller music room, dominated by the black baby grand.

Brett sat in the bend of the L-shaped, black polished cotton sofa which was littered with geometric shaped pillows in colors from a child's crayon box.

Brett removed a smoky Lucite box from the fawn leather shopping bag that sat next to her on the floor. David sank into the far end of the couch, placing his iced tea on the glass topped, marble "V" which balanced on its apex to form a coffee table.

"The phone numbers of every person I know, every company I do business with or hope to do business with, and every deli and restaurant in the vicinity of the studio that delivers should be in this box," Brett said, handing the file to David.

"Good. I can have this back to you in two days, and the telephone readout and your appointment information should be merged by the end of the week. Then we can see if anything significant shows up," David said.

"Part of me wants it to give me the answer and part of me doesn't want to know, but I'll cross that bridge when I get to it."

"How was your respite at Cox Cove?"

"Productive."

"Productive? I was expecting restful or invigorating, but not productive." David leaned back and pushed some buttons in a wall mounted console behind him, adjusting the room's recessed lighting to replace the rapidly fading sunlight and activating the stereo in the music room. The sliding clarinet glissando that begins "Rhapsody in Blue" came from the tiny but powerful speakers suspended unobtrusively at the corners of the room.

"I decided some important things."

"Such as?"

"I really need to work again, and I'm willing to start at the bottom, if that's necessary." Brett explained working on spec, her story ideas, and detailed her location-scouting trip to Santa Verde.

"Good for you. I think it's great that you've got so much fight, but you will be careful, won't you? You still don't know who's been sabotaging your work," David said.

"I'll be fine. Jeffrey's got some contacts down there at a new resort, and he's handling all the details." Brett rose and wandered over to a powder blue, marbleized bowling ball, mounted in a wrought-iron stand, like a piece of sculpture. She fit her fingers in the holes, lifted it as if to aim down the alley, then returned it to its cradle. "I made another big decision."

"And what was that?"

"Jeffrey and I are getting divorced," she said in the most neutral voice she could manage. She had admitted to herself that marrying Jeffrey had been a way of saying to David, 'See, I don't need you. Somebody else loves me.' She had proved her point, but it was childish, it hadn't made David's abrupt departure any less painful and she had hurt Jeffrey in the process. Now, telling the person who had prompted that lapse in judgment was hard. "I married him for the wrong reasons," she added honestly.

The music spiraled through the room, filling the momentary silence.

"I'm sorry that it didn't work out. This must be very difficult for you." And David was sorry. But inside, he wondered if it was crazy to hope that Brett could forgive him and care for him again.

They talked for a while longer about Cox Cove and the further adventures of Emma and Cameron, then Brett left.

David wandered aimlessly through the apartment. He pulled some technical journals from his briefcase and attempted to read, but the words did not compute. Then he changed into gym shorts and a Stanford tee shirt and headed for the mini spa that was off the master bathroom. He set the Lifecycle to the most arduous terrain and rode until the sweat drenched his clothes, then he did strokes on the rowing machine until it seemed he had paddled at least once around Manhattan. The smooth rhythmic motion usually relaxed him, but it wasn't helping now. Draping a white towel around his neck he grabbed a handful of M&M's from the etched crystal globe that rested on a fire engine red lacquered Parson's table in the foyer and headed for the music room. Popping candy in his mouth with his right hand, he aimlessly played scales with his left.

He loved Brett, in a way that was as natural and irrepressible as breathing, and he had never stopped, even after he had left her. He knew that he had to tell her—that even if she laughed at him, he had to say what his heart could no longer keep secret.

"Come on in, David." Brett answered the door wearing a violet sleeveless cotton jersey jumpsuit. Her thick braid was slung over one shoulder and she carried an eight-inch utility knife in her hand.

"Do you always answer the door so well armed?" David asked.

Brett looked at the knife and laughed. "I was slicing zucchini when the bell rang. I guess I forgot to put it down."

David followed her upstairs, aware of how much he had missed this house. Brett swung open the refrigerator and pulled out a bottle of white zinfandel. "Want some?"

"Sure," David said. "I brought your file box back. I'll start running everything tomorrow."

"That's great." Brett gave him a glass of wine. Their hands touched briefly in the exchange, but neither acknowledged the spark that passed between them. Brett took a sip from her own glass. "I was just starting dinner. Would you like some?"

After Jeffrey's departure, Brett was happy for the first time in months. She had learned that being true to herself was more important than anything else in the world.

And she was glad she finally understood why David had bolted. What had hurt as much as his abrupt departure was the feeling that she had been so totally wrong about the kind of person he was. It had shaken her faith in human nature and her ability to judge it. She was glad that he had silenced his personal demons and that she had her friend back again.

When she reflected on the bliss they had known together it no longer made her sad. It had taught her what love was like and she could never settle for less again.

"Sounds like a good deal. Lunch was the other half of my breakfast bagel, and that wore off hours ago. What's on the menu?" David asked, not really caring. The only thing that mattered was that she had asked him to stay.

"Today we have cappellini primavera, made with a delicate garlic butter sauce," she replied like a waiter reciting the house specials.

"How would you feel about a chef's assistant?" David offered, reversing their former roles. He unbuttoned the cuffs of his tattersall shirt and rolled his sleeves to just below his elbows.

She looked at his sun-bronzed arms and tried to dismiss the memory of how they had felt when they had circled her waist or gripped her shoulders. Pulling a second knife from the block, she said as lightly as she could, "Go for it!"

They talked and whittled vegetables as if it was the most natural thing in the world. Having plunged the fine straws of pasta into rolling water, she sautéed the vegetables until they were tender and finally, arranging all of the ingredients in a white pottery bowl, she said, "Dinner is served."

They ate with relish, enjoying the faint scent of herbs that lingered in the air. After the meal, Brett squeezed lemons and made *citron pressé*, then suggested they go downstairs to enjoy the unusually breezy summer evening in the garden.

"I'll show you the best spot," Brett said once they stepped outside. She led him to the lacy white gazebo that was centered toward the back of the yard.

All evening, David had fought the urge to stroke her face and hold her. They were privileges he had relinquished, and he had to be granted the right to enjoy them again.

In his mind, he thought it was too soon to let her know the way he felt. But then, while standing next to her in the kitchen, talking during dinner, he had been possessed by the feeling that his declaration was really a year late and that he could not spare one more day.

"I think I'd like a birdbath by the walkway," Brett said, turning to face David. She was taken aback by the intensity of his gaze and the way it seemed to look into her soul.

"Brett, there's something I have to tell you. I'm not sure you're ready to hear it now, or if you'll ever be ready, but it's something I should have told you long ago."

"Then, tell me now," she said quietly.

David took her glass and placed it on a low wood table, then took both her hands in his. "I love you, Brett—so much that it frightened me before. I have no right to expect that you feel the same. I just want the chance to prove my love to you—to prove that I'll never run away again. Will you give me that chance?"

Brett felt dizzy from the sudden rush of emotions. She looked down at her hands in his, as if to steady herself, then up into his eyes. "Yes," she whispered.

David cradled Brett in his arms like a lost treasure that he had never hoped he would retrieve. Lovingly his fingers traced her eyebrows, her cheek, her chin and Brett felt as if he cleared pathways overgrown from neglect. Then their lips met, and speaking in a language that needed no translation, expressed the joy for which neither could find words.

David stood and pulled her close, his hands gratefully reacquainting themselves with her soft skin, her firm roundness. Soon their bodies began to undulate as though dancing to some well remembered music and Brett felt a place deep within her open wide and a powerful need for him to fill it. She took his hand and led him inside, but as soon as they crossed the threshold, she turned and threw her arms around his neck.

"I've missed you so much," David murmured.

In a rush of hands anxiously tugging at buttons and sleeves they undressed and he began to bathe her with kisses. Each caress awakened a new pleasure center in Brett. She closed her eyes and buried her fingers in his hair, basking in the sensations.

He traced lazy circles around her breasts, saving her stiff, reddened nipples for last. Brett's insides began to liquefy.

He fell to his knees and traced a line down her stomach, past her navel, finally reaching her perfect triangle of curly dark hair. He parted it at the crest with his tongue, and Brett gasped as his kiss found her sensual core. When the currents of pleasure threatened to overtake her, she whispered, "David, I want you." He stood, carried her into the reception area, placed her on the sofa, then covered her with his body and slowly eased himself inside her, as if afraid that the resulting explosion would be too strong for either of them to bear. "Yes," Brett murmured, and their bodies guided them to the sweet release they had been seeking.

— *Chapter 34* —

Only the eerie green glow of the computer terminal illuminated the room as David entered the last date on Brett's appointment calendar into the memory banks and followed up with a series of commands that would start the search. Glasses perched on the end of his nose, he ran his fingers through his already rumpled hair, wheeled the chair back, and put his feet up on the console. A steady crawl of phone numbers and dates rolled up the monitor. It was after ten o'clock, and thirty-eight stories below, traffic still inched its way across the glittering span of the Fifty-ninth Street Bridge.

David swiveled his seat slightly and turned his gaze just in time to catch the Goodyear Blimp floating past his windows. Its sign flashed on and off and in between blinks the side of the aircraft displayed a series of colored light patterns which resembled psychedelic pop art. He returned his attention to the screen as the computer began its second run. Munching on the hamburger he had ordered, he thought about Brett and knew that this time it would all be right. He was finally free from his self-imposed guilt and soon she would be free from Jeffrey.

Brett had already found an attorney, the wife of one of Lizzie's colleagues at GNSN, to handle the divorce. Jeffrey had agreed to the generous settlement she had offered, and now it was just a matter of time.

On the computer's sixth run, David slammed his feet to the floor and bolted upright in his chair. There were at least a hundred calls to the same phone number, most of them made on days and times when Brett was out of the studio. He cross-referenced the number with Brett's Rolodex file; the match took only seconds. "I'll be damned," David said aloud as he stared at the screen. He couldn't think of any reason why Jeffrey had been called that frequently. He was a busy man, and Brett would never have instructed Thérèse to make those calls. Were Thérèse and Jeffrey having an affair? David wasn't sure what the calls meant, but he wanted to know more about Jeffrey Underwood.

He stored the information on a floppy disk, locked it in the wall safe and erased the memory. All the way downtown to his apartment, he debated whether he should tell Brett or not. He really didn't know anything yet.

He didn't know much about Jeffrey Underwood—only that he was an attorney who worked for Brett's grandfather. He hadn't even met him. But he suspected that ace reporter Liz Powell would know more.

"Hold on a minute, David," Lizzie said the next morning. He could hear her in the background, scolding the twins for dumping their breakfasts on the floor. "Honestly, if one does something, the other has to do it, too," she said when she returned to the phone. "What can I do for you?" she asked brightly.

David didn't tell Lizzie of his discovery last night—he merely asked her what she knew about Jeffrey. All she remembered was that he was about forty-one and he had gone to Yale Law School. David thanked her and promised to visit on Sunday.

On Saturday morning, David drove to Connecticut and parked his Saab a few blocks from the Yale campus. The university was almost deserted as David strolled toward Sterling Library. The imposing gray stone structure was as hushed as a cathedral inside, and his footsteps echoed on the tile floor. He approached the desk and asked the young, freckle-faced, red-haired girl behind the massive counter if she might tell him where yearbooks were kept. She asked him what years and directed him, with amazing accuracy, to the stack and shelf where he would find them.

David didn't know whether Jeffrey was advanced or a late bloomer so he took the dusty yearbooks from 1965 to 1975 to a table. He worked his way back to 1968 before he hit pay dirt. He had only seen the photo Brett kept of Jeffrey in her office, but this was clearly the same man. Here he was younger, but his keen features were exactly the same; even the hairstyle was remarkably like the one he wore now.

It didn't take him long to read the entry. Jeffrey had no club memberships or activities. His bio simply gave his name, his law review years, and his hometown of Warren's Corners, Minnesota.

For three hours on Monday morning, David tried to track down the Warren's Corners town clerk. It seemed that she also served as postmaster and county fire marshal, and she was conducting her semiannual fire safety seminar at the Fielding County Fair. When they finally spoke, David asked her if she could check the records for an Underwood family and if she could tell him if there were any family members still in Warren's Corners. "I don't have to check no records," she informed him. "I've had this job since 1932, and my daddy had it before me. It was a real pity about those Underwoods—such a shame. Mama, papa, and the little boy, all killed in a wreck on the interstate in 1948. I remember because we'd just gotten the big road through here. You know, it was one of them projects after the war, to put our boys back to work."

"All of them died? Are you sure?" David asked, stunned.

" 'Course I'm sure. That funeral was one of the saddest things I ever laid eyes on."

"Do you remember the little boy's name? Was it Jeffrey?" David was afraid he already knew the answer.

"Yeah. That was him all right. He had the prettiest brown eyes you ever want to see."

"Well, thank you for your time. You've been very helpful."

If Jeffrey Underwood is dead, then who is Jeffrey Underwood? He didn't know what was going on, but *something* was wrong. He didn't have enough information to go to the police, and he had no evidence that Jeffrey had done anything illegal, but now he was sure Thérèse knew more.

He called her home number the rest of the afternoon but got no answer. At the end of the day he went to her apartment on West Twenty-First Street, and luckily met a neighbor sweeping the stoop in front of the building. "I've lived here forty years—I like to keep the place clean," she said.

"It looks like you do a pretty good job," he said. "Do you know Thérèse Diot? I'm a friend of hers, in from out of town. I'll only be here a few days, and I haven't been able to reach her."

The elderly woman eyed him suspiciously, then, deciding he didn't look like an ax murderer, said, "She's away 'til next week. She asked me to water her plants; said she was off to see the U.S.A. Nice girl, for a foreigner. At least she speaks English."

"Thank you. I guess I'll have to catch her next time," David said.

He walked across town from Chelsea to Gramercy Park, trying to think of how to tell Brett what he had found out.

"David! What a nice surprise." Brett smiled as she answered the door. She was dressed in emerald green cotton shorts and a matching shell. With her hair spilling from a ponytail on top of her head, she looked like David remembered her as a teenager. Her smile faded as she noted his dour expression. "Is something wrong? Did something turn up from the lists?" she asked as they climbed the stairs.

"Well, something surely isn't right." David slumped in the middle of the sofa.

Brett perched on the arm of the sofa and faced him. David looked tired and slightly disheveled. His khaki suit was wrinkled and limp, and his shirt was open at the neck. The ends of his loosened tie hung unevenly, and as a result of the August heat, his curly brown hair clung damply to his forehead and neck. "You look wiped out. Can I get you something?"

"No, I'll be fine, but I am glad it's cool in here."

"All right, what is it?" Brett asked.

"How much do you know about Jeffrey?" David asked.

"The regular stuff, I suppose. He's worked for Grandfather fourteen or fifteen years. He went through Yale Law on scholarship and insurance money. His parents were killed in a car crash when he was fifteen. He's from a small town in Minnesota. It's known for something odd, like—sunflower farming, that's it!"

"And town clerks with excellent memories. It's Warren's Corners."

"Yes! That's it! What does that have to do with anything?"

"I called there today. Brett, according to their records, Jeffrey Underwood was killed in a car accident when he was two years old."

"But that's impossible. It must be another Jeffrey Underwood."

"From a town of eighteen hundred people? Come on, Brett, I know it's pretty strange, but I talked to the town clerk today and she gave me the whole story. She went on about how cute little Jeffrey was, with his big brown eyes. There's something shady going on here, but I still don't know what."

"How did you find out where he was from? What made you investigate Jeffrey?"

David told her about the calls to Jeffrey's private number at Larsen Enterprises from the studio, and the conversation with Lizzie that led him to Yale and, finally, Warren's Corners.

"Do you really think that Thérèse and Jeffrey had an affair?" *That might explain his sexual indifference toward me*, she thought. *But not why he wanted a child so badly*. Brett had not confided the intimate details of her failed marriage to David, so she kept these thoughts to herself, as well.

"I don't know. That's the problem. I tried to see Thérèse this afternoon, but she's away until next week."

"I could just call Jeffrey and ask him. There's probably a simple explanation." Brett tried to convince herself that was true. Had she really known Jeffrey all this time, married him, and he was someone else? It was too implausible for her to believe.

"You can't do that. What if he's involved in these incidents that have been happening to you? I think you should postpone your trip to Santa Verde until we know a little more."

"David, it's my career. I don't have time to waste. Santa Verde is a resort. Just because Jeffrey has some secret past doesn't mean he's out to harm me."

"I still think you should put the trip off. Just until I can talk to Thérèse."

"What would you say if I told you that you shouldn't go to Sunnyvale or Seoul because there might be an earthquake or a student uprising? You would tell me that you had to go because it was your business, wouldn't you?"

"This is different, dammit!" He wanted to convince her to take his suspicions seriously, but he did not want to alarm her unnecessarily. "What difference would another week or so make?"

"Obviously, you don't understand how important this trip is to me. Nothing will happen. I'm only going to scout the location. There are no models to be canceled and there is no equipment, to speak of, to be sabotaged. I'm staying at a lovely new hotel right on the beach. I'll rent a car, pick out spots that will make great photographs, swim a little, and come back. LARSair is pumping a lot of dollars into this place. It's going to be a major resort and the Board of Tourism is helping to plan my itinerary. What could go wrong?"

"All right . . . but promise me you'll be careful," David said hesitantly. "I love you."

Thick humid air still hovered over Manhattan when he left the house. *I just don't like the way this feels*, David thought.

— *Chapter 35* —

"Your visa is good for two weeks, *señorita*." The immigration clerk was charming and professional, and he smiled at Brett cordially as he stamped her passport with the official seal of Santa Verde.

"I'm only planning a four-day stay this time. But if I like it, I'll be back." Brett returned his smile and he directed her to baggage claim and customs. She had only a carry on and her camera bag, so she proceeded directly to the customs line.

The LARSair 727 had been almost full, but most passengers were continuing on to more well known destinations. Brett stood in line with the dozen other travelers giving Santa Verde a try, noticing that more than half of them appeared to be businessmen anxious to cut deals in the new resort.

The terminal was a one story building with pre-fab walls set on a cinder block foundation. Two gates, one for departures and one for arrivals, had large windows that looked out onto the lone runway, recently extended to accommodate big jets. There was the requisite duty free shop, gift shop and a tiny counter with a soda dispenser and packs of chips and peanut butter cheese crackers, that aspired to be a snack bar.

She cleared customs and carried her bag, bearing a chalk X, out into the bright midday sunshine. It's cooler out here than inside, she thought, enjoying the balmy air. Squinting against the glare, Brett could see the mountains, actually very tall hills, and a rising peak to the south that had to be Mt. Drado, Santa Verde's requisite inactive volcano.

"Miss Larsen?" inquired a mustached gentleman wearing sunglasses and a white tropical suit.

"Yes," Brett replied.

"I am Manuel Cissaro from the Board of Tourism. Welcome to our humble country. The car is just this way." He showed her to a Mercedes-Benz limousine, which looked out of place. Most of the other cars and pickup trucks appeared ready for the junkyard.

They must be pulling out all the stops, Brett thought as she settled into the air-conditioned cool of the car. Manuel Cissaro chattered on about the great future of his country, now that they had so much help from American businesses. Brett had been told that the ride to the hotel took about fifteen minutes, so she divided her attention between Señor Cissaro and the passing scenery. Children played by the side of the road and cows, each tended by its own egret, flicked their tails lazily, discouraging flies from lighting too long.

There was little traffic on the two-lane road, but the car was forced to pause several times. Once, a small herd of reluctant goats was coaxed across the road by a young boy wearing a tee shirt, gray trousers cut off to make shorts and a blue baseball cap. Then their progress was halted when a large truck with wood-slatted sides, loaded with farmworkers standing shoulder to shoulder, backed across the pavement and drove off in the opposite direction. Before long a runty litter of black pigs followed their mother, whose distended teats indicating feeding time, to the other side of the two lane highway.

Brett glanced at her watch and realized that they had been riding for over half an hour and there was no hotel in sight. "Shouldn't we be there by now?" Brett asked.

"There has been a slight change in plans, señorita, but we should be there soon," Señor Cissaro said.

"What change? Take me to the hotel—now!" Cissaro pushed her down across the seat and forced a chloroform-soaked handkerchief over her nose and mouth. *David was right*, she thought just before she lost consciousness.

When she awakened, she found herself lying in a dark room. Her head throbbed, her sweaty clothes hugged her body, her jaws ached, and her mouth was sore and dry. With a start, she realized that she was gagged. She tried to roll over and get up, but found that her wrists and ankles were bound to an old iron bedstead. She flailed and tried to free herself, but the scratchy ropes dug into her flesh, and the rusty springs creaked in protest.

The door opened and a tall lean man wearing jungle fatigues walked into the room. "So, you are awake. I will remove the cloth around your mouth, but do not bother to scream—no one will hear you. Would you like some food?" He nodded his head toward the scarred metal table by the bed. On it was a tin plate with a mound of rice and a mango.

As soon as he removed the gag, Brett screamed. He shrugged his shoulders, replaced the gag, and left the room. In the dim light, she watched as the flies enjoyed her supper.

"What do you mean, kidnapped, Jeffrey?" Sven Larsen had retired to his bedroom suite after dinner, and at eight, when the phone rang, he was already attired in bedclothes.

"Brett left this morning for Santa Verde to scout locations. When I spoke to her at six o'clock, everything was fine. She was in her room, about to change for dinner. Then, a short while ago, I got a call from a man with some kind of thick accent, maybe Spanish. He said he had Brett and she would be dead if I didn't do as he said," Jeffrey explained excitedly.

"How do you know he's not bluffing?" Sven asked, a slight quiver in his slow, steady voice.

Jeffrey paused. "He let me speak to her. She was crying so hard that I could hardly understand her. She told me she had tried to get away, but they had caught her and beat her." Jeffrey's voice cracked. He cleared his throat and continued. "He didn't let me talk to her long. He came back on the phone and warned me not to call the police. He said we would never find her alive if we did."

"What does he want?" Sven asked.

"Money. He wants ten million dollars. I have five—the money you gave us as a wedding present."

"I'll wire you the ten million dollars, Jeffrey. Spend whatever is necessary. We have to get her back," Sven said, the urgency apparent in his voice. Sven had lost everyone else he loved and the thought of losing Brett was unbearable.

"Thank you, sir. The man instructed me to have the money wired to myself at Banco Santa Verde tomorrow. He said he had ways of checking if it came through. I am to arrive after five tomorrow evening and check into La Reina Hotel. Someone will be in contact with me there."

"How do you know you're not in danger? How can he be trusted?" Sven asked.

"I don't know, but I don't have any choice. Brett's down there, and I have to go get her back."

"Take one of the corporate planes. Jeffrey, just get her back. We have to . . ." Sven's voice dissolved. "Does Lillian know?"

"No, but I'll take care of that. We'll get her back, sir. I believe in my heart we will. I will be in touch in the morning, or if there are further developments."

"Yes," Sven said weakly, then hung up.

Jeffrey was sprawled on his imposing gothic bed. The ornately carved mahogany headboard looked like a panel ripped from the walls of a cathedral.

She left me no choice, he reasoned. Divorce was out of the question. He could never relinquish his hard won position as the grandson-in-law of billionaire Sven Larsen and next in line to run Larsen Enterprises. If he and Brett were no longer married he was sure Sven would find a way to humiliate him.

Jeffrey sat up, opened the burled mahogany commode by his bed side and removed the locked steel box. He fished in the pocket of his robe for the key. Again he fingered the yellowed and crumbling articles. *He humiliated my father, but he won't do it to me*, Jeffrey thought. He had gathered enough information to bring Sven Larsen down, but that was no longer enough. He had to supplant him. With Brett dead, and he the grieving widower, he could succeed in doing that.

It all seemed so neat, and since Cissaro only wanted five million dollars, Jeffrey would make a profit on the deal. He replaced his mementos in the commode and settled into bed. The next day would be a long one.

"What do you mean, her reservations have been canceled? She's there—I know she is. I saw the plane off myself," David shouted into the phone. "Another hotel? How many are there?" His heart raced as he called the five numbers the man had given him, but when none of the hotels had a Brett Larsen registered, he knew she was in trouble.

At eleven o'clock he arrived at Thérèse's building on West Twenty-first Street and found the same elderly woman out front, this time sitting on the stoop. "Oh, you're still in town. That's nice. I bet she'll be happy to see you."

Not likely, David thought as he took the stairs two at a time and pounded on Thérèse's door. "Let me in, Thérèse. It's David Powell."

The door opened a crack and he shoved it the rest of the way, wrenching the security chain from its mooring. "Monsieur Powell?"

"What have you done with her?" He grabbed her by the shoulders and his fingers dug into her flesh.

"What are you talking about?" she asked, her eyes wide with fear.

"I know you and Underwood are in on this. Now, tell me where she is." He shook her roughly. "If he's done something to harm her, I'll . . ."

"*Oh, mon dieu! Mon dieu!* What has he done?" Thérèse moaned.

"Come on, I know you two had something going on. Now Brett is missing. She left for a trip this morning, but she never arrived!"

"He is crazy, that one. You are right, I did work for him, but no more. He paid me to spy on his wife."

"And the canceled models, the destroyed film—did he pay you to do that, too?"

"Yes, I did that, too, but I know nothing about this. I have been away." The tears started to roll down her cheeks, but they only infuriated David more.

"You helped him? Why? What did Brett ever do to you?"

Thérèse explained that she had done it for money, nothing else, and that if Jeffrey had done something to Brett now, he had done it without her assistance.

"Okay, then, you're coming with me." He grabbed her by the arm and pulled her toward the door. "You're going to tell the police what you know."

Their story led them through the ranks at the police precinct, until the precinct captain closed them in his office and lectured David about the seriousness of his accusations.

"I wouldn't be here unless I believed it was serious," David said.

With that, the officer telephoned the local FBI office. "I've got something here that I think requires your attention."

David led Thérèse down to the offices of the FBI where, detail by detail, they related all they knew once again. After waking the town clerk in Warren's Corners and receiving her corroboration of the death of Jeffrey Underwood, the agent decided to put a tail on the man using that name. He also contacted the CIA, since he didn't know whether Brett's abduction had occurred on U.S. or foreign soil. Thérèse was held for additional questioning, and David left with the assurance they would keep him informed.

Although it was two in the morning, David went straight to Lillian's. She needed to know what had taken place.

That night, the supervising agent authorized wiretaps on Jeffrey's home and office phones, and after confirming Jeffrey's presence in his East Sixty-eighth Street apartment, two agents were posted outside the building. Jeffrey did not leave his home until the next morning. The agents followed him to Larsen headquarters and waited by the elevator banks in the lobby, but it was the phone surveillance that paid off. They taped two conversations between Jeffrey and Sven Larsen. Sven confirmed that he had wired ten million dollars to Jeffrey at Banco Santa Verde and told Jeffrey to do whatever was necessary to get Brett back. It was the confirmation they needed. They also recorded a call to the LARSair terminal at Kennedy Airport, where Jeffrey ordered a corporate jet fueled and ready for take-off, destination Santa Verde, then verified that a flight plan had been filed. At ten-thirty, Jeffrey left Larsen and was followed back home. He emerged forty-five minutes later carrying two suitcases and entered a waiting chauffeured car, which they followed to Kennedy. Then they called David.

"What do you mean, you can't stop him? Are you going to follow him down there? . . . His plane is scheduled for takeoff at one o'clock and you can't go until the next regularly scheduled flight at seven tonight? You'll lose him—we'll never find her. What if I charter my own damn plane? . . . I'll call you back in ten minutes."

He called back in seven. "Meet me in front of West Way Airlines at one-thirty. We leave at two-fifteen . . . Oh I'm going all right." He called Lillian, advised her of his plans and promised to call again when they got to Santa Verde.

The Santa Verdian authorities had been faxed photographs of Jeffrey and Brett by the time David and the agents left New York. They would immediately investigate her whereabouts, and planned to follow Jeffrey upon his arrival.

Agent Walker, a tall young man about David's age, slept on the pullout bed in the rear of the airplane cabin. David paced the length of the Lear's center aisle, almost believing that his efforts could speed their journey. Agent Morgan had tried to engage David in conversation, hoping to ease the tension he could see in him. He was a stocky, thirty-year veteran in the service of his country, and he told David that he had learned long ago not to let his nerves get the best of him. "I'd never have survived if I hadn't discovered that you can't do anything until you can." He hadn't expected his advice to make a difference and it didn't, so he played solitaire and whistled show tunes until he could do something.

When the sun rose the next morning, Brett had been awake all night. Sounds she couldn't identify penetrated the darkness, and scurrying that she surmised came from rats added to her misery. Now the daylight peeked through the spaces in the windowless plank walls, and she was relieved to still be alive.

Almost immediately, as if he had been watching her, the man from last night came in and replaced her uneaten meal with a chipped enamel pan of water and a rag, then untied her right hand and left the room. She mopped her face with the water, glad it was cool. She bathed her swollen wrists and, as though awakened by the water, they hurt even worse. She desperately wanted to dribble some of the water into her mouth, but decided that it might not be safe.

He returned after ten minutes and explained that she would now sit in the chair. Without ungagging her, he loosened the rest of her bindings and helped her to stand. Then Brett struck out, hitting the man's face with all her might as she tried to get to the door. He wrestled her arm behind her back and she moaned in pain as he steered her to a splintery chair in the middle of the floor, retied her, and left, shaking his head.

When she quieted down, she surveyed her prison. It appeared to be a one-room shack with a sheet of corrugated steel for a roof. It contained only the bed, a table, the chair on which she sat, and a big pot in the corner she guessed was her bathroom.

It had to be Jeffrey, she thought. *Why would he do this?* She had given him plenty of money, so that wasn't it. She had done nothing to him but be unable to return his love. There had to be something else—something she didn't know about. *David knows I'm in Santa Verde, and Aunt Lillian knows, too. They'll find me. They have to find me*, Brett thought, and gasped as an iguana scampered across her feet.

Several hours later, her limbs were almost numb and she desperately had to use the bathroom. She pounded her feet on the floor to summon her guard. Still gagged, she nodded toward the corner.

"I will untie your feet, but not your hands. Just as I warned you not to scream, I will warn you not to try to run. You are far up in the hills, in the back country. It is treacherous, and you cannot get away." With that, he unbound her ankles and left her alone, but he returned a short time later and secured her to the chair again.

Shortly after sunset he came back with the tin plate. This time it contained rice and breadfruit. He uncovered her mouth. She did not scream, but she did not eat.

"I am Colonel Monterra. I am sorry your visit to our country is under such unfortunate circumstances. We are really quite a friendly place." The colonel was trim, tan, and appeared to be in his early forties. His dark hair was combed straight back from his face and it gleamed from his generous use of pomade. Since the police in Santa Verde were soldiers, he was dressed in full military regalia. They were at the Santa Verde police headquarters, a concrete barracks that had been painted pink. The colonel's office had been freshly whitewashed and a wooden ceiling fan revolved slowly.

"Have you found out anything?" David asked anxiously. "Do you know where she is?"

"Let's take this one step at a time," Agent Walker interrupted. "I'm sure the colonel here will tell us everything he knows, won't you, Colonel?"

Agent Morgan remained silent, but David began to pace.

"Mr. Underwood has arrived and he is staying at La Reina, a hotel not far from here. It is not the usual tourist spot, but it is across the street from Banco Santa Verde, where I am told the money is being wired. We have a man watching him. So far, he has done nothing out of the ordinary. We interrogated airport personnel, and the young woman in question did arrive yesterday. However, she was seen leaving the airport in the company of Manuel Cissaro. I am afraid that Señor Cissaro is, as you Americans say, bad news. He is a well-known broker of arms, ammunition, and American dollars. Usually he will sell to whoever is willing to pay, but he has a brother who is suspected of planning a military takeover of Alletia, our neighbor to the south. And lately Señor Cissaro has been unusually active."

"So what you're saying is that she's in more danger than we thought. And we're sitting around here talking about it!" David shouted.

"If he is holding her where we think he is, we can have the place surrounded by morning. We should have word soon."

"Up in the hills would be my guess—someplace nearly inaccessible unless you know where you're going. It's probably laid out to make finding it easier than getting out." Agent Morgan's recitation was made with his eyes closed and his hands folded in his lap. He started to whistle again.

"Exactly. We have to plan this carefully, so as to minimize injury to all concerned. Unfortunately, your hotel, the Casa Verde, is in town also. It is two blocks from La Reina. What a shame you will not see our beautiful beaches. But we will meet you in the lobby at seven-thirty. The bank opens at eight, and we expect that to be Mr. Underwood's next move."

They left the police station and took a taxi to their hotel. "The colonel knows what he's doing," Morgan said as they bumped along the dusty road.

"He looks like a dandy who doesn't know his ass from a hole in the ground," Walker replied.

David said nothing, but he thought the colonel sounded like he worked for the chamber of commerce. David tried to imagine the terror Brett must be feeling.

They exited the taxi in front of the fading pink hacienda that was the hotel, and David registered in a daze. He presented his passport, paid for the room in advance, and was presented the key. "Be ready to roll by seven," Walker called as David plodded up the wide center staircase.

When he entered his room the musty smell of humid air trapped in damp bed linen met his nostrils. Not bothering to turn on the light, David dropped his black bag from his shoulder and fell, face down, onto the woven spread covering the lumpy double bed. White light from a street lamp shining through the shutters fell across David's body, striping him in alternating dark and bright bands. He reached for the phone and called Lillian to report the sketchy information he knew.

David had not slept in nearly forty hours. His eyes felt filled with grains of fine sand, the muscles in his neck and back were rigid with tension, and he could smell his own sweat.

Yanking the pillow from under the spread, he shielded his face from the light. Soon he was overwhelmed by a deep, dead sleep, but a short time later his own muffled cry awakened him. David had dreamed that he was falling, deeper and deeper into a cold, dark pit. He flailed his arms and legs, trying to catch hold of the craggy walls and stop his descent. He failed, and his wild plummeting continued.

Head pounding, sweat coating his body, David stumbled to the tiny bathroom, turned on the cold water in the tub, and stuck his head under the faucet. After several moments he turned it off, then sat on the closed top of the toilet and buried his head in his hands.

All day, David had been plagued by the aching feeling that he had seen the disaster coming, but had failed to avert it. If only

Thérèse had been home sooner, he would have had the pieces he needed to convince Brett of the danger.

At the airport yesterday she was buoyant with hope and excitement.

"I'll bring you a surprise," she had said playfully.

"You're always full of surprises," he had said.

She had kissed him and ruffled his hair, then disappeared down the jetway. And at this moment, the only thing David wanted was to see that face again.

But he couldn't let thoughts of the peril she was in paralyze him. He had to summon all of his energy to think of how they were going to save her, and he knew that to be ready for tomorrow he had to get some rest, so he stripped off his wet shirt, returned to the bed and made himself sleep.

Jeffrey hated the tropics. The heat and dampness made him feel limp, and he could never take enough showers to feel clean. He stayed in his room, entertaining himself by imagining the torture Sven was enduring, miles away, completely unable to affect the outcome. He slumped in a bald gold velvet chair, his feet propped on the bed, tying and untying the belt of his robe. In a few hours, Sven Larsen would be sorry he had ever met Karl Holmlund. "The bastard will never even know what happened," Jeffrey said under his breath and closed his eyes, thinking of his father and enjoying the bitter ecstasy of the moment.

Sven Larsen had known Karl Holmlund since they were boys. They were both children of hard-working Swedish immigrants who had successfully staked claims in the Midwest. Their families had been among the wealthiest in Racine.

Each grew up to head the company founded by his father. Karl, always steady and conservative, built Holmlund Metal Works into a midsized company, employing a hundred people. The company primarily provided precision equipment for the automotive industry, concentrated in nearby Detroit.

Sven believed that diversification was the route to success. He took his company, then known as Larsen Rail Transport, from a rail freight carrier servicing the lumber and mining industries, and expanded into air freight and eventually to passenger travel. In the process he began acquiring smaller companies—often, his suppliers. He looked for firms that were in dire financial straits but had the potential to be profitable, and among them was Michigan Tool and Die, an undercapitalized facility located in Clemens, Michigan, not far from Detroit. Larsen had pumped money into the ailing firm for five years, but it had yet to show a profit.

In the early sixties, Holmlund engineers developed a prototype for a precision gauge that Karl realized had far-reaching applications in automotive manufacturing. Seeing it as the way to expand his business, Karl poured all of his capital into refining the device. He borrowed additional money, based on projected sales increases that the equipment would generate, and put Holmlund Metal up as collateral.

Sven had been at the point of closing Michigan Tool, an uncharacteristic and bitter admission of failure, when he got wind of the developments at Holmlund Metal. He, too, saw the profit potential in the new device and recognized it as the means to salvage his investment in Michigan.

By bribing a Holmlund employee, Sven was able to obtain copies of the plans for the gauge, which he filed with the U.S. Patent Office before Holmlund.

Karl was devastated. He knew that Sven had stolen the information, but he had no way to prove it. Without the patent, he could not generate the capital to repay his loans. Eventually, his company was seized and the assets auctioned to repay his debts.

Lars had been fifteen at the time. He had been yanked out of the military school he had attended since he was ten years old and watched as his father dissolve into a bitter, gin-drinking recluse.

In his drunken state Karl would cry and berate himself for losing the business entrusted to him by his father. He felt ashamed and responsible to all of the people put out of work by the company's failure. And then he would curse Sven Larsen's treachery.

Eventually, Karl drank himself through what money he had left and they moved to Minneapolis, where they stayed with relatives, but Karl continued to deteriorate.

The winter that Lars was seventeen, his father wandered away from home and was missing for days. Lars finally found him, in an alley behind an abandoned factory, with a bottle of gin between his knees, frozen to death.

"Jeffrey, have you heard anything?" Sven asked.

Jeffrey had waited until ten at night to call Racine, allowing Sven the full day to stew. "I received a call just ten minutes ago. I am to be at the bank when it opens tomorrow and collect the money. There is a church, down a side street, a block away from there and someone will meet me and take me to Brett."

"What can I do, Jeffrey?" Sven asked.

"Nothing but wait, sir. I'll call you when I have her."

Sven hung up the phone with shaking hands. He had spent the whole day waiting. For the first time in forty years he did not rise at dawn, drink a cup of black coffee and drive to his office. He lay in his bed, in the dark, thinking.

Several times before he had been forced to wait for those he loved, and it had not gone well.

He had waited in the parlor, listening to Ingrid's moans and screams, while a doctor tended to her labor. Then he told him she was gone.

Barbara had sworn that she would return from school and he waited, but it was only through his intervention that she came home. He had not intended for anyone to die, but at least he had gotten Barbara back, and Brett.

Sven remembered how happy he had been when he first saw Brett. She looked like his Ingrid, with shiny dark hair and green eyes, but she was gone out of his life soon, too, and he could only love her from afar. But now all he could do was wait, and he was afraid.

The stagnant tropical darkness weighted Brett's chest like a millstone. She was no longer gagged, but she felt as if she would smother under the oppressive heat. A scream rested quietly in the back of her throat, afraid that once swallowed into the black night it would be gone forever. *I have to stay awake. I have to stay awake*, she chanted silently. The guard had barely spoken to her, nor had he tried to harm her, but the night held unseen threats that daylight minimized. She could hear howls and calls from far away that stalked through her imagination and fed her fear. As though timed to add to her discomfort a mosquito orbited her head, its incessant whining buzz an instrument of torture that would leave her unmarked. *I have to stay awake.* Then she was overcome with the sensation of insects crawling across her skin. *There's nothing there, there's nothing there*, she told herself. She lay still and willed the sensation away. *Tomorrow someone will come*, she thought as hope timidly edged despair aside. *But what if they don't?* Terror seized control once again.

— *Chapter 36* —

David lazily rubbed his eyes, and only when they focused did he remember where he was. He looked at his watch and realized he was supposed to be in the lobby in less than ten minutes. When he met Walker and Morgan his body ached, the result of troubled sleep.

Colonel Monterra picked them up in a green 1959 DeSoto. "We will look like everybody else," the colonel said in response to their quizzical looks. "Do not worry, the engine is in top condition," he assured them as they drove the two blocks to La Reina and parked a discreet distance away, behind a battered pickup truck. "We will stay in the car. There are two men on foot who will follow him for now."

Jeffrey emerged from his hotel looking well-rested and crisp in blue cotton twill trousers and a white shirt. Carrying a Mark Cross suitcase, he crossed the street and walked into the Banco Santa Verde just as the guard unlocked the doors.

Energy surged through David at the sight of Jeffrey and he fought the urge to leap from the car and pummel him right on the street.

"I know. You want to beat the shit out of him," Morgan said, reading David's thoughts. "This isn't the time." He began to whistle the "toreador aria" from *Carmen*.

"I could pick him off right from here," Walker said as he peered through an imaginary gunsight on his finger.

"We have many men in the hills. They have spotted the place where we think she is being held, but they have instructions not to move in until they receive further orders. So far our blond friend has committed no crime in Santa Verde. We must wait," said Colonel Monterra.

David felt they had waited an eternity before Jeffrey came out of the bank an hour later, suitcase in tow, and stepped into a Jeep that pulled to the curb.

"This is it," the colonel said. "But we will not follow until they are beyond the outskirts of the city. For several miles there is only one road. My men will let us know which turnoff they take."

Waves of nausea rolled over Brett and she tried to breathe deeply, hoping it would settle her stomach, but the dank, musty smell that permeated the shack only made her feel worse. Sweat trickled down her brow and only tossing her head from side to side kept it from accumulating in her ears.

When the nausea passed a few minutes later, she wondered if she should eat the next time the man brought her food. She had no idea what time it was, but the previous morning he had brought her the pan of water and a rag, and later he had brought fruit and rice, which she did not eat, and a small tin cup with water, from which she had taken two sips—enough to wet her lips, she had decided, but not enough to make her sick. But maybe it had—maybe it was the water. It was also time for her to be moved to the chair. It was uncomfortable and she was still tied, but she looked forward to it.

She waited, but no one came. When she heard the voices, Brett thought she was hallucinating. The man had not spoken to her since the first day and she hadn't seen or heard anyone else. She inclined her head toward a crack in the wall and tried to quiet the beating of her heart, so she could understand what they were saying. There were only two voices to follow, and their conversation was liberally peppered with English. ". . . shoot her." Why? She began to thrash and struggle, trying to break free. *No one is going to come*, she thought. Then she heard a car engine, followed by other voices, and she lay quiet again. "He just wants to make sure we uphold our part of the bargain," said a vaguely familiar voice. "That's right," said a voice she recognized clearly. Why, Jeffrey? Her wrists and ankles were already raw and bruised, but as the tears began to roll down her cheeks, she tugged and twisted, oblivious to the pain.

About halfway up Mt. Drado, Monterra picked up the Jeep's tread marks on the dirt road. When the colonel saw that they veered off through a tangle of brush and vines that almost hid a narrow trail, he said, "They are going exactly where we thought. We are in luck." Grabbing his walkie-talkie from the dashboard, he gave instructions to his men, a dozen of whom were already in position. Farther along the trail, long-abandoned fields of sugar cane gave way to dense undergrowth and mahogany trees, and the car bounced over ropes of liana that, in its search for trees to climb, had grown across the ersatz road.

Finally, when the thick vegetation completely obscured the road, they continued on foot. Colonel Monterra and agents Walker and Morgan checked their revolvers, and David, feeling inadequately armed, hefted a fallen tree branch, carrying it like a club. Their progress was slow and the piercing calls of macaws proved the birds' presence, even though they could not be seen. Bamboo plants, trees laden with green oranges, and huge bunches of plantains were within arm's reach. A sudden rustling in the tall, thick grass prompted them to crouch in silence. Several feet in front of them a wild pig darted out, then disappeared again into the dense ground cover.

Monterra led, establishing a footpath with his thick-soled, high-top leather boots, but fifty yards farther in the topography changed and the trail ended. Now they pushed their way through land completely claimed by vegetation.

"The place is just on the other side of this rise," Colonel Monterra said, and then spoke into his walkie-talkie. "I will approach and identify myself. If they cooperate, stay in your positions until I signal you. If they resist, in any way, you know what to do," he instructed his men.

Just as they reached the perimeter of a man-made clearing, David could see two ramshackle wooden structures. He lunged forward, only to be stopped by the colonel, who motioned to him to stay down and to the agents to fan out on either side of him.

Manuel Cissaro and another man, whom the colonel recognized as Manuel's brother, squatted on the ground behind the Jeep counting packets of money. Jeffrey leaned against the side of the Jeep, cleaning his fingernails. The only other man they saw stood by the door to one of the shacks, tossing a knife at a target carved into the narrow trunk of a Castilla tree and the milky latex dribbled from the slits.

His gun drawn, the colonel stepped from cover and announced, "I am Colonel Monterra of the military police. Throw down your weapons and . . ."

Before he finished, Manuel Cissaro reached inside his jacket and pulled a gun. He was shot through the head before he could fire. For twenty seconds, the air rained bullets, then frantic birdcalls punctuated the hollow silence. David dashed across the clearing, his tree branch in hand, and burst into the cabin.

Brett lay drenched in her own sweat, sobbing hysterically.

"It's me. It's David. You're going to be all right," he said as he gently untied her. "We're going to get you out of here." He smoothed the wet hair away from her face, kissed her softly on the forehead, and lifted her from the bed.

Brett wanted to reach up and put her arms around his neck, but she did not have the strength. "David . . ." she whispered hoarsely right before she fainted.

"Put her in there," the colonel said, pointing to the Jeep. "We won't have to walk out of here now. They are all dead, except him . . . but it doesn't look good."

Jeffrey lay in a heap on a bare, sun-baked patch of earth. A red-brown stain marked the front of his white shirt like an insignia.

Walker, still gripping his .38 automatic, crouched next to him, applying two fingers to Jeffrey's neck to feel for a pulse, then turned to walk away.

"Wait . . . come back," Jeffrey called. When Walker stood above him, Jeffrey said, "I have to tell you why I did this . . . in case there's no time later." He clawed at the hard ground with his fingernails, as if to hold on against the pain that tore through his chest. "Sven Larsen . . . you have to get Sven Larsen. I have tapes . . ."

"Who are you?" Walker asked abruptly.

"Lars Holmlund . . . the son of Karl Holmlund. That's what this is for . . . to make Sven pay for what he did to my father."

By this time, Morgan and Monterra had come and they formed a circle around Jeffrey.

"It was the plans. He stole the plans . . ." In gasps and spasms Jeffrey filled in the details of the Holmlund theft and his mission to avenge his father. "And there's more. Barbara, his own daughter, told me that he had her husband killed. It's all on the tapes. I never wanted to kill Brett. She just got in the way." Blood now soaked his shirt and he was pale, but for the first time, a peaceful look crossed his face.

Monterra had two of his men carry Jeffrey to the car, but he died before they reached town.

"It's all so crazy. How did he fool everyone for so long?" Brett's voice was weak, and she looked pale and exhausted. Her wrists and ankles were swathed in gauze bandages and an IV dripped fluids into her body.

"I don't know, Brett. It's like he lived his whole life for revenge, and I'm not sure anyone understood but him." David sat in a chair next to Brett's ancient hospital bed. His eyes were red and a thick growth of stubble covered his chin. "I sensed something was wrong. I only wish I had stopped you."

"You tried, David. It's not your fault. I didn't want to believe that Jeffrey could have been behind those crazy things that happened to me. His story about my grandfather having my father killed would explain why my mother hates him, but it's so ugly. I don't want to believe any of it."

"You'll have time to put everything into perspective. Right now, you've got to rest and get your strength back."

"Excuse me, señora," a doctor wearing a white lab coat interrupted them. "I have your test results. Aside from a little dehydration, you are fine. You are likely to feel lethargic, so you should get plenty of rest when you leave here, but you should feel no long-lasting physical effects from your ordeal. And do not worry. We gave you sedatives when you were admitted, but nothing that will harm your baby."

"Baby?" Brett said hesitantly. "What baby?"

"You did not know, señora? It is the early stages, but you are very definitely pregnant. Congratulations. And to you, too, señor." He shook David's hand. Before he left the room he added, "We will keep you overnight, but you can leave in the morning."

Brett remembered her nausea; it hadn't been the water. "I didn't know, David—honestly, I didn't." She looked down at her hands. "I stopped using birth control after Jeffrey and I . . ."

"You don't have to explain." David reached out and gently lifted her chin. "And I know you've been through a horrifying experience, but when I told you I love you, I meant it with all my heart. I want to be with you always." Brett's gaze met his; she saw the emotion in his eyes and the tears rolled down her face. "Maybe you need some time to sort out your feelings, but I want you to know that nothing could make me happier than the chance to love you and our baby."

One of David's hands rested on the bed and Brett lifted it, kissed his palm and cupped it to her cheek. "David, I need time to sort out a lot of things, but right now, the one thing I'm sure of is that I love you." Brett smiled and drifted back to sleep.

Brett slept during the four-hour flight back to New York. David watched her, just as he had their first night together. He couldn't believe that he had come so close to losing her.

When she opened her eyes, just as the plane began its descent into Kennedy, the first thing she saw was David, and she smiled. "Hi, I guess I missed the ride."

"There wasn't much to see. We were over the Atlantic most of the flight. Agent Morgan has arranged for us to clear customs on the plane since there's an army of reporters waiting for you. Aunt Lillian will pick us up on the tarmac as soon as we land."

Colonel Monterra had been more than happy to give an interview about his part in the rescue of the kidnapped American heiress, and he spared no details of the gruesome story, down to Jeffrey's confession and his allegations against Sven Larsen. The press had become relentless in its pursuit of the story. One reporter even tried to bribe Lillian's doorman for information, but changed his mind when the stalwart attendant threatened to break the reporter's nose. Reports from Racine indicated that Sven was in seclusion, unavailable for comment.

Lillian wept copious tears of relief when she saw her niece. "Oh, child, thank God you're all right," she said as she drew Brett to her bosom.

Even Albert allowed himself an uncharacteristic display of emotion, and discreetly wiped the tears from the corners of his eyes as he welcomed her.

Only when she sat in the backseat of the Bentley, between Lillian and David, was she finally certain that it was over and no more harm could come to her. The sight of the New York skyline brought tears of joy to her eyes.

As Albert approached the San Remo, they could see news vans in front of the building, so he turned the corner and let them out at the service entrance.

Brett walked through the apartment running her hands over the familiar furniture and objects, comforted by their reassuring presence. Lillian and David watched her progress silently. "I'm not going to break, you know," she said, turning to them. "It's just good to be home."

Hilda had prepared a smorgasbord of Brett's favorite foods. She downed a bowl of vegetable soup, two chicken breasts with dill sauce, an extra helping of cold new potatoes, and a dish of vanilla ice cream. David watched her ravenous zeal with amazement, and when she spied him out of the corner of her eye, she winked.

"I'm going home to shower and put on some clean clothes," David said when they finished their meal. "Then I'm going by to see my parents. I have a feeling they've been a little worried."

"I know that feeling, David, and you're right," Lillian said.

Before David left, Agent Morgan called to tell him that they had found the tapes Jeffrey had referred to and they did corroborate his allegations. An agent from their Milwaukee office had been sent to question Sven Larsen. He also told David that the tapes indicated that Jeffrey had been having an affair with Barbara in order to obtain information from her.

Brett had gone to lie down. David and Lillian discussed Morgan's call, and decided they would tell Brett about it when David returned.

Lillian was standing at the window, looking out onto the park, when Hilda called her to the phone. "It's long distance, Mrs. Cox—your brother's housekeeper."

A few minutes later, Lillian peeked into Brett's room and found her awake. "May I come in?"

"Of course, Aunt Lillian. I was just thinking about everything that happened. What's wrong?" Brett asked, sitting up in bed.

"It's your grandfather. He died a short while ago. I guess all this was too much for him. I didn't know whether to tell you this or not, but he called this morning. He said he knew it wouldn't make any difference, but he wanted me to tell you that he was sorry."

"Grandfather's dead? I don't know what to say. I mean, I'm sorry. But what if the things Jeffrey said are true and he did kill my father? I know he's your brother . . ."

"Hush, child." Lillian took Brett's hands in her own. "My brother was a very disturbed man. Agent Morgan called while you were resting. They found the tapes."

And the tears came, not out of a sense of loss or bereavement, but the addition of one more ponderous burden to the load she was already struggling to carry was more than she could bear.

Lillian cradled Brett in her arms and they both wept.

"When are you going out there?" Brett asked a few minutes later.

"Sven made his own arrangements years ago. There is to be no funeral and he will be cremated. I'll go out next week and close up the house until we decide what to do with it." Brett's phone rang. It was Lizzie.

"Brett. Are you okay? We just got a story over the wire about your grandfather. Do you know . . . ?"

"Yes, Lizzie. Thanks. We got a call about half an hour ago."

"And, one more thing. Your mother gave a statement to the press late this afternoon. I haven't seen it, but it will be on the six o'clock news. I don't know if you want to watch. The story of your kidnapping and Jeffrey—well, you know, it's the lead. Brett, I love you and I'm glad you're safe. I talked to David and I'm going to stop by tomorrow. You should be feeling better then."

"Aunt Lillian, what time is it?" Brett asked when she hung up.

"Almost six. Why?"

"Lizzie said that Barbara gave a statement this afternoon and it's going to be on the news."

Lillian got up and switched on the set.

"Updating our earlier story, Barbara Larsen North, the mother of the kidnapped heiress, Brett Larsen, and the daughter of Sven Larsen, the billionaire transportation magnate who died in his home today, apparently of heart failure, made this statement just a few hours ago."

They rolled a tape of Barbara standing amid a swarm of reporters in front of her apartment building. Deep creases marred her forehead and dark circles were evident beneath her eyes. She had made no attempt to conceal them or to prepare for television cameras, and she wrung her hands nervously. "I am ashamed that I have to admit I was involved with Jeffrey Underwood. I loved him and I thought he loved me. He promised to help me get my rightful inheritance from my father." Barbara looked away from the camera a moment, then resumed her statement. "Everyone keeps asking me about tapes. I don't know about any tapes, but if there are some, and if they say my father was responsible for the death of my first husband, then it's true. I have proof of that and he admitted it to me. I should have spoken up years ago." Her voice wavered, but she continued.

"I also knew that my father did something to Karl Holmlund, but I didn't know what until Jeffrey's confession. I didn't know that Jeffrey planned to kidnap and . . . kill my daughter." Tears coursed silently down her cheeks. "My daughter deserves this explanation. For many years she has paid a debt that she didn't owe . . . I'm sorry."

When she finished, she pushed her way through the crowd and disappeared into her building.

The anchorman commented. "Sven Larsen died today. His debt to society and to his family will remain unpaid . . ."

Brett had been mesmerized during the segment. As soon as it was over, she got up. "Aunt Lillian, I have to see her. I have to go over there."

"Brett, child, let it wait. You can't be up to it now."

"It can't wait. Nothing can be harder than what I've gone through in the last few days." She pulled on a shirt and pair of slacks. "I have to go."

"Why don't you wait for David?" Lillian asked, but Brett was already on her way down the hall.

"He can't help me with this—no one can." And she was gone.

Even though it had begun to rain, she had the cab let her off at the service entrance on Sixty-third Street. Brett huddled in the doorway, but by the time the building superintendent answered the buzzer, she was soaked. When she got upstairs, the maid informed her that Mrs. North had left strict instructions not to be disturbed.

"I'm her daughter, dammit! I have to see her!" She pushed past the startled maid and ran into the living room. "Where is she?" Brett demanded.

"She went upstairs a couple of hours ago, miss. She hasn't been down since then."

Brett ran up to her mother's room and knocked on the door. "Barbara, it's me, Brett. May I come in?" She rapped again, louder this time, then tentatively turned the knob.

Barbara lay in her bed with the white ruffled covers pulled snugly under her arms and the delicate white lace from the collar of her nightgown framing her face. At first Brett thought she was asleep, then she saw the empty pill bottle on the bedside table. She grabbed her mother's hands. They were cold, and in her left hand, Barbara clutched a gold signet ring. "Mother, wake up!" Brett lifted Barbara by the shoulders and shook her. She put her ear to her mother's chest and could barely hear a heartbeat, and her breathing was shallow. "Get help! Call an ambulance!" she screamed.

— *Epilogue* —

David burst into the waiting room, his hair and clothes wet from the rain. "What happened? Are you all right?"

Brett recounted the horrifying discovery, the frantic efforts of the EMS crew, and the race to the hospital. "No one's told me anything yet. David, I don't know what I'll do if . . ." Brett couldn't finish the sentence.

"From what you've told me, she couldn't have taken the pills more than a couple of hours before you arrived. They should be able to save her," David reasoned as he took the chair opposite her. "Let's try to stay calm and wait. At least the reporters can't come in here."

Lillian arrived a short time later and the three of them kept a vigil. After an hour, David made a trip to the vending machines in an alcove down the hall for overcooked coffee and a bag of salty popcorn. Periodically, Lillian went to the nurses' station to see if there was word.

And throughout the long night Brett was riveted to her seat, as if by concentrating all of her energy on Barbara she could will her not to die.

It was almost dawn when a doctor came to the door.

"She's out of the coma," he said, "but she'll be on a respirator for at least twelve hours, possibly the next twenty-four. She took a lot of pills, and she already had a fair amount of alcohol in her system, but it looks like she's going to pull through."

"Oh, thank God," Lillian said.

"When can I see her?" Brett asked anxiously.

"She's still pretty groggy. You can go in, but only for a few minutes. She won't be able to talk for several hours yet."

Brett squeezed Lillian's hand, then David's, and followed the physician to the intensive care unit.

She looked at Barbara through the glass for a minute. A mask covered her nose and mouth and was linked to the respirator at the head of her bed by transparent plastic tubing. Her eyes were closed and her wrists were secured to the steel bars of the bed with bands of cloth. *We never had a chance until now*, Brett thought as she listened to the rhythmic wheezing of the respirator. There was still so much they didn't know about each other, but maybe they could heal their wounds together.

David and Lillian tried to convince Brett to go home for a few hours, but she adamantly refused, so they waited with her.

When Brett crept into the cubicle, it was nearly five that evening. "Mother," she whispered.

Barbara's eyes flickered open. When she registered that her daughter stood beside her, she turned her head away. "I couldn't face you."

"You've punished yourself enough." Brett looked at her mother and years of anger and confusion subsided.

"You should hate me." Tears seeped from Barbara's eyes.

"I don't hate you . . . I never did."

Slowly, tentatively, Barbara turned to face her daughter. "You look just like your father—you always did. He loved you, Brett, even before you were born. What day is this? It's your birthday, isn't it?" Barbara's voice was weak and hoarse. "It was so hard . . ."

"Mother, save your strength. We can talk later." *How strange that with everything going on, she remembered my birthday*, Brett thought. Neither Lillian nor David had, and she herself had forgotten until she sat waiting in the hospital.

"No. I'm sorry. I wanted to be a good mother, but every time I looked at you . . . I'm sorry."

Brett brushed the tears from her mother's face. "You just get well. It'll be all right."

The October day had dawned bright, and now the afternoon sun cast a glow as warm as a blessing over Cox Cove. The garden was abloom with Japanese anemones and marigolds and the trees formed patches of red and yellow around the property. The house brimmed with bunches of autumn foliage and fragrant bouquets of white roses.

"I'm so excited I can hardly stand it," Lizzie exclaimed as she fastened the hook at the neck of Brett's dress. "My best friend is marrying my brother."

"And we're making you an auntie—don't forget that." Brett stood in front of the cheval mirror in her room at Cox Cove, patting her still-flat stomach. Sheer ivory silk chiffon bordered in bands of satin formed the full bishop sleeves of her dress. A satin portrait collar framed her shoulders, and the bodice tapered to a fitted waist that gave way to a full ivory satin skirt with a silk chiffon overlay. Brett's hair, parted on the side, fell in soft waves.

Lizzie adjusted the strand of pearls around Brett's neck. They had belonged to Lizzie's grandmother and she had worn them on her own wedding day. "There—something old and something borrowed. You look like a princess," Lizzie said as she stood back to survey the whole picture.

"You told me that a long time ago, right in this very room. I didn't believe you then, and I'm not sure I believe you now." Brett laughed. She was happier and more content than she had ever been in her life.

Her grandfather's legacy had presented a formidable challenge, and after weeks of meeting with Larsen attorneys and division heads, she had discovered that the corporation was structured in a way that virtually ensured its perpetuity. After conferring with David and Lillian, Brett had decided to take the next six months, until the baby was born, to learn everything she could about the inner workings of her company. She had already begun the arduous task of reading her grandfather's annual reports. At the end of that time she would select a president who would handle the day-to-day operation of Larsen Enterprises, and would then divide her time between her family and her own career. Brett knew the task was difficult and that she had assumed an awesome responsibility, but she also knew she could do it. The past, for so long a dark, shadowy blotch, had been exposed, and although it would take time for her to understand all that had been revealed, the knowledge freed her and lit the path to the future.

"Come in," Lizzie responded to the knock on the door.

"Oh, my!" Tears welled up in Lillian's eyes at the sight of her grandniece.

Brett put her arms around her aunt and hugged her tightly.

"I just came up to bring you this." She handed Brett *The Book of Common Prayer*, bound in ivory satin ribbon, to which a tiny nosegay of white roses had been attached. "I carried it when I married Nigel. I hope that you and David will be as happy as we were." She kissed Brett lovingly on the cheek.

Lillian turned to leave. "Wait," Lizzie called. "Brett, I'll be right back, but I have to see how Joe is doing with Emma and Cameron."

She had only been alone for a moment when she heard the door open. "Can I come in?" Barbara asked.

"Of course, Mother!"

Barbara took her daughter's hands, and when she looked at her, she saw all the years she had missed. "You're beautiful, just beautiful!"

And for the first time in her life, Brett believed it.

"You'll be a wonderful wife and mother . . . and I love you. I'll see you downstairs." She kissed Brett and left.

The living room had been cleared of its regular furnishings and several rows of chairs were now filled with family and friends. Brett had decided not to be given away. She and David were giving themselves to each other. So as the opening notes of Beethoven's "Ode to Joy" filled the stately mansion, Lizzie and her father, David's best man, took their places in front of the fireplace. David, resplendent in a navy blue suit with a single white rose in his buttonhole, waited calmly at the bottom of the sweeping staircase as Brett confidently descended. They looked into each other's eyes, expressing in a glance the joy in their hearts, and as the music swelled, Brett took his arm and they headed down the flower-lined aisle.

"We have come together to witness the union of Brett Larsen and David Powell," the minister began. "May this marriage be a course of unconditional strength and will; a perpetual haven from strife; a tranquil reflection of connected lives, and a ribbon of bright love through all their tomorrows. . . ."

GET LOVESTRUCK!

AND GET STRIKING ROMANCES FROM POPULAR LIBRARY'S BELOVED AUTHORS

Watch for these exciting romances in the months to come:

March 1990
EXPOSURES by Marie Joyce

April 1990
WILD GLORY by Andrea Parnell

May 1990
STOLEN MOMENTS by Sherryl Woods

June 1990
NIGHT FLIGHT by Eileen Nauman

July 1990
BEYOND THE SAVAGE SEA by Jo Ann Wendt

POPULAR LIBRARY

GET LOVESTRUCK!

**BUY ONE AND GET ONE FREE!*
ORDER YOUR FREE BOOKS HERE...**

1) Choose one free title from this list 2) Complete the coupon
3) Send this page and your sales receipt(s) from two books participating in our LOVESTRUCK promotion to the address below. 4) Enclose a check or money order for $1.00 to cover postage and handling.

☐ *HEARTS OF GOLD* by Phoebe Conn
0-445-20812-0
A breathtaking tale of adventure and red-hot desire by the *New York Times* bestselling author of *Captive Heart*.

☐ *STOLEN SPRING* by Louisa Rawlings
0-445-20458-3
A young French beauty at the court of Louis IV becomes entangled in political intrigue and forbidden passions.

☐ *TWILIGHT WHISPERS* by Barbara Delinsky
0-445-20968-2 (USA) 0-445-20969-0 (Canada)
From the 1984 *Romantic Times* Best Contemporary Novel Award winner and the author of *Commitments* comes a compelling story of a young woman driven by love...bound by secrets...and freed by desire.

☐ *DESTINY'S DAWN* by F. Roseanne Bittner
0-445-20468-0 (USA) 0-445-20469-9 (Canada)
Spanning the untamed frontier from California to Colorado, here is the exciting third book in the turbulent *Blue Hawk* series about a family and a nation divided by blood and united by wild passions.

☐ *THE VIKING'S BRIDE* by Julie Tetel
0-445-20078-2 (USA) 0-445-20079-0 (Canada)
Set in 13th century York and London, here is a medieval battle-of-the-sexes between the beautiful owner of a shipping company and a mysterious trader known as the Viking, from the author of *Tangled Dreams*.

☐ *DARK DESIRE* by Virginia Coffman
0-445-20221-1
A spellbinding tale of passion and betrayal set in 19th century England and France.

☐ *DARE I LOVE?* by Gillian Wyeth
0-445-20557-1
A rogue's hungry kisses promise Jenna Thornton ecstasy and danger in this breathtaking tale of passion and revenge set in Victorian England.

☐ *THE WHITE RAVEN* by Mary Mayer Holmes
0-445-20660-8
The author of *The Irish Bride* weaves a magnificent historical romance in which a handsome bounty hunter learns the true meaning of love from his beautiful Cornish captive.

**Send to: LOVESTRUCK Promotion
Warner Publishers Services
c/o Arcata Distribution P.O. Box 393 Depew, New York 14043**

Name _____

Address _____

City _____ State _____ Zip _____

*Subject to availability. We reserve the right to make a substitution if your book choice is not available.